P9-CCV-346

Savage Liberty

A MYSTERY of REVOLUTIONARY AMERICA

ELIOT PATTISON

COUNTERPOINT
Berkeley, California

Savage Liberty

Library of Congress Cataloging-in-Publication Data
Names: Pattison, Eliot, author.
Title: Savage liberty : a mystery of revolutionary America /
Eliot Pattison.
Description: Berkeley, CA : Counterpoint Press, [2018] | Series:
    Bone rattler; 5
Identifiers: LCCN 2017050414 | ISBN 9781619027213
    (hardcover)
Subjects: LCSH: United States—History—Revolution,
    1775–1783—Fiction. | United States   History   18th
    century—Fiction. | Scots—United States—Fiction. |
    GSAFD: Historical fiction. | Mystery fiction.
Classification: LCC PS3566.A82497 S29 2018 | DDC
    813/.54—dc23
LC record available at https://lccn.loc.gov/2017050414

Jacket designed by Domini Dragoone
Front cover type treatment by Henry Sene Yee
Book designed by Jordan Koluch

COUNTERPOINT
2560 Ninth Street, Suite 318
Berkeley, CA 94710
www.counterpointpress.com

Printed in the United States of America
Distributed by Publishers Group West

10 9 8 7 6 5 4 3 2 1

This book is dedicated to Robert Kirkwood

ACKNOWLEDGMENTS

Special thanks to Amy Foster and the Boston Public Library

PREFACE

THE AMERICAN REVOLUTION IS TAUGHT to us in terms of well-chronicled battles and committees of Founding Fathers that were launched in April 1775 with what Emerson famously called "the shot heard 'round the world." Such lessons, however, teach us only about the final stage of the amazing story of the founding of the United States. They neglect the remarkable events and even more remarkable people who shaped the Revolution during the years before muskets echoed on Lexington Green.

Savage Liberty opens in 1768, when many of the inhabitants of the American colonies were struggling with what today we would call an identity crisis. They weren't thinking of themselves as Americans, they were just questioning what it meant to be British when their Parliament refused to treat them as full citizens. They were not seeking revolution, they simply wanted—and expected to be given—the same voice with their government that their counterparts in the British Isles enjoyed. During these years London had multiple opportunities to right these inequities, but at every step it chose instead to impose additional economic servitude. The British government was blind to a vital truth about its most important colonies: for six generations it had been creating a vast and potent pool of disenchanted colonists by pushing across the Atlantic those who complained about religious repression at home, those who had offended an overreaching criminal justice system, and those who sought to carve out an existence unharnessed by the rigid social and economic culture of Britain.

By 1768 the ranks of these colonists had swollen to nearly two million, many of whom were emboldened by their new lives and new land. British citizenship was becoming less and less meaningful to their daily lives. As their complaints were repeatedly met with new economic repression, they became more inclined to voice their opposition than to open their purses to arrogant bureaucrats across the sea.

The Massachusetts colony, where Duncan McCallum finds himself in the novel's opening, has felt more than its share of London's punishment, but the residents of Boston are still not speaking openly of rebellion. Their angry words are aimed at legislators and customs commissioners, not the king, who still embodies their national identity. They are discovering the power of standing together in dissent, not just on the cobblestone streets of their hometown, but across colonial borders. They are slowly awakening to a new common identity that bridges long-standing cultural and political differences among the colonies. This awakening was not decreed from above, nor could it be. It grew out of the personal struggles and experiences of individual men and women, not out of a common heritage, but out of common values. Before they glimpsed revolution, these colonists first had to discover that they were American.

Duncan, having painfully experienced London's brutality during the Stamp Tax crisis, wants nothing more than to return to his peaceful oasis on the western frontier. But he is in Boston, the hotbed of dissent, and his friends John Hancock and Samuel Adams have other plans for him. Before he can discover that he is on the path to revolution, he must endure wrenching lessons about the nature of treason, honor, and freedom.

Savage
Liberty

1

Spring 1768
Boston

IF YE WOULD FEEL THE PULSE OF HUMANKIND, Duncan McCallum's Scottish grandfather once declared, *just look to a busy harbor.* From his perch in the church tower overlooking the forest of masts in Boston harbor, Duncan indeed felt as if he were glimpsing the pulsing heart of the colony. In quick succession he pointed to three of the nearest vessels.

"Brig from Jamaica with a cargo of rum," the square-shouldered youth beside him eagerly answered, "next a fast bark just arrived from Liverpool with cordage and Dutch porcelain. And that filthy one with the wide beam, she's a banker fresh from the cod beds off the Newfoundland." Henry Knox was slow of body, but his mind was more agile than that of any eighteen-year-old Duncan had ever known, and he enthusiastically embraced Duncan's lessons about the architecture of visiting ships and the unique nature of each of the ports they called home. "Curaçao, Lisbon, Portsmouth, Recife, and Santo Domingo," Knox continued, pointing to ships farther out in the harbor before turning back to Duncan. "And I've heard that new cutter just arrived from Halifax carries a dozen twelve-pounders and a brass chase gun!"

Duncan smiled. The youth was obsessed with all things military, and on the nights when they climbed the higher steeple of the Old North Church to watch the stars, he often begged Duncan to describe his experiences in the last war with the French. Duncan glanced back at the small device Knox had strapped on the back rail of the narrow walkway that surrounded the tower of King's Chapel. "I need my lens," he reminded the youth as Knox stepped toward the contraption.

"Pray, just a few more moments!" the teenage scholar exclaimed, motioning to a pinpoint of light, sharply focused by the lens mounted above the rail, as it traversed the tin tray below the lens. As Duncan watched, the glowing dot of light reached a small mound of gunpowder, which abruptly crackled, then exploded with a small cough of smoke. "The zenith!" the youth declared triumphantly, pointing to the sun overhead, then toward the fortress on Castle Island. An instant later the noon gun from the fort echoed across the harbor.

Duncan extended an impatient hand, and Knox slipped the lens out of its harness and hurried back around the tower. "Prithee, Duncan, may I?" he asked, nodding to the telescope in Duncan's hands. Duncan hesitantly surrendered the instrument. Knox quickly reinserted the lens into the telescope and screwed the end cap back in place, then shook his long brown hair from his face to better examine the leather-bound tube in his hands, pausing over the inscription on the brass plate that adorned it.

"'With gratitude for services nobly performed, your servant, John Hancock,'" Knox read, and looked up, wide-eyed. "They say Mr. Hancock will soon be the richest merchant in all of New England!" the youth declared, then furrowed his brow as he read the inscription again and looked up with a mischievous grin. "It's like what a general would present to his favorite spy," he suggested. "Did you purloin a letter from the king's boudoir?"

Duncan cocked his head a moment, wondering if Knox had indeed pierced one of the many secrets he kept with Hancock. "Nothing so romantic, Henry," he explained. "The master of his trading sloop bound for Bermuda had a seizure the day before sailing. I was able to fill in." Something icy touched his heart as he spoke, and he turned toward the harbor to avoid further questions. The price he had paid for making the seven-week voyage out of American waters had been almost too painful to bear.

He raised the telescope to his eye and aimed it toward the northeast. "You said that burning ship went down past Shirley Point?" he asked the youth. Duncan had been on a wharf with his old friend Conawago, studying the luminescent jellyfish arriving on the spring tide, when a peal of thunder had rolled out of the clear starlit sky, followed by a flicker of flames. Fire was the nightmare of every mariner. Duncan had watched with dread in his heart as he saw the furled sails on two square-rigged masts ignite into flame. No ship could have survived such an intense explosion and the subsequent inferno, and the frigid, ripping currents off the Point would have dealt cruelly with any survivors.

"Have they named her yet?" Duncan asked. When Knox wasn't present at the bookstore where he had met Duncan, he was usually exercising his insatiable curiosity at the docks.

"No one is certain, but the harbormaster said a fishing boat that docked last night had exchanged greetings with the *Arcturus*, out of London, and told him to expect her soon."

Duncan fixed the Point in his eyepiece and slowly swept the telescope over the surrounding waters. The recently arrived revenue cutter, reviled by the many Massachusetts watermen who considered smuggling a God-given right, was anchored less than half a mile off the Point. Near the cutter, two of the small launches used by the harbor patrol were sailing in a search pattern, but nothing else. He would have expected a flotilla of boats from the neighboring fishing villages competing for salvage in the debris of the wrecked ship.

"*Arcturus*," Duncan repeated. "Not His Majesty's ship *Arcturus*, not a naval vessel. Why would the military keep salvagers from a merchant wreck?"

"A trading ship, owned by Mr. Livingston of New York, they say," Knox replied in a distant voice. Duncan turned to see him facing away from the harbor, toward the broad swath of green that was Boston Common. "The Sons are stirring the coals again," the youth observed, "in broad daylight this time." He spoke of the Sons of Liberty, who made sure that the customs commissioners dispatched by the king felt the colony's fury over the steep duties they were collecting. Duncan followed Knox's outstretched hand toward one of the streets that opened onto the rolling, grassy field. An untethered mule, grazing on the community pasture, kicked up its heels and trotted away. A flock of pigeons burst into flight and disappeared over Beacon Hill. As he watched, a small crowd emerged from the street, hoisting a long timber wrapped with ribbons, probably a wagon tongue, as a makeshift liberty pole.

Duncan grinned. No doubt several of those in the crowd were acquaintances from his months in Boston. He had grown to think of the town as an aged dowager who by force of habit and history knew that she owed loyalty to her king but who choked at the corset forced on her by his ministers. Sometimes the conflict in her emotions was so great she had to slip out the kitchen door and shout oaths to the sky. The liberty pole demonstrations were how the town vented its frustrations, and thus far the governor had wisely chosen not to interfere with them. The protests had become almost weekly occurrences since the arrival of the commissioners from London, though, until now, they had always been at night, torchlit processions that most often ended in good-natured revelry at a South Boston tavern. As another group entered from a second street, Duncan swung the telescope up and studied the compact brick house on a corner adjacent to the Common, where a slim red-haired woman emerged onto its steps, gazing at the converging crowds.

"The harbor watch!" Knox abruptly cried, pointing to a file of men in scarlet uniforms marching double time on the street below them. "The governor's called in the patrols from the waterfront! He's never done that before."

Duncan swung the telescope back toward the Common to study the second crowd, then shuddered as he saw the cart they led toward a solitary oak near the top of the hill. The troops were headed up Beacon Street, which would position them just above the tall oak. "The fools!" he groaned, then shoved the telescope into his pocket. "Go back to the bookstore, Henry, and stay there," he instructed Knox, then darted down the narrow stairs.

The crowds were merging, rapidly turning into a raucous mob as he reached the granite steps of the brick house. "Inside!" he said as he grabbed the woman's arm.

Sarah Ramsey resisted his push toward the door. "I, for one, am happy they are taking their protest into the daylight," she said as she pulled away from Duncan. "Look, it's the kind Mr. Sullivan the butcher," she said as if to reassure him, "and old Mr. Hansen the candlemaker—he's half blind, poor soul. I should go help him."

"Not today, Sarah." She may have been a visitor to Boston long enough to befriend a few tradesmen, but Sarah was a creature of the New York frontier, and though she was the esteemed proprietress of distant Edentown, she had no sense of the brittle tension between Boston's Sons of Liberty and the officials sent from London. He put an insistent arm around her waist and urgently spoke in the language of her youth, the tongue of the Iroquois, pointing to the oak tree, where several men waited, one of them mounted. Duncan turned her toward the horse-drawn cart, where a terrified man sat on a bed of straw watched over by two brutish-looking men armed with barrel staves. Finally, he showed her the file of infantry lining up along the crest of the hill.

Sarah pushed back a lock of auburn hair to see better. "The tree?" she asked.

Duncan handed her his telescope. "The low limb on the south side," he instructed.

She focused for a moment, then jerked back as if physically struck. "A hangman's noose? Surely they wouldn't—they can't!" This time she did not resist as Duncan pushed her back inside the house.

"Surely the king's soldiers will shoot if they do," Duncan warned. "It must be one of the customs collectors."

A sturdy middle-aged woman who had been reading in a window seat rose and guided Sarah to a table where a steaming pot of tea waited beside porcelain cups. The woman nodded to Duncan, and he dipped his head toward her. "Mrs. Pope, my gratitude once more," he said to their landlady, then spun about and darted out the door.

He paused halfway up the hill to catch his breath. The soldiers were deployed in a battle line. There were no more than a score, but each man carried a Brown Bess musket, and Duncan had seen in the French war how their heavy balls could rip apart a man's flesh at such a close range. The Sons seemed to think the soldiers were always bluffing, but an end to the bluffing seemed inevitable.

His heart lurched as he saw two men at the front of the crowd dragging the limp body of the customs collector toward the hanging tree, encouraged by loud cheers. The man on the horse, to which the other end of the rope was attached, waited eagerly for the order to spur his mount and jerk the rope upward, the moment of terrible strangulating death. He glanced back at the soldiers. The fuse of the governor's temper had been slowly burning as the assemblies of the Sons of Liberty grew more frequent and more vocal. With sudden dread, Duncan realized that the soldiers might allow the hanging to proceed just so they could at last inflict the governor's punishment. He sprinted toward the noose, weaving through the crowd, and was only fifty feet away when a foot shot out and tripped him.

As he pulled himself up, brushing dirt from his hands, the noose was fastened around the tax collector's neck. "No!" he shouted. "You don't understand.

The soldiers!" As if his cry were the cue he had been waiting for, the rider prod-ded his horse forward. The noose jerked upward. The tax collector swung in the rising wind.

Duncan burst forward, plowing through the line of jubilant onlookers, unsheathing the knife he carried in the small of his back. If he could sever the rope tied to the saddle, there was still a chance to save the man and avoid the massacre to come.

He was tripped again, and this time a boot pinned his arm long enough for someone to pry away his knife. "That'll do, Captain," someone said. He rose in a cold rage, ready to fight his way to the horse to save the man. He could not understand the laughter all around him. The soldiers would fire at any moment. Then someone sobbed, and he saw the cart only feet away, where the battered customs collector still sat, weeping. Duncan looked up at the swaying body and for the first time saw the straw extending from its ears and its burlap face with painted eyes and mouth. The collector had been hanged in effigy.

Duncan recognized the voice of his assailant and turned. Enoch Munro, the sturdy, aging Scot who had sailed as first mate with Duncan to Bermuda, nudged him and handed him his knife, then stepped back to yield to another man. Duncan had not seen his friend Conawago since the night before. The gentle old Nipmuc Indian was haggard, his face drawn with worry, his hands stained with fresh blood. He offered no greeting and spoke in Mohawk. "It is not the pretend death we need you for," the old man grimly declared.

2

WHILE LEARNING THE WAYS OF the wilderness from Conawago, Duncan had also learned to read the tracks of the old man's complex silences. Survivor of a nearly extinct tribe, educated in the best Jesuit schools, visitor to the courts of Paris and London, the aged Nipmuc often stilled his tongue, but never his eyes. Seldom had Duncan seen such intense emotion on his lined countenance. His deep, intelligent eyes were lanced with anguish, but an urgent fear also flickered in them. He responded to Duncan's questions with a dismissive gesture and a quickened pace, then slowed for a moment as he looked at his hands, as if just noticing the blood on them.

Duncan knew the old stone-walled warehouse next to Hancock Wharf, where Conawago led him, but he was not familiar with the small door at the north side that the old Nipmuc knocked on. He heard the rattle of a loosened dead bolt; then one of Hancock's Jamaican dockworkers, a huge man with skin the color of walnut, waved them inside and quickly locked the heavy door behind them, standing guard as they hurried on. Conawago led him down a set of stairs, past stacked crates and racks filled with casks of wine to an inner door, where another man kept watch under a hanging lantern, a heavy iron crow on his lap. He rose, tapped four times, and a moment later the door opened.

The chamber inside, with walls of blocked granite and a packed-earth floor, had no doubt been intended as a cellar storage vault, but a large canvas floor cloth, bright lanterns, an old sideboard, and a table with several chairs around it had transformed it into a secret but comfortable meeting place. For the moment it appeared more like a charnel house. A pile of bloody rags lay on the floor. An unconscious British solder lay on the long table, his right leg wrapped in blood-soaked bandages that were leaking onto the table, another bloody rag pressed to his ribs. The strip of silver lace on his cuffs indicated that the man was a noncommissioned officer.

"First the living," came a familiar voice from the shadows. The man who stepped forward was always well-groomed and clean-shaven, attired in the best Boston could provide. But today John Hancock was unshaven, his expensive clothes torn and soiled. His eyes looked older than his thirty years. A strip of linen was wrapped around a wound in his hand. Long strands of his brown hair had escaped the silk ribbon that bound it at the nape of his neck.

When Duncan reached for his bloody hand, Hancock gestured to the man on the table. "A none-too-sober Irishman decided to express his feelings about the new taxes with the end of a pitchfork. The wound to his side is a graze with a sickle, but the sergeant's leg wound has not staunched. I fear a blood vessel has been nicked."

Duncan pulled away the bandages. The gash in the man's side had stopped bleeding and would only need cleansing. The soldier's britches had been cut open, exposing a discolored thigh with three circular punctures. Bright red blood oozed out of the center hole. "An artery," Duncan confirmed. "The army has their own surgeons, John. He should be in the infirmary at Castle William."

"Not this soldier, Duncan," Hancock replied. "Not this wound." There was an unfamiliar tone of warning in his voice.

Conawago leaned over the sergeant's leg. "It will take more than cobwebs and moss," the old Nipmuc said, referring to the usual wilderness treatment for hemorrhages. "He's pale as a sheet, Duncan; he wouldn't last the time it took to transport him to the fortress. We need him alive."

A dozen questions sprang into Duncan's mind, but then he looked at the soldier's pallid face and lifted his wrist for a pulse. The man was dying. "I will have to cut into his flesh to get at the artery. I have no instruments. I need a razor or scalpel. And silk thread with a fine needle. And rip some clean linen for a bandage."

"A shipment of medical instruments from Amsterdam arrived last week," Hancock reported. "Just upstairs. You will have your pick," he said, and urgently spoke to the man outside the door.

"And strong spirits," Duncan added.

Hancock hesitated. "Surely you will need a steady hand if you—"

"To clean my instruments and the wound. You have some Scotch from the Hebrides, I recall."

"The most expensive crate in my cellars!" the merchant protested. "The governor himself ordered it."

"The governor is a mere Englishman. Top off the bottle with some tavern rotgut and he'll not gauge the difference so long as you charge him top price."

Hancock seemed to weigh Duncan's words.

"God's breath, John!" came an impatient voice from the shadows in the corner, "stop counting your halfpence and let the man live!" An elegant figure stepped out of the darkness, stripping off his stylish tan waistcoat as he approached the table. "I am a mere Englishman, Mr. McCallum, but I stand ready to assist." As he rolled up his sleeves, he saw the suspicion on Duncan's face. "I have heard of your many talents, sir, and of your secret errands for the Sons." He extracted an ivory-handled pocketknife and began cutting away more of the sergeant's britches, then glanced up as if in afterthought. "Livingston, sir, of the Hudson."

Duncan and Conawago exchanged an uncertain glance. John Hancock might have been a prince of Boston, but the Livingston family was the prevailing royalty of the Hudson Valley, proprietors of scores of thousands of acres on both sides of the mighty river. Duncan nodded toward the wounded sergeant. "Can I have his name?"

"Mallory. Does it matter?"

"It matters a great deal, since I will be speaking with him as I work. Now help me strip off his uniform coat."

Duncan forced himself to think of nothing but his patient for the next hour, first using the Scotch—a Skye malt, judging from its peaty taste—to deaden the nerves of the semiconscious soldier, then, as Livingston and the guard held down the sergeant's shoulders, to clean the wound before lifting the Dutch-made scalpel to open it. As he applied his medical skills, he spoke to the sergeant without expecting reply, asking if the scar on his leg was from a French bayonet, wondering aloud if he had fought in any of the northern campaigns Duncan had joined in the war, inquiring if he knew a Dr. Mallory Duncan had known in Edinburgh. "A habit I picked up in my medical studies," he explained to a quizzical Livingston. "One of my professors insisted that there was always a spark of consciousness alive in every patient. The talking keeps them distracted and interested in eventually awakening."

By the time he finished, his improvised equipment was strewn about the table, including a porringer filled with blood-tinged whiskey; a linen handkerchief with Hancock's initials, much soiled after use as a tourniquet; and the contents of an elegant sewing box imported from Germany.

He had tied and snipped the last delicate knot before he realized that he had not seen Conawago since he first bent over the wounded soldier. He was about to ask for him when Hancock pushed a cup of hot tea into his hand. "Will Sergeant Mallory live?" the Boston merchant asked.

"He lost a great measure of blood, and if he takes to the leg too soon, it could rip open the artery," Duncan explained. "But I've seen men survive much worse after battle."

"Praise God," Hancock rejoined.

"Praise God for saving one of the enforcers of the duties you so despise?" Duncan said in a low voice, for Hancock's ears only. "Who mysteriously shows up under your protection on business you don't want explained to the governor or the general."

"We are all God's creatures," Hancock said in a stern tone, as if scolding Duncan.

Duncan was tired and had little tolerance for the games Hancock liked to play. He wanted nothing more than to return to the boardinghouse for a quiet meal with Sarah Ramsey to plan their return to Edentown. "Need I ask whether I came here as a favor to the governor or as a favor to the Sons of Liberty?"

"Sergeant Mallory has provided valuable assistance to us, keeping us apprised of expected customs inspections."

"He'll have the devil of the time explaining himself when he shows up at his barracks."

"No, he won't," Hancock replied, warning back in his voice. "When he leaves here, he will leave his uniform behind."

Duncan sighed and looked back at the unconscious man's face. "A deserter, then. Even more dangerous. Did I save his life just so he could be hanged?"

Hancock's only answer was to pour two fingers of the smoky Scotch into a pewter cup for Duncan. When Duncan lowered the empty cup, the merchant nodded approvingly, then motioned him toward the shadows along the back wall of the chamber. The dim outline of a door became visible as Duncan approached. The merchant pushed on its iron latch and stepped aside for him to enter.

The chamber appeared to be a small workshop where casks and barrels were repaired, or perhaps spirits diluted and decanted into bottles. A long oaken workbench took up much of the dimly lit room, leaving only three or four feet of clearance between it and the walls. Conawago sat on a stool at one end of the bench, his head bowed, a string of white beads in his hand as he whispered in his ancient tongue. At the other end, a large man with a dark, fleshy face sat bent over his clasped hands as he quietly recited a prayer in Latin. Between them lay most of a dead man.

First the living, Hancock had said when he arrived. Duncan retreated a step. He did not understand what lay before him, except for the reverence, which he would not disturb. Hancock gripped his arm and pushed him back into the room. "I'm sorry, Duncan, but people talk. You may recall that there was an Indian on the crew you took to Bermuda. He said later that he had recognized you, that people on the frontier call you the Deathspeaker."

Duncan's breath caught. He desperately did not want to become Deathspeaker for the people of Boston, did not want the burden of grief and anguish that always came in speaking for the dead. "That's among the Iroquois."

As if in answer, Hancock swept his open palm toward the dead man.

Duncan did not understand, saying, "I prefer to help the living."

"And that, Highlander, is what we ask of you," came a gravelly voice from behind him.

There was only one man in Boston who used that name for Duncan. "Mr. Adams?" Duncan asked, half turning.

Samuel Adams's broad girth was draped in a cloak, his round face hidden under a large tricorn hat, which he removed as he approached. "These are desperate hours, lad."

Foreboding washed over Duncan like a dark, frigid wave. "I made a promise to Sarah," he protested. "We are going home."

"Of course, of course," Adams confirmed. "But first we just want to know about this man's death. We need you to"—he searched for words—"interpret his death in the manner of this mysterious Deathspeaker."

Duncan gestured at the stumps below the body's hips. "Perhaps you noticed he has no legs. He no doubt bled to death, if the shock of having them blown off didn't take him first. A common enough sight on a battlefield." He hesitated, weighing his own words. There were no battlefields in Boston.

"Tell us the story of his death, prithee," Adams pressed. "Casual appearances can be misleading, even with the dead. It is vital that we have the truth in this business. Much hangs in the balance."

"Business?" Duncan asked, then studied Hancock and Adams. The two men wore many hats in Boston, but he realized that here, in this secret subterranean chamber, they were the city's most prominent members of the Sons of Liberty. The Sons had been staging frequent public rallies and were not shy about leaving their name on broadsides throughout the city, but Duncan well knew that their most important affairs were conducted far from the public eye. Their numbers had been swelling after smugglers began benefiting from the Sons' secret warnings of revenue patrols and tradesmen received advance notice of the planned rounds of tax collectors. He turned toward Conawago, hoping for an explanation. The old man, who had steadfastly kept his head down, looked up, pleading in his eyes, then pointedly down at the white wampum beads he clutched in his hand. It was message enough. The beads represented a covenant with the tribal spirits, an obligation to speak the truth at the table.

"What was his name?" Duncan asked in a near whisper.

Adams nodded in gratitude. "Jonathan Pine."

Duncan glanced back at Hancock, now understanding his gesture when he had said his skills were used for the Iroquois. He did not know the dead man, but he knew the name. With renewed sadness he looked back at Conawago, who was bent over the bench again, reciting prayers of the forest. The dead man had a strong, leathery face, his black hair tied at the back in the short, blocked braid favored by seamen. Over his torso he wore a heavy woolen pullover that had rows of woven knots and cables, probably a product of Ireland or Scotland, which appeared perforated with small holes. His britches, stained with tar and singed at the uneven tears where they had been severed with his legs, were of heavy duck fabric, probably sailcloth. On the back of one of his hands crossed over his chest were inked the words *The Lord is my Shepherd*. On the other was a rattlesnake, so intricate it almost looked like scrimshaw work. Tattooed on his neck was a line of fish. The man was a sailor, a Christian, and a native of the woodlands. Jonathan Pine was a name commonly given to baptized Indians.

Duncan looked back at the gentle old Nipmuc at the end of the table. Conawago's words seemed to be drifting, the volume ebbing and rising, as he gazed desolately at the stumps of Pine's legs. At the end of each were splinters of bone and tangles of ligaments, muscles, and blood vessels. Duncan would have expected them to be bloodier. He ran his fingers over the charred remnants of the britches. The fabric was damp. Pine had been in the water after his legs were blown off. He turned to Hancock and Adams, who silently watched from the doorway. "The ship that exploded. Pine was on the *Arcturus*."

Hancock fingered his starched white collar. "Did he drown?"

Duncan moved to Pine's head, pushing down the dead man's abdomen as he bent over his mouth. Air rushed out of the lungs. "He did not."

"Did he die in the explosion?" Adams pressed.

"My God, man," Livingston, standing at Hancock's shoulder, inserted. "He was close enough to it that his legs were blown away. Do you even need to ask?"

Duncan saw the worry on Hancock's face and realized he did need to ask. He gazed at the dead man. He could not fathom the motives of the three men who watched so carefully, so nervously, and who were known for their clever manipulation of pieces on political chessboards. He felt Conawago's beseeching gaze. The old man knew that Duncan felt a duty to the dead, especially dead tribesmen and clansmen, and they had sometimes debated the reason why. Perhaps it was because nearly all of Duncan's own Highland clan were dead, slaughtered by the English, and though he still spoke to them, they never replied. Perhaps it was because the tribesmen who had become his de facto family believed that those who died unexpectedly had to be given resolution before they could move on to the spirit world. Perhaps it was because his medical education in Edinburgh had so acutely sharpened his curiosity about the human body. Whatever the reason, he was the Deathspeaker, and Jonathan Pine had a story to be told.

"I will need help with the body," Duncan declared to the onlookers.

Hancock stepped to the door and called out. A moment later Enoch Munro was at Duncan's side, nodding at Duncan's instructions for baring Pine's torso. With a cool, steady hand, Munro cut away the pullover, revealing more than two dozen splinters that had impaled Pine's chest and abdomen. None of the puncture wounds looked fatal, but the splinters had been driven deep into his flesh. Duncan extracted a two-inch shard of wood from his belly. It was oak, and slightly curved, as if from a barrel or keg, probably from the keg of powder that had exploded.

Pine may have been a Christian, but he had not forgotten the tribal ways. The tattoos on his chest were aligned along either side of a cross over his heart, but the life they reflected had not always been sanctimonious. The story of his existence began on his right shoulder, with small images of a stag and a pumpkin over a larger one of an eel, domestic images of life as a member of the eel clan. Then came a figure standing over a bear, another standing in a canoe with a massive fish, then the same figure standing over a dead soldier, and a final one leading a roped chain of prisoners. Underneath the row of images was inked a strand of wampum beads. Duncan studied the pattern of dark and lighter beads and looked up at Conawago. "Seneca?" he asked. The old man confirmed with a nod.

On the other side of the cross were images of a different life. Oddly, in the first, a man was dancing with a bear. In the second, a man climbed the shrouds of a square-rigged ship, then aimed a harpoon at a great whale in the third. The last, which Duncan could make no real sense of, was of a seagull carrying a snake.

He straightened and studied parallel scratches along the edges of Pine's rib cage. Spreading the cold flesh with his fingers, he discovered that they were precise cuts, shallow five-inch-long slices made by a thin blade. They were not death blows, nor wounds incurred from the explosion.

Duncan paused, looking at the strongly featured face, then at the tattoo of the warrior standing over a dead soldier. The Senecas were the westernmost tribe of the Haudenosaunee, the Iroquois Confederacy, so closely aligned with the French that many had fought against the English in the recent war. He could not discern whether the uniform on the dead soldier inked on Pine's chest was French or English.

The hands of a man tell his life story, one of Duncan's Scottish professors had told him. But Duncan found that they more often told a man's death story. Pine's hands surprised him. Their backs had been perforated by tiny splinters. The palms bore the usual calluses of the seaman, but the long, well-proportioned fingers gave them an oddly graceful nature, like those of an artist. *The Lord is my Shepherd*, he read again on the right hand, then turned it over. The palm was sliced so deeply that the ivory white of a carpal bone could be seen. Munro took his cue and reversed the left hand for Duncan, then abruptly dropped it. A sea worm was writhing inside a deep puncture in the heel of the hand. Duncan plucked out the creature and probed the wound. It had been a stab with a thin blade, like a dagger. He paused over the fingertips of the three middle fingers, which were badly burned. The wrists of each hand were severely chafed, the skin broken in several places.

"Bindings," Munro whispered.

Duncan considered the conclusion in silence, then bent over the dead Seneca's neck. It was bruised and chafed along one side, to the front of the windpipe. He lifted an eyelid. The eye was red from burst capillaries.

"Over," he instructed the Scottish sailor.

They turned the big man onto his belly and pulled away the tatters of his clothing.

"A defiant bugger," Munro muttered as he saw Pine's back. The long, narrow scars were overlapped so heavily that it seemed almost as if Pine had scales on his back. The Scot glanced at Duncan. He had seen similar striations on Duncan's own back.

"Pine jumped ship in Jamaica five years ago," Hancock said over Duncan's shoulder. "He had sworn off whaling after two years in the Pacific, saying he could no longer take part in killing the gods of the seas. After his whaler returned to Nantucket, he signed on to the first ship that would have him. He didn't understand what she was until they reached the coast off Gabon and traded their pipes of rum for human cargo." Hancock stepped closer, holding a lantern over the ruined flesh. "Merciful God," he groaned, and did not speak for several long breaths. "On the crossing, he was repeatedly caught taking extra food and water to the slaves belowdecks, and he was whipped more severely each time. In Jamaica he joined with one of my captains, who tried to pay him off when they reached Boston so he could go see his family. But Pine said his family had all been killed by the king, and he signed on for more voyages after we promised we did not run slaves."

Hancock hesitated, realizing that Duncan was staring at him.

"So one of your seamen was serving on a Livingston ship," Duncan declared.

Hancock shot a glance at Livingston, whose eyes filled with warning. "He was trusted," was all Hancock said.

Duncan directed Hancock to hold the lantern over Pine's head. He silently probed the Seneca's scalp, finding first a soft, abraded spot just above the braid. He pushed away a lifeless arm and bent to study a wound between Pine's ribs. The blade had been narrow, the stab expertly made to reach a kidney. He sighed, then straightened. "This is what killed him, at least why he didn't drown. His tormentors wanted to be sure he was finished. Pine would have had only a few minutes after this dagger entered his ribs." He signaled Munro to help him turn Pine over again.

The Puritan at the end of the table had not stopped whispering his Latin prayers, still carefully avoiding eye contact with Duncan. Conawago no longer spoke, and now he just stared at the white beads in his fingers.

"He was a fighter, to the very end," Duncan whispered, struggling with an intense and unexpected grief for this man he had never known. He and Conawago had put to rest far too many members of the tribes. The noble face of each one still lingered in Duncan's memories, and sometimes in his nightmares.

"Jonathan was slow to anger," Munro volunteered, "but when he did, he had the ferocity of a bear, in both body and mind, if ye ken what I mean."

Duncan looked up in surprise. "You knew him?"

"It's why I was sent to recover his body last night," Munro replied. "We made several crossings together. If a sail needed trimmin' in a blow, Pine and me be the first to go aloft."

"Sent last night?" Duncan asked. The ship had exploded only a few hours after dark. It was as if Munro had been standing by to meet the *Arcturus.*

"Afore the navy could get there," the Scot confirmed. "Not a task I'd care to ever do again," he added in a hollow voice, "floating through that tide of death, lighting up the wretched faces with a lantern. That cutter had everything shut up tight an hour after dawn. The salvagers are furious, say it ain't right for the navy to deprive them so."

"Enoch!" Hancock warned.

"Then they would have been watching for anyone sailing in from that direction this morning," Duncan suggested.

"Aye, had to stand off until the harbor patrols were summoned away." So far in Boston, the only regular patrols by the military were along the waterfront, to discourage smugglers.

Duncan stared at Munro, then followed Conawago's gaze back to the beads in his hand. The Nipmuc was reminding him that the truth was owed to the dead Seneca. Duncan turned to Hancock and Adams. "The Sons never marched in daylight until today," he said in an accusing tone. "You arranged it, you put that customs man through that horror so the troops would be called away from the docks so you could steal Pine into your warehouse."

Neither man returned Duncan's gaze.

"The wounds on his chest," Adams put in. "Could they have been caused by the explosion?"

"The punctures? Of course. A powder keg exploded only a few feet from him. He shielded his face with his hands."

Hancock looked at Duncan, his face pallid. "So he was alive when the keg was exploded?" he asked.

"Barely, but yes. He died before inhaling any water. Did you cause that public protest as a subterfuge to get his body here?"

"Is that important?" Adams asked impatiently. "How exactly did he die?"

"It is important if you manipulate the Sons of Liberty to the gain of your personal affairs," Duncan shot back.

The guilty glance exchanged between Hancock and Adams filled Duncan with an urge to abandon them altogether. He should leave and keep his promise to dine with Sarah.

Suddenly the stranger by Pine's head looked up at Duncan for the first time. "*Veritas vincit*," he declared in a deep bass voice. "Truth conquers."

At the other end of the table, Conawago shook the white beads and likewise stared at Duncan. The two men were saying the same thing. Conawago extended his hand, and Duncan accepted the beads, weaving them around his fingers as he had seen old sachems do at Iroquois council fires. He was deeply suspicious of the motives of Hancock and Adams, but the dead Seneca deserved the truth.

"Pine was attacked and overcome, probably by at least two men," he explained. "They tied him to an upright in a hold. He knew he was a dead man, but with his last breath he tried to save his shipmates."

A low moan escaped Adams's throat.

"Jesus, Mother Mary," Munro muttered, then added in a hiss, "Damn the bastards who did this! May they rot in hell!"

"Prithee, Duncan," Hancock said in a voice tight with emotion, "suffer us the details."

"His washing in the ocean makes his body poor evidence," Duncan warned, "but there is enough to understand his last moments." He turned over Pine's right hand. "The slices in the palm show no swelling, little bruising, meaning they were done just before his death. They suggest that he was fighting someone who had a blade, having no weapon available but his hands. He may have been successful, except someone hit him on the back of his head, a blow hard enough to disable him. That is probably when they drove the blade into his ribs." Duncan pointed to the chafed skin at the wrists and neck. "These say he was tied, probably bound to a post, his hands behind him, his neck secured tight to the post. The scorched fingers," he continued, gesturing to the charred fingertips, "show that at the end he was grasping at something that was burning intensely. We won't ever know with certainty, but I suspect he broke his hands free and desperately reached out to try to snuff a burning fuse. The fuse eluded him, and at the last moment he raised his hands to his face, hence the splinters on the backs of his hands and torso and the absence of any in his face."

"There was more damage to his chest than splinters," Hancock observed.

"That," Duncan replied in a pointed tone, "is no doubt why we are here." When his companions offered no reply, he indicated the parallel slices on either side of the Seneca's chest. "Pine had something fixed to his chest, something secreted and held there by strips of cloth, I suspect. It was cut away by those who attacked him after he was struck on the head. Then they lit the fuse. They didn't just want it, they wanted to destroy all evidence that they had taken it."

"Dear Lord," Adams groaned. "All is lost."

Duncan's pity for Jonathan Pine was slowly being replaced with anger. "They blew up the ship!" he reminded his companions. "Are you the reason? Are you why all those lives were lost? How many good men died?"

Hancock shut his eyes. Adams looked down at the floor.

"Thirty-eight," came a weak voice from the door. It was the taciturn Mr. Livingston. "Her crew was thirty-eight all told, including a ship's boy. Without the log or the purser's records we won't know if she took any passengers."

Livingston. Duncan recalled the words of Henry Knox in the church tower. The *Arcturus* was owned by Mr. Livingston. Duncan and Sarah lived in Edentown, inland from the Hudson. Everyone in the Hudson Valley knew the great manor family who owned a third of its lands and had ruthlessly dealt with squatters in recent years. "And what was a New York ship doing sailing into Boston?" he asked. "Why wasn't its owner waiting in its home port?"

Livingston turned away. He staggered, steadied himself on the back of a chair, and sat, gazing emptily at the table. "Thirty-eight," he repeated in a desolate voice, as if the scope of the tragedy had finally struck him.

"What was he carrying for the Sons of Liberty?" Duncan asked in a harsh tone. None of the three men would meet his gaze. He pulled the beads from his hand and moved them in front of Hancock. "Do you know what these are? They are touched by the Iroquois spirits. The man who touches them must tell the truth or feel the wrath of those spirits."

Hancock visibly shuddered as Duncan put the beads into the merchant's palm and closed the man's fingers around them. "Was he a messenger for the Sons, sailing from London?" he demanded.

The color drained from Hancock's face. Duncan pointed to the seagull and the snake inked on the man's chest. "This is the story of his life, and that image tells the tale of his life since leaving the whaling grounds. Birds and snakes are both messengers of the gods. His bird was a seabird. He was saying that he was a messenger on the sea, a messenger for very important people, almost godlike people. He was very proud of it." An unexpected vehemence heated Duncan's voice. "Would you deny him the truth of that now, as he lies here dead because of a task he was performing for you?"

Hancock suddenly dropped the beads on the table as if they had burned him. "Yes, Duncan. He was bringing something vital to the Sons."

"Something worth thirty-eight lives?"

Hancock, Livingston, and Adams had no answer. They looked strangely frightened now. Adams glanced at the door, as if about to bolt.

Duncan gestured to the slices in Pine's chest. "It was bigger than a letter. A small book. A journal or a ledger perhaps?"

"Not a journal," Hancock murmured.

"A ledger then," Duncan concluded. "An account book."

No one disagreed, but Adams and Livingston turned their backs to Duncan and stepped into the larger chamber, as if trying to ignore Duncan's words. Hancock simply stared at the dead man.

Duncan sighed and put a hand on Pine's shoulder, as if to comfort him. "His body needs to be cleansed," he declared. "I would like to remove the splinters and stitch his wounds." He glanced at Conawago. "There are more words of the tribes to be spoken."

Suddenly the broad-shouldered Puritan at the end of the table spoke. "He will be given a Christian burial."

"His blood was of the Haudenosaunee," Conawago stated, challenge in his voice.

"Jonathan Pine was anointed with the words of the Lord Jesus," the big man pressed.

Duncan braced himself as he saw Conawago's mouth twist. The old Nipmuc almost never lost his temper, but when he did, it was best to keep a distance. "And his ancestors in the Haudenosaunee heaven never learned those words," he rejoined in a voice like ice.

"Surely, Reverend Occom, such a soul would want to hear the prayers of his natural fathers as well as of his spiritual father," Hancock nervously offered. "I will see that he has a coffin of fine cherrywood," he added.

"Haudenosaunee!" Conawago growled.

As the big-shouldered man named Occom leaned forward, Duncan had the impression of an angry bull about to launch itself at a rival.

Conawago leaned forward himself, as if eager to accept the challenge; then Duncan set the white beads over the old man's wrist. The Nipmuc looked down at them, and his fire dimmed. "Oak, not cherry," he said in a hollow voice. "Red oak."

"Of course, whatever you—" Hancock began; then Adams grabbed his arm and pulled him out of the chamber.

"I will clean the body," Conawago declared, fixing the pastor with a cool stare. There was an argument between the two men that Duncan did not fully fathom. Defiance ignited again in Occom's dark eyes; then he gripped the cross that hung from his neck and quieted. He placed a hand on Pine's forehead for a moment and removed his jacket. "I will help you, my chief," the puritanical Occom said.

Duncan stared in utter disbelief. Revealed on Occom's wrist was the tattoo of a fish. He had spoken the last words in the Nipmuc tongue.

3

Boston Harbor slept under a blanket of fog as Enoch Munro guided their gig away from Hancock Wharf. Duncan and Conawago used oars to push past the hulls of the closely packed merchant ships as they coasted into deeper water and then, with a nod from Munro, hoisted the small, solitary sail. The breeze flexed the canvas, and the sturdy little boat swung to the northeast, ghosting past half a dozen huge square-rigged vessels recently arrived from the Wine Islands and the West Indies. No one spoke. It had been a grim, debilitating night, and now they were proceeding toward more death. Conawago settled into the bow and stared straight ahead, as still and somber as a figurehead. Duncan lowered himself against the slender mast. The gentle rocking of the boat soon lulled him to sleep.

"Captain McCallum, sir, if you please," intoned the sailor hovering over him.

Duncan stirred with the confusion of slumber, then recognized Munro, who had been his first mate on their voyage to Bermuda. "Captain no longer, Enoch," he replied, "just Duncan."

Conawago now had the tiller, and Enoch was lowering the sail. Shirley Point was less than half a mile away off their port bow. The sun was nearly an hour above the horizon, the fog reduced to a few wisps in the inlets.

The Point was alive with activity. Duncan had expected to see the usual scavengers of nature who descended on shipwrecks, pecking at ruptured barrels of meat or other ship's stores, but he was not expecting the huge flock of the human variety that scrambled along the tideline. A sunken ship often yielded little more than the flotsam from its open deck, but a ship that had been ripped apart like the *Arcturus* offered vast quantities of floating treasure. The broken hull was yielding up not just mangled sections of its oaken hull, some of which might still be put to good service by onshore carpenters, but also spars, chairs, and unopened trunks and crates. Most of its bounty, though, consisted of kegs, casks, and barrels. Men and women, many of them soaked to their waists after leaping into the water to claim their prizes, were calling out their discoveries.

"Salt pork!" shouted a corpulent woman whose calico dress clung unflatteringly to her body.

"Madeira!" exclaimed a bearded man nearby.

Watching over all was a sloop of war, a large cutter designed for swift sailing in coastal waters. The revenue cutter, which had arrived from Halifax the night of the sinking, was anchored in the center of a roughly quarter-mile circle in which there was no activity except for two naval launches dragging lines through the water, equipped with swivel guns and manned by marines who kept muskets at the ready. His Majesty's Navy may have yielded the beach, but it was not letting anyone near the site of the explosion.

As Conawago guided the gig into shallow water, Duncan leapt off with a line and secured it to an overhanging pine. Minutes later the three men were in the middle of the salvage frenzy. A farmer was loading casks of molasses onto an oxcart, laughing at another man whose own too-full cart had become mired in the soft sand. An aged man bent with a keg on his back, exhorting his wife to tie it tight to his spine. Cats, gulls, and a few scrawny dogs worked at the hundreds of herring that had been killed in the explosion and washed onto the wrack line. It had been more than a day since the disaster, but much of the debris, having been pushed out on the tide, was now washing back toward the scavengers.

At the end of the narrow beach, larger horse-drawn wagons waited, and as the three men continued down the beach, a line of carriages became visible, carrying onlookers who stared grimly at the dark shapes that had been assembled along the edge of the sand. The dead had been laid out in two rows on the off chance that a Massachusetts waterman might recognize a fatality from the New York ship.

Conawago, Munro, and Duncan stepped slowly along the beach, each now at his own pace. Conawago paused to help two children load pieces of shattered wood onto a milk cart pulled by a large dog. Munro waded into the shallows to help a struggling gray-haired woman tie a line around a drifting barrel. Duncan walked purposefully toward the rows of dead.

He counted two dozen bodies. There had been thirty-eight crew members, but some no doubt were trapped in the wreckage and others may have been taken out to sea on the shifting currents. The bodies were men of all ages, colors, and shapes. An African youth with a circular pattern of scars on one cheek stared lifelessly toward the sky, a long length of kelp wrapped around his neck like a scarf. A man with a balding head wore a leather apron. A crab scurried out of the mouth of a sailor with curly blond hair who clung with a desperate hand to the trunk of a gnarled pine, meaning that he had made it to shore before dying. A foot-long splinter of wood pierced his back. At least a dozen had most of their clothing burned away, one so completely that someone had draped his privates with seaweed.

Duncan's heart was a cold, heavy stone as he paced along the bodies. He had grown up in the Hebrides with men of the sea, his own beloved grandfather had been one, and he knew most to be bold souls who embraced the rigors and joys of the mariner's life with equal zest. These men would never again hold the hands of wives and lovers, never again embrace daughters and sons. All that they ever were and ever hoped to be had been snatched away by cowards who had lit a fuse in the bowels of their ship because of a parcel cut from Jonathan Pine's chest. A cold, helpless rage was building inside Duncan against the anonymous killers who had lit their spark in the night and fled.

"God was looking the other way when this happened," came a tight voice at his side. Munro too looked out over the grisly line of death. "The peace of the running wave to you," he murmured in Gaelic, "and the peace of shining stars." It was a Scottish prayer for mariners. The old Scot was a hard-boiled, practical man, but his eyes often betrayed a contemplative spirit.

Duncan stepped on, pausing by a red-haired man much his own age who wore a little bunch of dried heather on a leather thong around his neck and a sash of plaid around his waist. He knelt for a moment, pushing the hair out of the dead man's eyes. "*Cadal ann an sith mo bhrathair,*" he whispered to the Highlander. *Sleep in peace, my brother.* He felt the cool gaze of the onlookers and studied them. It was not simply fear of the dead he saw on their faces. These too were people of the sea. Fishermen, lobstermen, clam haulers, and boatwrights. They had not come as scavengers. They wore somber clothing, their Sabbath clothing, and had come to bear witness to the death of fellow mariners. As he watched, a handful stepped out of the ranks and began following his example, straightening the dead and pulling away the seaweed that covered some of their faces.

Suddenly a woman screamed. Another swooned and collapsed onto the man beside her. Several in the crowd pointed excitedly toward the water. Duncan spun about to see a hand rising up out of the water fifty yards offshore, shaking, rising, the arm making struggling movements toward the shoreline. He had unbuttoned his waistcoat and was about to kick off his shoes when the arm abruptly shifted direction and began wrenching back and forth. He saw now the gray fin four feet behind it. The shark was large and relishing the meal offered by one of the drifting bodies. Seagulls reeled overhead and dove for the gobbets of flesh in the water.

Duncan found himself advancing toward the water in mincing steps, without conscious effort. He did not know the man, but knew him to be a fellow voyager of the sea, and knew the bond between those who experienced the rage and beauty of the earth far from safe shores. Being ripped apart by such a beast was the common nightmare of all such men.

A hand clamped around his arm. "No, my friend. He is beyond your help." Conawago fixed Duncan with a weary but determined gaze. "There's more than enough death on these shores already."

Duncan made no response, just kept staring at the shark. The old Nipmuc maintained his tight grip until finally, as the thrashing in the water subsided, Duncan retreated to the dry sand. "Men die like this in war," Duncan said, "but in war they knowingly face the risk of death. These men had no chance to fight, no chance even to pray. They were homeward bound, in sight of a safe haven at last, the trials of their journey behind them." He gazed at the rows of dead. "It's cruel hard, Conawago. The king must make the vermin who did this swing from the gallows."

"It's cruel hard," the Nipmuc echoed.

The wind ebbed for a moment, and they could hear both the orders being shouted in the navy launches sweeping the wreckage grounds and the weeping prayers of those who had begun tending the dead. The two men tilted their heads in the direction of a clump of twisted spruce trees that grew hard in a patch of rocky shoreline.

"'Farewell and adieu to ye ladies of Spain . . .'" came a tiny voice cracking with grief. They pushed through the brush to see a boy with shaggy black hair, knee-deep in the water, fending off a small shark with a shattered oar as he retrieved something from the bay.

"'We'll rant and we'll roar across the salt sea,'" he hoarsely sang as he turned back to the beach, paying no mind to the sharks circling behind him, less than a stone's throw away.

Duncan darted to his side, pulling him free of the water. "Lad, don't bait the monsters," he warned. "You mustn't go into—" His words choked away as the boy dropped what he was carrying. It was a human foot, severed at the ankle.

The boy spoke with his head bowed as he pointed to the foot, which had only four toes. "I think I know him," he said of the foot. "Jesus Fusca, the Portugee, who lost his little toe to frostbite on a whaling trip to the ice sea." He looked up at Duncan with empty eyes. "Is that a Portuguese foot? Most of the others I can make a better guess at."

"Others?" Conawago asked.

The boy, who could be no more than twelve years old, made an absent gesture down the spit of sand. "My friends," he declared.

Duncan shuddered. The boy was pointing toward bloody arms, legs, hands, and one head lying in a row along the tideline, some being pecked at by fish crows and gulls. He indicated the first three of the body parts. "That tattoo of the dolphin, that's Ezekiel Grant, the cutlass scar on the leg, that's Peter Fife, who once fought pirates. And that ring with the cross," he continued in an empty voice, "that's my friend Adam."

Conawago grabbed the boy, wrapped his arms around him, and pressed him against his chest. The boy weakly resisted for a moment, then began silently sobbing.

Duncan picked up a handful of pebbles and began throwing them at the birds that scavenged among the boy's grisly salvage. He walked to the end of the row of body parts, scattering the birds, then turned toward the water as an officer roared through a speaking trumpet at a dory that rowed too close. "No farther, or we shoot!" Duncan heard with surprise, and saw the officer in the launch direct two marines to raise their muskets. Why was the navy so vehement about protecting the site of a wrecked merchant ship?

The dory was slow to respond, and the two muskets roared, hitting, as they were aimed, the gunwale near the waterline. Wood splintered at the impact of the balls, and the man at the dory's tiller responded with a sharp turn and a sharper curse.

Conawago was sitting with the boy on a driftwood log when Duncan returned. The Nipmuc introduced the youth. "This is Will Sterret, Duncan, ship's boy on the *Arcturus*."

The dark lump that was Duncan's heart lightened for an instant. The death count had gone down by one. He sat on the sand before the boy. "I was seven years old, Will, when one of my grandfather's sloops went down off the Hebrides with all hands, most of them my cousins. My grandfather didn't sleep until he had accounted for all the bodies. I was with him much of the time, cruising where the currents took the bodies, then coming into shore with the corpses to the wails of their families. My grandfather said that when the sea means for a man to feel her embrace, she will never be denied."

"T'weren't the sea who took 'em," the boy replied in a choked whisper. "T'was the demons who stuck a flint on a fuse." The words, and the boy's desolate stare, twisted Duncan's heart. Then, as they sank in, Duncan and Conawago exchanged a surprised glance.

"My friend Conawago here and I spent last night with the body of Jonathan Pine," he said. "Did you know him?"

Will slowly nodded. "'Flee,' Jonathan told me," the boy said. "'Launch yourself over the rail in a long dive like I taught you in the Azores. No time to raise the alarm. Just save yerself and stroke for the shore,' he said, 'and don't stop there. Make for Boston and Mr. Hancock and tell what happened.' Then he cursed me for lingering. I was nearly onshore when she exploded." His voice drifted away for a moment. "Then I ran like a demon and finally collapsed and hid under a fallen log until it was safe. I did not go to Boston, I came back to find Jonathan. I thought I saw his body and pulled it to shore, but it wasn't him, it was the third mate. Then there was the carpenter, and the cook, and another, and another. I guess I didn't really think they would all die."

"You should go to your family, boy," Conawago said. "Leave this to us."

"My uncle is all I have left. He wants us to pay off in Boston and buy a little pinnace, then sail it down east to the Maine country. Says we will start a sheep farm like my grandparents had once in Cornwall. He's keen as mustard about it, and is working the accounts to see how many ewes our coin might fetch."

"A good plan," Conawago declared with a nod. "We can get you to him. Where is he?"

"Not far." The boy looked down the beach with an empty expression. "I lost count. I think his was the fifteenth body I pulled out, maybe sixteen or seventeen. All of his hand bitten off except the thumb. Some shark has my grandfather's silver ring in his belly."

The brittle silence was broken by a shout from another dory that had ventured close to the navy boats. The wind minced the words, but Duncan could hear "Godless devils!" and "Rot in hell!" coming from the dory. Its occupants were not interested in salvage. A solitary man rowed while another, in austere black clothing, stood in the bow shaking his fist at the king's sailors.

As Duncan watched, a middle-aged woman ran into the water, shouting frantically, gesturing the dory back. The marines raised their muskets.

"Why do they do that?" Duncan wondered out loud.

"We thought the navy was trying to help, to recover more of the bodies before the sea wolves took them," the boy said in a hollow voice. His strength and spirit were drained. "But they ain't keeping them."

"I don't understand," Duncan said, then followed the boy's hand as he pointed toward the closest launch. A body, sprawled across the gunwale, was being searched by the officer in charge. As Duncan watched, the officer straightened and snapped an order, and the body was dumped over the side.

"Defilers!" the man standing in the dory shouted as he shook his fist again. "Spawn of the devil!"

The officer looked at the man with obvious disinterest, then gestured to his marines. The two muskets fired, and wood splintered on the dory's hull. As the dory retreated, the man in the bow still shouted his curses.

"Tell me something, Will," Conawago asked in a contemplative voice. "What did you mean when you said you ran until you were safe? Surely you were safe once you touched the land."

The grime on the boy's face was streaked with tears shed over the past hours, but his eyes were red and dry. He had no more tears left. "I called out when I touched the sand, grateful that they had reached the shore, too."

Duncan knelt by the boy and placed a hand on his shoulder. "Men from the *Arcturus*? You mean there were others who escaped?"

"They were rowing away already when I dove off the rail, but I'm sure it was the captain's little skiff, the one with the brightwork he's so proud of. They disappeared around that long spit," the boy explained, pointing to a pine-covered tongue of land that jutted into the bay a quarter mile to the north. "I had recognized Mr. Oliver by the light of the flames—my friend the boatswain's mate—so I called his name and began running toward them, but he stopped and yelled at me. 'Run, Will!' he shouted. 'Run and hide!' Then the others hit him and shoved him forward like he was their prisoner. I was confused, 'cause I thought they was all friends, so I followed, real careful like. They went into that line of trees, and I quickened my pace so as not to lose them. Then came a terrible Indian war cry and a scream. I ran in the other direction and hid like Mr. Oliver said."

"A war cry?" asked Conawago. "How could you know of such a thing?"

"Oh, Mr. Oliver, he was a great Indian fighter in the war with the French, one of those amazing rangers. Sometimes on fair-weather nights we would sit on deck and listen to his tales. He would act out pieces of them and always give that bloodcurdling cry when he told of the attacks of the savages. At first I thought Mr. Jonathan would take offense, seeing how he was of the tribes, but he just laughed and said Mr. Oliver was a good mockingbird. He said if I ever heard that sound in the real world, I must run, because it meant death was stalking near."

"So you mean you heard Mr. Oliver from the shadows?" Duncan asked.

"I don't think so. It seemed of a higher pitch, and angrier. I don't know. I told you, I ran, and hid 'til first light."

"So it was two of the other crewmen you saw with him?" Conawago probed.

"Not crew. The passengers from Halifax."

Conawago and Duncan rose at the same instant, both studying the point of land with the eyes of frontier scouts. Duncan realized that his hand had gone to his knife. It was impossible that there would be raiding warriors on Boston harbor, but clearly the boy had heard something that had given him a deep fright. And if men had been fleeing the ship before Will, they must have known about the fuse, even been the ones who lit it.

"'Hoy the shore!" boomed a voice behind them. Duncan turned to see the little ketch that Hancock used to visit his warehouses in Salem and Portsmouth. Munro was running to their gig as the ketch lowered its anchor.

"Stay here," Duncan said to Conawago and the boy, then trotted down the beach. He leapt onto the gig as it was coasting off the sand, and five minutes later they nudged the side of the ketch.

"Just needed a quick ferry to shore, Duncan," Hancock declared. Robert Livingston stepped out of the small cabin.

"No," Duncan replied, and pointed toward the two-masted naval cutter that was directing the searches. "The prince of the Boston merchants and the owner of the lost vessel are going to consult with the authorities," he said, and motioned them to climb down into the smaller boat.

"I don't see that—" Livingston began, but he was cut off by Duncan.

"We have little time," Duncan told him, "and you need to get me to the officer in charge. They won't stop us when they recognize the two of you."

By the time they were within hailing distance of the cutter, the two launches had flanked them, marines with muskets at the ready. "You intrude in the business of His Majesty's Navy!" barked the lieutenant at the rail of the cutter. "If you have inquiries, the commandant at Castle Island will be happy to entertain them, I'm sure."

"I am Mr. Hancock of the Boston merchants, and the *Arcturus* was owned by my friend here, Mr. Livingston of New York," Hancock called out, quickly grasping his role. "She was carrying important cargo destined for my warehouses. This is where we need to make our inquiries. Our insurance association will need notifications and certifications."

Hancock's words caught the officer by surprise, and he looked back down the deck as if for an answer. "Then surely where you need to be, gentlemen, is with that association," he replied. "We will supply the required paperwork in due course."

"We will learn what you have learned, sir," Hancock replied in a well-practiced peremptory voice. "Lower your ladder."

The lieutenant seemed distracted as Hancock, Livingston, and Duncan climbed onto his deck, his eyes shifting again and again to the launches and to another officer standing at the cutter's stern rail. He finally took notice that his junior officers had assembled in a line, as if to welcome high-ranking visitors, and he dismissed them with an awkward gesture.

Livingston did not wait for introductions. "What is the news of my vessel, sir?" he demanded.

The lieutenant glanced again toward the figure at the rail. "The *Arcturus* suffered a grievous misfortune. An overturned lantern perhaps, or a seaman careless with the ashes of his pipe. She is no more."

"And the noble souls who manned her?" Hancock asked.

The officer gestured over the water. "See for yourself. They have surrendered to eternity."

Duncan kept an eye on the nearest launch. It had thrown out a grappling hook to haul another body on board. He watched as the dead man was spread like a side of beef over the gunwale and the officer in charge ripped open his shirt, touched his pockets, then motioned to the two seamen who steadied it for him. They upended the man, headfirst, back into the sea.

"Christ on the cross!" Duncan spat. "You recover them from oblivion only to toss them back into it!" He could not contain his anger. "These were fathers and sons and brothers! Show some compassion!"

The figure from the stern was at the lieutenant's side now. The tall, dour man also wore the uniform of a naval lieutenant, though it seemed strangely new, bearing none of the blemishes from tar and salt that were inevitable at sea. "His Majesty's Navy has a duty to investigate maritime incidents," he declared in an aloof tone. He stepped forward and fixed Duncan with an inquisitive gaze, his long, aquiline nose raised in the manner of a predator fixing the scent of its next meal. "Not run a damned charnel house."

"You are feeding men to the sharks."

"While we are the most potent force on the oceans, sir, I admit that we have yet to find a way to subdue the wolves of the sea. The dead receive their due. Have you not observed that the current is casting them onto shore?"

"In bits and pieces," Duncan shot back. He had taken an instant dislike to the haughty officer. "What are you searching for?"

The tall lieutenant winced, as if he had bitten something sour, then turned to Hancock. "You must teach your servants better manners, sir, before bringing them onto a king's ship."

"Mr. McCallum is not my servant," Hancock replied in a level voice.

The officer repeated the name with oily disdain. "McCallum. Should have known. Another Highland heathen."

"Mr. McCallum assists us with the insurance survey," Livingston asserted, and stepped between Duncan and the officer.

"I am sure Lieutenant Beck meant no offense, sir," the cutter's commander nervously injected. "It has been a stressful day for all of us." Lieutenant Beck, Duncan realized, was an outsider, not part of the cutter's regular crew.

Duncan watched as the nearer launch approached another floating corpse. As one sailor prepared to throw the grapple at it, another called out, pointing to a second body wearing a blue jacket. The man with the grapple turned and snagged the second body.

Duncan turned to Lieutenant Beck. "You are looking for the bodies of officers. Why?"

Oddly, Beck looked to Livingston and Hancock, as if they might explain; then he answered with a cool, thin grin. "There's a press-gang over at Castle Island. They always know how to deal with a wild Scot in need of discipline." He turned to Duncan with an annoyed expression. "I wager they could find a berth for you on a ship bound for the yellowjack islands."

Duncan was only half listening to the arrogant officer. From the skiff, Munro was gesturing urgently to him. When he caught Duncan's eye, he pointed into the water forty feet from the cutter. Something was suspended a few inches below the surface. Another body, Duncan realized, clad in one of the dark blue jackets that Livingston, like Hancock, required his fleet officers to wear.

"Leave now," Duncan heard Beck say to him, "or you'll spend the night in the fort explaining why you choose to obstruct the business of the navy."

Duncan returned Beck's icy gaze. As Livingston asked the officer whether any cargo had been recovered, Duncan furtively slipped out of his shoes, whistled to Enoch as he threw them into the gig, and pointed to a large fin breaking the water two hundred feet away.

"Get down at once!" Lieutenant Beck snarled as Duncan leapt onto the rail. "You insolent dog, I will have you—" He had not finished his sentence before Duncan dove.

Duncan had reached the spot where he saw the officer's body when Munro gave a frightened cry. "Duncan! Forget it, I pray ye! No time! Back to me or yer in the belly of the beast!"

Duncan twisted on the surface to see the fin speeding toward him. He marked the position of the gig and curled into a powerful body dive into the depths.

The dead man hovered two feet below the surface now. Duncan came up under the body, hooked a hand under its shoulder, and pulled it toward the gig, breaking the surface thirty feet from Munro. Sailors on the cutter were shouting, pointing behind him. A musket fired from the cutter, then two more in quick succession, slicing the water behind him. Marines were firing at the shark. Lieutenant Beck was shouting furiously for the nearest launch to intercept him.

Duncan was the swiftest of swimmers, more so since accepting from Conawago as his totem the spirit of the furry swimmer of Iroquois lakes, though he knew he was no match for a large, angry shark. But the creatures were dim-sighted, and although this one could scent death and blood from afar, there was such a confusion of blood and death in the cove that, Duncan prayed, the predator would be distracted in its course. His strokes were powerful but only one-handed. Salt water stung his eyes. He heard voices in the gig, terrified calls from the sailors on the cutter. The sound of the launch's oars came close behind him.

"Sweet bleeding Jesus!" Munro cried out as he threw a rope into the water, Livingston and Hancock beside him now. "Don't look back, Duncan! Blessed Michael, don't look back!"

Shaking his head free of the surface in time to see Lieutenant Beck pushing away the barrel of a musket being aimed at the shark, Duncan grabbed the line. Several hands heaved him up as Munro violently slammed a heavy oak oar into the thrashing water just behind him. As the oar split with a sharp crack, Duncan twisted about in time to see a row of razor-sharp teeth and the bright anklebone of the foot the shark had ripped from the body. A huge black eye, fixed on Duncan, glided past.

Suddenly, arms were pulling him and his grisly cargo into the boat. Munro stood with the split end of the oar poised in his hand, ready to launch it like a harpoon. Then, to Beck's furious curses, the gig was drifting free and the officer of the launch was shouting at his men to board it. But not one of the seamen bent at his oars. Some stared at the big fin, some at Duncan. The sailors, ever a superstitious lot, had witnessed something extraordinary between Duncan and the shark, and they were loath to interfere.

"You are completely mad, McCallum," John Hancock said, still holding the oar he had used to push away from the cutter.

Livingston gave a final shove with his own oar against the hull of the ship and turned toward Duncan with a mischievous grin. "That was most satisfying!" the New York merchant exclaimed, then motioned to the body. "Now pray tell us why this dead man is worth incurring the wrath of His Majesty's Navy."

Duncan shed his waterlogged waistcoat. "I think you had already incurred that wrath," he suggested, suddenly feeling very tired, "but until now, neither side would admit it." Hancock and Livingston stared silently at the corpse, refusing Duncan's bait. He knelt by the dead man, rolled him onto his side, and delivered a sharp blow to his back. Water drained from his lungs. "This one drowned, probably while trying to escape the wreck twenty fathoms down. You can confirm he was an officer on your ship, Mr. Livingston?" he asked as he pushed the long brown hair from the man's face.

Livingston bent to look at the ghastly face. "The ship's sailing master, yes. For God's sake, close his eyes."

"The officers expected to arrive at the harbor before midnight," Duncan said as he pushed down the eyelids. "Why would they all have donned their uniforms at such a late hour?" He looked up at the two merchants with challenge in his eyes. They clearly had no answer. He looked back at Beck, who was shouting at the cutter's captain now, and answered his own question. "Because the cutter was going to board her."

He touched the blue jacket trimmed with silver thread. "This jacket makes the dead officers readily identifiable, and the navy has a particular interest in the officers. At least Mr. Beck does. Why?" Duncan began unbuttoning the jacket. "Because," he suggested, "he was led to believe that missing ledger is on one of them."

Hancock and Livingston looked at each another, and not at Duncan. "We should just take the body to shore," Hancock said in an uneasy voice. The merchant turned and made an awkward show of helping Munro with the oars.

Duncan straightened, noticing how neither Livingston nor Hancock would meet his gaze. "What do you mean?" he demanded. Neither man replied. In his mind's eye he recalled what the officers in the launches had done with the bodies they had recovered. Each corpse had been spread out, his clothing slashed open to expose his chest. "You know I'm right!" he spat. "They are looking for what was taken from Jonathan Pine before he died his horrible death."

"Please keep your voice down," Hancock chided.

"You let me dive in after this body," Duncan said, his resentment mounting, "let me recover it despite the stalking shark, all the while knowing there was no reason for me to do so."

To Duncan's surprise, Hancock showed middling skill at rowing. He took several long strokes before replying. "Actually there was a very good reason. You couldn't have played your part better had we rehearsed it. Now there is but one remaining act in the little drama you have improvised. Let Beck think you found the ledger on this man." The merchant slipped a little account book from inside his waistcoat and covertly dropped it on the bench beside Duncan.

Duncan pushed down his temper and saw that Beck was indeed watching, now through a telescope. He placed the body on the bench beside him, pulled open the dead man's tunic, and with a deft movement lifted the little book—as if from the body—before stuffing it inside his own waistcoat.

He did not have to turn back to Beck to confirm that he had seen. Beck began screaming for the launches to intercept their gig. Not a sailor moved. They were, Duncan realized, watching their commander, himself at the cutter's stern, speaking with his officers. He seemed to have found his spine, perhaps after seeing Beck stop his marines from shooting the shark. It was as if he decided that Beck's mission with the cutter was over. Had the cutter been stalking the *Arcturus* all the way from Halifax?

Duncan turned back to Hancock and Livingston. "You knew they sought it," he ventured, "and you wanted to pretend that you too were trying to find it. You were toying with my life—"

"You hardly gave us time to react, McCallum," Livingston interjected. "As it was, we were forced into an overly hasty retreat from the ship." Duncan had to admit the truth of Livingston's words. "My God, man," the New York merchant added in an admiring tone, "you swim like a fish!"

Duncan touched the little doeskin pouch, adorned with Iroquois quillwork, that hung inside his shirt. His spirit totem was sleeker than a fish. "Why?" he asked. "Why the charade of searching for the ledger you know was stolen by Pine's killers?" Another uneasy glance passed between the two merchants, and Duncan realized he had asked the wrong question. "Why does the navy so desperately want it?"

"Not the navy as such," Livingston murmured, earning a censoring glance from Hancock, who stood and tossed a line to a man standing in the shallow water of the beach, then quickly climbed out of the gig. Livingston, silver-buckled shoes in his hand, was a step behind him.

The onlookers had gathered now and were being led in a hymn over the rows of dead by a burly man with disheveled black hair. As Duncan approached the gruesome lines of corpses, looking for Conawago and Will, he recognized Reverend Occom, the man who had stood by Pine's body, and halted. He was not sure why the broad-shouldered pastor unsettled him. It was enough that Conawago clearly distrusted him, and it was unlikely that his friend would be anywhere near the stiff parson. He retreated to the little point where he had left Conawago and the young survivor of the *Arcturus*. There was no sign of them other than a few pieces of bent marsh grass leading in the direction Will Sterret had said the fugitives from the ship had taken.

Duncan felt a tremor of fear as he recalled the boy's description of a war cry in the night. He broke into a slow trot, then a long, loping gait over the soft ground. He passed into the thin strip of forest, then emerged on a narrow strip of land that descended into a marsh, where a wide river emptied into the bay. Standing on a fallen log, he surveyed the marsh and the clumps of trees and was about to shout for Conawago when he heard the two-tone whistle of a towhee, one of his friend's forest calls. Following the sound, he quickly found the Nipmuc and Will standing in a grove of pines near a ring of stones that had recently been used for a campfire. They were examining a crude lean-to constructed of conifer branches. Beyond the lean-to was a small, sandy flat that opened onto the river.

"The boy was sure the captain's skiff came down this river," Conawago explained. "If so, someone was waiting for them here. This camp has been used for several days, abandoned only hours ago, as if someone here was anticipating a party from the *Arcturus*."

The words sent a chill down Duncan's spine. It seemed to confirm that the sinking had been planned well in advance. "Waiting for it to explode," he declared, and bent to study the ground.

"All the tracks around the camp are the same," Conawago explained. "One pair of shoes with soft soles, perhaps moccasins. Many trips down the path to the river landing." The Nipmuc motioned Duncan toward the edge of the little clearing. "He caught fish and at least two rabbits," the old man said, indicating small bones tossed under a bush. He nodded toward the path to the water. "Then three men arrived by boat, all in heavier shoes."

"This can't be far from farms, perhaps even a village," Duncan observed.

"He wanted to stay close to watch the bay," Conawago suggested.

Duncan silently studied the campsite and a nearby tree that showed signs of being repeatedly climbed. "He picked a site hidden by the trees and the low hills toward the mainland, cut off by the marsh. There are other places he could have kept watch, but they would have made him conspicuous."

"Here he could hide," Conawago suggested, "and be ready to jump in the skiff as it traveled up the river."

Duncan saw that Will now stood at the landing, looking past the mouth of the river toward the bay beyond. "Not this river," Duncan said, recalling the maps he had seen of the area. "It can't go more than a couple miles at most, surrounded by marsh all the way."

"Here," Will called from the edge of the beach, and pointed to the ground at his feet. The track of packed sand indicated the dragging of a small boat, the path of its narrow keel making a tiny trench in the still-packed sand.

"And dragged here," Conawago suggested, indicating a roughly circular patch where the grass had been crushed by the press of heavy weight.

"Too uneven for a boat," Duncan said as he reached his friend's side. "More like stones, as if the man using the camp brought large stones here from the woods farther inshore."

"Stones?" Conawago asked, foreboding creeping into his voice. "But why? Where did the stones go? And why destroy the ship when they were barely an hour from anchorage in the harbor? They didn't leave the ship for a pile of stones. Why not just meet in Boston?"

Duncan paced along the narrow strip of sand, then squatted at the river's edge and carefully studied its ripples and eddies. "There," he said, and pointed to a patch of water a hundred feet away where there was a slight, unexpected twisting in the smooth water.

"It could be anything, Duncan," Conawago said. "An old stump, perhaps."

Duncan handed him his waistcoat. He stripped off his shirt, slipped off his shoes, and made a running dive into the river.

Duncan had sometimes tried to explain to Sarah the exhilaration he felt when swimming underwater, but words could never capture its full magic. Even this shallow, turbid water offered another world below its surface, and he glided through it with a carefree abandon. A school of minnows scattered at his approach. He smiled as an old turtle looked up from its muddy bed. Here he experienced life in an entirely different dimension, and though he could not always understand the ways of the native spirits, he was convinced that since accepting the totem that never left his neck, he felt an added energy, even a strength of perception when gliding through the depths. In one fluid motion he exhaled a string of bubbles, surfaced only for the instant it took for a new breath and to fix his destination, then slipped underneath again.

The captain was proud of its brightwork, Will had said of the officer's personal boat. Something red flickered at him through the swaying river grass; then, with two more strokes, he was on it. The boat wore a yellow-and-red checkerboard pattern along its gunwale, with little black anchors painted on the yellow squares. It had been holed, then sunk with the missing stones. Duncan quickly pulled out half a dozen of the big rocks, then surfaced for another quick breath and returned to the bottom, working at the stones. After one more dive the boat rose a few inches, and with a shove he sent it coasting back toward the campsite.

He surfaced twenty feet from the bank. Will gave him an enthusiastic wave, but his delight gave way to a startled cry as the boat ghosted to the surface beside Duncan.

Within a few minutes Conawago and Duncan had removed the remaining stones, and with a mighty heave they pulled the boat onto the sand. As the water drained out through the hole that had been chopped in its bottom, Duncan paced around the boat. She had been a trim, sturdy vessel. The busy yellow-and-red checkerboard did not make her elegant, but it certainly made her distinctive. As he stood at the edge of the water staring at her stern, twigs snapped near the campsite and he heard someone complaining about a tear in his new linen shirt. Enoch Munro appeared from around a thicket of alders, followed a moment later by John Hancock and Robert Livingston. Brambles had been trapped in the hair of both merchants, and they wore exhausted expressions. They were not accustomed to excursions in the field.

"They wanted to find you," Munro reported in an apologetic tone.

"You abandoned us, McCallum," Livingston groused, "with all those bodies."

"You asked me to discover the truth," Duncan stiffly replied. "Not to play the nanny." Hancock, despite his wealth and frequent arrogance, was still genteel and compassionate enough for Duncan to think of as a friend, but he was not warming to the New York aristocrat.

Livingston swatted peevishly at the flies that were landing on his shoulders. "Prithee, sir, why do we find ourselves in this bug-infested wilderness?"

Duncan, his britches still dripping river water, pulled the boat higher up on the sand and silently pointed to its stern.

With low grumbling, Livingston stepped down the narrow path, Hancock at his heels. "So you found a fancy dinghy," the New Yorker said in a chiding tone, batting at another fly. Hancock pushed past him to reach Duncan's side.

"Robert," Hancock said, nodding at the boat, "if you quit complaining, you'll find out sooner why we are here." Across the black-painted stern, painted in bright yellow letters, was the name *Arcturus*.

A small, confused sound came from Livingston's throat. "It's odd that it drifted here, I grant you," he finally said. "But it is just more salvage."

Duncan chose to speak to Hancock. "Three men left the *Arcturus* after the fuse was lit in the hold. They rowed here, met someone, then staved in the boat and sank her to cover their trail."

Hancock's brow furrowed. Livingston threw up his hands in exasperation. "McCallum, you can't just conjure up wild theories. Your imagination is obviously fertile, but—"

Duncan interrupted. "There was a witness," he said, nodding to Will.

Livingston's protest died on his lips. Conawago pulled the boy to his side, as if to protect him.

"A child?" Livingston asked.

"The ship's boy. A boy no longer. Will found Pine in the hold, but Pine demanded that he flee to save himself. When he was swimming to shore, he saw the captain's skiff pulling for this inlet."

Hancock's usually composed countenance twisted as confusion, then anger, and finally something like fear crossed it. "They're here?" he asked, glancing nervously at the sandy forest.

"Gone this past day," Duncan explained. "The man who had been waiting for them here was their guide, I suspect."

Livingston bent and ran his fingers over the yellow letters, then finally found his voice. "Accept my apology, sir. But guide to where? Surely not to Boston when the city is in plain sight."

Duncan watched a pair of gulls sweep low and land in the high grass two hundred feet away. "No way of knowing," he replied. "Will thinks a Mr. Oliver was rowing this boat. Did you know him?"

Livingston stepped to the youth and put a hand on his shoulder. "Brave lad," he said. "I am so sorry." He reached into his waistcoat and handed the boy a coin. "Daniel Oliver, the ranger?" he asked Will. When the boy, his eyes fixed on the shilling, nodded, Livingston sighed. "A solid, reliable man. Signed on to one of my molasses ships a couple years ago, then asked for a transfer to a North Atlantic ship after half the crew died of yellowjack. Made boatswain's mate on the last voyage."

Another gull landed on the riverbank near where the other two had alighted and disappeared into the reeds. A fish crow wheeled overhead. "Go up to the campsite," Duncan told the two merchants. "Conawago can explain what he found there."

Livingston frowned. "John," he asked Hancock, "do you always take orders from your man like this?"

Hancock winced. "I think we have established that Duncan is nobody's man, Robert," he replied as Duncan turned to walk along the riverbank toward the gulls. "He takes orders only from an auburn-haired beauty named Sarah. Now, up to the campsite."

Halfway to the gap in the reeds where the gull had disappeared, Duncan halted to study the line of trees. The senses he had shaped during years of running the woods with Conawago and the Iroquois were sounding an alarm, but he was not sure he could trust them here. This may be a place of tragedy, but surely there could be no imminent danger. He studied the woods and then, satisfied that his friends were safe, continued along the muddy river. He marked the spot where, startled by his appearance, the gulls flew up; then he stepped into the bed of reeds.

The body had begun to ripen enough to attract scavengers. The man still had his eyes, and only small gobbets had been pecked out of his cheeks and hands. He had been a sturdy, muscular man of about forty years. Duncan looked back to the campsite, where Conawago, speaking with the merchants, kept an eye on him; then he made several quick hand signals and bent to straighten the crumpled body. He lifted the man's shoulders, freeing his head from the reeds that partially covered it, and with a groan dropped the head and stumbled backward. The dead man had been scalped.

He spun about and studied the tree line with new alarm, then leaned back to study the corpse. The man had the callused hands of a sailor, but the scars on his forearms were from the slashes of combat, the marks of a soldier. He wore two amulets on a braided leather strand, one of them a polished tooth of a shark onto which had been etched, scrimscraw style, the word *Never*. It was a sailor's ward against death by shark. The other was a small leather pouch, sewn closed, that had dried and tightened over a round object. Duncan did not have to open it to know what was secreted inside. The rangers and the Iroquois allies they served with were a superstitious lot. The primary threat of death, they would say, came from round red lead, meaning a blood-covered musket ball. If they carried such a ball, they would be immune from a fatal shot, so some would coat a ball with red ochre and wear it around their necks.

"Your charms worked," Duncan whispered to the dead man. He had not died from shark or ball. He had died from the hand ax, probably a tomahawk, that had smashed in the back of his skull and the knife that had sliced into his heart. The ax blow had likely come first, an unsuspecting blow from the rear, accompanied by a war cry. At the end, a cloth had been jammed into his mouth, shortening his dying breaths.

The reeds rustled, and Duncan looked up to see Conawago and Will staring at the body. The boy's face drained of color.

"I take it this is your Mr. Oliver?" Duncan asked the ship's boy.

The boy opened and shut his mouth several times. When he finally found his tongue, his voice was hoarse. "When I knew him," Will stated, "he had more hair."

Conawago leaned closer, chastising Duncan in the Mohawk tongue for signaling him to bring the boy.

"I had no choice," Duncan replied in the same language. "We owe the dead a name." He pointed to the knife in the dead ranger's chest, then with a chill saw the gaping wound. The killer had cut out part of the man's heart.

The old man studied the hilt for a moment, then looked up and cursed, this time in his own Nipmuc tongue. "It can't be," he said. "Someone deceives us." He looked up to Will, who still stared at his dead shipmate. "Is this perhaps the knife of Jonathan Pine?" he asked the boy.

Will's eyes were still round with the horror of their discovery. He did not answer right away. "No," he bravely said at last. "Jonathan's had a handle made from the antler of a stag."

Conawago, who had been studying the boggy ground around the dead man, pushed aside a clump of reeds and picked up a leather sheath. The killer had deliberately left it, like the blade, with his victim. Duncan took the sheath from his friend and studied it, then tried to bend the tough leather. "Too thick for deerskin. Moosehide," he concluded.

Conawago gave a reluctant nod.

Will noticed the cloth in the dead ranger's mouth. "He was a happy man," the boy said, "often laughing. But they stole away his laughter."

Duncan steeled himself, then pulled down the lifeless jaw and extracted the wad. The strip of brown cloth was adorned with intricate embroidery in the shapes of maple leaves and fish. He stretched it between his hands for Conawago to see. They had both prayed that such deaths would be finished at the end of the bloody war. Duncan suddenly was overcome with an irrational fear for Sarah's safety.

"Tattoo," Conawago said in a low voice, and gestured to Oliver's forearm, where an inked image edged out from under his sleeve. Duncan rolled back the sleeve, exposing the tattoo of a square-rigged sailing ship, and above that an image of a rifle crossed with a tomahawk. An arc over the weapons was inscribed *Rogers 1759*.

"Great Jehovah, McCallum!" came a voice through the reeds. Duncan looked up to see Hancock emerge from the dense vegetation. "This damned bog is going to ruin my shoes—" The merchant's words faded, and he clutched his belly as he saw the dead man. Livingston impatiently pushed past him, took one more step, and froze. The prince of the Hudson gasped, then doubled over and lost the contents of his stomach.

"Mr. Oliver left the *Arcturus* in time to save himself from the explosion," Duncan said, "but he was killed minutes later in this marsh by the man who had camped here."

"Your imagination—" Hancock began.

Duncan held up an impatient hand. "The man who waited here was a man of the northern forest, a man who could easily construct a secret campsite and forage for his own food. He didn't want to be seen by the local farmers and fishermen. Because he would have been conspicuous."

"I don't understand," Livingston, his hand on his belly, confessed.

Duncan placed one hand on the dead ranger's chest and with the other pulled out the knife. "He was rushed. His companions were no doubt eager to flee after destroying the *Arcturus*. Otherwise he would have taken time to cut out the entire heart instead of just eating a piece of it." He gestured to Oliver's bloody head, where portions of the skull shone through. "He lingered just long enough to take his trophy."

Livingston's hand shot to his mouth, as if he were about to retch again.

"This is from the strife with the French, a vengeance killing between warring enemies," Duncan explained. He indicated the distinctive pattern carved on the much-used knife hilt.

"Duncan, prithee," Hancock said in a trembling voice. "You speak to us as if we too were creatures of your wretched wilderness."

It was Conawago who answered. The Nipmuc stretched the cloth to show its pattern, similar to that on the hilt. "The knife, the sheath, this cloth. They are from the Abenaki, warriors of the northern Algonquins. In 1759 the rangers raided their town of St. Francis, in the Quebec lands, and massacred dozens. Abenaki warriors took blood oaths of vengeance. At campfires long after the war, men would say that an Abenaki would kill himself if he thought he had a chance of strangling the soul of a ranger on the other side."

When Livingston finally found his voice, he grabbed Hancock's arm. "A French Indian, John! God protect us!"

"Enough!" Hancock snapped. "This is Massachusetts. Don't speak of such distractions, Duncan. Focus on the lost ship. We have not known murdering heathens here since the last century. This can't possibly have anything to do with Pine's murder or the explosion of the *Arcturus*."

"It has everything to do with it," Duncan shot back.

Livingston gave an impatient snort and turned to retrace his steps through the bog. Hancock cast a disapproving frown at Duncan, then followed his friend.

"If the killers who took Pine's treasure needed this Abenaki, it was because they needed a guide into the north, into his homelands, the old French lands," Duncan called to Hancock's back. "The guide had his price. He wanted to eat the heart of a ranger."

Hancock did not acknowledge him. Conawago and Duncan watched in silence as the two stubborn merchants reached the campsite and continued down the trail through the trees.

Carrying the body through the mud to the landing, Duncan at Oliver's shoulders and Conawago at his feet, was a slow, stumbling effort. They were surprised to see Munro still there. The Scottish sailor was using a flat stone to carve out a long, shallow hole in the sandy soil. "Beg pardon," he said. "But we can't take a man who lost his scalp out to the salvagers very well, now can we?" Duncan found another stone and began helping. "We knew the war—the three of us and Oliver," Munro continued. "Better his brothers put him in the ground than some starch-collared prigs from Boston."

Duncan paused at the words and looked up.

"Ye can't ignore the truth of it, Duncan," the former soldier solemnly declared. "This man, and the others on the beach, died like so many others in the north years ago. The war isn't over . . ."

4

I T WAS LATE EVENING WHEN Duncan woke in a chamber lit by a solitary candle. He looked around, trying to recall how he had gotten into the bed, then paused as he saw the woman perched in the window seat. Sarah Ramsey seemed to glow in the soft light. He pushed back the blanket and was about to speak; then, with a smile, he realized she was asleep herself, her head against the sash. Duncan rose up on an elbow, silently gazing at her. Sarah was not just the inspired leader of the Edentown settlement on the western slopes of the Catskills, she was also a vital ambassador between the woodland tribes and European settlers.

Washed in the golden light of the candle on one side and the silver beams of the moon on the other, it seemed indeed that she was a creature of two worlds. As a strand of hair fell across her face, he saw the skittish, wild girl who'd been raised by the Iroquois. Seized by the loathsome British aristocrat who was her natural father, she had first been terrified of the European world, then furious at it for what it was doing to the tribes, and finally reconciled to a new life on the frontier. It was there, at the remote edge of the European world, that he and Sarah both thrived, and he knew she ached to return to it as much as he did.

He slipped off the bed and advanced, as stealthy as a ranger, to place a kiss on the crown of her head. She was never conscious of her beauty, and she shunned with self-conscious laughs the rouges and powders that the women of Boston society pushed on her. Her eyes fluttered open, and she offered a groggy smile, then pulled him toward her, pressing her head against his chest.

"Someone took me captive and confined me in her bed," he whispered.

Her low laugh was a salve to his battered spirit. "You were at the kitchen table waiting for some stew. But when I brought it, your head was on the table and you could not be revived."

"The past two days have been an ordeal."

"The three of us had a time getting you up the stairs."

"Three?"

"Ishmael and your new friend Will Sterret, who sleeps down the hall now. Later I brought up food," she explained, indicating a tray with a half a loaf, cheese, and a kitchen knife on the chest by the door, "but you would not be awakened."

"Ishmael's back?" Conawago's nephew had come with Sarah from Edentown but then promptly debarked for Nantucket to see its famed whaling fleet.

"He's says his calendar shows that we leave for the Catskills in two days." She gestured toward the candle. "He brought one box of the best spermaceti lights for the school, though I asked for half a dozen. He spent the rest of the money on a sea bear who apparently needed a home."

"Sea bear?"

Sarah stretched and smiled again. "You will meet her soon enough," she said, then looked up and fixed Duncan with a pointed gaze. "Two days, Duncan."

He kissed her on the crown again. "I promise, *mo chridhe*," he said. *My heart.* "Two days."

She tightened her grip on his waist. "We'll have more than a week on the road together," she said in a hopeful, almost mischievous tone.

"With Conawago, Ishmael, and apparently a creature called a sea bear who doesn't mind leaving the sea behind, and all the horses needing tending. We'll need at least two wagons for the supplies."

"Did I mention I bought a new clock for the school today, and several reams of good Dutch paper?"

"So maybe three wagons and a teamster to share the work. Just you and me on an idyllic stroll, with assorted human and four-legged companions."

Sarah screwed her face in exaggerated displeasure. "We can plan the crops. Maybe we can pick up a new milk cow from those Dutch farmers on the other side of the Hudson."

"And planting stock. We can buy apple trees in the Berkshires."

Sarah gripped his arm with a faraway expression. "The orchards," she said dreamily, and for a few heartbeats they were both lost in memories of walking hand in hand in groves thick with apple scent and the buzzing of bees. Sarah collected herself, then rose, fixing him now with a smile that had a surprising hint of melancholy. "We need you, Duncan," she said, as if he had been arguing with her. "You've been away too long."

"I promise," he assured her, "two days—and back on the road to Edentown." He playfully rubbed the top of her head. "Now I must retreat down the stairs before one of those Boston matrons discovers me in your bedchamber." He felt her stiffen and instantly regretted his words.

She released her grip on his arm and took a step backward. "You can't be a warrior forever, Duncan McCallum." They loved each other, but a piece of paper stood between them. Legally, Duncan was Sarah's indentured servant, and he had made it clear years earlier that he would not smear her honor by taking to bed together. Either she would be accused of misusing a mere servant or he would be accused of using her affection to ease his bondage. The parchment imposing his seven-year bond lay fastened to the lintel of her bedroom door, angrily pinned there by Sarah years earlier with her Iroquois skinning blade. They had avoided speaking of it, or of the newer magistrate's order that her father had imposed between them. Sarah had instead taken to reminding Duncan of the Iroquois warrior's way, in which valued warriors were not expected to marry until they reached their thirtieth year, Duncan's age. Duncan had stood alongside tribal warriors in struggles of many kinds, and when Sarah and he were alone on one of their private excursions into the mountains, she often called him her Celtic Mohawk. The ways of her beloved tribe signified much more to her than the vagaries of English magistrates.

Duncan broke off a piece of the bread and nibbled at it. "Did you mention stew?" he asked, forcing lightness into his voice.

She offered a half smile and motioned him toward the door. "I need to wash. I've been sitting here since—" She paused, as if not wanting to admit that she had been keeping vigil over him. "I need to wash," she repeated, then pulled at the top hook of her dress with one hand and pushed Duncan toward the hallway with the other. Duncan planted a playful kiss on her forehead and retreated downstairs.

•

IN THE KITCHEN, HE SAT at the end of a long table that was so battered, he suspected it may have arrived with the original Puritans. A nearly empty bowl had been left on the other end. He assumed that Ishmael had eaten and gone to sleep in the small stable, which the young Nipmuc preferred. Mrs. Pope, the widowed landlady who rented her house out to sustain her daughter and herself, served him a steaming bowl from the pot hanging over the hearth, then turned to shelving the dishes that had been left out to dry.

"You were entertaining, I see," Duncan observed between mouthfuls. He had seen a tea service waiting to be collected from the dining room table.

The compact, very round woman replied without pausing in her task. "Mr. Adams paid a visit."

Duncan looked up in surprise. "Samuel was here while I slept?" He did not miss her hesitation before speaking.

"Not Samuel," the landlady said, speaking over her shoulder. "His younger cousin from Braintree. Not as well fed. Not as talkative. But genteel enough and quite intelligent. He and Miss Sarah had a most congenial discussion."

"And why would she—" His question was cut off by a terrified scream from upstairs, followed by what sounded like a body hitting the floor. Duncan bolted out of his chair and was up the stairs in seconds. The young Miss Pope lay in a faint on the hallway floor, folded linens scattered about her. Duncan slowed at Sarah's door and reached for his knife, only to find it was not at his waist.

His heart lurched as he inched into the doorway and discovered Sarah in her shift, bent, her legs apart in the stance of a warrior in close combat. The kitchen knife from the tray left in the room was in her hand. The swarthy man before her was bent in a similar posture, a deadly, much longer blade in his own hand, amusement on his face as he pushed back a long braid of black hair that had fallen from under his tricorn hat.

Sarah's shift had a slice in it along the ribs, and Duncan saw small spots of crimson seeping through the linen. As he darted forward, she snapped an angry Mohawk word at him, a command for Duncan to back away, like a warrior claiming a prize. Her assailant's grin widened. He was obviously pleased to have his prey served up one at a time. Duncan eased along the wall, looking for something to use as a weapon, until Sarah growled at him to stop. She touched the patch of blood on her shift, then with the blood-tipped finger hastily drew two stripes on each cheek. "Come meet my blade!" she taunted her opponent in the Mohawk tongue. "Don't come sneaking in the shadows against my people unless you are ready to bleed!" she hissed.

When the man hesitated, Duncan assumed it was because he did not understand the words, but then he saw the intruder's treacherous grin and realized it was just his surprise that she was challenging him in the Iroquois tongue and had adorned herself with a warrior's stripes. Duncan stared in confusion; then, as the man pulled off his hat, tossing it out the window, he saw the tattooed fish on the stranger's neck at the end of a long, slanting scar that crossed his forehead and continued down a cheek, a wound from a sword. Despite his European clothing, the man was an Indian. Then Duncan saw that his tattered brown waistcoat wasn't worn over britches, but over deerskin leggings, and on his feet were moccasins. A piece of fur dangled from his belt.

As Duncan grabbed a heavy pewter candlestick and perched on the balls of his feet, ready to spring, the warrior lunged at her. Sarah avoided his blade with an effortless twist of her body. She taunted him with a Mohawk curse about his mother in her afterlife then, as she spoke, made a surprisingly high leap and came down at the stranger's side. The Indian smiled again, then hesitated and touched his shoulder. His hand came away bloody. She had nicked his arm.

Duncan had not seen this savage side of Sarah for years. Captured at an early age, she had been raised by an Iroquois sachem, a spirit chieftain who was revered and feared throughout the tribes. He had bestowed his love and wisdom on her but also his bearlike ferocity, which she had amply displayed when struggling with the Europeans who tried to keep her from her beloved tribes.

"Duncan, get back!" Sarah snapped as she inched sideways.

The intruder paused, looking at Duncan for a heartbeat; then Sarah waved her knife in the man's face. The stranger lunged again, but feinted, twisting and thrusting his blade at Duncan's belly. As quick as a cat, reacting faster than Duncan, Sarah kicked the man's hand away and delivered a downward blow, cutting into the man's upper arm deeply enough to bring a surprised gasp.

The stranger straightened. There was still amusement in his face as he studied Sarah, but also a new respect. His gaze drifted to the amulet that hung from her neck, now spilled out from her shift, and he froze. His eyes went round. The amulet, whose contents not even Duncan knew, was decorated with ornate quill-work depicting a human eye flanked by a serpent and a bear, fastened at the top with the talons of an eagle. It had been worn by Sarah's Iroquois father, Tashgua.

The intruder retreated a step, whispering what sounded like a prayer in a tongue Duncan did not recognize; then he lowered his blade. He cast a long, disappointed glance at Duncan and in a flash of movement disappeared out the window. Duncan closed and locked it behind him.

Sarah dropped the knife to the floor and accepted Duncan's embrace.

"*Mussh, nighean, mussh,*" he whispered in Gaelic as a silent sob racked her body. *Hush, lass, hush.* They stayed locked in each other's arms for several long breaths.

"There!" Sarah said as she pushed away and straightened her shift, not realizing she was leaving bloodstains with every touch. "I'm finished with Boston!" she declared. "I need the forest around me. Too many people," she added, as if the Indian intruder were no more a concern than being splashed by a passing wagon.

"How did you discover him?"

"I had opened the window for the cool breeze and was drying myself after using the washbasin. I heard the creak of a floorboard, and when I turned, he was there."

"What exactly was he doing? Looking to attack you or get past you?"

Sarah ignored the question. "We're packing tonight," she said in an insistent voice.

"But the preparations are for dawn the day after tomorrow."

"Tonight. This is the last night I spend in this city."

"You know he wasn't from Boston, Sarah. What did he want?"

She shrugged. "The city attracts his type. Thieves, pickpockets, beggars, people who take advantage of open windows. He didn't expect to feel the sting of a Mohawk," she declared with a proud glint. Suddenly her head snapped toward the hallway. "Margaret! I heard Margaret scream!"

"She fainted," Duncan explained. He heard Mrs. Pope's comforting voice in the hallway. "Her mother has her." As he spoke, the voice in the hall paused, then grew louder and closer. They looked up to see a fearful Will Sterret in the doorway, with Mrs. Pope placing a hand on his shoulder. Duncan had forgotten the boy had been sleeping in the extra bed down the hall.

"There, there," the matron said to Will, patting his back. "Nothing for a wee one here." The boy, who had seen so much death that week, stared round-eyed at the blood on Sarah as Mrs. Pope led him away.

Sarah's gaze fell to the hand that had held the knife. It was shaking.

"Sit," Duncan said as he pushed her down on the bed. "You're bleeding."

"I will just wash up and join you as you eat."

Duncan retrieved the towel she had left by the basin and rubbed at her cheek. "Perhaps before you go to the kitchen, we should remove your war paint." He had cleaned the first cheek when he paused. "I didn't understand his words," he said.

"The coward. If he had tried that in the north, a war party would be chasing him already. Some hatreds never die."

"I don't follow you."

"He was from the Canada country, Duncan. An Abenaki."

THE APPEARANCE OF AN ABENAKI so soon after one had scalped a ranger from the *Arcturus* was simply a coincidence, Sarah tried to convince him, but Duncan's instincts screamed otherwise. Loading one of the new pistols they had bought the week before and returning his knife to his belt, he slipped outside, first going to the stable, where he was disappointed to find no sign of Ishmael, then circuiting the house twice, pausing each time to study the sturdy ivy-covered trellis that rose up to the edge of the roof, past Sarah's window. It could be no coincidence, yet it seemed impossible that the Abenaki killer would seek them out or even know how to find them. The Abenaki had seemed to recognize Duncan, or at least his name, but he had no connection to the killer, except, he reminded himself, through Hancock and Livingston. Gooseflesh rose along his spine as he recalled how the Abenaki had cut out part of Oliver's heart. He circled the block, his hand on the pistol tucked in his belt, before returning to Mrs. Pope's kitchen, where Sarah and the shaken proprietress waited with a fresh bowl of stew and bread.

His nerves had settled enough for him to eat, and censuring glances from Sarah made it clear that he was not to contradict her explanation that a drunken reveler had climbed the trellis looking for a free bed for the night. Duncan kept quiet, focusing on his meal, and Mrs. Pope soon retired upstairs to her own bedroom, carrying a rolling pin against future intruders. Sarah was filling their cups from a crock of water when a sharp, urgent rap on the door broke the stillness.

Henry Knox let himself in without waiting for an answer. "I wouldn't trouble your household so late, Miss Ramsey, but I saw the light and—oh, Duncan!" said the youth as he spied Duncan behind Sarah. He dropped three books onto the table, bound by a leather strap. "I had to search in every store, Miss, and they came dear. Three shillings eight pence, I fear."

Duncan grabbed the strap to pull the books closer, but Sarah self-consciously pulled them away, though not before he glimpsed the titles of the buckram-bound volumes. *Pamela* by Samuel Richardson, *The History of Tom Jones* by Henry Fielding, and Daniel Defoe's *Robinson Crusoe*. Famous books about a servant, a rogue, and a hermit.

"For the school," Sarah explained with a blush, then pulled down a pouch from the mantel over the hearth and extracted a handful of coins. As she counted out his payment, Knox took a seat at the table and accepted a slice of the bread from the plate Duncan nudged toward him.

"Is it true that you have trees in your wilderness that two men can't span with their arms spread wide?" the youth asked as he chewed.

"Oh, aye," Duncan replied with a grin. "On the Monongahela I camped once beneath a giant sycamore that took six of us to span."

Knox's eyes went wide, then he offered a solemn nod. "Someday I will cross the Hudson myself," he boldly vowed, as if the great river marked the edge of the civilized world.

"If you can work up such bravery, Henry," Sarah offered, her eyes sparkling, "then you must come visit us in Edentown. We can show you wonders of the forest that you have never even imagined,"

Before Knox could answer, a crash came from outside the door as someone missed his footing, falling on the step, and then Ishmael stumbled inside. The young Nipmuc seemed to see only Duncan. Like his great uncle, Ishmael seldom betrayed his emotions, but now his eyes were lit with alarm. "Mr. Hancock says come quickly!" Ishmael declared breathlessly. "He says the killers have breached the stronghold!" The young tribesman paused, wrinkling his brow, then gulped a breath and continued in a more tentative voice. "And a banshee has trapped Reverend Occom in the cellar!" He aimed his confused expression at Duncan, as if hoping for an explanation.

Henry Knox shot up in excitement, only to be pushed down by Sarah. She fixed Duncan with a gaze full of warning, which Duncan returned without expression. "Go," she said in a peeved whisper; then, more loudly, "Henry will keep me safe."

"The day after tomorrow," Duncan replied, as if in apology. "Start your packing, *mo leannan*. One more day, and we leave all this behind."

The warehouse that Duncan now knew to be a secret meetinghouse for the Sons of Liberty did indeed look like a fallen fortress. Outside the side door, the big Jamaican had collapsed against the stone wall and was pressing a bloody rag to his temple. The heavy door beside him hung open.

Duncan placed his hand on his knife as he followed Ishmael inside, cursing himself for forgetting the pistol in his haste. Two more of Hancock's men were at the end of the corridor, wearing the stunned, empty expressions Duncan had last seen on men in the aftermath of battle. One was bandaging the arm of the other, who used his good appendage to point down the cellar stairs.

As they descended into the cellar, an ungodly screech rose up from the shadows in the far corner. "Duncan, the banshee!" Ishmael moaned, clamping a hand around the amulet that hung from his neck.

"McCallum! Praise God!" Hancock called, rushing out of his secret meeting room. "Munro discovered your wretched heathen"—he paused with a guilty glance toward Ishmael—"the Indian intruder, and then fought him to a standoff at the chamber door. God knows what other casualties may been inflicted elsewhere." He wiped at his brow with a linen handkerchief, then touched the butt of a large pistol he had shoved into his belt. "I was just behind the door! But for Munro, I too would have been at the devil's mercy."

Duncan saw now the figure slumped unconscious against a barrel. "Enoch!" he cried as he darted to his friend's side. Munro had a lump on his temple and did not respond as Duncan lifted an eyelid. His pulse, though, was strong and steady.

"What Indian?" Duncan asked. Men from a score of tribes, most just wanderers in need of work, could be found working on the waterfront on any particular day. "Why here?" His questions were overwhelmed by another ungodly screech from the far side of the cellar.

"I fear the reverend is . . ." The ever-loquacious Hancock was at a loss for words. "Pinned by a demon," he finally offered, though through the fear on his face Duncan thought he saw a flicker of amusement.

Duncan straightened, drew his blade, and stole into the shadows, Ishmael a step behind him.

The sound came more frequently now, varying between a high-pitched scolding cry and the nerve-rattling shriek Duncan had first heard. It was unlike anything he had ever heard in his life, and he could not push the memory of Highland tales of flesh-eating banshees from his mind. They were small but could devour humans, a great-uncle once told him, because their shrieks robbed men of their senses, and the old man had never gone out in the night without holding a nail, a horseshoe, or another piece of protective iron in his hand, the traditional charm against evil. Ishmael fearfully clutched his totem but kept pace with Duncan. They advanced stealthily down an aisle between stacked casks toward the awful racket until, in the dim light of a cellar lantern, he discovered the besieged Reverence Occom.

The pastor did indeed seem paralyzed, sprawled as he was against the wall and staring up in mute horror at the pile of upturned crates from which the shrieks originated. Duncan saw movement to his right and discovered that Conawago had arrived and was staring at the reverend with undisguised mirth. With a quick glance, Duncan understood instantly what the old Nipmuc was thinking. The surface of the self-righteous tribal seminarian had been scratched, and the superstitions of the forest had left him cowering in the corner.

The banshee, seeming to react to Duncan's arrival, quieted.

"Surely such a formidable man of the faith is not frightened of a petite capuchin," Conawago observed to Occom, whose fear was quickly being replaced with resentment after Conawago's appearance.

"A monk?" Duncan asked in disbelief. The Order of the Friars Capuchin, he knew from his early days in Holland, were an offshoot of the Franciscans. He had never seen one of the barefooted, hooded ascetics in Massachusetts or anywhere else in the New World.

Before Conawago could answer, Occom attempted to move, triggering a new round of the awful screeching. As Duncan tightened his grip on his blade and advanced another step, a stranger in a dark cloak darted past him to stand before the crates, facing Occom. "*Suficiente de tu canto, me querida,*" he called over his shoulder, toward the crates.

Instantly the noise ceased. Duncan had the impression that he may have just witnessed an act of the dark arts. Then the Spanish words registered. *Enough of your singing, my dear.*

The sorcerer threw off his cloak and bent solicitously over the fallen Occom. "A thousand pardons, sir! This is most uncharacteristic, I assure you. She is out of sorts over the violence. Perhaps Sadie misunderstood when you knocked me down with that bottle." As the stranger grabbed Occom's hand and hauled the confused minister to his feet, Duncan saw a bloody bruise on his forehead.

The samaritan was a lean man, almost as tall as Duncan, with long black hair and a short beard of the same color. His eyes were bright, his countenance warm. He bent to lift a book from the floor and handed it to the minister.

As Occom collected himself, he flushed with embarrassment. "It is possible I overreacted, sir. When I first saw you with that intruder, I thought perhaps you were in alliance with him, and then that . . . that creature gave me a start."

Hancock appeared, rushing to Occom's side with anxious apologies. The merchant nodded to the dark stranger and turned to Duncan and Conawago with a peeved expression. "The reverend is an esteemed leader of the faithful," he chided, as if they had not shown him proper respect, then led Occom back toward the meeting room.

The stranger lowered himself onto a crate and gave a short whistle. A gasp rose from behind Duncan, and he turned to see Ishmael pointing in astonishment. A small head with dark brown hair on its crown had appeared over the edge of a crate. Its pink face put Duncan in mind of a newborn human, though its active, inquisitive eyes gave it an air of conspicuous intelligence. It inched over the box, revealing rich golden fur on its jowls, shoulders, and upper arms. The man on the crate spread his arms, and with a single leap the animal sprang several feet into his embrace. The stranger cradled the creature with obvious affection, whispering words of comfort into its tiny ears before extending it to examine its body. As he did so, the animal's tail, as long as its twelve-inch body, wrapped tightly around his arm.

Satisfied that the animal had suffered no injury, the man shifted it onto his shoulder. "Excuse our rudeness," he said with a bow of his head to Duncan and the two Nipmucs. "My name is Solomon Hayes, and this is Princess Salome Alexis Bergerac, though her friends call her Sadie."

Ishmael took an uncertain step forward, his eyes filled with wonder. "She's a . . ." he began, obviously having trouble fitting the creature with the fauna he knew from his native forests. "Part squirrel, part weasel," he tried, "like the gods assembled her from leftover parts." Ishmael paused and his eyes grew still rounder. "A *jogah*!" he exclaimed, referring to an impish spirit of nature in Iroquois legend.

"A monkey," Duncan explained, and bowed his own head. "Honored to make your acquaintances."

Hayes grinned and returned the bow. "*Cabus capucinus*, to be more precise. A capuchin, so named because the Spaniards who first encountered the creatures likened them to the old hooded monks of their homeland. Born on the shores of the Caribbean, where she mischievously decided to stow away on a New England merchantman. Sadie," he added with a gesture toward their new friends, "where are your manners?"

As Conawago gave a long, wheezing laugh, Duncan stepped past a still-uncertain Ishmael and extended his hand, introducing himself. The capuchin grasped his fingers and bent her head to touch it to them. Ishmael gave a cry of delight and pushed forward for her to repeat the gesture. "Princess Salome," the youth said with a deep bow. "I've never met royalty before." Conawago likewise presented himself, still chuckling. The capuchin had made a staunch ally in him by shaming Occom.

"A profound pleasure," Duncan said, question in his voice, "but I was summoned because of an attack by a human."

"The northern warrior," Hayes confirmed. "I had to leave Sadie to run after him, but then I lost him in one of those political marches."

Duncan's confusion was obvious. Hayes shrugged. "Perhaps we'd best collect our colleagues."

Minutes later the strange crew had assembled in the meeting room. Occom, his bulk settled into a chair that seemed too small for him, glared alternately at Hayes and Conawago. Hancock and Livingston sat at the end of the table, exchanging worried whispers until they saw Duncan. Enoch Munro, apparently none the worse for his injury, had revived and now produced a dusty bottle with a wax seal, which he was prying off with his knife. Ishmael lingered on a barrel outside the door, mesmerized by Sadie as she swung from rafter to rafter.

Duncan broke the silence. "I warned you yesterday about the warrior."

"You said he wouldn't come into the city," Hancock rejoined. "Take a seat, Duncan, please."

"What I said," Duncan corrected, "was that those who destroyed the *Arcturus* did not need him as a guide to come to Boston. So why," he asked, aiming an accusatory gaze toward Hancock, "did he suddenly need to come here?"

Hancock and Livingston glanced at each other.

"Why?" Duncan pressed. "Why did he seek out Sarah Ramsey in her bedroom an hour ago?"

Hancock went pale. "Not Sarah!" he moaned. "Is she safe?" He still offered no answer.

"Then let the deaths be on you," Duncan growled. "I am finished in Boston."

"There was another secret here in this warehouse," Hancock said to his back. "But it was expertly hidden away. This building was secure and guarded at every entrance."

Duncan slowly turned toward him.

Livingston nodded his vigorous confirmation. "They could never have known about it," he asserted. "It was between John and me, no one else. We took precautions."

Duncan paced along the table, studying the two merchants. "Until two nights ago it was between the two of you," he suggested. "Before that ledger was stolen and thirty-eight died."

"The boy survived," Livingston corrected.

"Thirty-seven, then!" Duncan snapped. "You owe them the truth! What did those men find in that ledger that made them come to Boston?"

Hancock sighed. "When I was last in Halifax, I left a note with my agent there to give to Pine when the *Arcturus* called, because I didn't know when I would see Robert. But it was in code. It would be meaningless to anyone else, let alone some savage."

Duncan glared at the merchant, who cast a guilty glance at Conawago.

"Some savage like me and my wilderness friends?" Duncan snapped in the Mohawk tongue.

Hancock gaped at him in confusion, then seemed to grasp his intent and flushed with color. For the first time, Duncan saw a hint of a smile on Reverend Occom's face. He had understood Duncan's words.

"Besides," Hancock continued, "no one could get into the building. No one did get into the building. He just appeared inside, as if through some dark conjuring. He injured the guards only when leaving."

"Ishmael," Duncan said to the young Nipmuc, who now listened from the doorway. "How would you get into the building if the street doors were locked?"

Ishmael grinned. "The stone walls are high but rough, with deep mortar points. The back wall has ivy growing nearly to the roof. The second and top floors have windows with wide sills and lintels. Practically like a ladder. There's a watcher's walk on the roof to survey the harbor, which means there is a hatch into the building."

"But there were guards," Livingston argued.

"Who were watching the street," Duncan stated. "They would not be looking up. A quick diversion would pull them away long enough for the few seconds needed to gain the top floor."

"A pile of straw burst into flame at the stable next door," Munro recalled as he pulled on the cork of his bottle. "Everyone runs to a fire."

"But the guard at the door was injured," Hancock pointed out.

"Oh, aye," Munro confirmed. "The brute accosted all of us on the way out. By then the surprise was gone, no need to climb back down from the roof. But his blows were like lightning, aimed only to disable us. And it weren't us who made him flee, t'was the monkey, who started shrieking at him 'cause he hit her master when he tried to interfere. She followed him, up on the rafters, raising that racket of hers all the way. When he finally saw her, he lowered his knife and fled."

"You had a good glimpse of him?" Duncan asked.

"For a quick breath, aye. Wore a brown waistcoat and leggings."

"Duncan flattened his hand and slanted it across his face. "A saber scar."

"Aye, an ugly beast with eyes like a catamount, the kind of cool, cunning eyes that size ye up for its next meal. Wearing a stinking wee dead thing at his belt."

Duncan drew up a chair and sat. "He was at Mrs. Pope's house, attacking Sarah."

"Surely that is impossible!" Hancock protested; then his voice faltered as he saw the fire in Duncan's eyes. "Duncan, please know we never intended . . ."

"He was the one who killed that ranger?" Livingston asked.

Duncan nodded. He recalled seeing the patch of fur hanging at the Abenaki's waist. "The wee dead thing was Daniel Oliver's scalp."

In the stunned silence Munro extracted the cork from his dusty bottle and hastily drank.

"Munro!" Hancock protested. "The governor's whiskey!"

"And won't he jist have to hear from ye about the lamentable breakage that occurs at sea." The Scot extended the bottle to Duncan, but Hancock interrupted, raising his hand in surrender before retrieving several small pewter cups from the sideboard.

As Hancock poured, Livingston retrieved a tricorn hat from a corner chair. "He lost this in the scuffle with Mr. Munro," he explained, handing it to Duncan.

As Duncan examined it, Conawago bent over his shoulder. "Ever the dressers, the 'Naki," the Nipmuc declared. The Abenaki were fond of bright cloth and decoration and during the war were known for stripping off the scarlet uniforms of soldiers they had killed and adapting them to their own use. Although badly tattered now, the hat was of finely made felt, probably a war trophy taken from a colonial militia officer. Duncan recognized its stained blue rosette as one favored by Hudson Valley companies. Pinned inside the hat was another trophy, a tarnished brass badge that consisted of the numerals 42.

Duncan let Conawago take the hat as he exchanged a pointed glance with Munro. It was a badge of the Black Watch, the 42nd Regiment of Foot, which had first brought Munro to America. Abenaki had fought alongside the French on that terrible July day ten years earlier, when, obeying the orders of a mindless British general, more than half the 42nd had been slaughtered before the ramparts of Fort Ticonderoga. The Abenaki had scalped and plundered the casualties, not all of whom had been dead when the scalping blade was put to work.

The Scot's eyes flared as he saw the badge, and he grabbed the hat from Conawago.

The old Nipmuc saved Munro from mouthing the sentiment he clearly felt. "They were indeed savages that day," Conawago stated.

"He killed that ranger," Munro observed, fixing Hancock with an accusatory stare. "He wears the badge of dead enemies. Like I said, he's still fighting the war."

"Enoch, steady, old man," the merchant chided.

"Steady? Steady! I'll give ye steady, ye spoiled pup!" The former soldier tore off the cap he always wore and pulled back the long, gray-streaked hair that lay over the crown of his head. Hancock jerked back in revulsion. Livingston choked on his whiskey. The top of Munro's head was nothing but a mass of jagged scar tissue.

"I lay there for hours, shot in the leg, knowing if I moved 'afore those French muskets, I'd be the dead man they took me for. My best friend, Archibald Brodie, lay half on top of me, a bullet through one beautiful blue eye, the other staring at me from his death all those hours. Then the 42nd pulled back, those who could walk, and the 'Nakis came for our hair, hooting and hollering. If I had cried out, they would have slashed my throat quick as that. T'was the devil's own butcher's shop. Steady be damned! Ye let one of those devils in here!"

"I didn't . . ." Hancock muttered. "We couldn't have known, surely you see that. Christ on the cross, Enoch! I did not ask for this!"

The Scot seemed not to hear Hancock. He had dropped into a chair and was staring, stricken, at the hat. It too could have been taken from the battlefield at Ticonderoga, or in any of the bloody north-country raids the Abenaki had been famous for.

Duncan studied each man as he tried to make sense of the night's events. The mysterious Solomon Hayes, the only man who had given chase to the warrior, had said nothing, listening with intense interest. Reverend Occom, whose presence Duncan could not explain, had also remained silent, apparently nursing his injured pride. Duncan spoke slowly, insistently. "Why was he here, John?"

"I told you, Duncan. He came for a secret we had concealed here. The ledger was of interest because of the Sons. But this had nothing to do with the Sons. He must have misunderstood something."

"Where?"

Hancock glanced uncertainly at Livingston. "The code simply described where the secret cache was. But surely he could not have understood it—"

"If you recall," Duncan interrupted, working hard to contain his temper, "he was not alone. The saboteurs of the *Arcturus* are with him, walking the streets of Boston! They were watching Mrs. Pope's house! Show me the code."

Hancock looked stricken. His voice took on a whining tone. "Duncan, surely you understand I can't just . . ."

"Thirty-seven men died in the harbor. A butcher is loosed on Boston, and you will fuss over a secret between merchants? Show me, or we can go meet with the governor," he stated, raising a worried look between Hancock and Livingston. "Just give me the coded message, that's all. I would see it as the killer and his companions saw it."

Livingston leaned back in his chair, as if retreating from Duncan's heat, then nervously nodded at Hancock. The Boston merchant opened a drawer in the sideboard, produced a piece of foolscap, and leaned over it with a writing lead. When he finally looked up, Duncan lifted the paper from between his hands. "The best I can do, from memory," Hancock said in a tight voice.

Duncan shook his head in angry surprise and stretched the paper out for Conawago to see. The old Nipmuc muttered under his breath.

"You invited them here," Duncan stated. "You made it so easy they could not resist."

"Of course not, Duncan. We took great precautions by using this code," Hancock argued.

"It's a damned pigpen code! The military has used it for years! I could give this to young Henry Knox and he would crack it in minutes!" With undisguised impatience he took another sheet of paper and drew two sets of two vertical parallel lines, each intersected by two horizontal lines. Below these he drew two large Xs. He filled the top row of the first large hatch mark with A, B, C; continued down the squares; and wrote J through R in the second set. He positioned dots along the edge of each box of that set, then finished the alphabet by placing letters in each triangle formed by the Xs, adding dots to the last four.

"Each letter is outlined by a unique shape, distinctive to it alone," he explained. He drew a backward L with a dot in it, a U turned on its right side with a dot in it, an upside-down U, and a four-sided square with a dot. "That says 'John.'"

Hancock downed a shot of whiskey and poured another. The bottle shook in his hand. "An old bookseller in New York told us about it, said it was a secret of the Roman generals. He accepted a handsome fee to guarantee he would not share it with anyone else."

"I'm sure he did," was Duncan's only reply, knowing how Hancock and Livingston fancied themselves as Caesars of the New World. He flattened the coded paper inscribed by Hancock and began deciphering the angular shapes.

He had barely finished the first word when Conawago bent over his shoulder and slowly dictated, pointing to each group of symbols in succession. "South wall, center top rack. Portuguese XX," he recited, then looked to the much-diminished Hancock. "A cask of brandy? Or is it port?" Conawago asked the brooding merchant, then spun about and left the room.

Duncan followed the old Nipmuc out the door and toward the deeper shadows along the back wall, grabbing a lantern off its wall hook. "Smells like brandy," Conawago observed as they approached the south wall. The cask stood upright on the floor, sitting in a pool of the pungent liquor. On its side a double X had been marked in chalk. Duncan knelt to examine the cask and the shards of wood beside it. A heavy blade, probably a tomahawk, had shattered the top, exposing a shallow watertight compartment that had been cleverly built into the end of the cask, allowing a storage space three inches deep. Duncan fixed Hancock with a disappointed gaze as the merchant appeared.

"More good men nearly died tonight," Duncan declared, "for a parcel poorly hidden in a cask of brandy."

Hancock looked like a frightened boy whose mischief had just been discovered. "I had given orders to ship the entire cask to Robert if something happened to me." His voice cracked. "You have to get it back, Duncan!"

"What I have to do, John, is to go back across the Hudson with my—" He started over. "I have to return to Edentown. I told you. The intrigues of wine merchants are no concern of mine."

His words seemed to sadden Hancock. "I don't know how to—" the merchant began, looking back and forth from Duncan to Conawago. "I mean, Sam

Adams may be right. Who can do this if not the two of you? I need you to hear me out. I have been a fool. Men have died, and I am devastated by the loss." His voice choked with emotion and faded away. "This is something of your world, not of mine," he added after a few heartbeats.

"Samuel is right about what?" Duncan demanded. He was about to gesture Ishmael back up to the street when a new figure appeared on the stairs, his large frame silhouetted by the lantern behind him. Before the door outside was pulled shut, the angry voice of an infantry officer could be heard over the marching boots of soldiers. "Surely, Duncan, you can linger for a final dram," Samuel Adams said in a despondent voice, "on a night when the soul of liberty is being crushed."

The sound of the boots seemed to be a cue for Hayes, who bent to Hancock's ear, then quickly disappeared up the stairway, his capuchin in a pouch slung under his shoulder. As they reentered the meeting room, Duncan became aware of sounds from the chamber where Pine's body had laid. Impatient with the secrecy of his companions, he pushed open the door and stepped into the room. A bright whale oil lamp burned at the end of the workbench. Reverend Occom sat there as he had the night before, but now he was bent over a small stack of papers.

The native pastor, much recovered from his fright, cocked his head and returned Duncan's cool stare, then gestured to the empty place where Pine's body had lain the night before. "We surrendered him to Abraham's embrace at dusk," Occom announced. "I have left funds for a stone to be carved." He seemed to think he owed something to Duncan. "I asked that an eel be carved on his stone, with arrows pointing to the heavens."

"At the Old North Church?" Duncan asked.

Occom nodded.

"So the wandering, courageous Seneca is laid to rest among the Puritans," Duncan observed. He was beginning to understand Conawago's resentment of Occom, whose pious, superior expression seemed almost permanently etched on his countenance.

Occom bristled. "Laid to rest among his fellow lovers of Christ."

"The only member of his eel clan in the Old North yard, I wager."

Disapproval clouded Occom's face. "Who *were* his people, McCallum?" The question had a bitter tone.

Duncan heard chairs being pulled out at the table in the chamber behind him, but he did not turn. "Why are you here, Reverend?"

"I had an emissary on the *Arcturus*," Occom confided in a forlorn tone. "We are building a college on the Connecticut River for all the tribes. I arrived only last week after two years in England, for which Mr. Hancock paid the passage. My man was bringing the final drafts from our donors."

"You mean someone other than Pine."

Occom nodded. "The captain's steward."

"And he died. I am sorry."

"He kept the drafts in a sealskin pouch on his person." Occom gestured to the papers in front of him. "We recovered them from his body as it lay on the beach. All funds are now accounted for. Over twelve thousand pounds in total."

Duncan gazed in disbelief. The *Arcturus* had been overburdened with secrets. The sum was beyond extraordinary, enough to build a substantial institution and operate it for years. "And I thought you had gone to that beach to bless the dead," Duncan said, not trying to conceal the bitterness in his voice. "Men would kill for such money—even destroy a ship."

"The drafts are just for the final installment, as it were, and made out to me, to be deposited here in Boston."

"Which for now makes you very valuable and very vulnerable."

"Surely not."

"Someone could capture you and force you to sign them over. Someone could steal them and impersonate you."

"No one knows about them."

Duncan rolled his eyes. "Surely you understand that knowledge hidden in this house is about as secret as tonight's quarter moon." The reverent way Occom treated the drafts disturbed him. Some pastors were men of faith, some men of learning, others men of money. Duncan was learning which one Occom was.

"Why the *Arcturus*?" he asked. "Why put the ledger and the funds on board the same ship?"

Occom winced. "The captain and his steward were devout men who had been helping us for years. It seemed the safest route."

"They wrote letters," Hancock said over Duncan's shoulder.

Occom took the cue. "Letters in the sealskin. The last one from ten days ago. The ship called in Halifax. When it embarked, two new passengers were on board."

Duncan recalled Will's report, that the men who accompanied Oliver to shore had been passengers from Halifax. "Who?"

It was Hancock who answered. "Two men, very well dressed, their clothing a bit too fancy, suggestive of Paris, though they spoke perfect English. Midthirties, both of them, calling themselves Hughes and Montgomery, though the steward suspected those were but names of convenience. The letter says"—here Hancock seemed embarrassed—"they wore conspicuous fragrance, lavender scent."

Occom took up the tale. "The passengers, as is customary, dined with the officers, and they told a tale of being scholars from Oxford coming to visit colleagues at Harvard College, but they evaded all questions about Harvard and Oxford. That was all. The rest of the letter was about Scripture, suggestions for a sermon we might preach together when we returned to our congregation in Connecticut."

Another round of the smoky Scotch was being poured when Duncan stepped back into the meeting room. All eyes were trained on Samuel Adams, who sat at the head of the table as if presiding over one of his Sons of Liberty gatherings. As Duncan sat, Livingston pushed a dram toward him. Duncan quickly drained it, and Livingston poured him another.

"The governor says he is done being patient," Adams declared in a heavy voice. "He has begun a more aggressive campaign, giving orders this afternoon for Mr. Hancock's ship the *Liberty* to be towed out into the harbor and put under naval jurisdiction until a formal inspection of her books can be completed. There was some resistance when the navy arrived. Some heads were broken, and customs officials were accosted. The crowd chased them into the streets." Adams wrung his hands in worry. "We prayed to avoid the presence of more troops on our streets. But now marines from the ships have been called out. When word reaches General Gage in New York, he may well summon infantry from Halifax."

In the silence that followed, Adams fixed an expectant gaze on Hancock and Livingston. But Duncan spoke first. "Halifax," he said. "What, Mr. Livingston, was it about your ship that caused that cutter to follow it from Halifax? I thought it was following the ledger, but is it possible they were following those two passengers?"

"Is there a meaningful difference? Different hounds on the scent of the same fox," Livingston replied, then shrugged. "The captain is beyond our reach," he reminded Duncan. "And the ship's books are on the bottom with him. We will never know more."

"Two men got off before the ship exploded, helped by Mr. Oliver, who was likely deceived by them and then murdered for his trouble," Duncan replied. "I think they boarded in Halifax to intercept your secret ledger and then Lieutenant Beck pursued them, as if he had been watching them, with the cutter at his disposal. And if they were coordinating with the Abenaki assassin, they were planning this for weeks, if not months."

"Impossible!" Livingston protested.

"They knew Oliver was on your ship, and they knew he was a ranger. How would they know that?"

Livingston had no answer.

"They knew an Abenaki warrior who would do anything to kill a ranger from St. Francis, even knew where to place him and when, over a period of days, he might expect the *Arcturus*."

"My ships are punctual," Livingston said in a sulking tone.

Duncan ignored him. "They had help, in the north and probably in New York, where the records for the Livingston ships are maintained, as well as here in Boston. *Agents provocateurs*, we called them in the war." He met Munro's gaze. *The war isn't over*, the old soldier had said, although Duncan was beginning to wonder if they were witnessing the birth of a new war.

Hancock stared intensely at his dram, then abruptly looked up. "You must find the ledger, Duncan. I beg you."

"We have already had this conversation," Duncan shot back. "I cannot. I will not. These are Boston troubles, not mine. And even if I were to consider helping, I would never do so while you withhold the full truth from me."

Hancock threw up his hands in frustration. "Enough! The package stolen from the cask had a list and a small parcel given us by the widow of a ranger who recently died in Quincy. The list is of names we are compiling, only ten or twelve thus far, 'Spartans of the cause,' we call them. Leaders with military experience in towns of New England and New York who we think will not shirk the cause of liberty when it arrives at their doorsteps."

"Who would want a list of your Spartans?" Duncan asked.

"Our enemies," Livingston said in a curt, dismissive voice.

"Then by all means you should try to recover it," Duncan said with a chill in his voice. "For a few shillings Reverend Occom will no doubt pray for its recovery. And if you want everyone in the colonies to know of your quest, just explain it in one of your schoolboy codes." Duncan drained his glass and stood. If he hurried, Sarah might still be awake.

"Duncan, you misunderstand," Adams protested, then leaned toward Livingston, urgently explaining something.

"What, may I ask, was in the package from the ranger?" Conawago asked.

"We're not sure exactly," Hancock said, "though the widow considered it very important, very secret, and said she didn't know who else to trust. Her husband was a Sergeant Branscomb, who served as a ranger in the war with Major Rogers. There was an old gold coin in the packet, and a note that sounded almost like orders to report to duty, written very vaguely, very flowery. In purple ink, I recall, because I thought how very odd. Destiny will call, it said, and keep your powder dry, I remember that. And it said this coin is a reminder."

"And the coin itself?" Conawago asked.

"French, one of those old gold louis you used to see in French Canada. Quite valuable. Of course, we intended to give it back to her, as belonging to her husband."

"But who sent it? When?"

"Three or four months ago. From whom, we don't know. No signature on the note, just a word at the closing. *Saguenay.*"

A question flickered on Conawago's face and was quickly gone.

"I will see you at Mrs. Pope's," Duncan said to his friend, and took a step toward the door.

"Duncan, no!" It was, surprisingly, Livingston who spoke. His face was suddenly dark with worry.

"You misunderstand, Duncan," Adams said again.

"You keep saying that. Fine. I misunderstand everything but my need to leave."

"You misunderstand even that," Adams said. His voice had an odd hint of apology.

"I'm sorry?"

"You must leave, but to find these French saboteurs and the missing journal. You must clear yourself, Duncan. The navy won't act against us openly, but you made a quick enemy of that man Beck yesterday. He has convinced the governor that you stole the ledger, saying it was the property of the king."

"The governor will forget the lies of some overwrought lieutenant when I am gone."

"No, he won't, and Beck is not just some lieutenant. That uniform was a costume he put on for the cutter's crew," Livingston said as Duncan took another step toward the door, then quieted as Adams raised a hand. Livingston whispered into Hancock's ear. His words drained the color from Hancock's face.

"I am sorry, Duncan," said Adams. "There is a warrant for your arrest."

Duncan stared at the portly man. "Surely I did not hear correctly."

"You heard me. A warrant has been issued, signed by the governor."

Conawago and Ishmael moved to Duncan's side, as if to defend him. Duncan pushed down the anger rising within. Soon he would be rid of this city and its troubles. "A misunderstanding among local officials. You are in the legislature. No doubt you can correct the mistake." He paused, seeing now the shocked expression that lingered on Hancock's face.

"Duncan," Hancock said in a tight voice. "I'm so sorry. You have to go and find those responsible. To save yourself. Samuel thinks he can delay distribution of the warrant until midday tomorrow, but no longer. If Beck and the governor think the ledger is still in Boston, they will rip the city apart to find it. Soldiers will be sent to search houses, churches—anywhere there is a suspected Son of Liberty. They have to be convinced the chase lies elsewhere, that the ledger is with a fugitive fleeing Boston. For the good of the Sons, you understand. For the good of Boston."

"I am no fugitive."

The pleading in Hancock's eyes changed to despair. "Prithee, Duncan, understand that I did not know until this minute. That man Beck works for the minister of war, for important men close to the king. The governor is cowed by him. Beck thinks you have what he so desperately seeks. He swore out an affidavit. The charge is treason, and thirty-seven counts of murder. At noon tomorrow you will be the most wanted man in all the colony."

5

THE CONVOY FOR EDENTOWN MADE agonizingly slow progress in the early dawn light, having to yield frequently at the narrows of Boston Neck to the incoming carts delivering food to the hungry city. Already some mongers had set up stands and were shouting the virtues of their produce. As Duncan nervously watched from behind the seat of the first wagon, Enoch Munro reined in the dapple mare Sarah had purchased in the city and looked back at the three wagons behind him.

The sturdy Scot had offered his resignation from Hancock's employ to join Duncan, but Hancock, unable to look Duncan in the eye after delivering his shattering news, had refused, saying that Munro would continue to be paid so long as he stood at Duncan's side to protect him. With a determined glint, Munro had vowed to do so, for he grasped that they were not just fleeing Boston, they were seeking out the French killers, and he had a score to settle with their Abenaki assassin.

As Duncan followed Munro's rearward gaze, he realized that the Scot was not looking for troops, but simply gazing in frustration at the slow wagons. The first two wagons, covered with canvas, were packed with the vast quantity of supplies Sarah had acquired in the city. The third, much lighter, wagon had appeared out of an alley in the morning twilight, Reverend Occom driving its cargo of Bibles for his new school.

As Conawago coaxed the first team forward, Sarah examined a new atlas from London that she had bought for Edentown's schoolchildren. A huge dog with long black hair—Ishmael's sea bear—paced alongside the second team, keeping a faithful eye on Ishmael, who drove the team of four heavy horses pulling the wagon, under whose canvas-covered frame were bolts of English wool wrapped in burlap, crates of wine, spermaceti candles from New Bedford, and coils of rope fresh from the ropewalk behind Beacon Hill. Lying behind Ishmael, concealed from sight by carefully arranged crates of tools for the new forge, was the bandaged Sergeant Mallory. The deserter, now dressed in the simple brown woolen of a farmer, kept a wide-brimmed hat close at hand to pull low over his face if soldiers probed the wagon.

Walking between the wagons was Solomon Hayes. The tinker had shown up before dawn with a great sack of trade goods on his shoulder and a smaller sack hanging from his shoulder in which Sadie slept. The man, like so much else Duncan had encountered in the past three days, was a mystery, not the least because, despite his scholarly appearance, he had been the only one in Hancock's warehouse to pursue the Abenaki assassin. More than once, the big dog, whom Ishmael had introduced as Molly of the Newfoundland, sidled up to him to sniff the pouch under his shoulder, cocking her head with an inquisitive gaze each time two appraising eyes peered out over its edge. Duncan had accepted the inclusion of the tinker on the word of Munro, who explained that Hayes visited every few months to restock his bag and chat with Hancock about mutual friends in the Rhode Island colony. The tinker, Munro assured Duncan, had an impressive knowledge of the frontier communities, and in any event would be with them only a few days on the western road. The Scot had overcome Duncan's hesitation by explaining that the odd assortment of companions would be useful cover once constables and bountymen started seeking him.

As the rays of the rising sun lit the wagon from behind, Duncan pulled out the slip of paper he had brought from Hancock's warehouse. The Boston merchant, shamed and understanding Duncan's outrage, had asked Adams and Livingston to leave and then sat with Duncan and Conawago to answer their questions about the list that was stolen from its place of hiding in the warehouse. The names were of reliable, like-minded men who, based on assurances from mutual acquaintances, could be trusted to keep secrets and who had particular talents that might be useful if the Sons, as Hancock put it, were to expand their efforts. Hancock could remember only half a dozen names he had supplied for the list, three of which were former rangers and three town leaders in Western Massachusetts, New Hampshire, and Connecticut. Duncan had pointed to the first name, Sergeant Josiah Chisholm. Worcester wheelwright, it said. "You added 'Rogers 1759.' Why?" Duncan had asked.

"I recalled he was on both our lists, Livingston's and mine. A solid man who's well respected in his town. A wheelwright now, but a ranger in the war."

"The year 1759 was the year of Major Rogers's raid on St. Francis," Conawago had pointed out. "And the next?" he said, reading the second and third names. "Ebenezer Brandt, Rogers 1759." Then, "Daniel Oliver, Rogers 1759." The old Nipmuc turned to Hancock. "And the dead ranger whose widow came to you, Branscomb. You said he had served with Rogers. Perhaps his widow can confirm, but I suspect he too was there at St. Francis."

The words had brought a dangerous gleam to Munro's countenance. Hancock looked up with an inquiring eye.

"St. Francis is the capital of the Abenaki," Conawago explained. "A center for French irregulars during the war."

"Abenaki," Hancock repeated with a shudder. His hand shook as he poured another whiskey. "I shall put guards around my house tonight."

"Dark as a storm," Sarah said to Duncan late that afternoon as she urged the team up a slope. "It scares me. I've never seen Conawago so despondent," she added. "Except once." She paused and surveyed the low, flat valley that came into view as they crested the hill. "And it was here, in this very valley of Worcester, as we passed through on the way to Boston to meet you all those weeks ago. They were taking down some aged trees at the edge of the forest. It is always a bit sad to see the old ones fall."

Since leaving Boston, Duncan had developed a nervous habit of studying the road for signs of pursuit, but now his gaze stayed on Conawago, walking beside the wagon. His best friend, more like family to him than any living person, was usually so calm as to be unreadable, but since arriving in Boston, he had grown increasingly moody, sometimes even morose. He had barely spoken since leaving the city and, since he'd climbed down to walk, seemed oblivious to his companions.

"The land," Duncan observed, shaking his head. He felt an odd foreboding. "The land feels mournful here."

"The land?" Sarah replied. "Just more Massachusetts farmland. More rocky than ours, and thinner soil."

Not even Sarah, raised by the tribes, could grasp the intense relationship that Conawago, and many of the aged Indians Duncan had known, had with the land. Those born before the European occupation of their homelands, as Conawago had been, sometimes seemed to have an almost physical link with the earth, as if their native soil was somehow in their blood. Certainly it was in their souls.

"There are secrets, Sarah, between him and the land," Duncan said, knowing he could never find the words to explain what he sensed. "When I was last in Onondaga," he added, referring to the capital of the Iroquois League, "he rose up from the council fire as if in a trance and without a word disappeared into the blackness of the forest. After an hour passed and he had not returned, I was about to go search for him, but one of the grandmothers at the fire ring said no, it was like this when the elders of the oldest tribes, like the Nipmuc, reached their final years. She said the earth spirits would touch them in ways no one else could see or hear, that sometimes the old trees spoke to them with words only they could understand."

Sarah nodded solemnly. "My Mohawk father told me that when those of ancient blood approached their ending time, they could hear the strains of their death song coming through the forest. There were massive trees, sprouted when time was young, he said, where the oldest spirits lived, and they were the ones who whispered the songs. I asked one of the old matriarchs what he meant, and she gave me a sad smile and said it was because he was beginning to hear his own song."

Sarah's words were like ice against Duncan's heart. The old Nipmuc was his teacher, his confessor, his companion, his anchor. His relationship with Conawago was one of the great blessings of his life. For a moment, as he studied his old friend, he found it difficult to speak. "I think this is somehow different," he ventured.

"I pray that it is," Sarah replied.

They did not stop the team as the wagon rolled past Conawago, who now stood at the crest of the hill, transfixed, staring at the landscape below. The frame of a tall new steeple rose up above the trees along a winding river. On a knoll on the other side of the river the vanes of an old Dutch-style windmill slowly moved in the breeze. From the surrounding hills, teams of oxen were dragging massive logs toward the river.

Sarah gasped and clutched the totem hanging at her breast, whispering an Iroquois prayer. *They were taking down some aged trees at the edge of the forest*, she had said. But now there was no forest. For a mile, all the way to the settlement of Worcester, there was nothing but cleared land. Here and there, men worked at stumps with axes and mules. Some of the huge logs, four feet in diameter and more, were being dragged to what looked like a sawpit along the riverbank, while others were being floated for delivery downstream.

The tribes never objected to pockets of cleared fields here and there among the dense primeval forests—indeed, they cleared small fields for their own maize and squash crops—but this was different. This was wholesale destruction, annihilation of woods that had existed since long before Europeans walked the continent. Not all tribal members might believe in the possession of great trees by spirits, but all those Duncan knew were certain that the spirits that watched over the tribes took their nourishment from the wilds. Without the forests there were no wilds, and the spirits would drift away. Without their spirits, the tribes were lost.

THEY DREW THE WAGONS UP at the stable behind a prosperous-looking clapboard inn, and as Duncan negotiated for a few extra sacks of grain for the road ahead, Sarah secured rooms. They had pushed hard from Boston and knew they would be sleeping under the stars for much of the remaining journey. After Duncan checked Mallory's bandages and found him a hiding place in the stable, Sarah promised the others a good meal and made lighthearted conversation as they retrieved their bags, even humming songs of the Edentown schoolchildren. Her smile, even though he knew it was forced, briefly banished his worry and fatigue.

They had already turned onto the cobbled path that led to the inn when he heard the unmistakable click of a rifle hammer being cocked behind him. He swung about to see Munro two steps behind, carrying Duncan's own long rifle.

"Steady, lad," the old Scot said with a quick glance at the road. "Into the inn like nay's amiss." Two dark-cloaked men on bay horses were approaching, riding from the center of the settlement. Reports of the warrant against Duncan would have been dispatched throughout the colony, and more than one fleet post rider had sped past them on the road. The two men had the look of the thuggish deputies who did the constable's work or, worse, the bounty hunters who generally brought in their quarries beaten into submission.

"On wi' ye," Munro pressed. "I'll just tarry with a pipe." The canny Scot had kept a close watch over Duncan on their journey and had paused at the message boards outside the roadside taverns they passed. Broadsides with Duncan's description and details of his heinous deeds would soon be posted along every main road in the colony. Although Adams and Hancock had promised not to speak of Duncan's connection with Sarah and their westbound wagon caravan, tongues would soon wag feverishly in taverns, stores, and even churches over the alarming news of a vile traitor loose in the Massachusetts countryside.

Sarah hurried out of the inn and put a hand on his arm. He found himself unable to move as he stared at the foreboding figures. They made his nightmare true, his danger real. He recalled seeing a low-level tax collector in Boston being tarred and feathered. If he were caught and openly accused in a place like Worcester, with no recourse to the truth, curious onlookers could instantly turn into an angry mob. The boiling tar would be given little time to cool, and unless it was quickly washed off, its glutinous nature would adhere the scalding substance to his body, cooking the flesh underneath. The screams of the collector had been heard for days as his doctor tried to comfort him. If the same was done to Duncan, he would be thrown into a cart and sent to a cell while the tar still baked his limbs.

Sarah broke his dark spell with a more adamant jerk of his arm. As she pulled him inside, he caught a quick glance of Munro leaning the rifle against the building and pulling out his clay pipe, then of Ishmael and Conawago pausing by the roadside entrance to the inn like an outer guard, the big dog, Molly, set squarely between them.

"You cannot go down, Duncan," Sarah stated as he looked out the window of her upstairs room minutes later. "You must stay in this chamber. You can make up for all the sleep you missed the past nights. Please!" she implored, coaxing him away from the pool of sunlight. "The innkeeper boasted of his kitchen," she tried. "Sleep, then take a meal with us downstairs." Her voice trailed off as she saw the determination in his eyes.

"I have to find the old ranger while there's daylight," Duncan explained.

"Munro can go with me. He's a wheelwright here. His shop is likely still open. Would you rather I see him now or wait until dark, knocking on every door until I find him? Should I write that script now? Prithee, sir or madame, I am looking for a former ranger from the massacre of St. Francis who may have information that will clear me of those pesky murder charges. Oh, and don't believe what they say about me being a traitor. Long live King George."

Sarah shot him an angry glance, then gazed out at Ishmael, who had taken up a new position in front of the printer's shop across the road. "I will never forgive you, Duncan McCallum, if you get hanged because of those fools in Boston."

"They're not fools, Sarah. They are leaders of the Sons of Liberty."

"If they would put your life at risk to avoid some embarrassment with the governor, then they are damned fools and they misunderstand the entire point of liberty."

Duncan put a hand on her shoulder as she continued to stare out the window. He had no interest in opening their long-running debate about the nature of liberty. "Let's just say they've made me more committed to my mission."

"Mission?"

"I am not in flight, *mo leannen*, I am on a hunt."

She spun about, her tribal wildness flaring in her eyes again. "I know what liberty means. It means Edentown. It means you and me in our sanctuary. Once in Edentown, what do we care if the king sends troops to Boston over some tax we never see? When's the last time you saw a constable or a tax collector in Edentown? Never! A Massachusetts warrant will mean nothing to us there. This is not your hunt, Duncan McCallum!"

"A warrant for treason will not be lightly dismissed. It will not be difficult to discover where I live. And Edentown will suffer for it." He felt his heart twitch as the fire in her eyes ebbed, replaced with pleading.

"Then we will go live among the Iroquois," Sarah said, "or move into the Ohio country. There are places out there where Europeans have never been seen."

With a finger on her chin, he lifted her head. He knew that his own eyes reflected the mix of anger, sadness, and fear that tightened her face. "Edentown is like nowhere else on earth. It is a sanctuary, yes, and not just for us. It cannot survive without you. You are its soul, and it is the anchor of your heart. You cannot abandon it."

For the briefest instant her eyes flared again, despite the moisture that gathered at their corners. "More the fool you, Duncan," she said in a pained whisper, and wrapped her arms around him. "You are the anchor of my heart."

They stood in silent embrace for several breaths; then she pushed him away. "Take Ishmael and his big bear of a dog as well if you must go."

As if on cue, they heard Molly bark excitedly from behind the house. They darted to the back window just in time to see Munro lift Will Sterret out from under a blanket in the second wagon.

SOLOMON HAYES KNEW WORCESTER, HAVING sometimes called there for trading goods used in his far-ranging journeys along the frontier, and he reported that the only wheelwright he knew of was on the opposite bank, adjacent to the old, creaky windmill. Duncan was about to step onto the narrow timber bridge that had been raised across the river when Ishmael tugged at his sleeve.

Conawago was sitting on a ledge rock a stone's throw away. The old Nipmuc had disappeared after they reached the stable. It was a rare thing that he would not join them in the work of unhitching and feeding teams at the end of a long day, rarer still for him to turn away with sullen coolness when Duncan approached him.

"When you came through two months ago," Duncan asked Ishmael, "did you spend a night here? Did your uncle perhaps have words with someone?"

"No," the young tribesman replied as he studied his uncle. "We pushed on and camped just twenty miles west of Boston. But he was in a dark mood when we passed through. I asked him what had happened and all he said was 'Everything.' And he spoke no more that day." He turned toward Duncan with despair on his face. "Sometimes he gets this look, one I have never seen on any man. It lasts but a moment, yet during the moment he seems to be as fierce as a bear but somehow at the same time as frail as a young fledgling. But this is worse, like nothing I have ever seen before."

"He is finally feeling his age, and he resents it," Duncan said, hoping that was all it was. The old Nipmuc had been born in the last century, taken from his people by Jesuits, and transported to Europe for his education. When he returned years later, filled with dreams of a new life for his people, he could find no trace of them. He had spent decades searching for them, finding only the orphaned Ishmael. Now in his eighties, Conawago could usually pass for a much younger man, but lately it seemed as if something in his eyes had surrendered. Duncan knew he had the spirit of the bear, but he also knew that Conawago sensed the approach of frailty.

"Stay with him, Ishmael," Duncan asked the youth. "Or at least near him."

Ishmael gave a low whistle and stepped away from the river. Molly, who had been frolicking in the water, bolted out of the river to follow. She paused long enough to shake the water out of her thick black coat, propelling a surprisingly heavy shower onto Duncan and Munro, who laughed good-naturedly as he wiped his face, motioning Duncan onto the bridge.

The wheelwright's shop proved to be a series of connected sheds that sat in the shadow of the old mill, whose tattered canvas vanes rattled like loose sails in the light wind.

"No," Duncan said when Munro began walking on a path directly to the shop. "I want to know the lay of this land. One of the cardinal rules of rangering: know your quarry's terrain."

Munro replied with a grunt. "Forgot ye was a ranger yerself."

"I mean to know something of Chisholm before I approach him, and to assure that no one else is watching him. No more surprises," he said, looking back toward the inn, half expecting to see their stowaway following them. They had spoken hard with young Will, who was to have stayed with Mrs. Pope to become part of her household, but the boy had refused to be cowed. "Ain't going to spend my years emptying those ladies' chamber pots and having them scrub my cheeks every day." Munro had turned away, hiding his grin, and Duncan had placed his hands on the boy's shoulders. "Then it's Edentown, Will," he soberly declared, "at the edge of the great, dark wilderness."

"Will there be bears?" the boy asked in an uncertain tone, his eyes growing round. "And catamounts? And Indians?"

"Aye, I'm afraid so. Terribly fierce, the lot of them."

The boy's worried face had broken into a huge smile. "Best life for me, sure as eggs!"

With that business out of the way, Duncan had asked the question that had been nagging him all day. "You said Daniel Oliver was a ranger."

The boy nodded.

"Do you know when or where?"

"No, except he helped Major Rogers punish those Indians in Quebec in a famous battle." The boy looked away, as if remembering his friend Oliver's scalped corpse, and Duncan had not pressed him further. Oliver had been a ranger with Rogers at St. Francis, and Hancock had been given a package sent to another of Rogers's rangers, with a gold coin as an enticement to join a bold enterprise or campaign in the north. Duncan was eager to learn whether Josiah Chisholm, also a veteran of the St. Francis raid, had received a similar coin.

Munro nodded toward a cemetery on the rising slope behind the mill. "I'll go among those departed as if seeking a relative, watch the back side for a spell."

Duncan nodded, then gestured toward a small alehouse. "Meet me in half an hour." He watched Munro climb toward the tombstones, considering with a pang how much the graying Scot reminded him of long-dead uncles in the Highlands.

At the alehouse, he paid for a tankard of weak ale and took it outside to a bench in front of the building to study the prosperous-looking wheel shop, two-thirds of which consisted of bays that opened to the street. At one end were racks of aging oak planks, then a work area with a lathe and cradle on which the hubs were worked into shape. In the next bay, two benches were fastened with large vise screws into the heavy floorboards, on one of which a hub was fixed with spokes inserted. A lanky blond youth of Ishmael's age, no doubt an apprentice, was manipulating the last felloe, a wheel section, onto the spokes. Behind him, near a small, smoldering forge, was a door in the rear wall that Duncan took to be an entry to an office or living quarters.

As the last felloe was knocked into place, a strongly built man in his forties emerged from the rear door. He wiped his hands on his leather apron, then patted the younger man on the shoulder as if to commend his work. From a tool chest in the shadows he produced a small, foot-wide wheel on a handle, a traveler, and ran it along the outside of the wheel the younger man was finishing. He was measuring the circumference of the wheel so he could make the iron rim that would be fitted over it. Pausing to make a note on what looked like a small slate, he disappeared behind the door. Duncan signaled Munro, and they approached the shop.

The apprentice looked up from the vise as Duncan's shadow fell across his wheel. The lad stretched his neck, looking along the road, searching for Duncan's vehicle. "If it's an entire set of four that ye seek," he declared in an amiable tone, "I must warn ye that we are booked into August already. If only a broken spoke, I might get to it tomorrow morning."

The older man emerged from the door. He had removed his apron and was fastening the top buttons of his green waistcoat. "Run down to the smith, Sam," he told the young man at the vise, extending a slip of paper. "Tell him this be the length of iron I'll need."

Sam brightened and eagerly took the slip. "And afterward go help yer ma in her vegetable plot. See ye at dinner, lad."

The blond-haired youth offered a mock salute and sped off down the road.

"It must be a satisfying life, Mr. Chisholm," Duncan began as the wheelwright eyed him suspiciously, "bringing ease to people's lives with just wood, iron, and the skill of your hands."

"Aye, but you're not here for my trade," the man said. Duncan saw that one of his hands was inside his waistcoat. "Ye think I'm blind, not to see the two of ye watching me as if readying for an ambush? Ye," he said with a nod to Duncan, "took all that time to drink a small tankard, eyes on my shop the entire while. And ye," he said with a motion toward Munro. "A lot of folks come and go in that boneyard, but I don't recollect ever seeing one take a long rifle to mourn." The wheelwright paused, studying the weapon in Munro's hand. "A good Pennsylvania rifle. Lancaster, by the look of it, maybe Reading." His hand inside the waistcoat came out gripping a pepperbox pistol, designed to fire its small barrels in one discharge. "Now tell me what I can do to satisfy yer curiosity. And don't waste breath trying to drag me back into tenant wars."

Duncan hesitated, considering whether to try to wrestle the pistol away. Munro simply took off his hat.

The suspicion went out of Chisholm's eyes as he saw the mass of scar tissue. "Jesus bloody wept!" he spat, and lowered the pistol. "French Indians?" he asked Munro, then saw the brass numerals the Scot had taken from the Abenaki's hat and fastened to the breast of his waistcoat. "The Black Watch, was it?"

The former soldier nodded. "Left me for dead at Ticonderoga."

The wheelwright silently studied Munro, his eyes settling on the pouch of green-and-black plaid that hung from his belt. "The Abenaki dealt cruel hard with the Ladies from Hell that day," he said, using one of the army's names for the ferocious Highlanders in kilts. His appraising gaze shifted to Duncan, who extended an open palm, holding a bronze disk inscribed with an oak tree. Chisholm lifted it and stepped out into the sunlight to examine it more closely. "Ain't seen one of these fer years," he said with a faraway look. "Captain Woolford still running the forest like a deer?" he asked. "Best ranger officer ever was, next to Major Rogers himself."

"Deputy superintendent of Indians now," Duncan reported, "under Sir William Johnson. He's more Mohawk than English these days."

The wheelwright nodded, as if approving. "There was a wildness in that man that he always pushed too deep. The Mohawk will cure that."

"I think that's what he thought. But then he took a Mohawk wife."

Chisholm grinned. "Now that's a whole different kind of wildness." He gazed with a longing expression at the disk, then handed it back to Duncan. "I've been keeping some of last year's applejack," he declared, and motioned his two visitors toward the door.

They passed through a chamber with walls of rough-hewn lumber, with a sturdy rope bed in one corner, a table bearing scattered papers in another.

"My brother opened the shop fifteen years ago and built up a fair trade. When he died of consumption a couple of years ago, I came from New York and took it over. His widow, Jenny, said move in with her and the three young 'uns, but I said no, people would talk against her if I did that." Chisholm retrieved a ceramic jar and three horn cups from a shelf and led his guests out a back door that opened into a garden under construction. Half the plot was filled with late-spring blooms, but the other half was only soil, recently worked in anticipation of planting. A spade leaned against the wall.

"Jen's got lots of vegetables up in her plot at the house," Chisholm declared as he poured out the applejack. His voice had a gentle quality that belied his oxlike build. "But she loves her flowers. I sent for seeds from Boston. Says she dreams of a garden planted only with flowers mentioned in Shakespeare. She reads him aloud when I go up for Sunday dinners, after young Sam recites Bible verses to us. I'm going to have marigolds and pansies and daisies. Aye, and rosemary. Hamlet speaks of rosemary, if ye credit it. Rosemary is for remembrance, the young prince says. Jen says that's because rosemary retains its essence all through the winter."

Duncan found himself warming to the callused, battered Indian fighter who wanted to plant the flowers of the Bard to please his brother's widow.

"Christ on the cross," Chisholm muttered. "Listen to me prattle on about such things to total strangers."

"One ranger's no stranger to another," Duncan said.

The wheelwright drained his cup before speaking. "That's why yer here? Hadn't thought rangers had any unfinished business until recently. We signed the peace with the French five years ago."

"I'm sure that's what Daniel Oliver would have thought," Munro observed.

The wheelwright's brow furrowed. "Daniel be off at sea somewhere, probably on the t'other side of the world, frolicking with those Pacific beauties the whalers rave about."

"If only it were true. He was murdered last week in Boston," Duncan declared.

Chisholm's head snapped up. "To hell you say!" He seemed to weigh Duncan's words. "Nay, nay, people might talk, but ye don't know the man. T'ain't a cutpurse in Boston that would be a match for old Daniel."

"Tomahawked from the back," Duncan explained. "Scalped. This was stuffed into his mouth." He unrolled the strip of cloth he had taken from the dead man.

Chisholm went very still. "Abenaki!" he whispered.

"Oliver was at St. Francis," Munro observed.

The words triggered a storm of emotion on the former ranger's face. "Aye, he was there, both of us corporals then with Major Rogers. Pulling each other out of the muck of the swamps, building human chains to cross the fast rivers. The major drove us hard. 'We're gonna hit them where the raiding bastards least expect it,'" he told us that night we left Crown Point, rowing with muffled oars so as not to be heard by French spies. And blessed Mary, that we did. No one ever did such a feat, not before and not after."

"Were you with Oliver in the fighting?" Duncan asked.

Chisholm seemed not to hear. "We thought the stealthy journey there was the ordeal," he continued in a hollow voice, "but the return was worse by far, with the French and 'Nakis on our tails through the damned barren wilderness, no time to take a meal or sleep. The major split us into small groups so we might evade our pursuers better, told us to reach the little militia fort down on the Connecticut as best we could. We attacked with nearly a hundred fifty men and lost only one in the attack, but we returned with ninety, all those others taken in the pursuit. Afterward we heard about them the heathens captured. Burned alive. Skinned alive. Given to women with small knives who cut off little pieces for days of slow death."

In the silence they could hear the bees among the flowers. "Why would an Abenaki go to Boston to continue the war all these years later?" Duncan asked.

The former ranger looked up into the sky, as if seeking an answer from the heavens, then fingered the necklace of pewter and porcelain beads that hung from his neck. It occurred to Duncan that the necklace could be a trophy taken from an Indian foe. "The 'Naki are breaking up, I hear. Some moving farther north into the Cree country, some going west into the Ohio country and beyond." He looked back at Duncan and shrugged. "A solitary 'Naki? That's just an angry man."

"A warrior on a trail," Duncan said, as if correcting him.

"Surely it was Oliver's bad luck to run into him in Boston, and if he did commit murder, ye can bet he's hightailing it back north now." The wheelwright looked at his freshly turned soil. "What exactly did he do to my friend?" he asked in a tight voice.

It was Munro who replied. "Stabbed him and left the knife's sheath beside the body. Then he stuffed this cloth in Oliver's mouth and lifted his hair."

"He follows the old ways, then. The power is in the hair from the top of his enemy's head. He's taking Oliver's soul back north. He left the knife as tribute 'cause it belonged to one of his fallen warriors. Fulfilling some kind of vow, I wager."

"He left the knife in his chest," Duncan said. "After cutting out a piece of his heart."

Chisholm seemed to choke and had difficulty speaking. "Mog!" he finally spat in a haunted tone.

"Mog?" Duncan asked.

"Mogephra, war chief of the Abenaki—at least he was. Like a rabid wolf in battle. Collected scalps all over New England, more than fifty by his hand alone, he would brag, and if he knew the man was a ranger, he would eat the heart. The major had us give chase to him once, sent off a young scout ahead. We found pieces of the boy along the trail the next day. A hand, a foot, the liver, the head, then the torso, with a great hole in his chest where his heart had been. The major always said it was his biggest disappointment, not killing Mog that October day in '59. But we took his family, had to, so as to knock the fight out of him the way he had done to so many on our side. I would have thought he'd be gone out west by now, carving out a place among those warlike tribes."

"This Abenaki who killed Oliver had a scar," Duncan said. "I saw him." He slanted his hand over his face again.

A curse escaped from Chisholm, and he crossed himself. "A saber did that to Mog at Lake George, though the bastard killed the officer who gave it to him."

"He broke into a warehouse in Boston the day after he killed Oliver."

"After committing murder, a little theft wouldn't trouble him."

"The warehouse belonged to John Hancock."

Chisholm did not look up from his cup, but Duncan did not miss the way his jaw tightened.

"The ship Oliver served on was destroyed in an explosion outside Boston harbor," Duncan continued. "Oliver escaped just moments before, only to be murdered. The ship was owned by Robert Livingston."

A low, guttural sound rattled in Chisholm's throat, though Duncan was at a loss to know whether it expressed surprise, disapproval, or remorse. The wheelwright bent and pulled a weed from his bed of soil.

"You're familiar with the name," Duncan observed.

The former ranger sergeant frowned. He stood and retrieved the spade, then broke up several clods of earth before replying. "I was one of Livingston's men, ye ken. One of the score he promised for the first New York ranger company in the war, made up of volunteers from his tenants. He promised us each fifty acres, and he made good on the bargain for those of us who survived, good bottom acreage along the Hudson." He buried the spade in the earth and looked up with something like apology in his eyes. "Then the new troubles arrived, and he asked us to stand with him. Law-abiding men must stand together when the rabble rise up, he said. A pompous prig often, but he knew the right things to say."

Duncan tried to piece together the words with his memories of events in recent years along the Hudson. "You mean the tenant uprising?"

"Aye. Livingston raised his own private army. But I was loath to bust the heads of poor hardscrabble farmers wanting nothing more than a few acres to feed their families. It became like a battle among the great lairds in the old country. The lords of Massachusetts sent in their farmers to make claim to land all the way to the Hudson, while the lords of New York insisted that their colony ran east to the Connecticut. Mr. Livingston had the better of the argument, based on his grant from the king. One of the other former rangers sided with the tenants, and Livingston revoked his land grant. Men were dying needlessly on both sides, and I prayed for a way out. I ne'er wished ill of my brother, but when he died, it was like the Lord had intervened. I told Mr. Livingston I had to come here to support his family, and we parted on good terms. He gave me his best wishes, and I came to my new life." He gestured to his shop. "I like wheels. Useful things, wheels. Jen has a joke. 'Wheels make the world turn,' she says." With a forced laugh, Chisholm put the cork back in the crock, as if his hospitality had ended.

"Good men have died," Duncan pressed. "Your friend Oliver was murdered. I think you got a package sent from St. Francis just as he did."

The big man gave a heavy sigh. "I put him on that boat. At night in our ranger camps he sometimes said he had a notion to see other lands, and he asked me if I thought Mr. Livingston would ever have a berth on one of his great vessels." As soon as I told Livingston that Oliver had been a ranger, he agreed, and off Dan'l went across that saltwater wilderness. That's what he called it in a letter he wrote me from the Azores—the saltwater wilderness."

"Your work for Livingston did not end when you left New York, did it? Oliver and another ranger named Branscomb received secret packages recently. Did you?"

Chisholm winced. "It's a complicated proposition, ye might say. Livingston and Hancock have tasks from time to time, mostly Hancock, now that I'm in his colony. Go meet a cobbler in Providence. Go talk with a schoolteacher in Framingham. But that's not what the package was. The package came from the north. Knew as soon as I saw that purple ink. There's secrets in the north, and not all known to me." He leaned on the spade and looked back up at the boneyard. "Our fathers had kings," he declared for no apparent reason, "their fathers before them, and beyond, to before the tales of men began. How could it be otherwise? It shakes my bones to think on it."

"Yes, but where are those secrets?" Duncan asked impatiently. "I need to know where they are, how to find them," he pressed. "It wasn't just Oliver who died. After he left his ship, it exploded. Thirty-seven dead all told. I mean to find the killers."

Chisholm distractedly worked his spade for a few moments. "Who's a man to trust?" he asked, staring at the soil. "It's a long way to go, but there's debts to pay."

"Why would Oliver work with French agents?" Munro shot back.

"French? Don't know about French. If Daniel was with any French, it was to play them. It was a game he and the major enjoyed sometimes, just walk into the enemy camp plain as can be, acting like they belonged there. A ranger rule, know the land of yer enemy as well as ye know yer own. If Dan'l was with them, it was to reconnoiter, if ye get my meaning." He looked back up at the cemetery. "We got secrets, sure. Secrets within secrets. Secrets that can change the world."

Duncan contemplated Chisholm's words. *It's a long way to go, but there's debts to pay.* He remembered something else about the secret package that had been stolen in Hancock's warehouse. "Saguenay secrets," he whispered.

Chisholm stared at him, then seemed to relax. He nodded. "Saguenay." He studied his two new friends with an intense expression. "I wasn't going to tell, but I n'er expected two fellow Highlanders to come asking. *On fuil na Gaidhealtachd?*" he asked, and extended his hand.

He was asking for a vow of trust. *On the blood of the Highlands.* Duncan readily nodded and took the offered hand.

"Saguenay," Chisholm said again, as if to seal their bond.

"Saguenay," Duncan repeated, feeling shamed for his deception. "Tell me, do you ken an Ebenezer Brandt?"

Chisholm's lips curled upward for a moment. "Corporal Brandt? Not all who seem crazy are insane," he declared, then straightened. "There be time tomorrow to talk. It'll make more sense when ye see the package, but I can't fetch it today," he said. "Ain't here." He gestured toward the boneyard above his shop. "I'll get it for ye at first light. Now I've got a wheel to finish. Got to keep the world turning, ye ken." The wheelwright plucked another weed. "When Shakespeare's flowers start blooming, I'm going to have Jen sit here," he said with a self-conscious blush, speaking toward the log seat, "and ask her if the bard also had golden-haired beauties in his gardens."

6

"My uncle hasn't moved," Ishmael said in a forlorn voice when Duncan found him by the sawmill, still watching Conawago. "Except to reach into his pouch and put on an old wampum necklace. Every few minutes he lifts his amulet and seems to speak to it. I tried to talk with him, and he didn't respond, didn't even seem to know I was there."

Duncan sent Munro back to the inn and stayed with Conawago's nephew, watching in painful silence for several minutes. The men in the log yard were winding down their work for the day, gathering their long bark spudders and cutting tools in the fading light. As they walked away, Duncan moved in a wide arc that kept him out of Conawago's line of sight, stopping in the shadow of a stack of massive oak and maple logs.

"Git out, ye damned beggar!" a stout, bearded sawyer snapped in an Irish accent as he passed the old Nipmuc, then stopped and threw a stone. With a lurch of his heart Duncan watched as it bounced off Conawago's shoulder. His old friend had taken off his fine woolen waistcoat, pulled out the tails of his linen shirt, and untied his long hair so it hung unkempt over his shoulders. He did indeed look like one of the old natives who stayed alive by asking for alms in European settlements. It was as if he were doing penance.

Duncan darted toward Conawago and stood a few feet in front of him, blocking his assailant's aim. The man saw the fire in Duncan's eyes, tossed his next stone from hand to hand, then shrugged and hurried to join his friends.

When Duncan turned around, the old Nipmuc was walking alongside one of the great logs, one hand on its bark, whispering in his original tongue. Ishmael tried to pull his great-uncle back, only to have Conawago slap his hand away. Ishmael turned to Duncan with a tormented expression. Conawago looked frailer than Duncan had ever seen him.

"It's a death song!" Ishmael groaned. There was anguish in his eyes. "He is singing a song about joining spirits on the other side."

Duncan stepped to the end of the log and blocked the old man's passage. "It's been a long day, my friend."

Conawago blinked and rubbed moisture from his eyes, then looked up as if seeing Duncan for the first time. "There you are, then," he said, as if he had been looking for Duncan. "A long, long day, yes, and a longer night is coming," he said. The bleakness in his voice tugged at Duncan's heart. "But meanwhile I could join you in some nourishment," he suggested, forcing a small grin.

Duncan motioned him toward the inn. "Sarah's waiting for us," he explained, glancing up and down the street, remembering the warrant on his head. Munro had taken up a position in the shadow of a dovecote down the road, Duncan's rifle still in his hand. The old soldier had not stopped keeping watch.

They discovered Sarah at a long trestle table in the back of the tavern's barnlike dining chamber, chatting cheerfully with Solomon Hayes. As Duncan, Conawago, and Ishmael pulled out chairs at the table, the innkeeper put a hand on Ishmael's arm. "Beasts feed in the stable," the man stated, indicating Molly, at Ishmael's knee.

"Please do send the beasts away," Ishmael replied in a pointed tone, "but my gentle Molly stays with me."

Sarah cut off the innkeeper's protest. "She will be no trouble, sir," she promised as the Newfoundland slipped under the table. "Just charge her as another guest, and all will be fine, I am sure."

"No trouble," the innkeeper repeated uncertainly, then called for the barmaid to bring a pitcher of ale and a board of bread for his customers.

"My father just wants to keep the peace in his establishment," the girl explained as she distributed a tray of tankards. She had an open, amiable countenance, but her smile seemed somehow sad. "And I will nay charge for your handsome creature," she confided in a lower voice.

Conawago dutifully chewed his roast pork and mashed peas, but he did not partake in the conversation that Sarah led about plans for new buildings at Edentown and whether early or late apples should be planted in the new orchard. Duncan realized that the old man was not even trying to follow the discussion, and he followed his gaze across the chamber to where half a dozen rough-looking men had settled for a meal. With a chill, Duncan saw that they were from the sawmill. The bearded Irishman who had cast a stone at Conawago seemed to ignore the Nipmuc's stare at first, but when Conawago, after draining his first tankard, had not shifted his gaze, the man noisily pushed his chair back and marched across the room.

"I told ye," he growled as he reached Conawago. "We don't take to your kind in this town. Will ye go peaceable, or will ye do me the pleasure of going otherwise?" he asked with a malevolent grin.

The old Nipmuc motioned the man closer, as if he could not hear. As the man bent, Conawago moved with surprising speed, seizing a handful of the man's shirt at his neck and jerking him down while reaching for the ginger beer crock beside him. He smashed the crock onto the man's head so powerfully, the thick ceramic shattered; then he slammed the man's head sideways onto his plate.

"I am a chieftain of the Nipmuc tribe," Conawago stated in a surprisingly level voice. "Can you say that? Nipmuc! Shouldn't be difficult even for an ignorant fool like you."

The bearded man struggled, but Conawago kept a tight grip, twisting the collar of the man's shirt so tightly it began to choke him. He cursed and tried to rise, only to have his head pressed even harder into what had been a pile of mashed peas. Ginger beer ran down the back of his head onto his unshaven face. His hands, opened on the table, balled into fists as if to strike; then he went limp. The point of Ishmael's knife was pressed into one wrist. "Nip—muc," the Irishman sputtered through the peas.

Conawago kept his grip on the man but spoke in a conversational tone. "Long before Europeans arrived in this valley, it was the home of the Nipmucs," he explained. "For centuries, my people lived here, always honoring the spirits in the trees here because they were the biggest, most majestic trees in all the world. We called this place Quinsigamond."

The Irishman's companions had taken notice, and three of them were now angrily approaching the table. Enoch Munro materialized out of the shadows, Duncan's rifle in the crook of his arm, and positioned himself with his back to

Conawago's chair. Ishmael leaned toward his knife, still on the man's wrist, as if about to pin the hand to the table.

"Quinsigamond," Conawago repeated, heat in his voice now. "Try it, or do you truly have granite for brains?"

"Quinsmond," the sawyer muttered. Mashed peas matted one eyebrow.

"Quinsigamond. Try harder."

One of the sawyer's friends advanced, raising his fist, and before Munro could react, a black mass of fur appeared in front of him. Molly emitted a low, rattling sound and bared her teeth. The man halted.

Three times Conawago's captive spoke the word before the old Nipmuc was satisfied. "Excellent. Before you start cutting each of the great Nipmuc logs, I want you to put your hand on it and say that word to honor the old spirits. Defy me, and the spirits will know. Your wells will sour, your grain will get the mold, your saw blades will break, and your oxen will go lame. And every board you cut will split." He pushed the man's head up, then jerked it toward him. "Do you understand the words of this old Nipmuc?" he growled.

The man nodded through the puddle of peas and gravy on his face. Conawago released him, and he backed away, wiping away the remains of Conawago's meal, then stormed out the tavern door.

Conawago, his eyes much brighter now, extended a hand toward the pitcher near Hayes. "I find myself suddenly thirsty. Might I try some of that ale, Solomon? And if you're not going to eat your pork, I will make the effort."

They finished the meal without incident, Conawago joining in their discussion of the next day's journey and the plan to push as hard as possible to the Connecticut River. No one gave evidence of the episode except for Ishmael's rotation of his chair a few degrees so he could watch the still-fuming sawyers.

After Conawago downed his second serving of berry pie, Sarah declared the meal complete and, rising, bid the company good slumber. As she and Munro moved toward the central stairway, however, they discovered that the Irishman who had confronted Conawago now stood by the entry with half a dozen new allies. The tavern keeper, sensing trouble, motioned Duncan and his friends up the stairway, but the angry sawyer shoved the man aside and stepped toward Conawago.

"This be *our* town, damned ye!" he spat. His companions held barrel staves and other makeshift clubs at the ready. The innkeeper retreated to the large fortified cage in the corner of the chamber where his spirits were kept.

"Quinsigamond," Conawago replied with false cheer. "That's the name of this place. I think that tells us all we need to know about the founders of this town."

As the sawyers at the table by the far wall stood to join their townsmen, the door opened behind them.

"God's grace to you, gentlemen," Samson Occom's deep voice boomed through the crowd. Several of the men, seeing his clerical collar, muttered polite replies, then stepped aside. Strangely, Occom seemed to stumble as he walked through the men, knocking a barrel stave to the ground, then a piece of timber, both of which he kicked away. He was doing what he could to disarm the men. Occom turned, tossed his cloak on the bench below the stairs, and faced the leader of the sawyers. " 'Behold how good and pleasant it is for brothers to dwell together in unity!' " he declared. "So the Good Book tells us. Psalm 133, if I am not mistaken."

"If he's my brother, then I was born to a redskin whore," the man growled. Bits of smashed peas still clung to his beard. "Don't speak so of my mother!"

Occom's hand came up. A barrel stave seemed to have magically appeared in it. " 'Live in harmony with one another,' " the pastor recited as he tapped the club in his palm. " 'Do not be proud, but be willing to associate with people of low position.' Romans 12."

"Shut yer teeth!" the Irishman snarled. "Look at ye, red in your skin as well."

" 'Blessed are the peacemakers,' " Occom recited, " 'for they shall inherit the ale.' "

Several of the crowd laughed, then seemed to lose interest and dispersed in amiable conversation. Occom's words were having the opposite effect on Conawago. He leaned forward as if to rise, then felt Duncan's tight grip on his shoulder. Duncan well knew that the old Nipmuc had little stomach for being defended by a man of the cloth. That Occom himself was a native of the same tribal lands, sharing more in common with Conawago than with anyone they had met in years, only seemed to add salt to the wound. Duncan caught Ishmael's eye, making sure the youth was ready to help restrain his uncle if he rose to add his own fuel to the imminent conflagration.

Suddenly Conawago eased. They watched in surprise as Solomon Hayes stepped out of the shadows behind them and approached the angry ringleader. A small ball appeared in the air before Hayes, and another, then a third. The contemplative tinker was juggling. He stepped between Occom and the fuming Irishman, then halted in front of a stout sawyer beside the leader as the balls went ever higher, past the high rafters of the chamber. Three balls went up into the shadows. Two came down. Two went up, one came down. As the man looked upward, Hayes bounced the remaining ball off his belly.

"Surely this fine and ancient town deserves a more noble army," Hayes exclaimed. The stout sawyer gave an uncertain grunt as the ball bounced off him again; then, as his companions laughed, he grinned at the tinker. "'How now, my sweet creature of bombast, how long is't ago, Jack, since thou sawest thine own knee?'" Hayes said, dropping the ball into his pocket as Occom stepped back. "'A goodly portly man, 'n faith,'" Hayes continued, "'and a corpulent cheerful look, a pleasing eye, and a most noble carriage.'"

Conawago, watching with sudden interest, cast a knowing glance at Duncan. The itinerant trader and pot mender was quoting Shakespeare. "*Henry the Fourth*," the old Conawago whispered in amusement. The rest of the tavern had gone silent, enjoying the tinker's show.

Hayes tapped the man's prominent belly. "A sergeant if I ever saw one. Perhaps almost two!"

As laughter rippled through the company, the tinker turned to the barmaid, the innkeeper's daughter. "And every army needs its Helen, its Dulcinea, its Juliet." With a quick motion, Hayes's hand went above the woman's ample cleavage and seemed to extract a bright red feather from her bosom. "Such fine plumage!" Hayes declared to the delight of the crowd. The barmaid gazed in surprise at the feather, then at her breasts, and burst out in laughter. Hayes lifted her hand and kissed it. "The finest hand I ever touched. 'O Beauty, 'til now I never knew thee'!"

"*Henry the Eighth*," Conawago observed approvingly.

Hayes made a twisting flourish of his hand before the barmaid. "'Most radiant, exquisite, and unmatchable beauty'!"

"*Twelfth Night*," Conawago said, now enjoying himself.

"'Who art so lovely, fair, so sweet that the senses ache at thee'!"

"*Othello*, to be sure," came Conawago's whisper.

Hayes winked and gave the woman a deep bow. Almost every tavern customer broke into laughter as, balancing her tray in one hand, the maid curtsied. The Irishman did not share in the amusement.

"Ye do not buy our affections so lightly, vagabond," the sawyer said, spitting the last word like a curse. "Worcester don't take red beggars, and that's the fact of it. And what are ye, just a damned roving tinker, not worth a nit to the world."

Hayes was unmoved by the man's words or his glowering expression. He sighed and looked about with an exaggerated fear. "Shhhh," he said. "You're going to upset those ancient spirits my friend spoke of."

"The spirits be dead in the ground, like every good heathen should be." As the big man glanced up at a strange rustling noise in the darkened rafters, Hayes put a finger to his lips, then rotated with the gesture as if to silence his audience.

A high-pitched screech suddenly filled the tavern, sending tankards tumbling as several customers fled under tables or backed against the wall.

"Banshee!" a man cried, and crossed himself.

"Damned ye, Jocko!" an old woman yelled at the Irishman when the terrible piercing sound split the air again. "Ye've brought them out from t'other side!"

The innkeeper darted out of his spirit cage, a heavy club raised in his hand, then hesitated as Hayes turned and bowed to what seemed an empty corner of the chamber. "Oh, wise and terrible one, we salute you," the tinker called, then lifted a candlestick from a nearby table and raised it over his head.

"Mother Mary, protect us!" groaned one of the men closest to Hayes. As other customers followed his gaze, they backed away, several fleeing the establishment entirely. The old woman pointed a trembling hand to the rafter above Hayes. The tinker looked up, then gasped himself and took a clumsy step backward, stumbling into the bearded sawyer.

The round pink face, framed by thick sable-colored hair, extended outward from the rafter, its body so obscured by shadow that the face seemed to hover in the air. Its bright, intelligent eyes solemnly surveyed the company. Through the stunned silence an urgent prayer was whispered and quickly taken up by others. One of the sawyers beside the Irishman turned and fled out the door, holding his belly as if he desperately needed a privy. Half a dozen men dropped to their knees.

Hayes seemed to recover his senses and took a brave step toward the phantom. "Who?" the tinker asked in a trembling voice. "Who is it you seek, ancient one?"

A small leathery hand materialized in the pool of light and pointed to the Irishman, who began to cross himself frantically. The hand seemed to beckon to those below. Hayes collected his courage and reached up, touching the phantom's hand, then audibly gasped and turned toward the frightened assembly. A slip of paper was in his fingers. He extended it toward the Irishman, who vigorously shook his head, refusing to touch it.

Hayes turned to the innkeeper. "Sir, if you will. My hand is shaking too much for me to read this message from the other side. But surely the spirits intend for us to do so."

The innkeeper tentatively accepted the paper, motioning for his daughter to hold a candle near as he stretched the paper between his hands. He read silently, his eyebrows arching as he looked toward the rafter where the spirit, now gone, had perched; then he stepped in front of his remaining customers, turning the paper for all to read as he recited its single word. "Quinsigamond," he solemnly intoned.

A collective gasp rippled through the crowd. Several men repeated the Nipmuc word, like a vow. The Irishman retreated with an uncertain backward step, then turned and fled. The tavern keeper reached out to help customers to their feet and announced that the next round would be served gratis by the inn. The free ale eased the general anxiety, and soon men were grinning, passing around the spirit's note, reciting it again and again, their eyes round with wonder. The ancient Indian spirits had visited them, not to punish them, but just to remind them of a sacred duty.

Conawago, smiling for the first time in days, settled back into his seat. "Might there be some of that excellent pie left?" he asked no one in particular. The barmaid fussed over Solomon Hayes as he returned to his seat, setting an entire pie before him for the table, then bringing a pitcher of spiced wine. "There's a hint of chill tonight," she said. "I will put a mulling iron in the embers for you. Would be no trouble."

Hayes lifted her hand with a genteel smile and kissed it once more. "That would be delightful, lass. And I hope we did not give you too great a fright."

"Nay, sir. T'is the most excitement we've seen in this town in many a moon."

They sat a long time in idle conversation, sharing the spiced wine and passing around the hot iron to heat it, relishing in their temporary comfort that, if not quite contentment, was a least a welcome respite from a long day of worries.

The innkeeper did not approach them until the rest of the tavern had emptied, and when he did, he brought a bottle of fine port, which he poured out into small sparkling glasses. "Prithee," he said when everyone had been served, lifting a glass for himself. "This is my gift to you. T'ain't seen my daughter smile so since her mother passed last year." He drained his glass, then retrieved his heavy club and laid it on the table by Conawago. "T'was cut last year from one of those ancient oaks," he explained. "I wish ye to have it, sir."

The old Nipmuc stared at the club for several long breaths, then slowly reached out to touch it. Emotion washed over his face.

"Quinsigamond," the innkeeper said once more. "I am going to paint the letters on the wall above my counter," he declared. "I swear this to you, sir. And I wager there'll not be many of those grand trees cut again in this town." He filled Hayes's cup again. The tinker looked up as the innkeeper hesitated. "I sailed in the West Indies in my youth," he declared in a tentative tone. "Ain't seen one of the little monks since we made port in Panama all those years ago, but I recollect the lovely creatures were fond of vegetables. I've got some tender new carrots in the kitchen."

Hayes appraised the man in silence for a moment, then made a low, clicking sound. Sadie dropped out of the rafters onto the tinker's shoulder. She wrapped a long arm around Hayes's neck, then shyly peeked around his head at the innkeeper, who greeted her with a half bow. "An honor to make yer acquaintance, sir," he offered.

"Miss," Hayes corrected; then, gently easing the monkey off his neck, he raised his index finger twice. Duncan realized it was a hand signal. "Say hello to the kind gentleman, Sadie."

The innkeeper gave a heartfelt laugh as Sadie straightened and bowed back at him; then he excused himself to retrieve her promised meal.

"I beg your forgiveness," Hayes said to Conawago. "I meant no offense to your people."

"The evening was going badly," the old Nipmuc replied. "If you had not snuffed that fuse so adeptly, there would have been an explosion. I take it in the generous spirit it was intended."

"Your skills are most impressive," Sarah observed to the tinker. "You should be in the theater, not mending pots."

Hayes gazed out the darkened window as he weighed Sarah's words. "I think it was the Bard himself who suggested that all the world's a stage," he replied at last.

"I saw you writing something when the commotion started," Sarah said, clearly amused to be part of Hayes's conspiracy.

"And when you stumbled against the Irishman, you dropped that little red feather onto his shoulder," Duncan observed. "Was it a signal of some kind?"

Hayes stroked the rich hair on Sadie's head and nodded. "A little game we play sometimes. Point out the bright feather. And my little girl long ago learned to screech at my signal."

The innkeeper returned with a plate of raw carrots and fresh peas still in the pod, which Sadie eagerly consumed, making low, purring sounds of satisfaction between bites. As she ate, her host watching in great delight, Duncan touched the innkeeper's arm. "A question, sir. Do you know the wheelwright Josiah Chisholm?"

"The old ranger. Of course. A good, solid man if ever there was, though not beloved by the government, some might say. If you are here on his other business, pray keep it quiet. There are those in this town who correspond with the governor, seeking his favor, if you get my drift."

Conwawago leaned forward. "Not entirely, sir."

"I don't make a habit of speaking of my neighbors. My custom depends on everyone in the town feeling comfortable in my establishment."

"But we are just passing through," Duncan pointed out.

"Chisholm is a devout and honest man. That's what counts, I say. Loyal subject or nay."

Conawago lowered his voice. "Do you suggest he is not fond of the king?"

"He goes to Boston every few weeks. When he returns, we have meetings in the night, sometimes in my back room."

"But an innkeeper needs to be an obedient subject. You are beholden to the government for licenses and such."

"Render unto Caesar what is Caesar's, the Good Book tells us. The king is a long way from our little hamlet and shouldn't have his hand in every breath a man takes. I like to think of our meetings as a community improvement association. There's talk of organizing a pageant after the harvest."

"But others might call them the Sons of Liberty."

The innkeeper did not disagree. "We started meeting in the days of that damnable stamp tax. Only later did we hear the name of the Sons. Came from a Whig in the Parliament, I hear. Talk about irony, eh?" The innkeeper gazed into the eyes of each of those at the table, as if assessing them, before continuing. "The wheelwright is a gentle soul, with the strong back of an ox, but his strength sometimes seems to hang by a thread."

It was Sarah who broke the confused silence that followed. "You mean his is a troubled soul."

"Aye. There is sometimes torment behind his eyes. He was a ranger for Major Rogers, and my cousin from Rhinebeck, along the Hudson, wrote me that he was one of those who busted the heads of tenants for the great lord Mr. Livingston."

Duncan chewed on the words a moment. "Why did you feel reason to ask your cousin about him?"

"There's splits within the Sons—factions, ye might say. Most of the leaders are wealthy gentry. There are those who say they are just using us for their personal gain, that some invest in liberty the way they might invest in a cargo of rum or tobacco. I wanted to be certain we could trust him with our secrets and trust his offer of militia training to the local Sons. My cousin says he is an honest man of stalwart heart."

"Secrets of the Sons, you mean," Duncan whispered.

The innkeeper poured himself a cup of the spiced wine. Sadie, who seemed to be a creature of uncommon intuition if not downright wisdom, sat cross-legged before the man and extended the last carrot to him. He spoke his answer to the primate. "Those boys in Boston stir the pot of rebellion thinking it is just how they get the attention of the king, but sometimes I think we may be on a path toward a real fight. If so, it'll be the blood of a thousand villages like this that gets shed." He looked down into his cup. "When my wife was sick for weeks afore she passed, she started having terrible nightmares of blood on the fields. I told her it was just all the old stories of the Indian raids. But she said no, it was always brother fighting brother."

Duncan sipped at his own cup. "Weapons?" he asked. "Your secrets are about weapons?"

The innkeeper sighed, looked around the chamber to confirm that it was empty, and explained. "The king maintains arsenals in several towns in the New England colonies, usually manned by invalids and old soldiers ready for pensions. Their inventory counting would never pass muster in the lowest of village shops. Some arsenal guards just sleep away their watches; others gripe about the meager count of their pension to come and accept a coin on the side. Our militias are expanding, but most just carry sticks instead of muskets."

"Weapons are being stolen to arm the Sons?"

The innkeeper broke off small pieces of the carrot and held them out for Sadie to eat. "One or two, here or there. It'll never be enough, but if it comes to a fight, would ye just want a pitchfork or a little fowling piece against a heavy Brown Bess musket?"

SARAH LEANED AGAINST THE DOOR as she shut it behind Duncan. The contentment that had settled over her countenance at dinner had been banished by the innkeeper's words. "Stealing muskets from the king! Bribing army guards. This is how you will prove yourself innocent of treason! I beg you, Duncan, leave this behind before it is too late. Not only do you tarry too long, you tarry with men who will draw you deeper into danger. Hancock and Adams talk about building a strong hand for negotiation with Parliament. This is not what I heard in that dining room!"

"Every cause has its zealots, Sarah. I have never been one, you know that." Duncan tried to put a hand on her shoulder, and she pulled away.

"Ride on, Duncan, I beg you. Ride to Edentown as fast as you can," Sarah pleaded. "Forget the Abenaki! Forget the liars who wish to trap you. I will be not far behind."

Duncan held her gaze for a moment, then looked away. "This is the world where I must find the answers, Sarah, the world of the Sons, the world of zealots. I cannot be a fugitive the rest of my life."

"They are zealots for their own peculiar version of freedom. We have all the freedom we need already," she replied. "When has the king ever bothered us in Edentown?"

"Only when I find the answers will we be safe in Edentown," Duncan insisted.

Moisture welled in Sarah's eyes, and she looked away. "I am frightened, Duncan, so frightened for us." She let him wrap his arms around her, and after a moment she returned the embrace. They held each other in silence, pulling apart at a tap on the door. Munro appeared, carrying a sleeping Will Sterret.

"Ye said the lad should sleep in yer chamber," the Scot said with an awkward expression, "to keep him out of mischief."

Sarah forced a smile and pointed to a pallet by the hearth.

DUNCAN WAS SURPRISED AT HOW troubled he was over the innkeeper's words. He lay on a comforter beside Sarah's bed, listening to the slow, quiet breathing of Sarah and Will, recalling prior conversations in Boston. The arguments with the king would never come to violence, Hancock and Sam Adams always insisted. King George would soon recognize that the inhabitants of his most valuable colonies had to be given the same respect as Englishmen in the home country, and all would then rally around their monarch. But the terrible visions of the innkeeper's dying wife now visited him, vivid images of ill-trained colonists being massacred by British regulars, the massed bullets of their Brown Besses mowing down farmers and shopkeepers like the blade of a bloody scythe. Whenever a colonist fell, an Abenaki materialized to rip away his scalp.

At last, all prospect of sleep banished, Duncan rose and found his way to the stable. In the first stall, by the light of a dimmed lantern, he saw Ishmael, Molly, and Hayes sleeping on a pile of fresh, sweet-smelling straw. Sadie's bright, inquisitive eyes peered over Hayes's shoulder, as if she were standing guard. Munro slept propped against a barrel, Duncan's rifle across his legs. He found Conawago outside on a stack of firewood, where he had rearranged the logs into a makeshift chaise over which he had draped his blanket. Duncan silently settled on the ground beside him, leaning against the stack of cut logs. He knew instinctively that his friend was awake, though several minutes passed before the old man turned from looking at the stars to acknowledge him.

The night sky was a blanket of thousands of shimmering points of light, intersected by the long, glowing finger of the Milky Way. Duncan, his hands locked behind his head, had quickly found the anchors of the mariner's sky, Polaris, then Altair, Vega, and Deneb, the summer triplets, as his grandfather had called them.

"I came out to go to the wheelwright's house," Duncan explained. "There is more for him to tell us, things best spoken of in the shadows."

Conawago seemed uninterested in anything but the spectacle overhead. "An old Jesuit monk once took me to his workshop outside Paris. He was a renowned astronomer, had even constructed domed chambers at Versailles depicting the night sky in each season. He was obsessed with trying to explain why all celestial bodies do not move with the same motion. He had persuaded the king to lend him the royal clockmaker, jeweler, and silversmith. Together they made the most amazing machine. It was about to be shipped to the king, but the monk insisted on showing it to me, saying that once it arrived in the palace, any number of fools would probably break its delicate workings. It consisted of huge silver filigree rings defining several circular pathways set around a golden sun, the third one holding the earth, worked in copper with seas of inlaid lapis. Each of the other rings also held a planet, depicted as smaller orbs made of semiprecious stones. A movable half-dome cover laid with diamond bits represented the stars. Each ring moved around the sun, but in different directions, each according to its own rules—its predestined orbit, he called it. The movement of one body is always relative to another body, he said. The subtleties were lost on the Sun King, but he declared that he was happy to see the sun at the center and that it would be a delightful addition to his toys. He endowed a new monastery as the astronomer's reward."

Duncan looked at his friend in frustration. Over the years, he had spent many wonderful hours talking about the mysteries of the stars with Conawago, but he wished the old man would understand that, for now, he was unable to focus on anything other than the mysteries of the deaths in Boston and the warrant on his head.

The Nipmuc elder sat up and stretched. "I doubt there were more than half a dozen people in the palace who understood its lessons. Everything is correlated in position with everything else, and all actions can be understood if only one knows those correlations." He fixed Duncan with a pointed expression.

Duncan studied his wise old friend. "Are we still talking about astronomy?" he asked.

"I never was. How could I speak idly of the night sky when there are men who seek your death, Duncan?" he asked, lifting Duncan's heart. "You think the wheelwright knows something of the deaths in Boston?"

"I don't know," Duncan replied. "The correlation is the motives. Two Frenchmen destroyed the *Arcturus* for one motive. I think the Abenaki killed for another motive, but the French made it possible because they needed him. And I worry about what else they need him for."

"It started with the ledger," Conawago observed, "but we know so little about it, we will never find its orbit. It is dark to us. But there is another orbit intersecting it, affecting it, the orbit of packets with purple-inked letters sent to rangers. So why, I keep asking myself, would the French care about that list of rangers?"

"Because," Duncan suggested, thinking out loud, "either the rangers know secrets the French realize they need, or perhaps to the French they aren't rangers, they are lightning rods, sources of ignition they might use to start another war against King George. You heard the words about stolen muskets and bribes at arsenals."

"Don't speak nonsense. The French wouldn't . . ." Conawago hesitated, chewing on his own words.

"Wouldn't want an uprising against King George?"

He could sense the old Nipmuc's shudder. "Don't even speak of such things! Surely not. The rivers would run red with blood."

Duncan had no more words. Everywhere he turned, he found new fears.

Conawago climbed off the pile of logs and looked up the hill toward the other side of the river. In the light of the half moon, the vanes of the big windmill moved like a circling of ghosts. "The wheelwright would be a careful man. An old ranger always watches and weighs before acting."

"I fear this particular ranger watches too much for a blond widow and seeds from Boston. I'll have no more sleep this night, not until I speak with him. He is the link, he is the planet whose path explains the others." Duncan realized that Conawago had raised a pouch from the woodpile.

"Help me, Duncan, in one small task, and then I will join you in a visit to the wheelworks. Fetch a bottle of the inn's good ginger beer to loosen his tongue. You'll find me near the river."

Duncan could not see his friend when he arrived at the riverbank a few minutes later, but he heard the murmur of a Nipmuc prayer coming from the shadows. He discovered the old man kneeling along the bank, clawing at the earth, then pounding his club of ancient oak onto the spot. He watched in confusion as his friend rose, took two steps along the river, then repeated the motion. He was digging, depositing something, covering it, and sealing the hole with a thrust of his club. With a stab of pain Duncan remembered what was in the doeskin pouch. It contained strands of beads made by Conawago's mother and grandmother, given to him to keep tradition alive when he left his village in the prior century. He was burying artifacts of his clan on the site of the long-ago Nipmuc mother town. He was, Duncan realized with a wrench of his heart, closing the story of his life. For decades Conawago had searched for his mother and siblings, insisting that he would return the old beads to them for a still-younger generation; then he had sought only traces—at least a neglected grave where he could stand vigil and leave the beads with old bones. Now, here in ancient Quinsigamond, he was surrendering all prospects, all hopes of the quest that had defined his life, as if he were abandoning part of himself, the vital part of his existence that had now become hopeless. Duncan pushed down the agonizing question that rose from his heart. What, after this, would be left of the old man? He silently bent and took the pouch, reverently handing Conawago a bead from a broken strand at the next hole, and at the next, as the old Nipmuc returned the last vestiges of his family to the soil of his ancient tribe.

When they finished with all the beads of the broken strand, they stood side by side at the river, looking back along the nearly imperceptible circles of packed earth that marked the tiny burials. Conawago's voice was dry as twigs. "They'll probably just get washed out in the next heavy rain," he said.

"Not washed out and lost," Duncan replied. "This river was here long before your people were here."

Conawago looked out at the river, then back to Duncan. "I confess I do not follow."

"Your people were giving things to this river for centuries, accidentally and otherwise. There is a Nipmuc graveyard here. It is in the bed of the river."

Conawago silently weighed Duncan's words, then slowly nodded and dropped onto one knee. "Be at peace," he said to his ancestors. "I am coming."

As they watched the dark, flickering current, a figure moved out of the shadows of the stacked timber logs. Duncan's hand instinctively went to his knife, but Conawago reached out to restrain him.

"My boy," he said, and Duncan recognized Ishmael, the black shape of Molly a few steps behind him.

As they walked along the darkened street above the bridge, Ishmael suddenly pushed them into the cover of a clump of alders as a young groom, less than twenty feet away, walked four tired horses from the front of an inn to its rear stable. Ishmael's hand shot out. "There!" he whispered urgently.

Duncan did not understand at first; then Ishmael pointed three more times, to the rear flank of each horse. He was pointing to a large brand that appeared on each of the tall thoroughbreds. Duncan crouched, slipping alongside the nearest of the sweat-stained horses as it turned, exposing the brand in the moonlight. His heart sank as he recognized the broad arrow, the mark put on the property of the British military. He glanced into the anxious face of Conawago, who was gesturing him back to cover; then he casually stepped toward the groom.

"These mounts are cruelly used," he observed conversationally. "Who would treat them so ill?"

The teenage stable boy snapped his head up in surprise, then shrugged, apparently deciding that Duncan was just one of the many workmen who started their day before dawn. "Four soldiers, riding hard from Boston." He hesitated, then seemed to relax as Duncan began to remove the saddle from the nearest mount, a big, heavily muscled black horse. "Dragoons, by the look of their tack," Duncan observed. "I fought alongside some in Canada."

"You were in the war, sir?" The groom's caution was replaced by a boyish curiosity, reminiscent of Henry Knox.

"Aye, I was there when the French surrendered at Montreal." Duncan hoisted the saddle off. "Where do you want this, lad?" The boy pointed to a long trestle near the front of the stable aisle. "What possible reason would they have to run so hard over darkened roads?"

"Urgent business for the Crown, that lieutenant said. He pounded a tankard on the counter, rudely shouting until the innkeeper appeared in his nightshirt. I was sleeping by the hearth. The lieutenant demanded the best room, took a bottle of ale, and asked for a woman to be sent up. When he was told that this was not that kind of establishment, he cursed and climbed the stairs."

"The others?"

"In the tavern, downing the last of yesterday's stew."

"Did the officer give a name?"

"Only on the register, sir."

Duncan handed the boy a two-penny coin. "I'd like to know it. Might be an old friend of mine whom I could surprise at breakfast. Just a quick look, between you and me."

The youth's eyes went round and with a mischievous gleam he darted into the inn. Duncan and his companions ventured a look through the window. Three soldiers, seasoned, gristle-faced veterans, sat with legs stretched out toward the heat of the hearth as they nursed their tankards.

"It's hard to read," the groom said when he returned. "The Christian name Horace or Horatio, I think, then four letters. Bart maybe, or Berk."

Duncan's heart tightened. "Beck," he suggested, now realizing why they had not seen any warrant men on the road. Horatio Beck himself had come for Duncan.

"And he settled into his room for a rest?"

"Oh, aye, they were all exhausted. And their mounts were spent, though with a little grain I'll soon have them restored."

Duncan handed the boy an extra coin. "No need to speak of this with anyone."

"No need at all, sir," the groom confirmed with a conspiratorial grin.

As the boy disappeared into the stable, Conawago spoke with a new urgency in his voice and motioned Duncan around the back of the wheel shop. "As you said, best speak to the wheelwright in the night."

But the old ranger was not on the rope bed in the back shed that was his home.

"Maybe he's with his brother's widow," Conawago suggested as he stared at the empty bed.

"No," Duncan replied as he set down the jar of beer he had brought from the inn and put his hand on his knife. "You didn't hear the reverent way he spoke of her. He's planting the flowers of Shakespeare for her. That's not a man who would put a shadow over her good name by being in her house after midnight." He pointed to a blanket lying on the floor by the bed as if hastily discarded.

Back in the shop, they found scraps of iron on the packed-earth floor, dumped from a shelf. Conawago stumbled as he stole along the back wall, and from the deep shadows at his foot he lifted the object that had tripped him. It was the spade they had seen in the garden. Fresh dirt still clung from its iron-tipped blade. "He's retrieved the hidden package from the boneyard," Duncan observed. He pushed on into the shadows, the hairs on his neck bristling in alarm, then bent to pick up a braided leather thong and held it out, dangling the pewter and porcelain beads that had hung from Chisholm's neck. "Someone else was here. He would not have given that up voluntarily."

Conawago raised his club and with a low, warbling whistle sent Ishmael into the shadows of the trees between the shop and the street. Duncan stole forward, knife in hand.

Ishmael whistled and pointed to something shining in the moonlight, a patch the size of a shilling.

"Blood, freshly spilled," Conawago declared as he knelt beside the little silvery pool. Ishmael indicated a second pool, then a third.

With a sinking heart Duncan followed the trail up the little knoll to a larger pool in front of the old windmill.

"He couldn't just disappear," Ishmael said. "He must have been put on a horse or wagon," the young Nipmuc announced, and bent to search for tracks.

"There's a breeze," Conawago observed. As Duncan turned to his friend in query, they both heard a dull, repetitive thumping sound behind them.

"There's a breeze, but the windmill doesn't turn," Duncan said, grasping his friend's point. Then he noticed that his hand was wet. Something was dripping on him. Both men looked up.

The ghostly figure that looked over the town seemed to have been crucified on the topmost vane, his arms spread and tied to the frame, his body and legs carefully fastened so that when the gears were blocked, the dead man gazed out over Worcester from its highest point.

Conawago murmured a prayer and stepped inside the mill. A moment later a mangled pitchfork was thrown out of the door, and the great wind vanes groaned into motion. He and Duncan caught the vane that held the body as it approached and quickly cut it free. Chisholm's shirt was soaked with blood, still seeping from the hole where his heart had been cut out. His face had been viciously slashed, a piece of Abenaki linen stuffed into his mouth. Blood dripped from his eyes, each of which was pierced with a nail. His scalp had been taken. The old ranger would never plant Shakespeare's flowers for his brother's fair-haired widow.

7

DUNCAN REINED IN THE TALL thoroughbred at an opening in the thick brush of the ridge above the road, letting it rest after two hours of hard riding. He gazed eastward, not for the first time that morning, and considered abandoning his flight. Ishmael was in grave danger, and Duncan would never forgive himself if the youth lost his life on his account.

They had wasted precious time looking for clues in the wheel shop by the light of the lantern. There had been little more than drops of blood, one trail of which led to a numeral 4 scrawled in the moist soil along the beaten path to the mill, reddened by the bloody finger that had made it. Ishmael had discovered a powder horn under the pillow on the ranger's bed, with images etched into it in the style of frontiersmen. The images were of birds and deer, except for the outline of a lake that might have been Champlain, though without marks for the forts at Crown Point or Ticonderoga. There was a single notation, across the narrows where Crown Point should be. *"Chev"* was all it said.

"Go back to the inn," he had instructed the two Nipmucs. "Rouse everyone and get the wagons on the road. No breakfast. By dawn, this town will be in an uproar. Sarah and the others need to be gone."

"But you, Duncan—" Conawago had begun.

"I can't be with them, not with Horatio Beck so close. Go. I will find you on the road."

Conawago seemed about to argue when a woman pulling an early-morning milk cart began to scream. She had spied the body by the mill. "Murder! Murder most foul!" As the woman dropped her cart and frantically ran down the street, shrieking all the way, Ishmael whispered into his uncle's ear, then slipped into the shadows.

By the time Duncan had reached the stable behind the inn, the town had begun to stir. He was saddling the big black, the strongest-looking of the dragoon horses, when Ishmael appeared. The youth was stripping off his waistcoat and shirt. "Just cut the cinches of the other saddles," Duncan said, "and turn the mounts loose into the street." By the time he realized that Ishmael was ignoring his instructions, the young Nipmuc had saddled another horse and was putting bridles on the other two.

"The road follows the ridges to the west for the next fifty miles," Ismael explained as he surveyed the street. Men were stepping out of their houses in nightshirts, standing warily on their front steps, some with weapons in their hands. "There must be game trails above, on the ridges. Gallop along the road until the sun has fully risen, then take to the trails."

"This is not your fight," Duncan protested.

Ishmael tied his rolled shirt and waistcoat behind the saddle and began investigating crocks and tubs on a shelf along the aisle of the stable. With a grunt of satisfaction he reached into a tub and produced a finger covered with a white paste. He quickly applied two parallel stripes to each cheek. "This is Quinsigamond. Which makes it my fight. A Nipmuc warrior rides for the last time from here," he declared. Louder voices were raised in alarm out on the street. "I will catch up. Don't slow down for me."

Before Duncan could stop him, he had wrapped the reins of the two extra horses around his hand, mounted, and kicked his mount into an explosive leap out of the stable. As he reached the street, he gave a convincing impression of a bloodcurdling war cry and galloped onto the northern road toward the New Hampshire wilderness, the two remounts running at his side.

A pistol had been fired in his direction. "Indians!" came a fearful cry. "God protect us! The savages are raiding!"

Now Duncan ate a few bites of the dried sausage he had discovered in the dragoon saddlebag, contemplating the possible routes the killers might take to Canada, then remounted and continued at a more relaxed pace, letting his horse recover from the headlong ride from Worcester. When he halted in a patch of grass an hour later, he took the hobbles from the saddlebag and fastened them to the horse's front legs, leaving it to graze as he followed the sound of running water to a narrow eight-foot waterfall. He stripped and bathed under the falling water. A stench of death and deception seemed to have clung to him since first encountering the grisly line of bodies on the beach back in Boston, and he scoured his skin with sand and rushes, then rubbed his arms with leaves of the wintergreen that grew at the base of a nearby hemlock. He badly needed purification but had no time for a more elaborate ceremony.

At the edge of the clearing, he paused, admiring the tall, muscular thoroughbred, then bent and picked a handful of wild strawberries. "I mean no offense," he said to the horse as he approached and extended the berries. "You're a fine, handsome creature and I but took the loan of you from the king." The black horse cocked its head, caught the sweet scent of the berries, and stepped forward to eat from Duncan's hand.

"*Cabhlach aon*," Duncan said, *fleet one*, rubbing his hand over the thick muscles of its neck. "Goliath. I'll call you Goliath. He was a great, strong beast too. It fits you," he declared, then leaned to the ear of the gelding and whispered the Gaelic words of comfort used by his grandfather in gentling animals. The big horse listened for several breaths, then cocked its head as if in surprise and pressed its nose against Duncan's chest.

"Goliath it is, then," Duncan declared, and he remounted and eased back onto the trail. Although cutthroat bountymen and soldiers were in pursuit of him, he was loath to outpace the slow-moving wagons. Late in the morning, he hobbled Goliath again in a broad patch of sunlight and stretched out on a bed of moss. It was midafternoon when the horse nuzzled him awake, and they got under way at a slow trot. He had been dreaming, but every dream ended with him looking down to see the number 4 etched in the ground at his feet, sometimes outlined in mud, other times chiseled in stone or drawn in blood. Knowing that he was dying, Chisholm had left only one simple answer. Duncan kept revisiting their conversation, eventually convinced that there had been only two questions the ranger left unanswered when asked about the secrets of the north. Where in the north, Duncan had asked, and did he know Ebenezer Brandt. Had Chisholm answered both with his enigmatic 4?

When the sun was low over the Berkshires, he halted at a ledge from which the road could be seen for more than a mile in each direction, overlooking a flat with a stream that appeared to have often been used as a layover by travelers. He watched Goliath's ears frequently as he scanned the eastern thoroughfare, knowing the horse would hear the little wagon convoy long before he could see it.

Duncan was lost in thought once more, reviewing again the events in Boston and trying to understand how a numeral 4 could be the answer to anything, when Goliath's ears twitched and his head snapped toward the east. It wasn't the expected jingle of harness that Duncan heard a minute later, it was the laughter of a boy. Duncan grinned and pulled Goliath's reins, angling down the side of the mountain toward the clearing.

As the first wagon approached, Duncan watched from a clump of spruce and gave the call of a tanager, Conawago's favorite bird. The old Nipmuc showed no reaction other than a momentary lifting of his head, but he called for the wagons to pull into the flat. Duncan dismounted and waited as the teams were unhitched and led to the stream at the edge of the campsite. He was watching Conawago move inconspicuously toward the spruces that hid him, when an acorn hit his chest. Sarah, the dust on her face showing the dried tracks of tears, emerged from behind an oak. As he stepped toward her, Conawago also appeared, taking the reins from his hand, and Sarah rushed forward into his embrace.

No one spoke. There were no words, except Sarah's futile halfhearted complaints that Duncan had not fled and Duncan's own futile assurances for her not to worry. When Sarah finally moved away, she nodded toward the camp. "I have to go help," she announced, and pushed back through the trees.

"Ishmael?" Duncan asked, turning to Conawago.

The old tribesman shook his head. "Nearly every able-bodied man in Worcester seemed to be in pursuit of him. And every soldier is looking for you."

"Horatio Beck?"

"Those dragoons looked most comical mounted on conscripted farm horses. Caught up with us at midday. Brought half a dozen armed townsmen, local militia apparently, as if expecting a fight. They searched the wagons. Beck recognized Munro from that day in the harbor and shouted that he should arrest him for aiding in your interference with the navy. Munro clenched his hands together and said, 'At yer service, Lieutenant Becky.' Beck slapped him, but nothing else. Then he rode back east, furious because his escort from the town said they had to go dig a grave for the wheelwright."

Duncan suddenly remembered the deserter. "Sergeant Mallory?"

"The fools raised a cloud of dust you could see for half a mile. The sergeant was well hidden in the forest by the time they reached us."

"Did Beck wave the warrant in your face?"

"Funny thing. No mention of a warrant. Just looking for the killers of that leading citizen, Mr. Chisholm the wheelwright. The townsmen were furious, saying that Beck had wasted their time, that everyone knew the killers and horse thieves had been savages who fled north. The rest of the townsmen had pressed on north."

"After Ishmael!" The frantic whisper came unbidden from Duncan's lips. "I must go!"

Conawago reached out to grab Duncan's reins. "No. My nephew is a woodsrunner, as stealthy as a catamount. They will not find him. He will evade them, leaving them convinced it was a raiding party from the north, a vestige from older days. Their fears will fester and they will soon give thanks there was but one casualty. He will find us when the time comes."

"He took the king's horses. A hanging offense in itself."

Conawago gave an ironic grin and gestured at Duncan's horse. "A hanging offense."

"When Goliath chooses to return to the king, he is free to do so."

The old Nipmuc rolled his eyes. "You gave him a name," he declared in exasperation.

Duncan stroked the horse's neck. "Aye, well. We enjoyed our ride today." The horse softly nickered, as if agreeing.

Conawago sighed. "Please, Duncan, do not make so light of your situation, of even your life. You are sought for treason. Beck will probably decide by tomorrow to spread the word more broadly, with a bounty that will tempt half the men in the colony. When you value your life less than your friends do, you dishonor them."

The words bit deep. Duncan had been outrunning the stress and fatigue of the past day for hours, but suddenly they bore down like a great weight on his back. "It all has the feel of theater," he declared in a hollow voice. "As if I were an actor given a poorly written role."

"The obfuscation from Hancock and Adams feels like insincerity—deception even," Conawago said. "I know that is what troubles you most. But you aren't here evading bountymen and soldiers because of them."

"Aren't we?" Duncan gazed through the branches at Sarah, who had settled Sergeant Mallory onto a log and was changing his bandage. He could hear the soldier's loud Yorkshire voice, and Sarah's laugh in response to it.

"You may fool yourself, Duncan, but never me. I saw the way you looked at those bodies on the beach. Thirty-seven men lost. Brothers, husbands, fathers, uncles. You looked into every dead man's face just as I did. You and I both pulled seaweed from their mouths and knocked crabs from their eyes. I wished I hadn't. Now I see them in my nightmares. I tried to nap in the back of the wagon today, but even then I woke up gasping. One by one the dead were sitting up and pointing at you and me, as if blaming us. We are here because of them. Those thirty-seven. Thirty-eight now. You and I are going to avenge them."

Duncan hesitated, contemplating his friend. The old man had been so despondent the day before, surrendering the essential cause of his life, but today he was speaking more like a seasoned warrior.

"The warrant just adds emphasis to finding the truth," Conawago added.

"I keep thinking of Hancock and Livingston. It was all too convenient for them."

"They didn't know Beck had gone to the governor. If anyone bargained with the governor, it was Sam Adams, without their knowledge."

"But they probably could have stopped the warrant."

"Maybe they understood better than you."

"Understood what?"

"Just as Hancock said, these crimes are not of their world. It will not be logic or warrants or starch-collared dandies who solve them. I haven't entirely lost the instincts of the hunter," the old Nipmuc said. "And those instincts tell me there are secrets in front of us we have yet to decipher. Secrets that will let us avenge that company of the dead. Secrets that we must find to protect the Sons, that will let us return to the harmony of Edentown."

Duncan followed his gaze toward the encampment, where the company was quickly getting settled for the night. "Which world must we seek them in? That of Reverend Occom's vengeful God, who sent the *Arcturus* to the bottom? I forgot to bring my Bible. There was a verse about ships."

Conawago was watching Solomon Hayes now. "'Look to the ships,' it says in James 3," he recited, "'though they are so great and driven by strong winds, they are directed by a very small rudder.'" He turned to Duncan. "An invisible rudder, even."

"You're speaking of correlations again, like a Parisian astronomer."

Conawago frowned, then nodded back toward the camp. "Look at them. An itinerant tinker. An army deserter. A middle-aged Highlander who left his steady job to revisit his nightmare of death. An evangelist tribesman who sees no irony in becoming another of the instruments that caused his own tribe's destruction. Why are any of them with us? They were all in Hancock's warehouse. They are with us because of Hancock. Is he steering an invisible rudder? Those Boston gentlemen live in a world very different from ours."

Duncan shot him a worried glance, knowing from hard experience that he should trust Conawago's intuitions. He gazed back at Sarah, who was helping Sergeant Mallory out of his shirt so she could check the dressing Duncan had wrapped around his ribs. She paused over the long, narrow scars on the soldier's exposed back and looked back toward the trees. She knew Duncan was watching. Duncan's own back had once been shredded by the whip of a plantation overseer employed by her father. He was beginning to understand why Mallory had deserted.

"In what world should I be seeking?" he asked Conawago again.

"Perhaps," the Nipmuc said after a few breaths, "it's a new one, one we haven't encountered before." Then he dropped the subject, pointing toward a thick grove of spruce and hemlock up the slope that appeared to be the source of the creek the horses now drank from. They both knew Duncan could not risk staying with the others that night. Without another word Conawago started walking in a long arc up the slope that would take them, unseen, to the grove. As they reached the shadows of the evergreens, Duncan released Goliath, who eagerly stepped to a ten-foot-wide pool in the stream, and Conawago cut pine boughs for a makeshift bed. Then, with an apologetic shrug, he handed Duncan a pouch containing half a dozen ship biscuits, a handful of dried meat, and a small ball of cheese. As Duncan chewed on the meat and Goliath finished drinking, the old Nipmuc eyed the pool and produced a horsehair fishing line, which he dropped on a flat rock beside the water.

"There are three pieces of the puzzle that I cannot get any grip on," Conawago declared. "There was that attack at Mrs. Pope's house. Sarah wants to pretend it was just coincidence, but we know otherwise. Why was that Abenaki there?"

"The second?" Duncan asked.

In answer, Conawago extracted a piece of cloth from his belt pouch and stretched it out on a boulder. It was the long strip they had taken from Oliver's mouth, next to which he laid the very similar strip they had removed from the wheelwright's mouth. The second one wasn't merely the same size, with the same adornment of leaves and fish. The speckled trout ripped in half at the edge of the first matched the half trout at the leading edge of the second.

"A hem," Duncan suggested. "From the same dress."

"From the same woman," Conawago rejoined. "The killer left his calling card. He wanted the world to know they had died at the hand of an Abenaki. If this was 1760," he continued, "you know what we would think. The Abenaki were used for secret missions by the French, as the Mohawks and Oneidas were used by the British."

"The war's over. The treaty was signed in Paris five years ago."

"And for how many centuries have France and Britain been at each other's throats? Five years is but the click of a gear in that great clock."

"Two scalps don't make a new war."

"Nor even thirty-seven men lost on a single ship."

"Three. You said three things."

"The gold piece. Why does a retired ranger from the St. Francis raid suddenly get a French gold piece sent to him? I think if Chisholm had lived he would have showed us another this morning."

"And explained this," Duncan said. He dipped his finger in the pool and wrote a number 4 on the flat piece of granite at its edge. They stared at it in silence until Goliath finished his drinking and turned to a patch of grass.

Conawago uncoiled his horsehair line, tied a bit of bacon rind to its hook, and lowered it into the water before he spoke again, in a low voice so as not to frighten his quarry. "The last war was different from any fought before. It spanned continents. India, the Caribbean, Europe, Africa, North America. The British pushed in India, the French responded in Quebec and Flanders. Many leaders in Paris were furious that their king gave up all of North America but two tiny islands off the Newfoundland. They say he didn't understand this new game, the importance of keeping leverage on every continent. When the French act, they will be subtle. An Abenaki taking vengeance on old rangers seems most convenient just when these other events are taking place. Secrets within secrets. Like some great machine has been set into motion and all we can make out is one or two of its gears."

As his words hung in the air, Conawago's line drew taut and the old man turned to the shimmering pool, watching his prey, then deftly snapping the line as the fish turned, setting the hook. In a moment the big trout was on the grass, and nearly as quickly the hook and bait were back in the water.

"I keep asking myself, what if something else happened that horrible night at St. Francis?" Conawago whispered. "What if the rangers there saw something that the French desperately don't want them to remember now?"

"That doesn't explain why Mog was in Mrs. Pope's house."

Conawago flipped the line, and another fish soon lay on the grass. "I think we might agree that their interest was not in Mrs. Pope or her overfed daughter. It was about something that happened those last days in Boston, something we haven't considered yet. I wish I could feel we've left Boston behind," he added. "I can't shake the suspicion that we have brought the answer to that particular question with us." Conawago jerked his line, and a third big trout was on the grass.

Duncan looked down the slope at the campsite and watched its occupants go about their preparations for the night. Sarah bent by the kettle that simmered over the fire as Munro fed wood into the circle of stones. The infantry deserter, on his feet though limping badly, was playing a game of fetch the stick with Molly. Hayes was in the shadow of a wagon, where he seemed to be secretly watching Reverend Occom. The tribal evangelist was kneeling in his own wagon, where he had made a makeshift altar out of some of his Bible crates. He might have been praying or he might have been loading the little pistol Duncan had glimpsed under his waistcoat. Why, Duncan asked himself, had they burdened themselves with these strangers? Their connections were with Hancock, not with the travelers to Edentown. Hancock might have felt obligated to the deserter and might have had respect for the expertise of Hayes on the frontier, even some sort of spiritual bond with Occom, but they were not Duncan's obligations, his respect, his bond.

When he turned back, Conawago had strung his fish, now numbering four, on a piece of vine. The old Nipmuc did not miss the flicker of disappointment on Duncan's face. "I shall roll these in cornmeal and fry them with a little bacon, served with fresh watercress from the stream," he taunted. "If you are opportune, the wind may at least bring the delectable scent to you."

"You will take all four?"

There was only a hint of apology in the old man's exaggerated smile. "Surely you understand that you can't risk a fire here," he declared, still grinning, and handed Duncan another piece of dried, leathery beef.

DUNCAN SLEPT, AS HE OFTEN did in the forest, in intervals of two or three hours, gauging the time by the rotation of the Great Dipper overhead. It was perhaps an hour before midnight when he woke the first time. Goliath greeted him with a soft nicker as he approached and stroked the thoroughbred's neck, looking down at the sleeping camp, marked by a solitary thread of smoke.

His mind drifted back to the gentle wheelwright in Worcester. Chisholm had been soft-spoken, but Duncan knew that no one survived years as a ranger without a body and spirit of iron. The searing image of the savaged man they had pulled from the windmill had haunted him all day. Now, unbidden, came Chisholm's unexpected words from the evening before. *Our fathers had kings, their fathers before them, and beyond, to before the tales of men began. How could it be otherwise? It shakes my bones to think on it.*

They had been too pressed to weigh the words or ask his meaning. Duncan had ignored them, but after revisiting their time with Chisholm, he wondered now if they weren't the key, the closest thing to an explanation of some kind.

Chisholm had been a philosopher in his own way, fretting over the condition of mankind. It had been his reply when he grasped that Duncan had come on secret business for Hancock and Livingston. He had not been ready to turn over the secret parcel buried in the graveyard, but had he foreshadowed the secrets with his unexpected words? Chisholm had been suggesting that the secrets he was entrusted with, perhaps the very secrets that had made Duncan a fugitive, were linked somehow to the possibility of life without kings. And the package, Duncan suspected, would have contained a French gold piece and the mysterious word that echoed in his mind: *Saguenay.*

He went back and lay down on his bed of fragrant boughs, thinking of the unseen parcel of secrets from the north. If Hancock and Livingston had been involved, he would assume that the secrets referred to dealings with the merchant houses of Quebec and Montreal, no doubt rivals of theirs. But the packages had not been sent to the two merchants; they had acquired one only because the former ranger who received it had died.

Had the French identified the Sons of Liberty as the soft underbelly of the American merchants? Why would the secret ledger from the *Arcturus*—and now the secret packages for the rangers—be so important to King Louis if he was done with North America? When slumber finally found him again, it brought wrenching visions of dead men on fields of battle, not fantastical nightmares, but memories, long suppressed, of friends lost in the French war. Then came images, so seared into his mind that they might as well have been memories, of the heaped bodies of Highlanders killed by the French in the last war and by the English in the bloody Jacobite rebellion.

There had been other words spoken in Worcester that haunted him almost as painfully. Sarah had begged him to drop his pursuit of the killers. *I am frightened for us*, she had said. That afternoon, as he rested in the forest, he'd realized what she meant. She hadn't meant she was frightened for the two of them, she meant she was frightened of what was happening between the two of them, worried about their relationship, as if it were in grave danger. The agony of the death surrounding him paled with the thought of losing Sarah.

He awoke to a low, rattling noise. It was coming from Goliath, who was inching toward Duncan as if needing protection. Something was approaching in the night. Cursing himself for declining Conawago's offer to bring up his rifle, he unsheathed his knife and rolled into a crouch, ready to spring. It was not a man, he saw, as the creature crossed a patch of moonlight, but something low and bulky, setting itself directly for him. A bear. It had to be a bear. He rose, his heart thundering, knowing he would have to fling himself onto its back if he had any chance of surviving an attack.

Duncan raised his knife, ready to launch himself; then Goliath seemed to relax, and he heard a low, throaty greeting and saw a wagging tail. "Molly!" he exclaimed, and knelt to embrace the shaggy Newfoundland. She was dragging a piece of rope, ragged and still wet from where she had chewed through it. The big dog licked Duncan; then, with a series of sniffs, got better acquainted with Goliath, who, lowering his head to meet her nose, triggered another round of tail wagging. Duncan produced a strip of dried meat, which Molly eagerly downed. Then she circled his makeshift bed and settled down, taking up more than half of it. With a smile he lowered himself onto his side beside her and draped an arm over her, grateful for the warmth of her body.

He was awakened for the last time that night by a strange vibration in the ground. Sitting up groggily, he discovered Goliath beside him, slowly stomping a hoof near his head. Molly was up, sitting at the opening in the trees, staring out into the dim grayness that was the first hint of day. Suddenly he realized that horse and dog were watching not the camp, but a copse of alders near the stream. He calmed Goliath, checking his hobbles, then slipped down the slope, Molly close behind.

When he reached the alders, there was no one there. He knew it could have simply been someone in the camp answering a call of nature, or one of the night creatures that, having satisfied its curiosity, had slipped back up the mountain slope. Then he realized. Molly had disappeared.

The picketed horse teams began to stir, pulling restlessly at their lines. He stepped to the edge of the camp and gave the low call of a nighthawk. A solitary figure sat up from his blanket by the smoldering fire. Duncan held up a restraining hand, and Conawago stayed in place, listening. Molly barked at the opposite side of the camp, closer to the road. Duncan started toward the dog, careful to stay in shadows. Then Sarah screamed.

It was not exactly a scream, he realized an instant later, but one of her spine-rattling war cries. Sarah leapt out of the back of a wagon, a blanket flying from her shoulders. She hardly broke her running gait as she swooped down to pick up the short ax that was embedded in a stump. Conawago shot up, kicked at two sleeping figures, then raced with Duncan toward Sarah.

By the time they reached her, she was nearly at the road. "It was him!" she shouted. "I swear it was him, from the Pope house! He hasn't given up his—" Her words died as a figure appeared in the dim light of the open road, carrying a heavy sack on his shoulder. "Thief!" she cried, then erupted in a tirade of furious Mohawk as she sprinted toward the man. When she was ten feet away, she threw the ax with the skill of a forest warrior. The thief staggered as the razor-sharp blade embedded in his left thigh. The sack fell from his shoulder, and, extracting the ax, he half ran, half limped toward the thicket at the far side of the road.

"Mog!" Conawago shouted in challenge.

The Abenaki paused and looked back, but only long enough for them to make out the long, diagonal scar and the stripes of paint on his face before he disappeared into the shadows.

Duncan sensed Sarah's urge to follow, clamping a restraining hand around her arm. "We have the object of his theft," he said, "and he will suffer the effects of that wound for many weeks." He dropped to his knees and put a hand on the sack. It came away wet and sticky. "Blood!" he cried, and quickly untied the knot at the top. A tuft of hair appeared, soaked with more blood. The boy inside had been beaten so badly he showed no sign of life. The Abenaki had stolen Will Sterret.

$$8$$

WITH A DESPERATE SOB, SARAH ripped open the sack. Conawago helped her stretch out Will's limp limbs. Duncan searched for a pulse. "He lives," he announced, though the boy's heartbeat was as light as a feather.

"He's been beaten most cruel," Munro observed over Duncan's shoulder.

Will's bruised and bleeding face had received several violent blows. A gash on his left temple oozed blood where something had been slammed into his head. Duncan gingerly probed the wound, fearing a fracture. The boy's hand did not respond as Duncan pressed it, hoping for a returning grip.

Sarah saw the worry in his eyes. The thief may not have been successful in stealing the boy, but he may have stolen Will's life. She stood, calling for a blanket as the rest of the camp stirred, and a black shape wedged into the opening she made. Molly began gently licking the boy's face. Sarah bent to pull the dog away, but Conawago stayed her arm.

"She may be the best medicine we have," the Nipmuc said.

Will's fingers began moving, slowly curling inward, then reaching upward until they found the big dog's neck. Molly gave an acknowledgment that was half snort and half joyful yap, and she began licking more energetically.

The wagons were on the road an hour later, leaving Duncan and Sarah by the campfire, still tending to the unconscious boy. Sarah had insisted that the slow-moving wagons continue the westward journey, and Conawago had insisted that Duncan stay with her as he ventured into the forest, hoping to find sign of the boy's assailant.

"The ax sank deep in his thigh," the old tribesman said. "He left much blood on the trail, which means he won't be traveling fast this day and for many to come." He gestured up the slope. "But the number of bountymen will only increase as the broadsides are distributed more widely, Duncan. Bring down your horse in case you need a quick departure."

Sarah heaped the fire higher and reached for their copper teapot. "There's food," she said with a nod to a flour sack stuffed with biscuits and bacon.

Duncan warily eyed the eastern road and shook his head, knowing that neither of them had any appetite. When he returned with Goliath, Sarah had the boy cradled in her lap. "It's someone else's fight. Will is just a bystander. But he had to endure the horror on that beach in Boston—and now this." She clutched the boy close to her breast and rocked back and forth. "I told him he could join our school in Edentown. He laughed when I explained that sometimes the schoolchildren go out and sit on the broad backs of the oxen while they plow the fields. He's a good boy, a joyful boy. He'll like the maize pudding that the new cook makes," she said in a brittle voice.

It wasn't like Sarah to prattle on. She had been deeply shaken by the events of recent days but had maintained her usual reserve. Now, alone with Duncan, her guard was dropping. "You can run in the orchard with Molly, Will," she whispered. A single tear rolled down her cheek. "You will laugh to see the lambs play with the fawns in our back fields. We make gingerbread at Yuletime," she added, then changed from English to the tongue of her tribe. "*Jiyathontek.*" It was an invocation to the forest gods. She held Will out, for the spirits to take notice, and beseeched them. "Bring this brave warrior back to us," she begged, then paused and looked up at Duncan.

"He wasn't just stuffed in this bag and carried away," he said. "That Abenaki took him into the trees and beat him. I think Will knows something they desperately want to learn. I think he wouldn't tell them and just took the beating; then Mog put him in the bag for the French to interrogate."

"But Molly would have—"

"Molly came up with me last night," Duncan said, feeling shamed now at allowing the dog to stay with him. "But I don't think this was the first attempt, Sarah."

She scrubbed at her cheek. "Not the first?"

"We couldn't understand why this Abenaki, this Chief Mog, came into

Mrs. Pope's house. He didn't know you or me. But Will was sleeping in the room down the hall."

"Surely he could not have known that."

"The French were watching. They were already in Boston, probably looking for the Hancock warehouse. It's where we took Will when we came back from the shipwreck. They had but to follow us when we brought the boy back to Mrs. Pope's."

"But why?"

"He's the sole witness to their horrible deed."

"Then why not try to kill him here? Why do they need to speak with him?"

Duncan could only shake his head. He lifted his rifle and made a wide scouting circuit in the forest beyond the camp. When he returned, Sarah still held the boy close to her heart, but her eyes were closed as if in sleep. He opened the pouch he had retrieved from one of the wagons before their departure and extracted a small vial of amber liquid and a small muslin bag; then he poured a mug of hot water into which he dropped the bag and a few drops from the vial. When he finished, he discovered that Sarah was watching him, and she lifted Will's head. Duncan held the aromatic mixture under the boy's nose and gently lifted it to his lips. Will stirred and accepted the brew in slow sips.

Molly, who had stayed at the boy's side since the wagons departed, raised her head toward the forest and gave a tentative wag of her tail. Will looked pale and sapped of all strength, but his eyes had opened.

He stretched an arm out, as if trying to reach something in the direction Molly was staring. "Come back!" the boy said in a strangled cry, grabbing frantically at the thin air. "I did not mean it!"

Sarah stroked his head and murmured words of comfort.

"I can't see the face!" the boy cried, and looked frantically toward the shadows of the forest.

"Don't fret so," Sarah said. "We saw his face. We will not long forget it."

"So bright," Will said, still looking at the shadows. "The color of fresh snow! And when she approached and spread her arms, I saw the feathers! Wings!" Will twisted as if to trying to rise. "I have to go to her! Don't you see? It's my mother! She died when I was but four, but I am sure of it! Her face! I want to remember her face!" He grabbed Duncan's hand. "Why couldn't I see her face?" the boy asked in a forlorn voice.

Duncan found himself following the gaze of the boy and the dog back toward the trees, for a moment looking for the angel himself. He turned the boy's head and looked him in the eyes. "Because it wasn't time, Will. Because you're needed in this life for many more years. She just wanted you to know that, and that she will be waiting, biding her time for the blessed day in the next century when you're old and weak and surrounded by adoring grandchildren."

The boy chewed on Duncan's words, slowly calming. "The next century? Really?"

"I am certain of it. And an amazing time it will be."

"But will she know me then?"

"Mothers always know," Duncan assured him.

Will gazed back into the shadows, then accepted the still-steaming mug Sarah offered him and silently sipped. "Maybe it wasn't because it was not my time. Maybe it was to say there was still hope despite my sin. Maybe it was because of the way I killed all those others."

Sarah and Duncan exchanged an alarmed glance. "You're too young to be troubled by sin," Sarah said, encouraging the boy to drink more of Duncan's brew.

"What if Jonathan told her?"

With a chill, Duncan realized that he was talking about the dead Jonathan Pine speaking to his dead mother.

"Would he be there yet? Reverend Occom consigned his soul to the angels. I heard him say it in that Boston cemetery. You have to tell the important truths when you meet them. No secrets in heaven. Jonathan would have ciphered it out." The boy looked back toward the shadows. "She knew, that's why she turned her back on me. Fifty or sixty more years won't matter. She'll never want me again." Will began weeping.

Duncan braced the boy's head between his hands. "He would have ciphered what out? What secret sin?"

Tears streamed down Will's cheeks. "When those two were in Halifax, I thought they were so entertaining. They told me riddles when I met them on the wharf there. What cheese is made backwards, Philip asked me. Why, Edam, says he, and when I puzzled it out, that the letters are just reversed, I laughed so hard. The captain, he didn't like us speaking to strangers about the *Arcturus* and her ports, but I didn't mind telling them. They bought me candy in Halifax, and a whole orange from the Caribbean, just for me, my first ever. Henry wanted to know the captain's name, and whether we had sailed from London, and did I know the name of our shipping agent there. I asked them why they were writing all those things down and they told me more jokes and bought me a cup of chocolate. Once, Philip started telling me about a great circus he saw in Paris, with lions and elephants, but then Henry cut him off, though I didn't think anything of it then. Later, they asked if we was carrying military supplies, and they watched as the army loaded a few barrels of gunpowder, supplies for the fort in Boston. Then they asked if we had any of those remarkable natives of America who sometimes went to sea, and I told them of my good friend Jonathan. Next day they were there with a letter, addressed to the captain. I didn't think anything of it until we sailed with them on board, but I realized it was curious that they didn't know the captain's name one day and had a letter for him the next. Then they had more candy, sweet molasses candy, and after the first day they observed that Jonathan Pine worked long hours, standing double watches, and they asked why he didn't strip off his shirt like most of the other men." Tears began flowing down the boy's cheeks again. "Don't you see! He died, they all died, because I wanted molasses chews."

"I don't understand," Sarah confessed.

"I said it was a secret, but they were my friends and each of them told me a secret, like how Philip had shot off his own toe once, and I wasn't sure about it so he showed me. So then I told them about Jonathan, explaining that he didn't take off his shirt because he had important papers strapped to his chest, that very important people waited for his secrets in America. I was prideful because I knew such a secret and wanted to let them know I could be trusted. And then they killed everyone, took away everything my friends ever had with a spark on a fuse." Will wiped at his tears. "Don't you see? I am a sinner who sold my friends' lives for a handful of candy." He buried his head in his hands as a long sob racked his body.

Sarah pressed the boy to her shoulder. "Will," she said, "those men were going to have those secrets no matter what. They left you in that boat to die with the others. But you showed them you had a different fate. Better for the world that Will Sterret lives. Your mother came to tell you that, and that she and your uncle and all the Sterrets who ever lived count on you now."

The boy lifted his head. "Count on me for what?"

It was Duncan who replied. "Count on you to help us find justice for all those new angels, so they can find peace. Tell me, Will, did those men want to know something about Mr. Oliver? What was the Indian asking for today?"

"My uncle said no one was to know."

"Your uncle is one of those angels, Will. You have a piece of the key that will unlock the puzzle of his death so he can find rest on the other side."

The boy reached toward his britches, but the effort caused his face to screw up in pain. "It's there, in the pouch inside my waist. My uncle said to keep it for us. Mr. Oliver gave it to us for our new life in the Maine country, saying that it would mean a lot of ewes for our flock. Mr. Oliver said the major would understand, and maybe we'd go thank him in his new mountain home one day."

"The major?" Duncan asked.

"That's all I know. It came in a parcel to Mr. Oliver last time he was in port. I had a whale tooth. I thought I would take that to the major to show our thanks. I told Philippe and Henry one night, 'cause we shared our secrets. I boasted that I had a golden king and showed them."

"Golden king?" Sarah asked.

Will nodded. "It was funny. They got very excited and went off and spoke to each other, and when they came back, they asked where it came from, and I just said the north. They asked if my uncle was a ranger too, like they knew Mr. Oliver was a ranger already. Then today, that Indian, he kept asking who sent it, and did I get it from a ranger, and where in the north did it come from, but I would not tell the bully." He swallowed and fixed Duncan with a sober gaze. "I will tell you, though, because we are going to find justice. Mr. Oliver told us. It came from the place of the heroes of Quebec, from St. Francis."

Trying hard not to provoke the boy's pain, Duncan pried the pouch out and handed it to Will, who upended it onto Duncan's palm. "Ain't it grand?" the boy asked. "And the seawater didn't stain it at all."

Duncan stared in mute amazement. It was a gold coin bearing the image of the King Louis of France.

THEY BROKE CAMP IN MIDMORNING, Sarah on one of the two horses left by the convoy, holding Will and leading the second by a lead rope. She insisted that Duncan stay out of sight, and he followed slowly, often walking beside Goliath, who registered his sentiment about the turtle's pace with impatient shakes of his head, as if to suggest that Duncan had confused him with a plow horse.

Duncan finally relented and cantered ahead half a mile. As he reined Goliath in, the horse spun about, his ears bent sharply toward the eastern road. Two riders emerged, riding fast out of a cloud of dust. With an explosion of instinct, Goliath stamped the earth with a front hoof and burst into a gallop despite Duncan's strenuous effort to hold him back. He had recognized two military horses and was charging to battle.

Sarah threw up a frantic hand as Duncan approached. He slid off his saddle, rifle in hand, and disappeared into a clump of brush before the dust around Goliath cleared.

The two horses were indeed from dragoon stables, but to his relief, Duncan saw Ishmael mounted on the first, though he could not understand why Sarah, clutching Will tight to her, hesitated when she saw the young Nipmuc. Then Ishmael inched forward, and Duncan saw the musket aimed at his back. It was held by Sam, the dead wheelwright's nephew.

"Is it only you then, Duncan?" Ishmael called as Duncan edged out of his cover, his gun aimed at Ishmael's captor. The click of a second hammerlock came from across the road. "Not just, nephew," came Conawago's voice from the shadows. "And you'll not be able to take down both of us," he warned Sam.

To their surprise, Ishmael laughed, then leapt off his horse and ran toward the sound of his uncle's voice. Before dismounting, Sam grinned, opened the pan of his musket, and turned it over, showing that it was not primed. He quickly explained how the young Nipmuc, having led his pursuers on a hot chase up the northern road, had circled back around them the next night to return to Worcester, hoping to secretly return two of the stolen horses after having given the third to an ecstatic northbound farmer on the condition he ride it hard into New Hampshire, then keep it out of sight once back on his farm. Ishmael had hoped to find more evidence of the killer at the wheel shop but instead had found Sam.

"He knows, Duncan," Ishmael explained. "Sam didn't just make wheels with his uncle."

"If he's with the Sons, then why treat you so?" Sarah asked Ishmael, still uncertain of the newcomer.

"In case someone encountered us and recognized me. Sam would say he had captured me."

"Captured you, then headed in the opposite direction of the magistrates?" Duncan asked.

"It was the best we could think of. We had to come. Sam has news and something to give you."

The apprentice explained that he had gone back into town the night of the murder after his mother and siblings had retired for the night. As usual when going to see his uncle on Sons' business, he had kept to the shadows. "But I wasn't the only one. As I was passing the first inn, two men came out, both wearing cloaks, one with a thin beard that he kept trimmed close."

"A soldier from Boston?" Duncan asked.

Sam shook his head. "If I understand what happened, this was before the soldiers arrived."

"Tell him," Ishmael urged the youth.

"Tell me what?" Duncan asked when Sam remained silent.

"They were speaking fast and urgent-like, sixteen to the dozen, and in French. I know just enough to recognize the tongue. My uncle Josiah knew it, from the north, and sometimes sang French songs. And for a moment I smelled lavender, if that means anything."

Duncan gazed into the shadows as he considered the news. Mog's French masters had been in Worcester with him the night Chisholm died. "What did they do?" he asked.

"I don't know," Sam said, pain now in his voice. "My uncle had a rule, one he said I must never break, just like the ranger rules he would talk about. If anything ever seemed amiss in town, I was to run back to protect my ma and the family. I didn't linger."

"Did you understand anything they said?"

"No, only their names. Henry, he was the one with the beard."

"And the other was Philip! It's them!" Will cried out, then held his head from the pain of the effort. "Hughes and Montgomery, or so they called themselves! The devils who sank the ship!"

Sam gazed at the boy and nodded. "Philippe. That's what the bearded man called the other. Philippe pointed down across the river to where your wagons were, and Henry said no and pointed to the mill . . . or maybe"—Sam paused, collecting himself—"maybe I guess the wheel shop."

Duncan saw the agony in Sam's eyes and put a hand on his shoulder. "You did nothing wrong." He shared the boy's pain. The French had been right there. If he had known, or if he had warned Chisholm, the wheelwright might still be alive.

"There's more," Ishmael said with a worried look back up the road. "Tell them, Sam."

"Next morning the lieutenant posted a bounty before he left. But not for my uncle's killer, as everyone expected."

Sarah and Duncan exchanged worried glances. "We know of that bounty, Samuel," Sarah said. "Believe none of it."

The apprentice looked away from Sarah, as if in embarrassment. "You don't understand, ma'am," he said in a near whisper. "A new one. Ten pounds sterling. For ten pounds a man wouldn't have to work for a year or more, or could buy a fair piece of land." He looked back at Sarah with wide eyes. "For you, ma'am. It's for Sarah Ramsey, on charges of harboring an infamous traitor. Aiding and abetting the notorious Duncan McCallum, the broadside says."

Duncan heard Sarah's sharp intake of breath. Will put his arms around her and patted her back. "It's a lie, Miss Sarah. We all know it is a lie."

She pushed the boy away and took several steps toward the forest. Duncan followed her, stricken at the thought that he had brought such trouble to her. When she turned to face him, her countenance was calm again. "It's just a way of distracting you, Duncan," she declared as she returned his worried gaze. "You must run faster than ever. Go."

"With you, yes."

"Impossible. Will needs me. We'll catch up with the wagons by nightfall."

"I followed a trail of blood to a camp where Will's abductor went to meet with two other men," Conawago reported as he approached. "He was still bleeding from the ax blow. If he is their guide, they'll not make quick progress. We may catch them yet."

"Go," Sarah said again. "The world is against us, Duncan, don't you see? If they take me back to Boston, I'll have my Mr. Adams, John Adams. But you must recover that damned ledger to be free again."

•

AN HOUR LATER, CONAWAGO AND Duncan were scouring the campsite the old Nipmuc had discovered. Three men riding three horses had indeed used the camp along the high game trail, one wearing moccasins, the other two in expensive shoes with stitched leather soles. The three had departed in a hurry, alarmed no doubt that the mission of their guide had failed.

Duncan extracted a broken pipe bowl from the ashes, then two pieces of its clay stem. It was as if someone had thrown the pipe down in anger. On the bowl was stamped a small fleur-de-lis. Conawago pointed to chestnut-red spots on a frond of ground cedar. It was drying blood. "Sarah slowed Mog down. I think an artery was nicked. He'll need a doctor or risk losing the leg—or worse."

"And if their guide's truly disabled, they'll be wary of staying in the forest," Duncan said as he pointed to more drops of blood on the trunk of a maple.

"Meaning they'll take to the road, or follow close to the road, to the next settlement, to Agawam on the Connecticut River. That's where we can intercept the killers."

THE SUN WAS SETTING AS Duncan and Conawago, leading their weary mounts, gazed down on a tidy little farm joined to the western road by a narrow, winding lane with a cow pasture on one side and maize field on the other. With rising alarm, they had searched in vain for any sign of Sarah and Will. Ishmael and Sam had, as agreed, lingered behind to slow down any pursuers, but Sarah had not, as agreed, gone to meet the wagons.

In the last of the light they warily approached the farm, studying the horses by the small stone-walled barn. The dapple mare Sarah had been riding was tied with five other horses in what appeared to be a military-style picket line. The pursuers had caught up with her.

Duncan and Conawago quickly conferred, then dismounted and advanced on foot, circling through the pasture to the stone wall nearest the barn. Exchanging a sober glance, they checked the priming charges in their rifles. If they could surprise her captors, the two of them had a reasonable chance of rescuing her, though that was only if all the captors were in one place. They paused at the barn, looking for evidence of whether she was held in the barn or the white clapboard house.

Through the solitary window on the east side of the house they could glimpse figures inside, though the only person who was plainly visible was an unfamiliar woman in a linen cap who was bent at the hearth. Conawago pointed to the smoking chimney and made a downward motion with his palm before nodding toward the big oak beside the house. Duncan nodded and pointed to a blanket airing on a clothesline. If he blocked the chimney, they could disable the captors one by one as they fled the smoke.

Duncan had begun inching toward the blanket when a long moan rose from inside the barn. He instantly shifted direction, slipping into the shadows of the forebay, then easing through the open double doors of the entry.

Sarah was sprawled, unconscious, on a pile of hay in the center aisle. A man in a black hat was grabbing the wrist of an equally comatose Will Sterret.

All the anger and frustration that had been boiling inside Duncan erupted in a white-hot fury. He raised his rifle and rushed forward, slamming the rifle butt down hard on the back of the man's head, then standing over Will with his rifle aimed in case the man rose to resist.

Sarah stirred, rubbing her eyes, then gazed in confusion at Duncan and the fallen stranger. "What have you done?" she gasped, and darted to the unconscious man, pulling away the hat that had fallen onto his face. An angry chatter rose from above, and Sadie swung down onto Duncan and pounded his back with her tiny fists before slipping onto her prostrate master. Duncan had attacked Solomon Hayes.

The capuchin and the proprietress of Edentown both offered comforting strokes on the tinker's shoulders, then looked up with accusing stares.

"I—I didn't know," Duncan muttered to Sarah. "I thought you were . . . What is he doing here?"

"What is he doing?" Sarah shot back. "Helping us, unlike you! My God, Duncan, you may have killed him! Look what all those fools and their talk of liberty is doing to you!"

Duncan was rescued from the sharp edge of her temper by Molly, who gave a quick yelp of greeting and bounded over to him. Ishmael appeared in the doorway with a pot of steaming water, his uncle close behind.

The young Nipmuc explained that they had caught up with the wagons by midafternoon, but Will had shown no sign of improvement. Hayes was acquainted with the owner of the farm, who readily agreed to let them spend the night, in the hope that a few quiet hours in a bed might restore the boy. Sarah had ordered the wagons on, hurrying them toward the safety of the Hudson Valley and the New York colony.

Duncan knelt by the still-unconscious Hayes. In his fury, thinking that the man was threatening the boy, he had hit him a desperate blow with the brass butt plate of his rifle. At the back of his head his black hair was matted with blood over a disturbingly large lump.

Duncan's face was flush with guilt as he turned to Sarah. "I didn't . . ." he began before she cut him off.

"He had been so kind to us today, carrying Will on his back to get him here because he said the horse was too rough a ride. We were trying to wash the grime off the boy before getting him to a bed." Her eyes brimmed with tears again. She shook her head despairingly at Duncan, gathered up her skirt, and marched out of the barn.

There was movement in the hay. Will Sterret was staring at Duncan with narrow, disapproving eyes. "How do you feel, lad?" Duncan asked.

"Mr. Hayes needs that bed more than me now."

Duncan met Conawago's worried gaze. "Help me carry him to the house."

"Ishmael and I will take him," his friend insisted. "You must go. You should have been a hundred miles away by now. Every minute you linger brings the noose closer."

Duncan looked back at the comatose tinker, whose face was ghastly pale. "If I let him die, the noose will be the least of my problems."

He exchanged no words with Sarah, who pointedly ignored him as they carried Hayes inside and laid him on a cot that had been brought to the back of the kitchen. They installed Will on a folded quilt on a long deacon's bench, with Molly lying beside him.

"Poor Mr. Hayes," the farmer's wife declared as she brought a pillow for the boy. "He collects tragedy like a fresh pie collects flies. How awful if he were to perish like this after all his travails."

Duncan looked up. "Travails?"

The farmer put a hand on his wife's arm. "Don't know that he would want us to speak of them, Judith."

The woman pushed away her husband's hand. "You know he's lived with one foot in the grave all these years. He takes so many risks."

Duncan looked from the farmers to Sarah and back to their hosts. "He's a tinker."

"Yes, yes," Judith agreed. "He can be a good tinker. Or a juggler. Or an actor. Or a teamster even. But he had much nobler beginnings. A prosperous merchant, son of one of the most successful merchants and shipowners in the Rhode Island colony. But seven years ago he had a notion to expand his business into the New Hampshire colony, at the edge of that wild country they call the Hampshire Grants, up between New Hampshire and New York. Decided to take his young wife and son up the Connecticut River after his new store was built. The war wasn't quite over, but they took no notice, acted as if they were still in Rhode Island. The raiders came at dawn, as is their way. Hayes's two hired men were killed. The Indians took his wife and six-year-old son. He managed to raise a party out of Charlestown, and they took off in pursuit a day later. The savages left a warning on the trail fifty miles to the north—his young son's head on a pole. Solomon called off the pursuit, fearing they would kill his woman."

Duncan glanced at Hayes. Sarah was still at his bedside, listening closely.

The farmer's wife pressed her hand to her heart and sighed. "Oh, he loves her so much, like in one of those romance tales. He won't speak much of it, but over the years we've heard the story. He abandoned his comfortable life in Rhode Island and spent months looking for any sign of his dear wife. Rebecca, as she be named. After not finding any sign the first year and barely escaping captivity himself several times, he went back to Rhode Island, then sold his holdings to his brother, we hear. He made himself up to be a tinker and trader so as to move unsuspicious-like among the tribes and villages in the north. The second year, he showed up with darling Sadie," she added with a nod toward the monkey, who laid curled up beside Hayes, "and they've been like father and child ever since. Only real family he has now."

As the woman stirred the steaming kettle that hung in the hearth, Duncan examined Hayes once more. Sarah, on a stool beside the bed, held the tinker's hand. As Duncan lifted the other hand, Sadie stirred, snuggling closer to her master.

"His pulse is stronger," Duncan reported. "A good sign."

When Sarah did not acknowledge him, Duncan turned to his second patient. Will lay with his head propped up by pillows, watching the low flames of the hearth. Duncan sat beside him.

"You must wish you had stayed in Mrs. Pope's house," he suggested to the boy.

"Never in life, sir! It's been such an adventure! A monkey befriended me! I got a sea bear companion and got to feed dragoon horses! And then an Indian kidnapped me and Miss Sarah saved me! Ain't it grand!"

"TABLE'S READY," CAME THE FARMWIFE'S call as Duncan and Conawago returned from rubbing down and feeding their mounts. Duncan watched, his heart aching, as Will rose, steadying himself on chairbacks at first, and went to lead Sarah to the dinner. She steadfastly ignored Duncan. Hayes did not stir.

The party of travelers ravenously consumed the thick soup and fresh-baked bread. When Duncan reached for his pouch and offered to pay, the farmer held up a hand in protest.

"We had a bad time of it two years ago," the man said. "Cow died, half our wheat failed. Mr. Hayes stopped over on his way west and saw our shame when we could only feed him half-rotting potatoes and some wild onions. He gave us five guineas out of his own purse, enough to get us a new cow and see us through that long winter. He and his friends will ne'r owe a pence for the hospitality of this house," he declared as his wife poured out servings of buttermilk.

Duncan encouraged Will to drink two cups, then looked back at Hayes. He knew the tinker lay perilously close to death. "I fear there is a swelling in his brain," he said. He had seen more than one man die from such an injury. "We need to keep cool compresses on his head, from buckets of fresh spring water."

"There's ice," the farmer offered.

"Ice in May?" Duncan asked in disbelief.

"Aye, we have a pond out back with a cellar dug into its hillside."

Ishmael followed Duncan out to the ice cellar. The tomahawk the young Nipmuc had put away while in Boston had returned to his belt, and he now used it to chip away at one of the large blocks at the rear of the low stone-walled chamber.

"They're coming, Duncan," he said as he helped fill a bucket with the chips.

"The men from Worcester. We slowed them down, but not for long. There'll be soldiers next."

"You mean I shouldn't be anywhere near this house."

"It would go bad for our hosts if you were found here. And no sense in making it easy for those looking to cash your bounty." Ishmael returned the tomahawk to his belt. "But I'm coming with you."

"No. Stay with her. Keep her safe. I'll not be far."

"No. You must clear your name. Go north into the Abenaki lands. My uncle and I will find you."

"Not until she is safely past the Hudson."

"Then you are a fool, Duncan McCallum," the young tribesman said, and grimaced at his choice of words. "The wise warrior stays away from danger until he understands it. You are just running headlong into it." Ishmael lifted the bucket and cocked his head at Duncan. "My uncle speaks of the great Battle of Culloden, where Highlanders ran foolhardily into rows of English cannons with nothing but swords and wooden shields. Is that what you seek, a proper Scottish suicide?"

"Your uncle teaches you too much," Duncan muttered, as if the battle where so many of his clansmen had died was somehow his personal secret. He dropped the last of the ice chips into the bucket. "Those men were brave, fighting for a noble cause."

"And such a fine line it be between stupidity and courage. You need to find those Frenchmen and let your friends handle these problems," Ishmael said as he closed the cellar door and turned to the house.

Duncan lingered at the cellar, weighing Ishmael's words. "Wrap the ice in a piece of linen," he called to the youth's back. "If he wakes, make him drink."

The young Nipmuc paused, then spoke over his shoulder, sounding uncannily like his uncle. "You won't reach Sarah by pushing toward her."

GRIPPED BY AN UNFAMILIAR TORRENT of emotion, Duncan watched as the dark of night settled over the little farm. A deep anger had taken hold of him, anger at the florid merchants, anger at the French for refusing to accept their defeat, anger at the killers, anger at the ruthless Horatio Beck. Most of all, he was furious at himself for keeping the Edentown party for so long in Boston against Sarah's wishes just for the pleasure of its many ships and books. At his core, though, it wasn't anger that tormented him, it was the ache from the withering looks Sarah had thrown at him, stabbing deep into his heart. She had often been distant during their time in Boston, often reluctant at his touch, but tonight she had refused to even acknowledge him. Hearing the tragic tale of Hayes's quest for his wife and his charity to mere acquaintances had only hardened her toward him. If Hayes died, that ice would be in her gaze forever.

Goliath responded to his warbling whistle by trotting out of the shadows of the pasture, standing eagerly as Duncan saddled him. He tied on his rifle and mounted, then eased out into the moonlight in front of the cabin. Someone looked at him from the dimly lit interior. He saw only a silhouette but knew well that gentle shape. He stayed motionless, praying Sarah would come outside. She did not wave, did not hold an open palm to the glass as she had so many times in Edentown for a final farewell. He lingered, too long to avoid more pain, then dug his heel into Goliath's flank and they sprinted to the top of the hill above the farm, where he dismounted and sat on a ledge rock, gazing down on the farm with an unexpected desolation.

He steadied himself against the memory of that bleak day back in March when Sarah wouldn't speak with him when he returned to Mrs. Pope's house, would not even answer his knocks on her bedroom door when he heard her weeping inside. When she arrived at breakfast the next morning and saw him at the table, she had abruptly turned and gone back up to her room. He had never seen her like that, had indeed expected that her visit to Boston at the end of his five-month stay would be five weeks of joy, as his indenture would expire soon and he would no longer be her bonded servant.

To his great irritation and his great shame, it had been John Hancock who explained Sarah's distress. The merchant had been unable to look Duncan in the eye. He had found him on the Hancock Wharf, where Duncan was directing the unloading of cargo from one of the merchant's coastal ships. Duncan had given the tally board to Munro and followed Hancock to a private place between stacks of crates.

"Duncan, a solicitor came to our offices—" Hancock began as he nervously flattened a torn label on one of the crates. "He had me sign an affidavit he had already prepared. I thought it was just another dispute between consignees of cargo, in which the court often wants to confirm particulars of shipments or of a voyage. It seemed just a confirmation that one of my sloops ran to Bermuda and back, with a list of the cargo and confirmation of the officers."

Duncan tried to look interested. Hancock's legal affairs were of no concern to him.

"It stated that you were the captain, that you left Boston on such a date and returned on another. My clerk confirmed the details, and I signed. I get documents every day to sign, you know. Now I feel practiced on. If anyone had explained the point, I never would have signed, you have to believe that."

"The point?" Duncan asked impatiently. He was eager to return to work.

"That it was about you, not the cargo. You and Sarah," Hancock added, and quickly looked away.

Duncan went very still. "Sarah?"

"I just found out this very hour. My own solicitor was in court yesterday when the proceedings occurred."

Duncan pushed Hancock down on a crate. "Stop looking away, John," he demanded, "and speak to me straight."

"A gentleman in London, a lord of some rank, had been paying someone to watch your comings and goings. The affidavit was used as proof that you left the territory of the American colonies. Apparently you have an indenture with Sarah, who is this lord's daughter, an indenture imposed as a condition of your transportation to America. As a condition of your release from prison. I never knew, Duncan. You never told me."

Duncan found his hands curled into fists. "And?"

"And you broke your bond by leaving America. When a servant breaks bond, the indenture renews upon his return, that's a standard term."

"Speak plain!" Duncan growled.

"The indenture started over the day you returned to Boston. There's a magistrate's order. You are bound for another seven years."

Duncan had collapsed onto a crate, not even realizing that Hancock was gone until several minutes later. He stayed out late, wandering the streets, lost in despair, and when he returned, Sarah was shut in her room again, weeping. He had not even knocked, just sat on the stair near her door. They had gone seven years without joining as man and woman, without consummating the love they felt for each other. Their relationship could not survive another seven years.

Sarah did not speak until the following day, when she asked to walk with him on the Common. She was wearing a colorful new dress, and she tried hard, but failed, to put the same brightness on her face. "I had a note from Mr. Hancock," she reported. "He says you know what Lord Ramsey did with a magistrate here." She almost never referred to the aristocrat as her father.

Duncan tried hard to push his heart back down his throat. "Seven more years," he murmured.

"And who cares what some old Boston nabob with a frayed wig says?" she asked, forcing a smile.

Duncan stopped, pulling her to face him. "Everyone, when that nabob is the law."

"But I don't!" she protested, moisture filling her eyes.

"Sarah, I would not shame your honor by—"

He would not have been surprised had she run away or put her hand over his mouth. He did not expect her to slap him. "Damn you, Duncan McCallum! We are not talking about my honor, and we are not talking about the vile creature who calls me his daughter, may he rot his eyes in a cold, hollow tree," she snapped, conjuring a tribal notion of a particularly unpleasant hell. "We are talking about your stubborn Scottish pride that makes you a slave to a piece of paper! You would make me a slave to it as well. But I am no such slave! I am a woman full in my years, if you haven't noticed!" Tears flowed down her cheeks, and Duncan pulled her to his shoulder.

"I've well noticed, *mo leannan*. I notice every day of my life, and when you are not there, I still set your image in my mind so I can get through my day." He patted her back, but her fire would not be quenched.

"Stop it! Stop using your Gaelic words of love when you do not mean them!" She pushed away. "I wonder more and more, do you like the image of me more than me in real life? Is that the way of it, that you like the concept of my love better than the imperfect, tattered, fatiguing way of love with a real woman? I think you just harbor me the way you harbor your damned honor, like some trophy that can never be tarnished!"

The tears were flowing fast now, but she did not wipe them away. "You will have to decide, Duncan. Every time you swell your honor, you shrivel my heart." And she turned, looking frail, and walked back to the house alone.

He had not gone back that night, but walked to the waterfront and sat on a pier until sunrise. She had spoken no more of indentures but mentioned more frequently the Mohawk way, in which a warrior just acknowledged that it was time to set aside his war ax and take a wife.

DUNCAN DID NOT KNOW HOW long he sat staring down at the farmhouse, but Goliath finally pressed his muzzle into his back, and he climbed into the saddle. He rode hard up the shadowed road, savoring Goliath's power as he gave the horse his head. A special air of wildness seemed to settle over the forest at night, and he drank it in like a raw, renewing liquor. They had gone miles before he reined to a halt at a flat at the top of a mountain with a view of moonlit hills for miles to the east. He was alone and heart-weary, on a stolen horse, with men coming to kill him, but he found a weak smile on his face. If he squinted, the scene merged into an image of the Highlands, and in a distant memory he heard bagpipes.

He had learned much about freedom since arriving in America as a virtual slave, and the most important lessons had come from his tribal friends. There were freedoms in this continent that were unimaginable to the inhabitants of the Old World—freedom to earn your own way as an equal among men, freedom to travel the vast open spaces, freedom to cherish and worship whatever things a man held sacred, freedom to make your voice heard—but most powerful of all was the freedom he was beginning to sense now, the freedom of the land itself. The leaders of the Sons were fond of speaking of freedom, but he was no longer certain they understood it. The freedom spoken of in Boston taverns did not taste like what he found here. Was there a city freedom and a country freedom, he wondered, or did ten men have ten different notions of freedom, each his own?

Duncan bared his spirit the way Conawago had taught him, stretching out his arms and opening himself to the moon and the mountains, and he felt the power of the earth course through him. He calmed himself, knowing what Conawago would say if they were together. He did not know if he could outrun the noose, could not tell if the woman he loved was abandoning him, did not know if the lies of Beck and his invisible conspirators would destroy his good name, but no one could steal this, the freedom of his soul.

He found himself stroking Goliath's neck, speaking low words that came unbidden, some in Gaelic, others in Mohawk. Despite their rash galloping, the big horse's breath was still deep and steady. Goliath gazed out over the shining hills, and Duncan was convinced he too felt the power of the land. "Easy, boy," Duncan chided. "You belong to the king."

They continued westward until, perhaps an hour before sunrise, Duncan spied the camp of the little caravan. He slipped off Goliath and approached on foot, studying the sleeping shapes about the camp. The metallic click of a weapon being cocked froze Duncan in his tracks.

"Like a highwayman in the night," came an amused voice in a Yorkshire accent. "Do you have any notion of the grand size of that bounty on your head, McCallum? You would addle some brass for me, as they would say back home in York."

"Enough to set up a deserter in a new life," Duncan suggested as Sergeant Mallory stepped out of the shadows, a pistol in his hand. "Glad to see you've recovered."

"A new life? Gawd, a new world! I could set myself as a gentleman merchant in Savannah. New Orleans, even." Mallory gave an exaggerated sign and eased the hammer back. "But where's the honor in that? You saved my life, I seem to recall."

"The bounty on deserters be almost as high," came Munro's voice. The old soldier had circled behind the sergeant. "And a thousand lashes would wait ye, if not the noose."

The deserter turned to see the rifle Munro aimed at him, and he lowered his pistol. "Alas, McCallum and I are at your mercy. With McCallum's bounty I could be a gentleman on a southern plantation. With both our bounties, you could be a prince of the frontier."

"Already got a job, thankee," Munro rejoined, nodding at Duncan as he lowered his own weapon. "Keeping this fool Highlander alive."

Mallory tucked his pistol into his belt. "Better to aim for a less difficult challenge, sir, like keeping the sun from rising. His Britannic Majesty seeks McCallum's head, and I fear that when the king wants something so desperately, he tends to get it."

Munro stretched languidly. "I look forward to debating King Jordie about that particular notion. Now, do ye suppose there's some of that good bacon from Boston left?" he asked, and marched off toward the smoldering fire.

Duncan helped Mallory feed grain to the horses as Munro and Occom prepared breakfast over the replenished fire. If the weather held, the reverend declared over their bacon and corn cakes, they might make their rendezvous with the Wheelock party on the Connecticut by nightfall.

"Wheelock?" Duncan asked.

"Oh, ye did not hear?" Munro said. "A messenger met us on the road. The eminent Eleazer Wheelock and his disciples are expected in Agawam, the settlement on the banks of the Connecticut."

"He is my guiding light," Occom declared. "The man who made me who I am. The tribal college I raised funds for these past two years was his inspiration. I was honored to be the instrument of his charity."

Duncan had heard of the famous Reverend Wheelock. "But he already has a school for natives, in Lebanon town, in Connecticut."

"That was but the start, a trial, as it were," Occom proudly explained. "We will build a vastly bigger institution that will shine like a light in the wilderness. It will change the destiny of thousands of our tribesmen."

Duncan pieced together what he remembered of the tales about Wheelock. "He is a man who inspires zealous loyalty, I hear—"

"The Apostles," Munro interjected. "That's what they call the stern tribesmen who escort him."

"A man who earns zealous admiration," Occom said, as if correcting them.

Munro cocked his head. "And perhaps ye were one of those Apostles yer own self once?"

"I was honored to serve at his side for many years," Occom said, a bit too defensively.

"Then your reunion in Agawam will no doubt be joyful," Duncan said, and motioned Munro away on the pretense of getting the horses ready.

"Something happened that night of the St. Francis raid," Duncan said to the Scot as they hitched a team to one of the wagons.

"A lot of people died, that's what happened. Loved ones were taken. The Abenaki have blood feuds that last for generations. That assassin isn't killing randomly, he's killing rangers who were there."

"His masters left Halifax in pursuit of that ledger. But they found something in that unexpected code, and they took the package from the warehouse, a parcel that went to a ranger with a gold coin in it. Daniel Oliver got a gold coin from the north and gave it to Will and his uncle. Josiah Chisholm had a parcel from the north he had hidden in the cemetery. All three from the ranks at St. Francis with Major Rogers. That parcel from Hancock's warehouse put the killers on a new scent, a scent that led them to Will Sterret. I thought they wanted him because he was a witness. But now I think it was because they wanted to learn all they could about old rangers and French gold. What do you know about St. Francis? Is it connected to the Sons of Liberty?"

"Not possible, Duncan," the old Scot replied. "No one had even heard of the Sons of Liberty back in '59. Took the stamp tax to bring the Sons out, and that was just three years ago."

Duncan stared at Munro in confusion. The Scot was right. The ledger may be about the Sons, but the parcels from the north were not. If the pieces of his puzzle were not fitting together, perhaps it was because there were two puzzles.

Sergeant Mallory appeared, sharing the last of the morning tea with them. "Left sucking the bottom leaves, as we used to say at Fort Ti."

Duncan looked up at the soldier in surprise. "Were you stationed at Ticonderoga, Sergeant?"

Mallory jerked his thumb toward the north. "All over the Champlain Valley. Crown Point, Ticonderoga. Sometimes on those sloops of war that patrol the lake. The Ticonderoga navy, we called it, though it was mostly an army affair."

A thought occurred to Duncan. "Do they keep records at Ticonderoga? Archives from the war?"

"You're speaking of His Majesty's army, sir. Of course they have records. Rivers of records, oceans of records, all locked up in the clerk's office. The scriptorium."

"Sorry?"

"That's what the colonel in charge calls it. Colonel Hazlitt's a bit of a scholar. An office soldier, if you catch my meaning." The sergeant paused, weighing Duncan's question. "I worked in the scriptorium some days, 'cause I have such a neat and legible hand, they said. Sometimes visitors would go in to spend a day or two, hunched over old journals and such like old monks."

"Visitors from where?"

"Not for a lowly sergeant to be asking. Some high-ranking officers, even officers wearing civilian clothes sent from headquarters. I recall one from London a few months back, an arrogant, excitable cove who expected us to salute him even though he was a civilian. Bark, bark, bark, people called after him, though never in earshot. On account of him giving angry orders all the time and it sounding like his name."

"Beck? Was his name Beck?"

Mallory rubbed the stubble on his chin. "Don't recall for sure, sir, but yes, I think maybe so."

Duncan and Munro exchanged a worried glance. Horatio Beck had visited the record vault at the great bastion of the north, Fort Ticonderoga, before returning to Halifax to join the chase for Jonathan Pine.

DUNCAN RODE BACK ALONG THE trail above the road until, at midmorning, he finally saw the stragglers. Ishmael and Conawago rode ahead of Sarah, riding double with young Will, beside the slumped figure of Solomon Hayes. Duncan eased Goliath as close as he dared without disturbing them. Hayes wore his slouch hat pulled low, his face pale and twisted in pain, but the tinker was at least handling his horse, staying mostly upright in his saddle.

After a few minutes, Conawago, with his usual uncanny awareness of Duncan's presence, leaned to exchange words with his nephew, then left the road, urging his horse up the slope. Duncan waited for him behind a ledge rock that opened to a view of the empty road to the west.

"Hayes does not blame you, Duncan," Conawago said even before he dismounted. "He was confused when he awoke in the night, asking who had spared him from the assassin, as if that Abenaki had attacked him. After Ishmael explained what had transpired, the first words from his tongue were 'Tell Duncan not to feel at fault.'"

Duncan did not acknowledge the words. "Did you look into his eyes? Were the pupils still dilated? Was he seeing double at all? Was his pulse strong?"

"His vision seemed fine," the old Nipmuc replied. "He was understandably weak when he awoke. He asked for his hat, then some tea, and after sharing a slice of bread with his Sadie and downing a cup of that fine buttermilk, he announced that he was ready, if someone would just help him into the saddle, saying we must not tarry, for Sarah's sake. The farmer went out with us, with an ax. He said he needed wood and would cut a tree down by the road and make a convenient mistake, letting it fall across the road. It wouldn't be much of an obstacle, but it would encumber pursuers, and when they asked, he would say he saw us yesterday, splitting off the road to flee into the Berkshire heights."

"She must leave the tinker," Duncan stated. "Does she not know the danger she is in?"

"She'll not leave him. Asking will just stoke her anger."

"He's just a tinker." Duncan regretted the words the instant they left his lips. He could not explain the bile he felt toward the man.

Conawago shot him a disappointed glance. "Jealousy does not become you, Clan McCallum," the old Nipmuc said, addressing Duncan as the head of his nearly extinct clan.

Duncan muttered in Gaelic.

His old friend frowned, not understanding the words, but hearing the sarcasm. "Lesser men are always tempted to hate the ones they wrong."

The words tore at Duncan's heart. "I'm bone-weary," he said after a long and painful silence. "I'm soul-weary. Since that day walking among all those bodies on the beach, I have been adrift, without a compass. I don't know whom I can depend on except for you. The warrant that would have me hanged is based on lies, but I don't know why."

"You know a good man was murdered in Quinsigamond. You know you attacked Hayes only because of the killers. You know liberty is worth fighting for."

"No, I don't. Liberty this, liberty that. So many invoke it for so many reasons that I don't know what it means anymore. In Boston it seems just the name of some game being played by politicians. If more men minded their honor and less about some mob's notion of liberty, this world would be the better for it."

"Fine. Your honor is worth fighting for. And Sarah's. And Ishmael's and mine. I don't know about the Sons of Liberty. But I do know about our small tribe, and its liberty is its honor."

They nudged their horses up the narrow game trail to keep parallel with the little party below. "I recall," Conawago observed, "that the river is just a dozen miles from here. Occom says he will prepare his friends to offer comfort when we reach the Agawam settlement. Hayes and the boy can take to bed. Let Will recover, and we can talk with him further when his mind is clear."

Duncan was surprised at the suggestion. "You mean to turn him over to the missionaries."

"I've nothing against a proper measure of Christian charity."

"Some say those Apostles are more like riders out of the Apocalypse."

"I believe they take their role as Christian soldiers most seriously," Conawago said. "Shepherding eternal souls is a somber business." A question seemed to linger in his tone.

THEY WAITED, WATCHING THE LONG stretch of road that led to the final rise before the river, until the weary riders appeared. Even from a distance Hayes, Ishmael, and Sarah, holding Will now, looked fatigued from their arduous ride, but once they crested the final ridge, they would have less than a mile to Agawam, the community nestled on the western bank on the Connecticut. Conawago, after scouting ahead while Duncan rested with Goliath, reported that it appeared to be a surprisingly large, prosperous settlement. The old Nipmuc had ventured far enough to confirm that the Edentown convoy had already been ferried across and was setting up camp along the riverbank by one of the three white steepled churches. Duncan relished the idea of a good night's sleep and a chance to mend things with Sarah. Wary of the reception she would give him, he resisted the temptation to ride down the road to meet them, but he reconsidered as they passed his observation point, and he eased Goliath down toward the road, keeping pace behind them.

Relief washed over him as the stragglers began climbing the last long slope that would lead to the promised help in Agawam. Duncan paused, letting Goliath nibble at the grass of a small clearing less than half a mile from the crest of the hill. He was about to urge the horse on, to catch up with Sarah, now only fifty yards away, when a strangled cry rose from the woods. Conawago was recklessly galloping down the mountain toward the road.

Ishmael had wheeled his horse about and was gazing defiantly at a dust cloud in the east. Sarah pushed her horse into a trot and shouted for Hayes to hurry, but the tinker seemed not to hear her.

Conawago burst out of the woods and reined in beside his nephew, lifting the club he had tied to his saddle. Sarah grabbed the reins from Hayes's limp hands, leading his horse as she hastened up the hill. Duncan dug his heels into Goliath's flanks, and the big horse, as if sensing a battle, snorted and stomped the ground before lunging into a gallop.

By the time Duncan reached his friends, the roiling dust on the road was only a quarter mile away and half a dozen riders could be seen. The bounty riders from Worcester had not given up.

As Duncan, Conawago, and Ishmael blocked the road, the riders slowed. Another four men came into view as the dust settled.

"She's there! The red-haired bitch!" one of the men at the back shouted, pointing toward Sarah, who was now a few hundred yards from the crest, struggling to keep Will balanced while still leading Hayes's horse. "And that's probably the damned traitor with her! We're rich, boys!"

Unexpectedly, Ishmael dismounted as the riders trotted eagerly forward. He bent into his horse's neck, whispering into its ear, then slapped its flank.

"T'is one of them stolen army mounts!" a man yelled as the horse ran past them, up the mountain trail. "Five pounds reward!" Four riders broke away, racing to claim the army's bounty.

"Don't let them get to the river!" shouted one of the remaining men.

Duncan jerked Goliath back and forth across the road to impede the riders. As a bountyman kicked his horse into a burst of speed, Conawago raised his oaken club, and in a blur of motion the old tribesman intercepted the man, leaning low to thrust the long club between the horse's legs. Rider and horse tumbled to the ground, the man groaning in pain as his shoulder slammed against a rock. As a second rider tried to run past Duncan, Goliath instinctively lunged and clamped his jaw around the man's arm. Conawago gave a triumphant cry as the big horse tossed the man from his saddle. "A horse bred for war!" Ishmael called out. The stunned rider gazed up in terror, gripping his arm, all the fight gone from him. The remaining mounted men, however, charged past with a cry of "'Ten pounds for the wench!"

Conawago was spinning his horse, about to give chase, when one of the men who had ridden into the woods reappeared, holding up a loop of rope as he charged Ishmael. As the old Nipmuc changed course to protect his nephew, Duncan and Goliath charged up the hill.

Sarah and Hayes were only a stone's throw from the crest when Hayes sagged and slowly slid to the ground. Sarah instantly leapt off her horse and ran toward the tinker, grabbing his arm in a vain attempt to drag him uphill.

Duncan burst through the group of riders, reins in his mouth, flailing out with a fist to bloody a man's nose; then he leapt off Goliath and planted himself between Sarah and her pursuers. To his surprise, they halted, looking up in confusion. Will threw a stone that hit a rider on his shoulder, but the man seemed not to notice. As Duncan raised his fists, fear began rising on the riders' faces. He grinned, thinking they may have tasted the fury of a Highlander before. He shouted his grandfather's battle cry and was rewarded to see two of the riders turn back.

"Duncan," Sarah said behind him.

He took a step forward, hoping to push more bountymen back, but then realized they seemed not to see him.

"Duncan," Sarah repeated. In the corner of his eye he saw Will step closer to her, as if frightened of a new threat. Conawago trotted up, Ishmael riding double with him, but as he passed the bountymen, he too halted, looking uphill with new worry on his weathered face.

Duncan slowly turned. In a row along the crest of the hill were half a dozen very large bronze-skinned men, all on black horses and all wearing black coats, with raven feathers in their long, braided black hair. Mr. Wheelock's wrathful Apostles had arrived.

9

THE VOICES OF ELEAZER WHEELOCK'S congregation drowned out the little pianoforte that played accompaniment to their hymns, rattling the glass globes over the wall sconces. Duncan had forgotten that the day was Sunday, and he'd only begrudgingly agreed to put on clean clothes and accompany Sarah, who insisted that young Will needed to go to the service because the singing would be good for him.

Agawam was a thriving town, larger than Duncan had expected, a crossroads community that lay at the junction of the Albany road and the busy north–south thoroughfare of the Connecticut River. To his surprise, there were two doctors in the town, and Duncan had introduced himself to both by delivering Hayes to one and asking the other for help in replenishing his own store of medicines. Neither had treated a traveler with an ax wound to his leg, but Duncan and Conawago kept a close eye on them, knowing how many doctors refused to speak of patients to anyone other than family members, let alone total strangers. Hayes lay recuperating at the house of Dr. Simons, and the other now sat two pews in front of Duncan. He had asked both not only about a wounded man, but also about strangers, perhaps French. Dr. Simons, who was treating Hayes, had dismissively observed that Duncan was a stranger himself and reminded him that Agawam, at the juncture of the east–west road and the river, was a town through which dozens of strangers passed every week. The second doctor, eyeing him suspiciously, had asked why Duncan would presume to ask him for medicines and suggested that he consult the town constable about strangers, leaving the impression that if pressed further, he might ask the constable about Duncan himself.

He had been left to roaming the town, watching its inns and public stables, altering his appearance by changing hats and waistcoats. In the afternoon of his first full day, after Ishmael reported that a band of bountymen had passed through, galloping westward, he had tied a band around his forehead and joined a crew unloading kegs from a flatboat. There he learned that vessels often sailed for Saybrook, at the mouth of the Connecticut, where fast boats were always available for passage to New York town. No one recalled seeing two Europeans and a wounded native taking passage on one, but Duncan showed a shilling and announced he would pay for the information if they did.

The big church they sat in had been opened for use by the much-revered Eleazer Wheelock and his escort of stern Indian Apostles and had been sealed off during Occom's reunion with Wheelock, which, Munro reported, had turned into an extended and surprisingly heated discussion. At its conclusion, the Apostles had filed out with expressions of regret and confusion. Reverend Occom had apparently been struck dumb by the encounter, not speaking to anyone afterward, then returning to the church to sit in prayer all night long, emerging at dawn looking troubled and exhausted.

When Sarah, in a voice that brooked no opposition, declared that they would be taking Will to the service, Duncan found himself anticipating Occom's sharing the pulpit with Wheelock. But the tribal pastor had been absent from the nave, not to be seen anywhere near the pulpit. When the congregation began its first hymn, Duncan recognized the deep bass voice behind him. He tried to turn, and Sarah pushed him back with a chiding glance. Defying her, he turned again to see the big man with long black locks on a back pew, alone. Occom sang with his usual energetic volume, but there was a new tightness in his voice, something that strangely hinted at suffering.

Sarah, clearly peeved at his staring, turned to follow his gaze, squeezing his arm in reprimand; then she too paused and gaped as a newcomer arrived to stand beside Occom. Conawago and Occom did not acknowledge each other, but the old Nipmuc solemnly joined in the song.

After the services, when Will pulled Sarah toward the river landing to see a team of majestic red Devon oxen that had arrived the day before, Duncan excused himself. He explained that he wanted to look in on Hayes, but he stood in the shadow of a nearby stable and he watched Occom and Conawago step out of the church, the last of the congregation to do so. Four of the tall Apostles, dressed as always in black, seemed to be waiting for them, and they walked around the church to the old barn that had been converted to rough sleeping quarters for Wheelock's traveling flock. Duncan looked back down the street—where Wheelock had disappeared in the company of a wealthy merchant family—then stealthily approached the barn.

The Apostles seemed to strike fear in most of the townspeople, who always gave them a wide berth, even though some had passed the prior afternoon in acts of charity, cutting firewood for a widow and replacing the rotten corner post of the schoolhouse porch. They had frightened not just the bounty riders from Worcester, who quickly fled after encountering them, but even Will and Sarah, who had carefully stayed behind Duncan as the Apostles silently led them down to the ferry to the western bank. In those first hours the Apostles struck Duncan as something of an imperial guard for the self-important Wheelock, but he had come to see them more like muscular monks in the service of charitable works.

They had all been together that first night in Agawam, at a dinner hosted by the Reverend Wheelock, and several of the Apostles had opened up with animated questions about Occom's travels through England, where he confessed that he had sometimes been paraded onto stages to demonstrate how the hand of God could not only tame the savage but could teach one to speak Greek, Latin, and Hebrew. Occom took it all congenially and even assented to Will's request to bring Sadie to the table, where she walked along the linen, pausing to clasp her hands as if in prayer and bow before each guest. Only when she jerked a solitary red feather out of the hair of one of the Indian elders was there a flush of disapproval, which quickly faded as Will called her to his side with one of the whistle commands he had learned from Hayes.

The Apostles, who seemed to all belong to the Mohegan, Pequot, and other southern New England tribes, grew even more sober after the meeting between Wheelock and Occom. Duncan had watched Conawago speak with two of the austere men as they were admiring a huge fawn-colored mule. Whatever they told him seemed to have struck him like a physical blow. He slightly staggered as he walked away from them and went to sit alone on a ledge overlooking the river. He had not spoken with Duncan since.

As Conawago and his new friends disappeared into the barn, Duncan pulled down the new tricorn hat Munro had purchased for him and made his way to Dr. Simons's house, where Hayes still lay in a front room next to the surgery. He knocked on the door, then, hearing no response, let himself into the short outer hallway that allowed visitors access to invalids without disturbing the main residence.

Hayes was sleeping as he entered and did not react when Duncan lifted his wrist, finding a strong pulse. He lowered himself into the ladder-back chair by the bed and studied the secretive tinker. His guilt over nearly killing the man had clouded his perception of him. Duncan saw now that the man's strong, thin face was nicked by several small scars, as if from close infighting. Laying two fingers on Hayes's forehead, he found him too warm and flicked off the woolen cap on his head. Sadness seemed etched on the man's long countenance, but even in this deep repose Duncan sensed a fierce determination.

Did Hayes, who had devoted himself to rescuing his lost wife, truly understand the brutal world of most Indian captives? The few who returned to civilization were often called ghostwalkers, for the dull, empty expressions that were often permanently fixed on their faces. Sarah had been one of the ghostwalkers, and Duncan's first encounter with her had been when he saved her from suicide in the middle of the Atlantic. Even if Hayes found his wife, she would likely be another ghostwalker when he brought her back to the settlements.

Duncan picked up a *Boston Gazette* lying on the nightstand. The newspaper was dated only a few days earlier, and it provided a detailed account of how the British navy had seized Mr. Hancock's sloop the *Liberty*. As usual, it reported the comings and goings of ships and the activities of the customs and tax commissioners, a topic that preoccupied many in the colony. The editor endeavored to set forth a chronicle of the feud between Boston's merchants, led by John Hancock, and the commissioners. Months earlier, Hancock's brig *Lydia*, he reminded his readers, had been illegally boarded by customs officials at her wharf in Boston. When they attempted to search belowdecks without a writ, Hancock had expelled them. When the commissioners tried to prosecute Hancock, the attorney general had sided with the merchant, infuriating the commissioners. They had lain in wait for Hancock's aptly named sloop the *Liberty*, which they immediately boarded for inspection. Hancock paid the duties on the wine that was unloaded and quickly replaced it with an outbound cargo of whale oil and tar, hoping for an early departure. The commissioners refused to provide the papers needed to clear the harbor, and days later, Duncan read, the government seized the vessel, saying that the *Liberty* was not licensed to receive cargo in Boston. The customs inspector from the original inspection claimed that Hancock had bribed him to turn a blind eye on cargo other than wine. The commissioners petitioned the navy to haul the sloop away, which had indeed happened the night that Mog had struck Hancock's warehouse.

The story closed with what read like a news bulletin. The publisher had just learned that the captain of the *Liberty* had mysteriously died the night after the sloop was inspected by the government.

"Why do you suppose the captain would die that particular night?"

Duncan's head snapped up. Hayes was staring at him.

"I've read that piece again and again," Hayes said. "Someone in government tried to search the *Lydia* and didn't find what they wanted. Hancock convinces the attorney general to take his side. Then the *Liberty* arrives after a stop in Halifax. The government seems to prevail in inspecting that cargo, but only later is it reported that the captain died. Then, the day after Hancock's warehouse is raided by the Abenaki, the ship is impounded, as if someone in government had to search it from keel to topmast. Hancock didn't know about the captain's death when we were there, only said that he had gone missing. Consider the sequence, McCallum. The *Arcturus* blows up, the wreckage is searched the next day. The Abenaki raids the warehouse; then the *Liberty* is searched and the captain dies. It had to be that man Beck. He is the fulcrum, the hinge on which these events turn. John said they tore that sloop apart. Ship's records scattered, crates of provisions opened, berths ripped apart. Just after, the *Arcturus* was sunk, as if Beck had to be sure that what he sought had not been hidden on her. Then the captain dies. Could it have been in a rough interrogation by Beck?"

As he spoke, Hayes touched his bare head, then rather urgently looked about for the cap Duncan had removed. He found it on his blanket and set it back on his crown. "Reverend Occom kindly bought it," he said, as if in explanation. "And it was a Hancock ship arriving from Halifax," the tinker added.

"Signifying what?" Duncan asked.

Hayes shrugged. "Perhaps I have too much idle time lying here on my back. But it would seem that Beck gave up on his search of the wreckage of the Livingston ship and went right to a Hancock ship. As if he knew that what he sought related to both merchant princes. As if," Hayes said pointedly, "he had learned that you didn't have the ledger at all by the time he searched the Hancock sloop."

Duncan chewed on the words a moment. "Are you suggesting that there was an informer in Hancock's warehouse?"

"If you consider the sequence, it would seem so. Maybe the captain knew something Beck didn't want shared with anyone else. Or the captain knew the secret that you didn't have the ledger despite the charade on the harbor, but Beck wanted to be certain it was shared with no one else."

"Why?"

"Because he planned on getting a writ against you. Beck gave up his direct approach against Livingston and Hancock and decided to apply himself to a surrogate."

"Meaning me. You are right—your idle mind works too much, I think."

"Perhaps. But I was in the warehouse having lunch with John after stocking up on trade goods when he received two separate reports about Beck asking questions pertaining to a Mr. McCallum who was associated with Hancock. Those asked tried to disincline him, to make him think you had nothing to do with Boston, so they told him you were a man of the frontier, someone who spent much time with the distant tribes."

Duncan was still suspicious of Hayes's motives in explaining his theory, but the explanation gave him pause. "So why didn't Beck drop his interest in me?"

"Because that was exactly what he wanted to hear, assuming by then that he had learned of the Abenaki and that the French spies were heading to the northern frontier."

"Impossible. That was far from public knowledge."

"How many were in attendance when you and Conawago discussed the Abenaki? Five? Six? Not to mention the guards coming and going. He knew, and he adapted his plans. Forcing you to go after the ledger makes his mission much easier. He could never follow the Abenaki, but he could follow you."

Duncan studied Hayes in silence, trying to convince himself that Hayes was playing his own peculiar game, but he could not deny that his words had a disturbing ring of truth. Still, although Sarah seemed to trust Hayes implicitly, Duncan found he could not. The secrets of their traveling companions, Conawago had said, may be the most important secrets of all. Hayes gave the impression of being an impoverished tinker, but he had given the astounding sum of five pounds to the starving farm family. Duncan's life had been saved more than once by the call of his instincts when danger lurked, and they always screamed when Hayes was near. Was it possible that Hayes himself was the informer?

He held up two fingers in front of the tinker. "How many?" At least he could be the man's doctor if not his confidant.

Hayes sighed, as if disappointed. "A pair. The fourth time you've asked in the past two days. How much longer must we play at this?"

"Until I know you are healed. Extend your arm, then touch your nose with your index finger."

"I assure you, my brain is not leaking out through some fissure in my skull," Hayes said peevishly as he complied.

"There is a membrane around your brain called the dura mater," Duncan explained. "There are blood vessels that feed it. If one ruptures, the hemorrhage will squeeze your brain. It can affect your sight, your breathing, and your ability to move your limbs."

"I am not blind, I am not suffocating, and I am prepared to waltz with Miss Ramsey the moment she asks."

"Have you been given any hellebore?" Duncan asked. "Or perhaps James's powder?"

He realized the tinker was looking over his shoulder, grinning.

"You are welcome to visit my patient, sir," came a gruff voice over Duncan's shoulder. "You are not welcome to play the charlatan."

Duncan turned to see a tall, ruddy-faced man in the doorway, wearing a deeply annoyed expression.

"I do not mean to presume, Dr. Simons," Duncan said. "But hellebore is often effective against swelling. And swelling is the great foe of the concussed."

The doctor stepped forward and lifted Hayes's wrist. "And where exactly did you study your medicine, sir?" he asked in a mocking tone.

"The University of Edinburgh," Duncan shot back. "And you, sir?"

The doctor lowered the wrist and fixed Duncan with a skeptical gaze.

"Such claims may buy you respect among the uneducated of the frontier, but they can get a man arrested in civilized society."

"Epidural *sanguinem* is what I fear most, though subdural remains a possibility. I think we would have seen paralysis if the bleeding were intracerebral."

"I warn you, sir," the doctor replied, suspicion still in his voice. "I had the good fortune to spend several months studying with Dr. Hunter at the very university."

"John Hunter or his brother William?"

The doctor could not hide his surprise. "It was John Hunter."

"I studied anatomy with William and assisted him in the Royal Infirmary there, before all those tales about the brothers and body snatching, but my real love was the botanical garden and the study of *materia medica*. I wrote recommendations for my friend Benjamin Rush of Philadelphia, who is now a student there, I am happy to say. Now, have you thought of a few drops of laudanum for the swelling?"

Hayes and Simons both stared at Duncan in astonishment.

"I—I have exhausted my supply of laudanum," the doctor sputtered. "I applied some Peruvian bark."

"But he shows no fever."

"What is a fever but a swelling, and you and I both fear epidermal swelling. I sent to Boston for—" The doctor was interrupted by a scratching at the window. Sadie, one arm around Will Starret's neck, was trying to get Hayes's attention. With a congenial laugh the doctor gestured the visitors to the door. As Hayes joyfully extended his arms to welcome the capuchin, the doctor motioned Duncan inside his sitting room. His housekeeper served them tea while they spoke of Edinburgh, then of Reverend Wheelock's very stern, very charitable Apostles.

"He's going to recover, McCallum," the doctor said of Hayes as Duncan glanced not for the first time toward the sickroom. "I didn't understand fully until Miss Ramsey explained the . . . incident. And I did not fully appreciate your professional interest."

"I will pay for his expenses," Duncan offered. "I have little cash, but my rifle is valuable."

"No need. Miss Ramsey has been most generous. After hearing of Hayes's tragic story, I said I would have extended my services gratis, but she insisted."

Duncan sipped at his tea, uncertain how to take the news. "I am curious, Doctor. Does Reverend Wheelock often stay in Agawam?"

"Not often. But always," the doctor replied, and seemed to weigh his words, "very conspicuously, you might say. He is a godly man but always seems to move with his disciples, as if he were royalty with his courtesans. And some of our self-righteous folks are quick to point out that they are all Indians."

"Folks?"

The doctor lowered his voice. "Mostly pastors and deacons. This time when he came, there was a delegation of them waiting for him, with special emissaries from afar."

"A Boston pastor?"

"Representatives sent by Governor Bernard and Governor Wentworth in New Hampshire." Simons raised a palm, as if to ward off further questions. "Don't ask why. I avoid politics like the scurvy." He sipped his tea and contemplated his visitor. "Did you find the tribal man with the leg wound?"

"No luck."

"I have been considering your quest. My housekeeper says that one of Wheelock's Apostles came to her and asked her for an old sheet."

"As if for bandages," Duncan suggested.

Simons nodded. "Sometimes injured natives prefer to take healing from their own."

DUNCAN RETURNED TO THE STABLE at the edge of town, where he had left Goliath. The owner had asked no questions about the government brand on the horse's flank, and later Ishmael had found some axle grease that, mixed with a dollop of pine tar, effectively concealed the brand to all but the closest examination. The horse offered a nicker of acknowledgment, and Duncan stroked his neck as he surveyed the stable for signs of Conawago and his nephew, whose packs lay by his in the next stall.

He dropped to a crouch as he heard someone in the aisle, then rose as he recognized the tan britches on the small legs that appeared on the opposite side of Goliath. Will Sterret jerked back in surprise as he saw Duncan. "Sorry, sir," the boy said. "The storekeeper gave me an apple, and I thought . . ." He shrugged and backed away, as if worried he was being too bold.

"I'm sure Goliath would be pleased to share it."

Will took a big bite of the fruit and held the remainder out for the horse. "No sign of soldiers anywhere," he reported in a low voice. "I keep watching, like you asked. Not at the inns, not at any stables, not at church."

"Bountymen?"

"That one party came through, heading westward without stopping. And a man rode in from Worcester. He ordered half a dozen broadsides to be nailed up. At the printing shop, at the mercantile, on the message boards by the churches."

Duncan's gut tightened.

"But Mr. Conawago went to the printer after the rider took the ferry back across the river. He said he was surprised that the printer would allow such a trespass on his domain, then pointed out that the broadside was printed in Boston, not even in the same county, and why should those city crusts take business from a good journeyman in Agawam? Surely, if it was so important, Mr. Conawago said, the government could find a few shillings for the town printer to take care of town broadsides. So the printer thought a bit, then gave me a ha'penny and told me to correct that rude behavior." With a mischievous grin the boy pulled out several papers from inside his shirt. "I got 'em all, Mr. Duncan," he declared, then handed Duncan one and began to rip the others.

Duncan's belly turned to ice as he read the announcement that was being circulated throughout the colony. Across the top of the broadside was a row of skulls. HEINOUS MURDER OF THIRTY-SEVEN! the headline read in one-inch font, then: *Treason! His Majesty's Royal Governor Bernard by the writ of his sovereign authority gives notice to the citizens of Massachusetts to seize and restrain one Duncan McCallum, late of New York colony, to be returned to Boston to answer for the heinous murder of the crew of the good ship* Arcturus *and treasonous theft of articles belonging to His Royal Majesty King George III, long may he reign.*

At the bottom was a description, fortunately ambiguous, of the fugitive: *McCallum, known to be of a violent nature, stands six feet tall. His reddish-blond hair hangs long down his neck when not braided, and he is known to hold sympathies for the Scottish Jacobite cause. We weep for the wives and mothers he has so cruelly deprived of love and comfort. All men be duty-bound to avenge his dark deeds by his capture and return for swift punishment.*

When Duncan looked up, Will was still smiling. He had a wad of four-inch paper squares in his hand. "I'll remember ye in the shack of convenience," he happily declared, and stuffed the squares back in his shirt.

"Tell me, Will, have you been inside the Apostle's barn?"

The boy's eyes went round. "Oh, never, sir! It's for the Apostles!"

"You make it sound like it's a nest of vipers."

"Just very holy men. Mr. Ishmael says maybe they was possessed by the souls of those Puritan beggars what hanged those witches at Salem in the last century. But Mr. Conawago cuffed him on the back of the head and said we owe them our sympathy, for Mr. Wheelock just wears them as gemstones of his pride, though I couldn't cipher what he meant."

Duncan tried to stifle his grin. "Think you can watch them for me?"

The boy's face clouded for a moment, then his eyes lit with a sudden memory. "Later I can, but Mr. Ishmael said if I found ye, to bring ye to the hidden sergeant."

Sergeant Mallory was on his feet in the tavern woodshed, where he had been hiding since arriving in Agawam. Duncan paused and watched as he threw a small tomahawk at a slab of wood, successfully lodging the hand ax in the center of the slab with each throw. He nodded at Duncan, then threw once more, leaving the blade buried in the wood.

You seem much recovered, Sergeant," Duncan observed.

"Thanks to the kindness of the lady and yerself, sir." He gestured for Duncan to sit on one of the two broad log cross sections that were used as chopping blocks, then sat on the second himself. "You know I got no coin to speak of, but I wanted to repay ye. I don't have much, but I do have my honor, mind." He reached into his waistcoat and extracted a folded sheet of paper, which he straightened and handed to Duncan. "T'ain't like I'm a scholar, but my mother taught me a solid hand, as she liked to say.

"Sometimes at the fort's record library, the clerk would have me list out contracts, transcribe accounts, organize files, and such. It got me relieved from digging trenches or hauling firewood, and out of the wind and rain, so I never refused an offer of library duty. I made a list for you of files I remembered, in case it might help."

Mallory's list confirmed that Ticonderoga was the administrative headquarters for all Champlain operations. *Quartermaster accounts, 1759 onward,* Duncan read, then:

Duty rosters
Barrack construction
Burial records
Battery construction
Requisitions
Campaigns: Quebec, Fort Richelieu, Cumberland Bay, St. Francis
Book of garrison orders
Artifacts

"These are all in the vault at Ticonderoga?" Duncan asked.

"Those and twice as much again, I reckon. Some are bound books, others are stacks of papers bound up with pins and those red ribbons the government likes to use."

Duncan's eyes went back to the entry that mentioned St. Francis. "Campaigns?" he asked.

"Oh, those be the ones most entertaining to read. The commanders made the officers in charge of expeditions write down their reports and recollections, and lists of soldiers injured or killed. Always need good records of the dead, the lieutenant in charge would say, it's a debt we owe them."

"You're saying the report of Major Rogers about St. Francis would be there?"

"Oh, aye, and as I recall, some from his officers too. They all split up on the return and had a rough go of it, I recollect. There was an investigation into it, into why one man died in the raid but thirty or forty perished in the retreat."

Duncan pointed to the last item on the list. "Artifacts?"

Mallory shrugged. "Mostly oddities brought back from the campaigns, such that no one claimed them or was scared to speak of. In two or three small boxes. I recall a lot of French military badges. Some decorated powder horns belonging to dead soldiers."

"What things that people were frightened of?"

"Old crosses from the Romanish churches up north. After bringing 'em back, some said melt 'em down but others said they be cursed. And Indian things. A turtle shell with some kind of water monster painted on it. A necklace of dried tongues. There was one box of shriveled things that an old ranger said was men's pricks collected by a 'Naki warrior. No one would touch it."

Duncan had visited Ticonderoga and was trying to visualize the fort on the shores of Lake Champlain. "Where is this vault?"

"Up on the northeast corner of the old barracks building, the big stone structure inside the gate."

Duncan listened carefully to Mallory's description of where the office was, and where a key was hidden in the hallway should it be locked. "You said there was a visitor from London. Do you recall what he was looking for?"

"I've been thinking on that. I do believe it was the St. Francis papers—and then some about the Montreal campaign."

Duncan studied Mallory's list, his mind racing. He was more convinced than ever that the Quebec town of St. Francis held answers to the mystery that had caused so many deaths.

"Now, don't even think of that, sir," the deserter said. Duncan realized that the sergeant was staring at him. "I see that look of yours. You don't think that warrant will make its way to the Champlain Valley? What do you think the army does to traitors? They don't wait for niceties of lawyers and writs. You might find some answers there, sure enough, but go to Fort Ti and you'll be dead bones within the week."

"BUT, DUNCAN, I HAVE THE stomach of a goat," Ishmael protested as Duncan explained his instructions. "Why would I tell the Apostles my bowels are suffering?"

"Because one of them is a healer. Because you are of the tribes, and they will want to help you. That Abenaki suffered a terrible wound. I'm convinced he came here, to Agawam, but the doctors here say they never saw him."

Ishmael gazed uncertainly toward the log structure beside the church. "You mean the killer might be in that barn?"

"I doubt he would think it safe to linger. But he may have sought treatment."

Ishmael weighed his words; then a mischievous grin split his face. He darted to a maple tree, pulled off some leaves, and stuffed them into his mouth. After a moment he returned to Duncan, green drool dripping from the corner of his lips.

Duncan rolled his eyes. "Don't overplay it. We want them to think you need some herbs, not last rites."

He settled on a shadowed bench in the cemetery and watched the door on the side of the barn as Ishmael spoke to an Apostle who was sitting on a keg reading a Bible. The man listened, then rose and stepped inside. Moments later he returned with one of the older Apostles, a particularly somber figure who wore his long, gray-tinged hair in a braid down his back and had a pattern of intricate tattoos in a line down one cheek. Duncan had noticed him before because of the distance he kept from the other Apostles. Ishmael clutched his stomach and spoke in a labored voice. The old tribesman studied him silently, then stepped inside and emerged not with a medicine bag, but with a wide-brimmed hat. Ishmael seemed confused, but he followed the healer as he strode to the cemetery gate. The tall elder stood as straight as a musket barrel. His solemn, weathered face had a quiet dignity to it.

Duncan made room as the healer reached his bench, and the old man sat down. "I saw this boy eat an entire venison pie last night," the healer declared. "I could believe it might cause discomfort, but not green spittle."

"I'm sorry, Grandfather," Duncan said. "We meant no disrespect. We have a problem of a different sort you might help with."

The man seemed to be giving them only half an ear. He was watching three figures walking down the street—Reverend Occom and two of the other Apostles. Something was different about the two. They were still somber, but they had removed their white starched collars, and each wore a necklace of white and purple wampum beads over his waistcoat. Worry grew on the face of the elder as he watched Occom and his companions. There seemed to be a schism in the group.

"You came with him," the Apostle said.

"The reverend? We traveled together from Boston."

The tribesman fixed Duncan with a chastising stare. "You did so knowing there was a bounty on your head. You might have thought about—"

"Grandfather," Ishmael interrupted. "You don't understand what—"

Duncan held up his hand to silence the youth. "Yes. They say I killed thirty-seven men and have acted against the king."

"Did you?"

"No."

The healer studied Duncan in silence. "No, I don't suppose you did," he said with a shrug. "But you drag scandal behind you like a shadow."

"I am shadowed by lies and deception, and men who want to kill me."

With a remarkably quick motion the healer reached out and grasped Duncan's totem pouch. Strangely, he clutched it in silence for several breaths, his eyes closed. When he opened them, he stared anew at Duncan, his face full of surprise. "Much power," he whispered. "Much pain."

Suddenly Duncan felt very small and not a little afraid. The man might have been a Christian now, but he had not always been so. In the tribes there were two kinds of healers, those who practiced earth medicine, using herbs and tonics, and those who practiced spirit medicine, shamans who might use herbs but also invoked the names of ancient gods and demons.

Ishmael sensed it too, for his eyes went round and he took a step backward. "I am called Ishmael," he said, and for a moment Duncan thought the young Nipmuc was going to kneel to the old man. "My mother named me Ojiwa," he whispered, "of the Nipmuc."

The healer nodded. "Reverend Wheelock decided to baptize me and declared that I should be Noah." He spoke his Christian name as if speaking of someone else, and Duncan had a sense that perhaps it had not been the first baptism for the tribesman. Surely it was not his only name. Some shamans, the most powerful, were given secret names by the tribes. They often terrified outsiders, tribesmen and Europeans alike, and some were killed out of fear. The few who survived sometimes hid behind new lives.

"I am seeking an Abenaki," Duncan declared. "He killed men in Boston and Quinsigamond. My fiancée . . ." He hesitated, not certain what he was to Sarah anymore. "The woman who leads our wagon convoy sliced open his leg with an ax when he tried to steal a boy. I think he sought help here. Did you treat him?"

Noah ran a hand through his thick hair. "Every man must find his own way to die," he observed.

Duncan exchanged an uneasy glance with Ishmael. It was a saying used by tribal warriors before battle. This old man with the stern bronze face and hawk-like eyes was not simply one more church elder. What was he doing with Wheelock's flock? "I did not hear a denial in your words," Duncan replied.

Noah surveyed the street, resting his eyes in the direction Samson Occom had gone. "Reverend Wheelock is fond of the parable of the Great Flood. Reverend Occom was his first disciple," he added, as if to explain himself. "I was his second. They are both men of great virtue. There are times for learning of the workings of this world, and there are times for learning of the workings of the spirit."

Duncan hesitated, not sure if he understood the man's intention. "You weren't always Noah," he asserted. He flushed as he saw that his words brought pain to the man's eyes.

"I thought we were talking about healing," Noah said.

"I was talking about an Abenaki murderer."

The old man's lips twisted into a sad smile. "Two kings sign a piece of paper telling the world they are ending a war. If you kill before the paper is signed, you are a hero. If you kill afterward, you are a murderer. It's one of the things I learned in European books. But I was taught to worship wise souls, not kings." He gestured toward Duncan's totem pouch. "Who do you worship, Duncan McCallum?"

Once again the old man was making Duncan feel very small. "I would understand if you helped that Abenaki warrior. He was in danger of losing his leg. A healer should not judge his patient."

"After the last war I was surprised at how many had lost legs and lived," Noah declared, looking out over the gravestones. "Because of the skills of British army doctors, I was told. They usually wound up in big towns like New York or Albany, begging for their sustenance. There was a score or more of them, Indians and English, who would sit along the outside walls of churches in New York and beg. Once, there was a terrible blizzard, and afterward I found frozen bodies of two one-legged Iroquois. The churches had let the English inside, but not the Iroquois. One of them had stripped to a loincloth. He had an old, battered war ax in one hand and his totem pouch in the other. He had known he would not survive the night."

"*Jiyathontek*," Duncan whispered. The word used for summoning of Iroquois spirits.

Noah grimaced. "Do not use that word lightly, McCallum." He looked up at the sky, then at the cemetery again, resting his gaze on a stone with a weatherworn angel carved at the top. "'I praise you, for I am fearfully and wonderfully made.'"

Duncan cocked his head. It was a Psalm, though a most unusual one.

Noah looked back at Duncan. "You say he is a murderer. Others may say he is a hero."

Duncan weighed the old man's statement and was reminded of Munro's similar words on that first day in Boston harbor. "You mean for some, the war has not ended."

"It never ends," Noah declared, then shrugged. "I treated a man with a mangled leg, sewed it up, and made a poultice for him. The fool had been walking on it for two days, as if he were indestructible, making it much worse. He was of the north, one of the Algonquin tribes."

"Abenaki," Duncan stated.

"He was in a great hurry, said they had to push on to the Hudson."

"They?"

"There were two well-dressed foreign gentlemen waiting for him, most impatiently. I told all three that if he kept using the leg before it healed, the poison would settle in and it would be the death of him. Then those two went off into the cemetery to talk, as if they had to debate whether it was acceptable for him to die."

Duncan found himself looking at the man's chest, wondering if his waistcoat concealed a totem pouch hanging from his own neck under the cross that hung on the outside. "They need him to guide them somewhere in the north."

Noah nodded. "They said they could not stay here. I told them their companion needed to stay off the leg, two weeks at least. *Merde*, the younger of them kept saying. *Merde*. I hadn't heard that since I was last in Canada. So I ventured that they could go upriver into the wilderness and over the mountains, where they would be digging a grave for their native friend. Or downriver. I said with fair weather they could be in New York town in four or five days, then catch one of the trade boats up the Hudson into the north country. How long then to Lake Champlain from New York town, the young one asked. Ten days perhaps, depending on your guide, your vessel, and your weather, I replied."

The old healer paused. Samson Occom and his two companions had come into view again beyond the row of houses. They were heading toward the river landing. Noah turned to Ishmael, who had been silently listening. "I have a cure for you, son. Abstain from eating maple leaves." With a nod, he rose. "I heard a name," he added in departing. "They did not know I had French. The older one, with the close-cut beard, was Henri, though the other one once called him Comtois, and he was arguing with the younger man over the importance of keeping their native companion with them. They decided to keep him alive, and they left by boat the next day."

Henri Comtois. At least Duncan knew the name of one of the French murderers. As Noah threaded his way back through the gravestones, he halted and half turned toward Duncan. "He was proud of his wound, that Abenaki. Said he had been attacked by an Iroquois witch and lived to speak of it."

Duncan lingered alone in the cemetery to read, for the third time, a letter Reverend Occom had handed to him the day before. It was from John Hancock, who had addressed it simply to DM, then put it inside an envelope for *Occom, care of Reverend Wheelock in Agawam.* Hancock begged Duncan's forgiveness, claiming ignorance of the scheme dreamed up by Livingston and Samuel Adams to use Duncan so, and promised he would do all he could to help Duncan. Meanwhile, he had made discreet inquiries about Horatio Beck among officials in Boston who had encountered him in other settings, learning that he was the son of a bankrupt lord who had sold his title and estate to settle gambling debts and then died soon after in a duel. Beck had navigated his way through London society despite the disgrace and earned a post as private secretary for the minister of war. After a few months he had taken on a new assignment, pursuing private tasks for the minister, including the successful interrogation of high-ranking French prisoners during the war. There were rumors, Hancock cautioned, that his prisoners had been horribly mutilated, and that the man who killed his father in the duel had been found dead in the Thames. During stays in Philadelphia and New York he had developed a reputation as a rogue who preyed on the daughters of wealthy merchants and left hurriedly after incurring gambling debts amounting to more than a thousand pounds, including a substantial sum owed to Robert Rogers. He had fled back to London, still in the good graces of the minister, though there were recent reports that he had been seen in the Champlain Valley. *You must at all costs stay out of the devil's grasp*, Hancock had closed in warning, over his elegant signature, then added a postscript. *Branscomb's widow says he served with Rogers at St. Francis.*

THE IROQUOIS WITCH MOG HAD spoken of was wearing a new calico dress and arranging a Sunday dinner when Duncan arrived at her inn. Sarah insisted that all the Edentown travelers attend, to fortify them for the hard push to the Hudson that would commence the next day. Munro had retrieved Hayes, whose color and energetic step showed that he was quickly recovering. Sadie too was invited, though the capuchin quickly retreated to one of the windows when Ishmael laid a plate of pumpkin seeds on its wide sill.

"I deeply regret it, Miss Ramsey," Occom said after heaping servings of chicken, potatoes, and beans in molasses had been distributed, "but as I mentioned at the outset of our journey, I part company here. It's upriver I travel now."

"To the site of your new school?" Sarah asked. "Truly I must visit the new institution someday. We may have applicants for you among our tribal orphans."

Occom's smile was forced. "Some of my flock are at the fort at Charlestown, in the New Hampshire colony."

"Oh," Sarah said, "is that where your school will be constructed?"

Occom glanced at Conawago before replying. "Just some members of my flock who were scouting a location. I owe them an explanation in person."

Sarah looked back and forth from Conawago to Occom. "Explanation?"

Duncan saw Ishmael carefully studying the beans on his plate. Hayes and Munro stared expectantly at the tribal clergyman. In the silence, they could hear pumpkin seeds cracking behind them.

"There's been a change in plans—" Conawago offered.

Occom put down his fork and knife. "It is my story to tell, friend," he interrupted in a forlorn tone, then for a long moment studied his companions. "There will be no college for tribesmen. Reverend Wheelock has changed his mind."

"But you raised all that money for a school," Sarah pointed out.

"And that was the message I gave to every donor, that members of the tribes would be raised up to do God's work by gaining the same knowledge as Europeans. It was the condition upon which Lord Dartmouth gave us such a lavish sum." He took a long sip from his glass. "But all I am I owe to Reverend Wheelock. He says he has a new vision, that he already has an Indian school in Connecticut, that what is needed is a school for the boys of good English Christians."

"He's taking your money?" Hayes asked in surprise.

"Everything I am I owe to Reverend Wheelock," Occom repeated. "He says he will appease the donors by naming his new college after the lord."

"He's calling it God's College?" Munro asked.

Occom offered a bitter smile. "The secular lord. Lord Dartmouth. It is to be up the Connecticut, near where I had hoped to . . ." Occom's voice choked away as emotion overwhelmed him. He had spent nearly two years of his life performing a miracle by raising a princely sum in England to help Indians, and it would now fund another man's dream for colonists' sons. Duncan recalled how Conawago had abruptly changed his demeanor toward Occom, had unexpectedly joined him at the back pew that morning. Conawago had known. The Apostles had known, which explained their sudden tension and divisiveness. Some were Wheelock's men, but others were loyal to Occom. Old Noah seemed to have had his faith shaken.

In the silence, Sadie, her eyes drooping after her meal, climbed up into Hayes's lap and disappeared into the sack that hung from his shoulder. Duncan saw the momentary smile of contentment on the tinker's face. Conawago had chastised Duncan again that morning for speaking with suspicion of Hayes, saying that he deserved nothing but sympathy, for he was a family man without a family.

Hayes sensed Duncan's gaze and looked up. "Dr. Simons says the aid you gave me that first night probably saved my life."

Duncan glanced at Sarah, who was watching him expectantly. "It was the least I could do," he began. Her expression was cool, with something that might have been warning in her eyes. "I am grateful for your recovery," he tried, and Sarah looked away, disappointed.

"The harnessmaker has a pet duck, raised by a hen," Will Sterret put in, trying his best to lighten the atmosphere. "It lands in the long watering trough at the village green and just swims back and forth. Some of the old horses are so used to her they just lift their heads to let her pass, then keep drinking!"

Occom smiled. "I saw that once at the Four."

Duncan's fork stopped midway to his mouth, and he exchanged an inquiring glance with Conawago. They had seen a numeral 4 etched in dirt with a bloody finger. "The Four?" he asked.

"Odd, I agree," Occom replied, "but that's the name of the old fort up the Connecticut that the rangers used, where Charlestown was built. The Fort at Township Four is the official name, but folks tend to just call it the Four."

AFTER THE DINNER SARAH FOUND Duncan on the porch, at work with a writing lead. She silently sat beside him and read the paper he handed her. "Black

Oxford and Golden Pippin," Duncan said. "The first for cider, the other for the cellar, for winter eating."

"Then I hope you will find good stock at the orchardist," Sarah said without looking up from the paper. "We should be there by late tomorrow if we get an early start. We can camp in the apple grove."

Duncan leaned forward, trying unsuccessfully to get her to look at him. "I won't be there. I must go north." He felt her shrink from him. He reached for her hand, and she pulled it away.

"Must you ever fight other people's battles?" she asked in a tight voice.

"The king seeks to hang me and arrest you. I tend to think that makes it my battle."

"My people—" Sarah began. "The Mohawk say that the more scars a warrior receives, the more foolhardy he becomes. You have too many scars already. Come home, Duncan. They can't disturb us at Edentown."

They paused, watching Munro, Occom, and Ishmael transfer a box of Bibles from Occom's wagon to one belonging to Sarah, who had accepted the gift of Bibles for Edentown. As Munro lifted the heavy crate, a cat ran between his legs and the crate dropped. Occom gasped in alarm, but Ishmael helped Munro lift it from the ground.

"Lord, Reverend, for a moment ye looked like the bishop who's been caught in a whorehouse," Munro said, laughing.

"Just concerned for the Good Books," Occom awkwardly rejoined, then turned to help pack the crate securely in Sarah's wagon.

Duncan touched Sarah's shoulder, and she twisted again out of his reach. "If I don't track this to the end," he said to her, "they will find me. Even at Edentown. I keep seeing those dead, Sarah, all those bodies on the beach at Boston. Those innocent dead are owed the truth. The truth belongs to the dead." It was one of the ancient tribal sayings Conawago had taught him. At first he thought it meant that secrets died with the dead, but as the Deathspeaker he had come to realize that it meant the truth was a debt the living owed the dead.

Sarah glanced at him and looked away. "Duncan, I have a terrible feeling about this. I've had wrenching dreams myself, about the tribes and us. I can't go on with this pain between us. You mustn't go."

In all the years he had been with her, from the day he rescued her from a suicidal leap into the stormy Atlantic, she had never used dreams against him.

It was a force of tribal culture. To those who had raised her, dreams were sent from the other side, sent by spirits and gods, and their messages always had to be respected. Dreams could stop a battle, could even force a village to relocate.

In the brittle silence Duncan sensed something rising between them, a new wall that might forever separate them. "These are not matters for the tribes," he tried.

"You are wrong. Whatever it is involves the tribes, too. In my dreams, I see you beaten and bleeding before a fire of death, with more death all around you. I see men bathed in blood and men burning, and a great, long beast lying in wait for you."

Duncan shuddered. He knew better than to treat such dreams lightly. These were powerful omens. "Conawago says that those of the tribes have more intense dreams because they are more respectful of the spirits."

"And so the spirits have stopped speaking to you?" Sarah asked. It was a profound accusation. "If you go north, your death is waiting."

Duncan sat in silence, fighting the pain. He was tempted to say that he had had a dream that he must go to the north, but he would never lie to Sarah. "I don't know how not to go," he said instead.

Without another word, Sarah stood and left him.

10

"No one but Patrick Woolford, do you understand?" Duncan demanded of Ishmael as the young Nipmuc tucked his folded and sealed message into the pouch that hung around his neck.

"Deputy Superintendent Woolford," Ishmael confirmed. "Captain of infantry," he added, referring to the rank Duncan's friend still held in the British army while seconded to the Department of Indian Affairs.

Duncan pulled on Ishmael's arm to get his attention. The young Nipmuc was watching the river docks, where two big whaleboats were being fitted out for Reverend Wheelock's party. "He has a new son, so he'll probably be close to his cabin, near his wife's tribe. If not, he'll be with Sir William at his manor house," he added, referring to Sir William Johnson, hero of the Seven Years' War and superintendent of all Indian affairs in the north. "It's a long way. I want you to take Goliath. He'll get you there in half the time. And carry more grease to keep his army brand covered." Duncan held up his hand to stifle Ishmael's protest. "We have time to go to the stables so I can get you two better acquainted. You take Goliath, and Sarah and Will take Molly, it's better for all that way. Get the message to Patrick, then speed back to Edentown. You need to keep Sarah safe." He paused over his own words. Sarah had her foreboding dreams, but he was fighting his own terrible premonition that he would no longer be in them.

The Agawam navy, as the former sailor who ran the docks dubbed the town's odd collection of river craft, seemed to have been sucked up by some Atlantic waterspout and deposited on the upper Connecticut. Crowding the waterfront were sailing dinghies, whaleboats, fishing dories, and long sailing gigs, most of which had seen heavy service, as if they'd been borrowed from oceangoing vessels.

Duncan surveyed the battered smaller boats with dimming hope, then studied the docks. When he left to see Ishmael off—Goliath had shied away from the youth until Ishmael whispered in his ear—Conawago and Munro had been on the bank, apparently negotiating with the old sailor. Now they had disappeared. As a loon called out from upriver, Duncan contemplated with disappointment the prospect of rowing one of the unwieldy boats for dozens of miles. He was approaching the first dock when the loon called again, and he realized it was a most unlikely spot for the bird. With a grin, he saw Conawago waving from farther up the bank. Munro sat waiting in a long, sturdy canoe.

THE POWER OF THE WATER restored him. The vision of Sarah, who had not returned his embrace when she departed at dawn, stayed with him, clouding his thoughts for the first hour. Then Conawago turned and with a single questioning eye banished his darkness. Duncan instinctively recognized his expression.

It was one thing to be distracted from the true things when in towns, the Nipmuc had told him once, but to be so in the wilds was offensive to their spirits. Take the truth of the forest, he would say, or, as now, take the truth of the water. Be here, be now, the old Nipmuc had said, for this is the moment the spirits of nature have given to you.

Duncan grinned, touched his totem pouch, and put his back into his paddle. Here were no bountymen, here were no assassins. Here was the shimmering river that bound sky and land together, here was the sleek silver flash of the hungering trout, here were the crystal drops that rolled off his weathered oak paddle. A stag paused from drinking to watch them glide by. A wood duck, ablaze with color, surfaced, cocked its crested head at them, and dove again.

"*Jiyathontek,*" he heard Conawago say, then "*Joskawayendon, yoyanere.*" It was a chant of Mohawk warriors, used in the rhythmic paddling of canoes. *Hearken ye*, it meant, summoning the spirits, then *here again is wildness*, always emphasizing the strong first syllable on the downward stroke, *it is good.*

"*Jiyathontek,*" Duncan echoed as he matched Conawago's powerful stroke. "*Joskawayendon, yoyanere.*" After a few minutes he heard Munro, at the stern, take up the chant. The old Scot wasn't familiar with Mohawk traditions, but as a veteran of the sea he recognized a good work chant when he heard it.

Here and there the woods broke into open fields. Men worked plows behind teams. A boy perched on an overhanging willow with a fishing line paused to wave. They passed a southbound shallop stacked with casks of maple syrup, judging by the fragrant smell.

The fort at Charlestown was nearly a hundred miles north of Agawam, and as they made camp on an island of birches, Duncan estimated that they had covered at least half in their long day of paddling, putting them near the border of the New Hampshire colony. They were cooking trout over their campfire when a long shadow glided through the night toward them. Any doubt as to who was on board was allayed when, with an excited bark, a big black shape leapt off the bow of the dugout canoe, splashing through the water to reach them. Conawago laughed good-naturedly as Molly nuzzled him so energetically, he fell off the log he was balanced on.

Duncan shot up to grab the bow of the dugout and dragged it onto the little sandy beach. He recoiled for an instant as a small, furry creature leapt at him from the vessel; then it landed on his shoulder and patted his head like an old friend.

"Good evening, Princess Sadie," he said to the capuchin, returning the gesture. Solomon Hayes climbed out, straightening his ever-present cap, and stretched tired arms. The tinker shrugged. "The dog wanted to stay with the boy, and the boy insisted on coming north," he explained as Will Sterret sat up from the bottom of the dugout, rubbing sleep from his eyes. Hayes extracted a frying pan from his huge tinker's pack. "I brought a ham and cornmeal," he declared in a hopeful tone as he looked at the fish still waiting to be cooked. With a gleeful murmur Munro balanced the pan on the stones by the fire.

DUNCAN AWOKE WITH A START, out of a dream in which Sarah danced with another man. Her face had borne a serene happiness that Duncan had not seen for years. The man, lithe on his feet, stubbornly refused to turn his head even when Duncan called out to them. It was a silly, trivial image that he knew he should ignore, yet it stayed with him, feeling like a stone in his chest. He finally sat up, pushing aside his blanket, and tossed another log onto the fire. Molly rose and sat beside him.

Several minutes passed before he realized that Molly had twisted her head toward the northern end of the quarter-mile-long island. Solomon Hayes's blanket lay in a heap by his dugout. Duncan stepped to the fringe of sand that outlined the island and followed a set of shadowed footprints.

He found the tinker in a tiny cove fringed with white birches, sitting on the ground and writing by the light of a small whale oil lamp. He had two papers in front of him and was working with a quill, apparently referring to the text on the left before writing on the paper at his right. From time to time Hayes looked heavenward and spoke, often with a question in his voice, as if needing to calculate what to write. Straining to hear the words, Duncan inched forward, Molly patiently following. He halted fifty feet away. Hayes's voice was clearer now, but his words sounded like gibberish. He seemed to be reading from a small book on his lap, and every few moments he would dip his quill into a capped pewter inkwell and write. With a chill, Duncan realized he had. seen such actions before. Hayes was writing in code, using key words from the text as anchors for an alphabet shift. Such codes were common in certain high government and military circles.

It made no sense. There was no one to receive a coded document, no one to deliver it. Then he realized that the next day they would arrive at Charlestown and the busy fort at Township Number Four. Such a place would attract traders, French trappers, militiamen, and probably British soldiers, even frontier evangelists.

Duncan tried to recall who might have heard him speak of Ticonderoga. Conawago of course, Munro, and Sergeant Mallory. But the sergeant was moving westward for sanctuary at Edentown, and Duncan was certain that Hayes had not heard of his plans. Had Will overheard? Hayes would have had all day in their dugout to coax the information from the boy.

As Hayes kept busy at his writing, Duncan ventured a step closer. Then the tinker's coconspirator made a soft, chattering sound. Sadie was somewhere in a tree, keeping watch. Duncan bent low and retreated, Molly steadfastly at his heels.

He tried to sleep again, but each time he gained slumber, it was threaded with fragments of nightmares: Conawago lay dead, scalped, in a canoe drifting down a wide river. He turned a corner on a wilderness trail and found Will Sterret's head on a pole. Sarah and a stylishly dressed man were being married in the Old North Church, with Samuel Adams standing nearby, nodding his approval. In a recurring dream, he kept pursuing a cloaked man down a shadowed road but could never quite reach him. He passed a farm where a young girl wept, and when he stopped, she pointed to the bodies of her family and said the wanderer had written secret words on a page and everyone who touched it died. He ran harder after the man, the sorcerer, and found that he was now carrying the ancient battle-ax his grandfather had kept in his thatched house by the water. A fog descended over the evil wanderer, but the one time it cleared, Duncan glimpsed his face. It was Solomon Hayes.

As they pulled their canoe onto the bank below the Fort at Number Four, a young piglet charged out from a berry bush, emitting a high-pitched protest that Duncan at first thought was a challenge aimed at them. Then a barefooted girl of seven or eight years darted out of the shadows and captured the feisty creature with a long flying tackle.

"Gotcha!" she chortled, then, with only a quick, uninterested glance at the new arrivals, ran toward a giant maple where a brindle sow rooted in the ground, accompanied by several other piglets. More huge maples rose up like sentinels in a line pointing toward the fort, each with a draft horse, ram, bull, or ox relaxing under its shade.

"A fair!" Will exclaimed as he pointed to tables and tents arrayed along the log wall of the fort.

"The midsummer barter meeting!" explained a teenage boy who was tending a red ox. "Folks come for miles to see the best creatures of the north valley." Suddenly his eyes went round and he darted behind the ox for protection. As if taking his words as a cue, Sadie had poked her head out of Hayes's side pouch.

Munro made a sweeping gesture that took in Molly and the capuchin. "And have we not brought our best creatures then?"

The boy bravely extended his head around the ox's neck. "Is it some kind of weasel?" Both the boy and the ox seemed to watch in wonder as Sadie curled around Hayes's arm and climbed onto his shoulder. "I've seen martens and minks before, but never such a being as that!"

"Well, lad," the old Scot solemnly intoned, "we put my old auntie in a coffin for her wake and next morning that's what crawled out."

"Munro!" Hayes chided, but not before the boy had let out a squeal and fled toward the fort.

The establishment at Township Number Four was more of a fortified village than a military structure. Rows of sturdy cabins with shared walls flanked a large two-story building at the rear, with a taller tower built onto its southwestern corner. Conawago had explained that the fort had a noble history, for within its walls a tiny garrison had withstood a siege by a vastly larger French and Indian force in 1747 and then provided the sanctuary desperately needed by Rogers's rangers on their flight from their famous St. Francis raid in 1759. Duncan was convinced that that night in October nearly ten years earlier had only triggered a different confrontation, one that had been slowly playing out in all the years since. Had Rogers simply inflicted a wound that continued to seep, Duncan kept wondering, or had he somehow cracked open a secret that was suddenly coveted by kings?

The gathering along the road outside the fort's broad, open gate seemed less a fair than an extended picnic that wound around the packed earth roads of the village known as Charlestown. A collection of settlers behind a gaunt-looking clapboard church was singing hymns. In front of the church two elderly women stood at a table made of planks and trestles, serving out slices of pie on shingles. Half a dozen young men competed at throwing tomahawks at wooden slabs. Older men in plain homespun were examining the hooves and teeth of several draft horses tied to a picket line. As Duncan approached the gate, several children called out, some in glee, others in fear, and he turned to follow their gaze. Even those with the tomahawks stopped and were looking behind him. Will was parading Molly, with Sadie perched on the dog's back, her head held high like some queen of the wilds.

"So much for an unobtrusive entrance," Conawago muttered.

Duncan kept his head down as he passed through the high gate into the inner yard of the fort. He had assumed he could just ask a guard on duty where to find Corporal Ebenezer Brandt, but there was no guard. There was in fact no garrison. The famous old fort had more of the air of a shantytown, with laundry hanging on lines stretched between buildings and chickens scratching at the weeds around a flagpole from which a tattered Union Jack flew. By the stable, swallows darted at flies hovering over a pile of manure that almost reached the roof. Only two inhabitants were visible—an aged, toothless man on the porch of a house who hummed loudly as he worked his rocking chair, and a spindly woman stoking a fire under a kettle of foul-smelling lye, in the early stage of soap making.

The old crone cackled when Munro asked for Corporal Brandt, as if the Scot had told a good joke, then began stirring the contents of the kettle with what looked like a salvaged canoe paddle. When he asked again, she scowled.

"Great Ebenezer. 'Samuel took up a stone and set it between Mizpah and Shen.' He named it Ebenezer," she declared with a grin that revealed gums with only three teeth. "Says so right in the Book of Samuel."

"We're just looking for a former Indian fighter, not a biblical lesson, ma'am," Munro patiently replied.

She offered her disturbing grin again; then her gaze drifted to Conawago, who had tucked a duck feather in his hair, and she straightened her dirty calico dress. "A lass likes a pretty feather," she declared with mischief in her eyes, patting her tangled coif. Conawago nervously handed her the feather, and she pointed with her paddle toward the upper floor of the two-story structure.

They warily climbed the stairs of the watchtower that adjoined the building, pausing at the landing to listen to the military drumbeats coming from the second story.

"Form up, ye lazy stoats!" came an angry, high-pitched voice from inside. "Shoulder those arms. On yer right shoulder, ye ignorant sot! Ye call yerself a soldier? If the king saw ye, he would weep his eyes out. God help the women and children of this colony if this be the best the governor can send!"

Munro, in the lead, inched up the stairs to the slightly ajar door, then pointed to a new broadside fastened to the door with a horseshoe nail.

INDIAN RAID! the sheet announced in large, bold type, under which was a report of the recent bloody raid on Worcester by a party of savages from the north. Governor Bernard had petitioned Governor Wentworth of New Hampshire to allow him to send a company of militia up the Connecticut.

They stared in silence at the paper.

"Sounds like the company's arrived," Munro whispered, then motioned to Duncan and edged open the door.

The only occupant of the cavernous hall was in fact a short, stick-thin man at the far end of the room, holding a musket on his shoulder. He jerked, starting with surprise as he spied them, then marched double time to a rack of arms in the center of the wall. Duncan reached him as he leaned the musket into an empty place on the rack.

"Exercising the guns. Got to exercise the guns," the scrawny stranger declared in his high voice. The stubble on his jaw was a salt-and-pepper mixture that matched the color of his unkempt hair. His waistcoat and britches were much repaired, with patches of various colors.

"Corporal Brandt?" Duncan asked as the man stepped to a workbench where a musket had been disassembled for repair.

He fixed Duncan with a hopeful expression, then straightened, tucked the powder horn that hung from his neck into his shirt, and tapped his forehead with a knuckle.

Duncan realized the man's assumption and shook his head. "Not the militia." As Brandt sagged, he added, "I served in Woolford's rangers."

Brandt brightened. "Cat in the night, we used to call Captain Woolford. The major's favorite officer for night scouts—said the Mohawks taught him well. He and the major would get drunk together whenever they returned from a mission. Never in the field, never touched a drop in the field. Cat in the night. Who comes to kill, who comes to kill," he cackled.

With a chill Duncan remembered the call, used by some rangers in the night, mimicking the rhythm of the barred owl's call, which he had learned as *who drank my tea, who drank my tea.*

"Major Rogers, you mean?" Munro asked.

"In the field," Brandt said with a distant expression. "That's where we do the killing. Got to wait for it, the major would say. Wait for it. Most men will shoot as soon as they see the enemy, but not us. We wait until they are almost on us." Brandt gestured to a tattered paper nailed to the wall, bearing a list of numbered items. "Rule thirteen. Reserve your fire 'til the enemy be near, then discharge and rush with hatchet or tomahawk." Rogers's twenty-eight rules of ranging had proved so effective that the British army had reprinted and distributed them to all its units in America. "Wait 'til ye smell the stink of sour wine on Frenchie's breath before ye announce yer presence, he would tell us, though he never wrote that one down," the jittery man said with a cackling laugh.

Brandt lifted a twist of tobacco, stained with gun oil, from the bench and bit off a piece. "They say those pretty white flowers grow where a man bleeds out. Bloodroot." Brown tobacco juice dribbled down his grizzled jaw. "We left snow-white flowers all over the north. No need to keep night watch anymore, I says to the major, cause the ghosts will keep 'em all away."

Munro stepped forward. "Do you know Josiah Chisholm?"

Brandt eyed the badge on Munro's waistcoat. "Forty-Second of Foot," he declared. "I came back to Ticonderoga from a scout that day in '57. Gawd, we dropped a lot of black-and-green plaid into holes that week. Took days to bury 'em all."

"I almost filled a hole myself," Munro announced.

Brandt's drifting, almost deranged demeanor suddenly disappeared, and his pale gray eyes took on a more calculating look. "I knew Chisholm, sure, made sergeant by the end of the war. The only one killed in that Worcester raid, folks say. Saved a lot of men on our flight from St. Francis." Brandt spat into a ceramic pot on the workbench, then, as if forgetting they were there, turned and set to work, lifting a cocking mechanism out of a tub of oil.

"I'd like to hear about St. Francis, Corporal," Duncan said to his back.

Brandt paused, but did not turn from the bench. "Two hundred fifteen of the enemy killed. One of us killed. Except for those eaten, hacked, or burned on the way back. They say that Italian fella Dante described all the levels of hell, but we discovered a whole new one that October. That's the telling of it."

"I was hoping for a bit more detail," Duncan observed.

Oddly, Brandt's hand felt for the powder horn he had stuffed inside his waistcoat. "That's the telling of it," he repeated, as if that was all a stranger deserved to hear.

Duncan extracted the strip of cloth with embroidered leaves and fish he had recovered in Worcester and dropped it in front of Brandt. "This was stuffed in Chisholm's mouth. Another one in the mouth of Daniel Oliver the week before. An Abenaki from St. Francis killed them both."

The corporal stared at the cloth for a moment; then his gaze drifted, and his eyes lost their focus. "No good. Just a town of death."

"Mog." Munro's single syllable sent Brandt instantly into a fighting crouch.

The former ranger slowly straightened, spat out his wad of his tobacco, and once more tightened his arm against his powder horn. "He be the animal we sought more than any, he be the reason why the major privately said the raid wasn't over even after we returned."

"He is the one who killed Chisholm and Oliver," Duncan explained.

"T'ain't a story for daylight."

"There must be a tavern near," Conawago suggested.

Brandt finally turned back to face them. "They call it the Bear's Tooth. Bring a bear tooth to the proprietor and he gives a free ale. A bear chewed off two of his fingers onc't. At the end of the street past the church. Don't kill the doves flying inside, they be pets of his wife."

"An hour after sunset, then," Conawago suggested.

Munro, who had been studying Brandt with an intense curiosity, hesitated as Duncan and Conawago headed toward the door. "Reckon I'll stay and help with the guns," he said, and the old infantryman lifted one of the dirty muskets from the rack.

Outside, the grounds inside the fort were still deserted except for the soap maker and the scarecrow on the porch, still rocking. Beyond the gate, however, the modest fair had become more festive. Will and Molly were on the steps of the mercantile, messily sharing a piece of blueberry pie. Two young men, wood chips clinging to their bare backs, were competing in a rail-splitting contest to hoots of encouragement from onlookers. Brawny farmers and their sons were engaged in a friendly tug-of-war. The older men, several smoking pipes now, still clustered around the draft horses, apparently engaged in trading. Duncan felt a pang of regret for not having Goliath as half a dozen younger men, and younger horses, assembled at a line of flour laid on the grass, readying to race. "A penny on the chestnut mare," he offered.

Conawago made no reply. Duncan followed his gaze toward a large pine, in the shade of which several men were gathered around someone sitting on a blanket. As he stepped with his friend toward the tree, he saw that several of the standing men wore their long hair in braids. They were natives, all but two wearing European clothing. At the edge of the group stood Noah, Occom's stoic elder. They were all listening to Solomon Hayes.

It was, he realized, the perfect venue for obtaining and sharing secrets from the north. His anger at Hayes rose like a slow fire in his belly. The likelihood that the tinker's nighttime code writing was for the benefit of the French had been gnawing at him all day. Duncan had been ill used for too long. He might not understand the strange game Hayes played, but he knew without a doubt the man had been deceiving them. Sarah was no longer there to protect the tinker.

He had begun inching toward Hayes when Conawago placed a restraining hand on his arm. "No," the old Nipmuc said in a surprisingly insistent voice. "Let him go about his business."

"He mocks us!" Duncan protested. "He keeps secrets from us!"

"As do we all," Conawago observed.

"He pretends to be impoverished, with patches on his waistcoat and holes in his shoes, but then he hands out guineas as if they were buttons." He saw now that Hayes had laid out goods on his blanket and was describing the redeeming qualities of his frying pans, sewing needles, writing quills, penknives, pewter thimbles, colorful ribbons, and strands of glass beads.

"He is a wretched soul who has lost his family," Conawago pointed out.

"He writes secretly at night, writes what Will says is gibberish. They are coded papers, I am certain."

A strange pain crossed Conawago's countenance. "Duncan, you don't—"

"Noah! You sorry piece of weasel gristle!" The thunderous voice that interrupted them belonged to an ox of a man who now pushed past them, his thick arms spread wide as he approached the native elder. Noah, standing straight and somber, betrayed his acquaintance with the stranger with only a momentary flash of amusement in his eyes. The big, black-bearded man pounded his back, then turned with exaggerated surprise toward Hayes. "God's teeth, boys!" he exclaimed to his two companions. "T'is the king of wanderers hisself!"

Duncan cocked his head at the rough-looking newcomer who, like his two companions, was clad in the leather jerkin favored more by wilderness trappers than by farmers. All three wore tomahawks and knives in their belts, and ornately decorated powder horns hung from their shoulders.

The bearded man turned back to Noah. "Is it true? Your soul snatcher has made it back across the Atlantic?"

Duncan saw both amusement and regret in the elder's eyes as he nodded toward the knot of worshippers behind the church. Occom and his own band of elders, split off from Wheelock, had arrived at Charlestown. He wondered why Noah was separated from the others, and as Conawago pushed forward to meet the strangers, Duncan retreated a few steps, then slipped away toward the church.

He worked his way inconspicuously along the street leading to the church, pausing at a table that was dispensing cider, then exchanging pleasantries with an old tribal woman who was selling exquisitely worked baskets. Something heavy pressed against his leg, and he looked down to see Molly nudging a greeting. He knelt and wiped away shreds of blueberry pie from her thick neck hair, and they both waited while Will approached, cradling a familiar bulge in his shirt.

"She's asleep," the boy said of Sadie. "Everyone loved her, gave us pie for free and cider for free, and I was thinking of charging a ha'penny for people to pet her when some old witch of a woman pointed at her and squawked that she was the imp of Lucifer. People began backing away; then she said she knew a prayer from the mountains of Wales that could turn the beast to dust. No one stayed then."

"Best get the princess back to Hayes," Duncan advised, the tinker's name bitter on his tongue.

Will nodded, but did not move. "Funny, ain't it. All the Indians are with the tinker, and the Indian preacher only speaks to Europeans."

Duncan hesitated and studied the two assemblies. The boy was right. "Best get her back," he said again, and gestured the boy toward Hayes. As Will hurried away, Duncan spied a fallen log on which articles of clothing had been left by the men stripped down for the tug-of-war. He glanced about, then borrowed a large tricorn hat and stepped around the little clapboard church.

Pulling the hat low, he stood at the edge of Occom's makeshift congregation. It wasn't a liturgy Occom was reciting, but something rather like the pitch of a merchant. Joining midstream in what was apparently a long speech, Duncan couldn't quite grasp what the native pastor was asking of his listeners. Occom spoke of the land to the north, the blessings of nature, and the importance of strong backs in building strong minds. Only when Occom summoned an Indian youth who had been sitting on a bench along the rear wall of the church did Duncan understand.

The boy began singing. "*Ehstehn yayan deh tsaun we jisus ahattonia,*" he sang in a surprisingly rich tenor. "*One watch wado-kwi norrwa ndasqua entri.*"

The words were Huron, but so many Christians along the St. Lawrence had adopted the song that Duncan had frequently heard it in northern longhouses.

The boy switched to English. " 'Within a lodge of broken bark the tender babe was found, a ragged robe of rabbit skin enwrapped his beauty round.'" It was called the Huron Carol and written by a Jesuit missionary living among the northern tribes in the prior century.

A woman near Duncan dabbed at a tear. "So beautiful," another whispered.

Occom laid a hand on the boy's shoulder as he finished. "The savage in all of us can be tamed," he declared. "The once-wild spirit can be a messenger of the Lord. Luke here would stand with your sons in the classrooms you will build on the banks of the Connecticut."

Wheelock's college. This was all about Wheelock's college, Duncan realized. Another man would have felt betrayed when the pious Wheelock proclaimed that Occom's dream for the funds he so painstakingly collected had been superseded by Wheelock's own dream, but Samson Occom had swallowed his bitterness and was now plowing the ground for Wheelock's college of the north, readying it for the seeds Wheelock would plant. He was also preparing the local population for the integration of at least a few tribal students with their own offspring. Occom had lost his war but was hoping to win at least one battle.

Duncan pulled his hat still lower as Occom surveyed his audience. "There will be a good living made for years by those who join in the construction of the great college," the pastor pointed out, "and opportunities for Christian charity at every step. There will be orphans of both red and white skin, like Luke here, who will be candidates for admission if they could but find good families to support them."

With an audible sob a sturdy-looking woman stepped from the crowd and wrapped her arms around Luke.

"Praise the Lord," Occom declared. The assembly quickly echoed his words. "And tomorrow," he added, looking directly at Duncan now, "when Reverend Wheelock arrives with the detachment of redcoats, they will gape in amazement at the prodigious size of Charlestown's heart."

Some of the assembly began clapping. One man raised an arm and shouted "Huzzah!" Occom kept looking at Duncan. He had recognized him and inserted a warning into his words to the crowd. Duncan backed away. He returned the hat to the log, stepping aside for a goat pulling a cart with two young girls in it, then decided to look for the tavern.

He was sitting against a big maple across from the tavern, sharpening his knife with slow, contemplative sweeps over his whetstone, when Conawago found him.

"Troops are coming," the old Nipmuc announced as he sat beside Duncan. "Regulars, from Boston they say."

"Who told you this?" Duncan asked.

In answer Conawago pointed to Noah, who approached now from between two heavy farm wagons. "The reverend warned me," Duncan said to the elder. "He must have spoken to the fort's commander."

"There is no commander, just that drunken old soldier who hasn't left Fort Four in nearly two years," Noah explained. "He is obsessed with the raid on St. Francis, according to a town councilman. We delivered a dispatch to the council, ordering them to make ready accommodation and fodder for a dozen dragoons."

"Dragoons would need a flatboat for their horses. There weren't any in Agawam when we left. That means they are a day or two behind us at least."

"The message said to expect Reverend Wheelock," Noah continued, "as if the soldiers were escorting him. But his followers tend to exaggerate things, to make him sound like some kind of royalty. Just a coincidence that they are coming together, I suspect."

His followers, Noah had said, as if he no longer counted himself among them. "Reverend Occom says that Wheelock's college will be an oasis in the wilderness," Duncan observed, to gauge Noah's reaction.

The tribal elder betrayed no emotion, only silently returned Duncan's stare. "The tinker leaves in the morning. He knows this land. Go with him."

"I do not trust the tinker," Duncan said. "He keeps too many secrets."

"Secrets of life, secrets of death, secrets of gods. Is that not why all of us go north?" Noah asked. "His secrets are only of his heart."

Duncan wiped his blade on the grass, returned it to his sheath, and looked up, not certain how to take the words.

"When I was a boy," Noah said, gazing at a distant mountain, "my grandfather would disappear for weeks at a time. Once, I asked him where he went. He said to the mountains because that's where men are free, where he could run with the stags. I grew up thinking there was some paradise in the wilds of the north where all creatures loved one another. Later I realized it was just a wide land where few people lived, white or red. But then the men from the north taught the world better," he said, gesturing at a boulder a few feet from where Duncan sat.

Duncan looked in confusion, back and forth from the big rock to the elder. Then he saw that the flat face of the boulder had letters carved in it. He rose and knelt at the stone, chipping away some of the encrusted lichen. "P-h-" he read, then peeled off more of the crust. "Phineas Stevens."

"This is where it began," Noah said. "Under this very tree."

Duncan looked up at the broad limbs as if he might find an answer there. "I don't follow," he confessed.

"When the distrust started, when the despair and hatred started. In 1746."

Duncan glanced at Conawago. It was the blood-soaked year of the Battle of Culloden, in the faraway Highlands, the year Duncan's family had been slaughtered by the English.

"Phineas was escorting some women who had been milking cows. Some French and Abenaki leapt out of cover and killed him in cold blood. A few months later, hundreds came from the north and besieged the fort. I met them on their way back after they had given up the siege. I asked one of the French officers why they had to kill all the time. He said because God and their king said so." Noah shrugged. "The war was long. Braddock's massacre. Lake George. Niagara. The Fort William Henry massacre. Ticonderoga. Quebec. St. Francis. I still don't understand it."

"The war?"

"Not war as such. The treachery men commit on behalf of gods and kings."

Duncan had no answer. He finished cleaning away the debris to make the name on the rock legible again.

"Is it true," asked the sachem in Christian clothes, "that all those men who died in Boston did so for a secret paper?"

"Thirty-seven. Most as they slept."

Noah gave a heavy sigh. "In the tribes we are taught that when a man dies in his sleep, his soul will be unprepared and confused. When my grandfather lay dying, he insisted that we hit him with switches to keep him awake until the end came." He seemed to consider Duncan's words. "And my friend Jonathan Pine?"

Duncan realized he shouldn't be surprised. Many of the Christian Indians in New England knew each other. "He died," Duncan said. "He wasn't asleep."

Noah held Duncan's gaze for several moments. "I don't know if I should resent you or thank you for saying no more than that."

"Thank him," Conawago inserted. "Just know that Pine died well, saving that boy's life," he added, extending a hand toward Will, who was now skipping along the street with Molly at his side.

"How do you know that big brute of a man?" Duncan asked after a moment, nodding toward the bearded figure who had greeted Noah earlier, now on the steps of the general store, laughing with his companions.

"A friend of the tribes. He brings food sometimes to the old ones in the winter, though I wonder if it may be just so they will sign his papers."

"Papers?"

"Papers for land."

"Deeds?"

Noah nodded. "Deeds. He collects deeds for land that no one has ever owned, then trades them in the settlements like animal skins. I said to him once that I do not comprehend how land can be reduced to a piece of paper, that the land belongs to the gods. He laughed and said no need for me to understand, only necessary that a proper English magistrate understands." He shrugged. "If not him, it would be another. He has a big heart." Noah glanced at the bearded frontiersman then fixed Duncan with an amused gaze. "Later I suspect he will take off his shirt, set a shilling on a stump, and invite all comers to wrestle him," he added, as if in invitation, then produced three apples from a belt pouch. He distributed two to his companions, then bit into the third. "In the mountains to the north there are places no man could track you," he said to Duncan in a pointed tone. "Mountains of bare earth and heather. Rather like Scotland, I fancy."

"I am not fleeing," Duncan replied.

"We are all fleeing something. Sinners flee their priests. Saints flee their temptations. That's what the Christians would say."

Duncan silently studied the elder, who had lived so many years as a Christian, had even joined the devout Apostles of Reverend Wheelock. Was he having a crisis of faith? Or had he worn the Christian clothes as a shelter, as a mask to flee something himself? His gaze drifted back to the boulder, and he realized that while those who carved the name meant to honor the dead man, there would be others, from the wilderness, who might see it as a monument to rebellion.

Conawago spoke in a near whisper. "We both had teachers before the Christians."

"Yes," Noah replied in a cracking voice. "The biggest mistake Christians make is to think only Christians can speak with gods." He looked toward Reverend Occom, and for a moment it seemed as though he would weep.

His gaze on the tavern entrance, Duncan lingered with Munro on one of the benches set up for an evening Scripture service, half listening to a pair of adolescent sisters sing old hymns. Will and Sadie tossed a hard-boiled egg back and forth on the torch-lit street, to the delight of a dozen boys. Hayes seemed to have disappeared again.

As the sisters concluded with an off-pitch rendition of the Doxology, one of the lay leaders rose and solemnly announced that he would lead a prayer for the brave.

"Pray keep courage and faith resolute in one who has given us so much," the man in dark homespun intoned. "In this hour of greatest need, may he who has given us so much know our faith in him remains steadfast."

It was not a prayer for the brave in general, Duncan realized, but for a specific brave man. "Beg pardon," he said to the young farmer beside him. "Who is it we are praying for?"

"The great hero, of course. May he be freed soon so those Worcester raiders can feel the same righteous fist that saved us from the devils of St. Francis."

"Major Rogers?" Duncan asked. "Freed from where?"

"Freed from his torment, freed from false accusation."

"Accusation?"

The man fixed Duncan with a reproving gaze. "Ain't ye heard? Major Robert Rogers, the great liberator of the frontier, is being held in Canada, kept in chains on charges of treason!"

11

DUNCAN SPENT ANOTHER AGONIZING HOUR waiting for Brandt to appear, his heart heavy with the news of Robert Rogers. Patrick Woolford had written to Edentown months earlier with the welcome report that Rogers, hero of the frontier, had won command of the garrison at Michilimackinac, the British fort in the far northwest. Duncan and Woolford had both assumed that Rogers would be there for years, for it was the ideal location for the major to pursue his dream of discovering the elusive Northwest Passage to the Pacific. But now someone in the government had decided that Rogers, like Duncan, should hang. Duncan had only briefly met Rogers in an Albany tavern years earlier. Horatio Beck, who had gone to Ticonderoga to examine records of the St. Francis raid, had surely known of the charges against Rogers. Did Beck think Duncan and Rogers were connected in some conspiracy?

His eyes kept drifting toward Hayes, who had resumed trading with the various strangers who wandered over to his outstretched blanket of goods. He was selling ribbons and writing lead and the odd spoon or fork, and from the snippets of conversation Duncan caught he seemed as interested in learning about conditions in the north as in selling his wares. He heard a solitary tribesman deny any interest in trading, but Hayes called him closer and spoke in low tones with the man, then gave him a slip of paper and a tin mug, which the man accepted with a nod, carefully stowing the note in a pouch at his belt.

When Brandt finally appeared, stiffly marching with a weapon on his shoulder, as if on a parade ground, Duncan was instantly on his feet. Munro put a hand on his arm. "Let him work on his thirst for a while. I gave him a half shilling as a token of our friendship, and he'll be eager to spend it. After three or four pints our conversation will go a mite easier."

Thirty minutes later they found the wiry corporal sitting at a table by the hearth, staring at his powder horn, which now lay on the table before him. From above came an unexpected cooing. Duncan recalled that the proprietor's wife kept pet doves.

"Sorry to hear of yer predicament," the corporal said as Duncan pulled up a chair.

Duncan cast an uneasy glance at Munro. The Scot, who had cannily worked his way into conversations with the townspeople, had told Duncan that Brandt, who had lost his family early in the last war, had long ago ceased being paid by the government. He had become a self-appointed sentinel at the fort, living on the generosity of the settlers, who would never let a St. Francis ranger starve. Recently, however, he'd been unexpectedly paying off all his old debts. Dismissed by many as a harmless fool, he was fastidious in his care of the modest arsenal, as if always expecting an attack. But what had Munro told Brandt of Duncan?

"I conveyed to the corporal how yer betrothed got dragged away by her unhappy father to his farm in the Champlain country," Munro explained as Conawago settled beside Duncan. "It's why ye need to hasten to Ticonderoga and find a boat to the north end of the lake," he added, and turning from Duncan's withering glance, he called for the barmaid.

Brandt drained his tankard and ordered another. "Must be a beautiful thing," he observed with a dip of his head.

The man's high, scratchy voice and his mannerisms so reminded Duncan of a rooster that he had to clamp his jaw to stifle a grin. "I'm sorry?" Duncan asked.

Brandt lifted his tankard to Duncan. "True love, son, true love."

Munro was able to turn the laugh that rose in his throat into a polite cough.

"I am eager indeed to reach Ticonderoga," Duncan said. "How is the trail?"

"Trail, you say? Nay, t'is a military road. Didn't the good major and I work to finish it, all the way to Crown Point. Good to have our hands busy after the return. Heavy hearts need busy hands, my ma used to say. Bless her soul." The corporal dabbed at an eye.

"Heavy hearts—after St. Francis, you mean," Duncan suggested.

"The 'Nakis had scalped and burned and butchered all across the frontier, from Maine to Champlain and down into Massachusetts. We stopped 'em good, didn't we? Never the same after that October dawn. 'Take 'em down,' the major says, 'take 'em all down. Too many of us have buried children and women. Let 'em choke on their medicine.' That was the speech he gave when we gathered in the dark. 'Let 'em feel the fist of good King George,' the major says. May God rest that royal gentleman," the corporal added with a dip of his tankard. That king, the second George, had died a year later.

Brandt quieted, and seemed to lose himself in the dancing flames of the hearth. He spoke abruptly, in a distant voice now. "The babies are screaming, but nothing like their mothers when they see them covered in blood. One threw her infant from her breast into the river rather than see it killed in front of her. I wake in the night hearing them screams. But we had to do it, don't ye see? 'They have to choke on their own medicine,' the major says. 'Have they not slaughtered the babies of settlers for decades?'" Brandt made a stabbing motion, as if with an imaginary knife. Conawago and Duncan exchanged a worried glance. Brandt did not seem entirely tethered to reality.

"'Just a little boy, he has a bad foot,' one cries. A woman holds up a papist cross over her breast. 'But yer Bible says an eye for an eye,' my lieutenant shouts to her."

"What did you find there?" Conawago asked. "In the battle, did you discover something surprising?"

Brandt hesitated. "They was dead, and then not dead." The corporal still spoke to the fire. "They ran into the Jesuit church for safety, but as the fire spread through the town, the blaze reached it, too. I saw several, a 'Naki grandmother with a gray streak on top of her head like a polecat, with a little girl clutching a cornhusk doll, and a Jesuit priest. But except for the back chamber of stone, the church was all wood. It went up like an inferno. God, the screams." Brandt went quiet and gulped down more ale. "We never wanted that, not for the church to burn, not for all those Christian women and children to die like that. But an hour later, as we formed up to retreat, there they were, on the slope above us, at the edge of the forest with their town burning below them. Alive again. That grandmother and the little 'Naki girl with her doll, and that priest with a bunch of children, all just watching him."

Duncan recalled what Chisholm had said when asked about Brandt. *Not all who seem crazy are insane.* "Him?"

"The major. I told him. Dead and risen again."

"They must have gone out a window," Munro pointed out.

"Nary a chance. We had posted men to be sure no one else escaped from the church. Several warriors had run in there at the beginning of the fighting."

They sipped at their ales. "Did the major acknowledge them?" Duncan asked. "As if he knew them?"

Brandt slowly nodded. "At least the priest. He seemed to be waiting. It was as if they knew each other." Brandt shrugged. "Know the land before ye attack, the ranger rules say."

Duncan chewed on a piece of sausage left by the barmaid, gauging the nervous corporal who had survived the St. Francis expedition. "You mean he had a secret informer."

"Wouldn't be doing his job if he didn't."

"You said the priest and the others waited, as if they had to confirm something?"

The old ranger frowned and sipped at his ale before replying. "When they saw him, they didn't run. That's why I remembered. Major Rogers, he was like a demon to most 'Naki. They were superstitious about him, truly scared of him. But not these, not that old woman and the papist. The major held something up above his head. A white doeskin pouch with those flowers that 'Naki women like to embroider with threads and quills. The priest held a hand above his own head and made a motion. Funny, I thought, it was like a ranger sign, made a fist, then spread his fingers as he waved in a spiral motion. For a ranger it would mean disperse and hide in the forest. But how would a priest know that?"

"Had Rogers gone into the church before the raid?" Duncan asked.

"Not that morning. But he made a reconnaissance the night before."

Duncan remembered the romantic stories that had been published about Rogers's grand St. Francis adventure. While they varied considerably, they all agreed on one thing, based on Rogers's own official report—Rogers had gone into St. Francis the night before the raid. He was fluent in Canadian French and passed himself off as a casual traveler. He had done so, he said, to assess the strength of the enemy, but what if he also met an ally inside the town and perhaps told him to ready a parcel for him to retrieve during the raid?

"Did the church burn to the ground?" Munro asked.

Brandt, staring intensely into his ale now, seemed not to hear. "People hide up in their rafters and lofts, thinking they'll escape notice. They'll have no chance when the flames engulf them." His face hardened. "There's trophy poles everywhere, even in front of the church. At least a score of scalps on every pole. Hundreds of scalps. The 'Nakis even ripped the hair off little girls. There's a special pole of nothing but scalps of long, straw-colored hair, some still with ribbons in them. God's blood, but they scream. The air is full of smoke and the stench of blood and burning flesh. A dog runs by me, all on fire. We gotta keep order, dammit, like good English soldiers. Ain't gonna be coming for us for a day or two, the major says, so we'll get a good start toward Number Four. Safe Number Four. Blessed Number Four."

The barmaid brought a plate of fried apples, but no one seemed interested in eating now. From the street came the ragged sound of fife and drums, inexpertly played.

"How would the major know that?" Conawago asked. "How would he know they wouldn't follow for a day or two?"

Strangely, Brandt suddenly became aware of the powder horn in front of him and, with a nervous glance at his companions, covered it with his hands. "The major, he knows everything." He looked about the tavern, back in the present now. "He's 'bout the greatest hero folks in these parts have ever known. I remember that day we finally arrived here. They didn't come after us right away, but when they came, they was an army of demons. We had to split up and take indirect routes to throw them off. We were more dead than alive, all played out, and near starved to death as we marched through the gate. Little more than a few mushrooms and raw acorns for a week and more. As soon as folks here see us, they begin cheering. 'Huzzah, huzzah, the saviors from the north!' they call, and we stood tall and straightened the rags of our uniforms."

"And you came back here after the war?" Duncan asked.

"It's the refuge, don't ye know. Rangers need a refuge to make ready fer the next battle. We ain't done with the 'Nakis, I know that in my bones. Gotta keep ready, wait for orders."

Duncan leaned toward Brandt. "So the next battle is to free the hero from his chains."

Brandt looked up in alarm, glancing nervously at the other tavern patrons.

"Keep yer voice down!" he whispered, and slowly nodded. "A misunderstanding is all. He ain't any more a traitor than you." Duncan and Conawago exchanged an ironic glance.

One of the resident doves flew through the rafters overhead, shedding a small downy body feather as it flew. Brandt stared at it with the fascination of a small child as it drifted over their table; then he made an unsuccessful attempt to grab it, his action pushing it in another direction.

Duncan gestured to the powder horn that Brandt kept fingering. "I remember rangers who etched their stories on their horns. Is that one about St. Francis?" As he slowly extended his hand, trying to reach the horn, Brandt snatched it away, tucking it under his arm. "Not yer nevermind, nevermind, nevermind," he echoed. His high voice was getting hoarse.

"I seem to recall," Conawago observed, "that Major Rogers tended to argue with British officers as energetically as he fought the French king."

The old corporal gazed at the Nipmuc with half-lidded eyes. He seemed to be sinking into an intoxicated torpor, and then he bent toward Conawago, his eyes burning with sudden energy. "T'ain't spit and polish what wins a battle, it's guts and vinegar, it's moving through the forest as stealthy as a catamount, it's standing to reload even though the bullets be flying around you and piss be running down yer leg." Brandt drained his tankard and grew more solemn. "The major won the battles, but the generals who despised him got all the rewards."

Conawago pushed the plate of apples toward the corporal and signaled for more ale. "It's enough to make a man bitter," the Nipmuc observed.

"It's him what wrote the book of ranging rules that the damned lobsterbacks now teach their own soldiers. He should have been made one of those knights or dukes or such."

Duncan leaned forward and whispered. "Is it the army that now accuses the major?"

"God rot 'em, yes! Because he wants to save this great land from the likes of those pissant generals!" Brandt looked down at the table. The stink of ale was heavy on his breath. "He sent me a letter a few months ago," the scrawny corporal confided.

"A letter from the hero of St. Francis must have been an occasion for all here at the fort to celebrate," Conawago suggested. "You probably read it out loud to all the town."

Brandt flinched at the words, and he craned his head, surveying the tavern's customers with sudden suspicion. When he looked back, his eyes narrowed. "Once a ranger, always a ranger." Brandt knuckled his forehead. "Knights of the forest," he recited. It was one of the slogans ranger officers used for recruiting.

"You make it sound like he gave you a mission, Corporal," Duncan observed. "Written in purple ink perhaps." He pushed down the temptation to ask if Brandt had also received a gold coin. He had been paying off his debts.

The grizzled ranger fixed him with a bristling gaze. "Ye'll get burned poking yer finger in someone else's fire."

"Once a ranger, always a ranger," Duncan repeated. "I was a ranger," he reminded Brandt. "So were Branscomb, Oliver, and Chisholm."

Conawago placed a hand on Duncan's arm as if worried that he was pushing the unsteady corporal too hard, but Duncan pushed anyway. "I supposed a man as cunning as Rogers could find ways to get messages even while he is in prison."

Brandt's eyes flared. Duncan had found the line he could not cross. The corporal pressed his arm more tightly around his powder horn. "Damned few he can trust," Brandt shot back. "Who else but the faithful from '59? Branscomb, Oliver, and Chisholm were with me in that special hell, sure. The man who stands beside ye when the 'Nakis come screaming down the hillside to eat yer heart, that's the one ye can rely on."

Duncan leaned close to the old ranger. "There's a new call from the north," he whispered. "Saguenay."

Brandt's eyes suddenly burned with a new light, and he began frantically searching the pockets of his much-patched waistcoat, finally extracting a leather-wrapped bullet like the one Daniel Oliver had worn around his neck. He stared at it, all signs of drunkenness gone, then gripped the ranger amulet tightly and stood, staggering only slightly. With a determined glint, he marched out the rear door of the tavern.

"Ten, eleven, twelve," Munro counted as the red-coated figures climbed out of the whaleboats on the river below them. "A dozen lobsterbacks plus an officer. Tough-looking bastards. They all have long swords. Dragoons, like Noah said. Dragoons like at Worcester."

Duncan and his friends had crossed the river in the dim light before daybreak. He pushed back an alder branch to see the soldiers more clearly. "Dragoons need horses," he observed.

Munro nodded. "Odd for them to arrive at dawn," he said. "They must have been rowing in shifts through the night." As he spoke, two more whaleboats appeared out of the river mist, one manned by a bedraggled group of men who wore red bands around their arms—the Massachusetts militia sent by the governor. Duncan puzzled over the black uniforms in the second boat. Then he saw the man sitting on the central thwart, a broad-rimmed hat on his head and a black book in his hand. Wheelock and his Christian soldiers were bringing up the rear of the flotilla from Agawam.

Someone on the fort ramparts gave a sharp whistle. Someone else near the gate began energetically blowing a tin horn. Men and women began appearing—some rising from blankets laid out near slumbering livestock—and watched as the soldiers marched in a column of two toward the fort.

"Wheelock's not going to have the pomp he was expecting for his arrival," Conawago observed, his words filled with foreboding. The soldiers had not waited for the reverend, for they had a mission and were not interested in ceremony. They had to be part of the dragoon company Beck had been riding with. Duncan nodded grimly, then pulled on his pack, lifted his rifle, and set out for Lake Champlain.

The rough track they followed could be considered a road only with the same hyperbole that the military used in calling a hill with a trench a fortification. No doubt the army had urgently dispatched troops to clear the path during the war to make it passable for wagons of materiel, but in many places it was now so heavily rutted by intersecting creeks and so crowded with undergrowth that no wheeled vehicle could pass. By midmorning they reached a verdant mountain range that stretched to the north, and they had to climb around a tangle of trees that had tumbled down a steep slope in an avalanche. They passed over enough straight, clear sections, however, that Duncan found himself pining for Goliath, who would have taken joy in stretching his legs over such terrain. The thought made him gaze westward, wondering if he would ever see the horse or even Ishmael again. The task he had given the young Nipmuc had been almost impossible, and more than once he chided himself for pushing the youth to undertake it on a stolen dragoon mount.

"So is he truly touched in the head," came a voice over his shoulder, "or was the corporal putting on a cunning act for us?"

Duncan paused to let Conawago catch up with him. The old Nipmuc had been lost in worried contemplation ever since they'd left the Connecticut. "I have been weighing our time in the tavern with Brandt," his friend said. "Is he a lunatic on a mission or a sane man on a lunatic mission?"

They walked a few more paces. A pine grouse flew across their path. "Perhaps both. He is a man alone," Conawago continued. "His life was defined by his time with the rangers, and the St. Francis raid has tainted his mind. He has lost the scent of battle, lost his commander, lost his brothers. The unsteady mind of the old ranger drifted without those anchors to hold it. But did you see his eyes when he rose from the table last night? You lit a fire in him that burned away his alcohol. Your words triggered something inside him, as if he suddenly had to commence his mission."

"I think Major Rogers, lying in chains, has finally given him orders, through the one who writes in purple ink."

Munro, now walking beside them, had been listening. "T'weren't no rough musket he brought to the tavern last night. It was a ranger's gun, a lovingly maintained long rifle that he leaned against the wall when he arrived. He was planning to leave, at least the part of him that's a ranger was planning so," Munro said, as if he had decided that Brandt, who had lost his family in Indian raids and experienced the horrors of the St. Francis expedition and who knew many other violent encounters, was made of several broken parts.

"And he kept his powder horn hidden," Duncan said. "He didn't want me to study it, snatched it away when I tried."

"But he showed it to me," Munro explained, "up in the hall when it was just the two of us. I admired the handiwork and told him I had etched my battles on my own, so he showed me. Seemed like the usual images a soldier in the field makes. A bear, a stag. A star-shaped fortress at one end and another box like a fort at the other, connected by a rambling line."

"Ticonderoga is star shaped," Conawago observed, "and Number Four is a box."

"Aye, connected by the line that is this road. And there were images spaced along the line."

"A map, you mean," Duncan said. "A map he needs for his mission."

Munro nodded. "Except surely an old ranger would know how to get to Fort Ti or Number Four."

"Rogers wants him to do something else, not at the forts. What else was shown on the horn—along the road?" Duncan asked.

Munro shrugged. "Trees. A mitten-shaped lake with little fish in it. Something like a chimney."

"A chimney? Why a chimney?"

"Don't know, Captain. Does it matter?"

"Whether Brandt's mind is cracking or not, somewhere inside it he holds a secret we need, a secret that has something to do with the sinking of the *Arcturus*, or at least the French who sank her. Rogers found something at St. Francis, something he could use in the war against the French. He came back to Number Four, then returned to Champlain over the road that was being constructed then. He discovered that the war was almost over and he did not need to use his secret, so he kept it for another opportunity. Brandt said the road was completed in 1760, a few months after the raid on St. Francis. By then the war was finished in North America. Odd that a man of Rogers's rank and his corporal would come to work on the completion of the road. It was a time of victory parades and celebratory balls in Albany and New York, where Rogers would have been feted, but he chose to come back into these mountains and build a road. That doesn't strike you as strange?"

Conawago grinned. "And tell me, Duncan. What would be your choice, a starched-collar ball in the city or a walk in paradise?" he asked good-naturedly, with a gesture that took in the rolling hills around them.

Duncan knew that Conawago needed no answer to that question.

" 'Heavy hearts need busy hands,' Brandt said," Munro recalled. "But why would Rogers have a heavy heart? He was a hero, perhaps the most famous man on the continent for months after St. Francis."

"He had a spy in the French camp, someone who had soured on King Louis," Duncan suggested. "Rogers had become a son of the New Hampshire wilderness. English walked those mountains, but so did French from the Quebec country. There's no clear border even now between Quebec and the English-speaking colonies. The outcome of the war was not certain then. His spy told him not to worry about immediate pursuit, but he also gave Rogers something that would help the British cause in the war, I'm convinced of it."

His companions had no chance to reply, for suddenly Molly ran past them, Will a few steps behind. As they rounded a curve in the road, they could hear men's voices ahead of them. Duncan and Munro instantly slipped into the shadows and checked their weapons, but Conawago, undaunted, continued and after a few paces began to laugh, bringing his friends out of hiding.

The scene reminded Duncan of an Italian circus he had once seen as a student in Holland, complete with clowns and a performing monkey. Ahead of them, where tall trees bent toward each other to turn the road into something of a tunnel, Ebenezer Brandt was clutching his belly, laughing hysterically. Solomon Hayes was repeatedly running up a fallen log that had lodged five feet up the trunk of a huge maple, then leaping, arm outstretched, up against the trunk as he tried to reach higher and higher. His hat moved up the side of the tree, always just out of his reach, seeming of its own power. Sadie was swinging back and forth on thin branches, squawking in alarm, her efforts to retrieve the hat as futile as Hayes's.

Munro instantly assessed the situation and raised his gun. "Spiny pig," he announced. "They'll go for anything that smells of salt." He lifted his rifle and fired, hitting the tree just above the hat. The frightened porcupine dropped its prize and scurried to the far side of the trunk.

Hayes darted after his hat and with a quick whistle called Sadie to his shoulder.

"I thought you were going north," Duncan observed icily.

Hayes hesitated, seeming confused by Duncan's tone. "Perhaps you hadn't noticed this is the only road that leads anywhere near north," the tinker replied. "Northwest to the lake, then north along the trails that follow its shore."

"The Connecticut goes north."

Hayes began extracting the short quills embedded in the inside of his tattered hat. "The northern settlements are not upriver, they are up Champlain."

"French settlements," Duncan shot back.

"I seem to recall a treaty that made King George their monarch."

"You know what they say about treaties. Just a means for each side to build strength for the next war."

"Mere tinkers are hardly engaged in affairs of state, McCallum."

"Mere tinker, Hayes? I saw you at Number Four. You were sending messages with tribesmen who had come to the fort."

Conawago produced a canteen and stepped between them, extending it to Hayes. "You know he seeks his wife among the northern tribes, Duncan. Of course he sends messages. To trappers, to Mohawks, to Micmacs, to Hurons and Passamoquoddy. What would you expect?"

Munro extended a twist of tobacco to Brandt, and the two old soldiers spoke in low tones, laughing as Brandt pointed to the splintered bark that marked Munro's victory over the spiny pig.

"I am not blocking your path, McCallum," Hayes stated in a brittle voice, gesturing up the road. "By all means, continue. My hat and my monkey are no concern of yours."

Duncan glanced at the tinker's shabby hat and pushed down an ungrateful remark about wasting everyone's time over an old rag. He was tempted to force the tinker to unpack his coded books right there.

"I believe the road passes by that lake in the distance," Conawago observed, pointing toward the north. "I wager the soldiers who used this road built a campsite there. We'll have a fire going and a hot meal ready at sundown. We'll look forward to your company."

Hayes impassively brushed off his hat and set it on his head. "Your Highland friend doesn't want me in his camp."

"But I do," Conawago cheerfully replied. "There will be room for all of us. And fried trout for all if I can arrive early enough."

Duncan shot his friend a petulant glance, then set off at a rapid pace up the road. He grew more suspicious of Hayes each day, angry at Conawago for defending the tinker, always despairing that the more he struggled to grasp the secrets that plagued him, the less he understood.

As Conawago had anticipated, there was indeed a campsite with a pleasant prospect waiting for them when they arrived at the lake hours later. They had made good time, and Duncan agreed to join Will and Munro in a swim while farther down the shore Conawago dropped his horsehair line into the current where a brook emptied into the lake.

Duncan felt an odd sense of urgency as he dove in, feeling a sudden desperation to be cleansed. Here in the depths was at least a world he understood, a world that his totem spirit and the Hebridean boy within him both adored. The tannin-stained water combined with the long rays of the sinking sun to create a vista of golds and browns beneath the surface. Speckled trout watched him, then lazily swam away. A huge pike, as old as the mountains, studied him, as if evaluating him as a possible meal, until four black legs churned the surface above, and with a powerful stroke it disappeared into the murk.

Duncan surfaced beside Molly and followed her as she retrieved a stick for an exuberant Will, who stood knee-deep in the water. The boy threw the stick again, and with a long, skimming dive Duncan raced Molly toward it. Dog and boy jumped up and down with delight when she returned with it clenched in her jaw. Duncan laughed and dove again, embracing the joy he felt in the watery underworld, letting it scrub away his fears and anger. A turtle scurried along the bottom. He glided through a school of sleek minnows and watched from below as a large trout shot upward past him, escaping the water for an instant to capture a midge before splashing back home. What did it think of the world above? He remembered afternoons on his grandfather's sloop, when whales or great basking sharks would follow the boat, one eye rolled up so they could examine the strange human world. More than once his grandfather had shouted the Gaelic war cry, "*Buaidh no bas!*"—*Victory or death!*—and leapt onto the back of a leviathan. The massive creatures seemed to enjoy the frolic, and with a laugh that echoed far over the bays, his grandfather would declare that they were undoubtedly distant relatives.

Duncan surfaced again, wearing a rare smile, to the sound of an excited call.

"There! In the water, Duncan!" the boy shouted, eagerly pointing. "A piece of treasure!" Duncan reached his side and followed his arm toward a tiny point of color on the bottom that sparkled in the long rays of the setting sun. Will grabbed Duncan's arm and pushed him toward it. With another laugh Duncan took a couple of steps and submerged again.

It did indeed seem to be a piece of treasure that Will had spotted, or at least a finely cut piece of crystal. Duncan studied it for a moment, then carefully pushed aside enough of the mud to see that it was part of a bracelet. It would be good for the boy to have a memento, something to distract him from his sorrow. He lifted the bracelet, then recoiled in horror. A skeleton arm rose up out of the muck with it.

As Duncan flailed in the water, still gripping the bracelet, the skeleton hand disintegrated, the bones disappearing back into the mud. He shot to the surface, his heart thundering, and treaded water as he calmed himself.

He knew not what to say, so he silently extended the bracelet to the boy, who grabbed it with a gleeful whoop and splashed back toward camp. Duncan, his joy withered, stared back at the patch of blackness where the remains of a woman lay.

The day was ending in a blush of purples and pinks over the western mountains when Molly sprang up to greet the last two travelers. Hayes and Brandt looked completely sapped from their long trek, and both collapsed by the fire, eagerly accepting the split wood slabs on which Conawago served his fried trout.

"What ye playing with, boy?" Brandt asked Will after wolfing down his first serving and extending his slab for more.

Will still beamed with excitement as he turned his bauble over and over. "Pirate treasure!"

"In the Hampshire Grants?" Brandt scoffed. "Not likely." The old ranger rose and stepped to the boy's side, gesturing for the piece of jewelry. He reached for it, but as he touched it, he seemed to shudder and abruptly pulled away his hand. "A bracelet? From the lake?"

"Mr. Duncan dove for it! He's like a fish!"

Brandt fixed Duncan with a look of sober inquiry. "How far out?" he asked.

"A stone's throw," Duncan answered.

"Give it back, boy."

Will looked up in alarm. "Back?"

"To the dark waters."

Conawago stepped to Will's side. "The boy's had a vexing time. Go lightly."

Brandt shrugged, exchanged a glance with Hayes, muttered something about ghosts, then silently finished his meal and carried his bedroll to one of the piles of fresh pine boughs Conawago had collected for bedding. He spoke no more, and Will soon followed his example, leaving the others staring at the bracelet he had left on a rock by the fire.

Munro produced his pipe and was coaxing the tobacco with a smoldering stick when Hayes suddenly spoke.

"Emma Fletcher," the tinker said.

Munro lowered his pipe. "Pardon?"

"That was her name. Emma Fletcher," Hayes replied. "Captured with several other women in a late-winter raid during the war. I made it my business to track down every tale of female captives, thinking I may find a thread of my Rebecca's fate. Before the army cleared this road, much of this route was a path used by Abenaki raiders when they came down from Champlain." He extracted his own clay pipe and lit it, then stared into the flames.

"And?" Munro asked.

Long moments passed before Hayes spoke. "She died," he finally said.

No one seemed inclined to push the tinker, knowing the pain it cost him to speak of Indian captives. The weary silence remained unbroken except by the haunting, echoing cry of a loon. Molly sauntered to Will and lay down beside him. Munro rose, completed a night scout around the camp, and returned, joining again in the silent vigil at the fire.

"Scarce out of her teens, they say," came a voice from the shadows. Brandt, in his blanket now, was still awake. "Fresh married. The raiders slaughtered her husband before her eyes. Took a dozen women up to the St. Lawrence, where the western tribes came to trade for slaves. One of 'em got bought by a Frenchie whose priest made him give her up. She told the story, how this Emma cried and tore at her bindings, even tried to bite open her own veins. They stopped here on their run north.

"There was a winter moon," Brandt continued, "shining on the snow and ice over the lake. Emma made like she had a call of nature, and her captor led her off with a loop around her neck. When they got to the lake, she jerked it from his hand and ran out on the ice. They could all hear the ice cracking, and the other women called and begged her to come back. But she kept going and finally turned. She stretched her arms out and called her dead husband's name out to the heavens, then started jumping up and down. After four or five jumps, the ice opened and she was gone."

Duncan sensed motion behind him. Will darted past them, snatching the bracelet from the rock and running toward the lake as if to pitch it back into the water. But as he passed the tinker, Hayes grabbed his arm.

"It's all that remains on earth of her, boy," Hayes stated. His voice was fierce. "She reached out to you today, to keep her memory alive. Only you felt her summons. Don't deny her this."

The sudden alarm in Will's eyes ebbed, and he stared at the bracelet in his hand.

"Say her name," Hayes told him. "Emma Fletcher."

The boy took a deep breath, then looked back at Duncan, who knew the boy was acquainted with angels. Will solemnly repeated the name and pushed the bracelet into his waistcoat.

As the boy settled again, Duncan wandered down the shoreline and sat on a ledge that had the shape of a natural chair, its granite still warm from the sun. He gazed out over the long, shimmering blade that was the moon's reflection on the lake and found himself whispering a prayer for the soul of young Emma Fletcher.

As he watched Conawago and Munro stoke the fire and lay out their blanket rolls, it occurred to him that he was witnessing an age-old ritual. The camp, the trail itself, had been established long before the army arrived, before colonists arrived. At the intersection of the route between the mountains and the fertile lake, it was a perfect resting place, probably once a perfect hunting place. Tribesmen had been coming here for decades, probably centuries. It had clearly seen tragedy and despair but also no doubt great prowess and celebrations. Secrets were soaked into the soil of such places, Conawago would say, and some might rub off on the observant.

Natives had no doubt been exactly where he was, sitting on this granite slab, the likeliest of perches, and fished, watched sunsets, made love, committed mayhem, and witnessed death. Duncan somehow knew that men and women sat in his stone chair long before anyone had heard of Europeans or conceived of their distant lands. It made him feel small yet somehow more alive, the way he felt as a boy when sitting alone by the ancient standing stones of Scotland. Something timeless surged through him, something fierce and free, something shared by the natives of this land and the Highland clans. These were people who would reject the harness of a distant king and laugh at those weak enough to let such kings steal their freedom and honor.

Duncan had felt adrift for too long, uncertain of anything anymore. He could not shake the feeling that he was losing Sarah. He had let himself become a minion of merchant lords whose motives he did not grasp. He had let himself be used and become a fugitive for reasons he did not even understand. But here on this ancient granite, with the moon slicing silver into the dark, remembering waters, he felt an unexpected strength. He was the head of Clan McCallum, and though it may be nearly extinct, he would keep its honor as long as his heart kept beating. He leaned back, feeling, if not contented, at least at peace, and he shut his eyes.

When he woke, the moon had moved more than an hour through the heavens. The loon's lonely signal still echoed across the lake, joined now by the questioning call of an owl. Duncan stretched, then paused, hearing a strange murmur along the shoreline. He stole toward the sound, which had the cadence of rhythmic speech, though in words he had never heard. They were harsh and guttural, nothing like the Gaelic, Mohawk, English, French, Latin, and rough Spanish he knew. He recalled that the tribes of the north spoke Algonquin, a unique and very different tongue with which he was not familiar.

It was several minutes before he located his quarry. Hayes was sitting on a different granite ledge near the lake, writing on a paper placed between two candles. The tinker wore his wool cap, and a shawl hung on his shoulders, though it was so small and thin Duncan doubted it offered much warmth. He seemed to be speaking to someone in the shadows, Duncan was sure of it, someone who did not want to be seen.

"*Barukh ata Adonai,*" Hayes intoned, "*eloheinu melekh ha-olam.*"

All of Duncan's frustrations surged within him. Here at last was an enemy he could confront. He sprang forward, shoving Hayes off his knees. "Enough!" he shouted. "You will poison us no longer!" His knife in hand now, Duncan reached for a candle and held it high in a futile attempt to see Hayes's secret contact. Failing that, he aimed the blade at Hayes, cautioning him to lie still, then looked down at the objects of the tinker's treachery. The paper he had been reading from was so long it was rolled at each end, held in place by two narrow metal bars bearing inscriptions. Above the paper was a morsel of bread and a small mound of salt, and beside them a sheet of paper and a writing lead.

"What treachery is this?" he demanded. "Who do you work for?"

Hayes slowly straightened, keeping his eye on Duncan's knife. "McCallum, surely you misunderstand."

"Who is it you communicate with?" Duncan pressed. "Someone from the French court? Or is it an agent of Beck's?"

"I speak to Him," came Hayes's simple reply.

"Who, damn it? Whom do you write to?" Duncan gestured to the paper scroll. "Is this your codebook, then?"

"I suppose in a way," Hayes said in a level voice. "Deuteronomy is filled with enigma."

"You will tell me whom it is you sneak away to write to, damn you!"

Hayes sighed. "My wife."

"So you have lied from the start!" Duncan accused. "She serves your masters in the north?"

Melancholy filled Hayes's face, and he looked down at the unfinished note beside the bread and salt. "It's difficult to keep track of the calendar sometimes out here, but I do believe this is Friday night," he said, as if this explained everything. "If you would just allow me to finish, I will answer your questions back in camp."

"You are finished now!" Duncan insisted. "I want your papers!"

"Not possible."

"I can't arrest you, but at least I can put an end to your deception. And if I find that you were involved in killing the crew of the *Arcturus*, I vow that I will—"

"You will let him finish, Duncan," came a voice from the shadows. Conawago stepped into the circle of light, Sadie asleep in the cradle of one arm. Duncan hesitated. The old Nipmuc had the air of a coconspirator. "As Solomon said," his friend continued, "it is Friday night."

Duncan's head swirled. He could not understand why Conawago would take the side of a traitor. "Look at this!" he said, pointing to the note. "A code! He is writing with secret symbols!"

Conawago sighed. "You are better than this, Duncan." He lifted the incomplete note. "I am rusty, but once I had a good Jesuit teacher. 'My dearest Rebecca,'" he slowly read. "'My Sabbath begins on the shore of a beautiful lake.'" The old man looked up. "Not code, Duncan. Hebrew." He looked back at Hayes. "*Barukh ata Adonai*," he said, repeating the words Hayes recited; then "*eloheinu melekh ha-olam*. Pardon me, Solomon, if I mangle the translation, but if I am not mistaken, it means, 'Blessed are you, eternal one our God, our universal ...'"

When Conawago hesitated, Hayes finished the sentence. "Our universal ruling presence."

Duncan's confusion was like a paralysis. He gazed in painful silence at Conawago, then at Hayes, then down at the items on the ledge, which suddenly took on the appearance of an altar. Memories flashed in his mind from his youth in Holland, where somber men wearing black shawls hurried down the street on Friday evening. "The Sabbath starts on Friday night," he said in a hoarse voice. He lifted the unfinished letter. It had been many years since he'd seen the strange language, written from right to left, and he had never expected to see it in America. As he handed the letter back to Hayes, more memories flashed before his eyes, of Hayes often reaching for a cap or hat even when one seemed unnecessary. "Your hat. Your wool cap. You always have something on your head."

Hayes nodded.

"It's why you struggled so when the spiny pig stole your hat. The night in the tavern you wouldn't touch the pork. The shawl. I used to see more elaborate ones in Holland."

"A tallith."

"They had fringes at the corners. And some wore something like aprons."

"I just frayed a few threads on mine," Hayes explained, and opened his waistcoat to show he was wearing a ragged cloth belt.

Duncan knelt and reverently rearranged the objects of the makeshift altar, then looked up to the tinker. "I have wronged you."

"I am sorry, Duncan," the tinker said. "My people have been forced into habits of secrecy, even in America."

Duncan found that he had difficulty speaking. "I am the only one here who has been shamed," he finally said. "I offer my apology, sir, though I don't expect you can ever forgive me."

"The Sabbath is the perfect time for forgiveness," Hayes replied, extending his hand.

Duncan accepted the handshake. He had so many questions. "You could have just told us."

"No, and even now, I must beg for your discretion," Hayes said with a sad smile. "The Jews were driven out of Massachusetts decades ago. The Puritans came to America to escape intolerance in Europe only to practice it themselves in the New World. It is not safe to advertise my faith outside of Rhode Island. I would only put my traveling companions at risk and assure that I was shunned in my journeys. It was a mistake I made all those years ago when I agreed to come into the Hampshire Grants with my family. We didn't hide our faith, for we never had to in Rhode Island. We had forgotten that in much of the world, my people are creation's scapegoats, blamed for every misfortune. Teamsters deserted us. Accidents happened. Sometimes I think we were deliberately put in harm's way in that Indian raid. No family suffered like ours that day."

Sadie stirred, and as Conawago handed her down to Hayes, Duncan's gaze settled on the writing lead and paper. "Will told me you wrote secret letters."

"Yes, as often as I can."

Conawago shot Duncan a cautioning glance.

"To do so in the wilderness seems odd," Duncan said.

"To my wife. My heart says she still lives. That hope is all I live for," the tinker confessed. He bent and opened the knapsack that lay near his altar, tipping it. Sealed letters spilled out, dozens of letters. "When we reunite, I will share all these years of my search with her. It will . . . help repair things, I think, bridge the gap so we can put these painful years behind us, and when we are old, we will take them out and tell our grandchildren about our grand wilderness adventure." He looked at Conawago and gestured to the letters. "Many are in English, some in Hebrew. Open one or two, my friend. You will find them filled with boring details of a solitary existence." He lowered his voice. "Sometimes I write of Sadie," he admitted, as if in confession, "and, fool that I am, speak of her as my child."

Strangely, his words seemed to stab Conawago. The old Nipmuc sagged, then slowly dropped to his knees before the mound of letters, each addressed simply *Rebecca*, with a date. He picked one up, and another, and Duncan saw that they were of many types and sizes of paper, with the message written on one side, then folded and sealed into an envelope. Some were jagged along one side, as if on paper ripped from bound volumes; others looked as if they had been salvaged from newspapers, with the typeset ink painstakingly scraped away so new words could be written.

Hayes wordlessly watched as Conawago emptied the sack. There were scores and scores of letters, the oldest ones, from the bottom, on good linen paper. Many were stained with sweat, with water, food, and sometimes blood. As the old Nipmuc ran his hands through the evidence of Hayes's solitary, secret existence, his eyes filled with moisture. When he finally looked up, he gave a long sigh that seemed almost a sob. His voice cracked as he spoke. "It doesn't have to be like this," the old Nipmuc said.

"Like this?" Hayes asked.

Conawago looked out over the shadowed lake. "Twenty-five years ago I went to Canada because I heard that one of my old Jesuit teachers lay dying. I thought I would comfort him, thank him by sitting vigil at his deathbed because all his other friends had already passed. But all I did was make him angry. He shouted at me so loud that nuns came running from down the hall."

Duncan could not recall ever seeing Conawago in such despair.

"I was a disgrace, he said. I had slapped away the hand of destiny, of greatness, that had been extended to me so many times. I had the best education a native ever received. I had dined with kings and great scholars. I had my feet well planted in both worlds, tribal and European, better than any man alive, he said. I could have built bridges between our peoples, could have prevented so many tragedies, he said. But I had wasted it, wasted everything on my ridiculous quest, which we all knew was hopeless from the start. It was a grave sin, he said, and he hoped the Lord would forgive me because he could not."

Duncan's heart seemed to shrivel. In all their years together, he had never heard this confession.

Hayes did not understand. "You knew kings?" he asked.

Conawago, staring at the letters again, seemed not to hear. "Don't you understand? This was what I did! For sixty years it was all I did! My people disappeared while I was enjoying the pleasures of Europe. For sixty years I searched for them. Don't do the same, Solomon, I beg you! Don't throw your life away. You're a good man, an educated man. You can still do great things with your life."

Hayes was silent for a long time. The lonely loon called from across the lake. "In the end," he said in a near whisper as Duncan helped Conawago to his feet, "a man's years are all that he has. How I spend them is between me and my God."

"Then your God is as irresponsible as you!" Conawago snapped. He kicked the pile of letters, sending several into the shadows, then stormed away into the night.

•

THEY MADE GOOD TIME THE next morning, skirting the north end of the lake on a sandy section of the trail before cresting a series of gently rising ridges. Duncan found himself often slowing, falling behind as he studied the forest on either side of the track. There had been no sign of Conawago since he vanished into the night. Duncan had heaped fuel on the campfire and futilely searched for his friend past midnight before surrendering to his fatigue. When he awakened, Conawago's bedroll and kit were gone.

"I'm sorry," Hayes said. The tinker had paused for Duncan at the side of the track. "I never should have argued with him. I didn't know about his life. It is a tragedy of Shakespearean proportion."

Duncan accepted a drink from the water gourd Hayes offered. "It's not that. He took no offence from your words, Solomon, it's just that they deepened his own pain. For weeks he has been out of sorts. Disjointed from the world. You saw him in Worcester. He is not by nature an angry man, but an anger has been growing inside him unseen for years. He grows bitterly angry at the world and doesn't know how to get past it. The way he finds his peace is by going deep into the wilderness and consulting the ancient spirits who dwell there."

"I thought he said he was a Jesuit."

"No. He learned from the Jesuits. But he is fond of observing that they don't know everything. He enjoys conversations with the European God, as he says, but his soul belongs to the ancient ones."

"Still, our conversation gnaws at me. I must apologize to him."

Duncan shrugged. "He's disappeared like this many times before. He could be back in a week, or a month. Once, it was six months. The last time, he had to go see the great inland sea called Superior because he had a dream about it." The words brought a stinging memory of his last conversation with Sarah.

"Indians seem to place a lot of stock in dreams."

"Dreams are messages from the other side," Duncan explained as he handed back the gourd. "And he's been having many bad dreams lately."

"They must have started in Boston," the tinker said as he heaved his huge pack onto his shoulder.

Duncan had already taken a step up the road, but he turned. "Why do you say that?"

"Two weeks ago I was out taking the air with Sadie. She likes the harbor. I think the tall masts with ropes remind her of her childhood among tall trees intertwined with vines. I saw him, though I didn't meet him until that night in Hancock's warehouse. He was sitting alone on a wharf at sunset and speaking toward the water." Hayes tightened the strap of his pack and fell in beside Duncan. "I remember because there was such despair on his face. For a moment I thought he was going to throw himself in. I began to quickly walk his way. But then he rose, stretched out his hands to the heavens, and shouted a word in a language I do not know. He threw something into the water. It looked like a necklace, a strand of beads."

Duncan stumbled as he fought down a wave of emotion. They walked in silence, passing a woodpecker hammering on a birch.

"*Jiyathontek*. Is that what he shouted?" Duncan finally asked.

"*Jiyathontek*," Hayes repeated slowly, then looked at Duncan in surprise. "I can't be certain, but yes, that was the sound of it. So you know what he was saying?"

"I know whom he was speaking to," Duncan said. "It's a summoning, in Mohawk, the tribal language he most often uses. It means *hearken* or *listen to me now*. It is used to get the attention of the old gods. He shouts it because he says the old ones are getting hard of hearing."

Hayes digested Duncan's words for several steps. "So he called on the gods to watch him dispose of some beads?"

Something squeezed Duncan's heart as he spoke. He recalled burying old beads by the river at Agawam. "No. He carries strings of wampum beads in an old pouch, some given him by his mother and some from his grandmother in the last century, who remembered seeing the Pilgrims land at Plymouth as a child. He was asking the gods to witness an ending, to accept his sacrifice. His people are all but extinct. He knows he has but a short time left in this world. He has taken on a somber responsibility."

"I don't follow."

"He isn't saying goodbye for himself, he is saying goodbye for his entire people. Though it rips his heart apart, he knows they are ended. But that isn't the worst of it. He has known about his tribe for years, but now there is something different, something we saw at Worcester. Now he fears their gods are dying, too."

It was midafternoon when Munro, on a rise ahead of them, yelled at their short column. Duncan followed his extended arm toward a cloud of dust behind them. "Riders!" the Scot shouted.

They were well hidden behind boulders and trees by the time the horsemen approached. To his surprise Duncan recognized the big bearded man from the Fort at Number Four, singing a bawdy song while leading five other riders. Duncan tried to recall the boisterous man's name. *Allen.* He seemed to have a personality as oversized as his frame, which itself made his horse seem too small. His song, extolling the contours of a barmaid named Maggie, faded, and he reined in his horse. He studied the track with the eye of a seasoned woodsman.

"Hell, boys," Allen called out. "We ain't the ones you want to be hiding from."

Corporal Brandt stepped out from behind a broad hemlock. "We ain't hiding, Ethan," he quipped. "We're just running from the stench of ye."

Allen gave a whoop and slid off his mount. "Ebenezer, you sneaky piece of gristle! You got a monkey, a dog, and a tinker with you?"

"Why?" Brandt shot back. "Ye grown particular about the company ye keep?"

Allen guffawed and tossed the grizzled corporal a canteen. "Hell, no. Now if you can just round up a drunken bear, we'll have a real soiree tonight."

Duncan, Munro, and Hayes ventured warily into the sunlight as the other riders dismounted. Allen muttered an urgent command, and they began quickly unloading their packhorse. The big man scanned their party and stepped toward Duncan, extending a hand. "You must be McCallum. Allen be my name, but you can call me by my Christian name, Ethan. Now mind me sharp and you'll survive the day. T'ain't their land to be riding so roughshod over." His men were straightening out a long chain of metal rods. "Know anything about surveying?"

"I don't understand," Duncan confessed.

"Those lobsterbacks, boy! More boats arrived yesterday with their horses. They weren't for the garrison at Number Four, they were dragoons coming this way with a warrant!" Ethan Allen urgently pointed to the southeast. A second cloud of dust could be seen now, moving rapidly toward them.

"We can hide," Duncan suggested.

"No. My way's better. Hide, and they'll be searching the road for days, doubling back and hounding your tail."

By the time the soldiers caught up with them, Allen had deployed their party across the landscape, stretching the chain of rods to its full length, then marking its spans with stakes. The big frontiersman had settled on a flat boulder with a ledger he produced from his saddlebag and was busily writing on its pages. He greeted the soldiers with careful disinterest, warning them not to disturb the true line he was measuring. "Tell me, General," he said to the officer in charge, "do you spell woodpecker with one *u* or two?"

His question took the young officer off guard. "I am an ensign, sir. And I do not follow."

"Woodpecker Hollow. That's what I'll call this tract when we finish the survey. On account of all the trees have holes in 'em. The great swordsmen of the feathered world. Lord, imagine if the king could train a company of woodpeckers, eh?"

The ensign shook his head as if to dispel his confusion. "I seek a fugitive from the king's justice," he sternly intoned. "Charges of treason are levied on his head."

Duncan glanced up at the riders, careful not to make eye contact with any. He had had only a quick look through the tavern window, but he was certain that the three soldiers riding behind the officer had been in Worcester with Beck.

Allen seemed reluctant to change the conversation. "How would you train 'em, I wonder. Aim to pierce the hands of your enemy or go straight to the eyes?"

"Sir! A man who is an enemy of blessed King George is known to be in these parts."

The alarm on Allen's face was worthy of the theater. "God protect us, sir! You should have said so! This traitor got a name?"

"I will have yours first, sir,"

Allen stood up and soberly saluted the officer. "Ethan Allen, sir, of the Hampshire Land Company." He gestured at his party. "And these be my mountain boys, as folks call 'em. Commissioned by the governor hisself to set out ten thousand acres in this paradise."

The officer narrowed his eyes. "The governor of New York or the governor of New Hampshire?"

"Why, New Hampshire, of course. He says New York lies over in the Hudson Valley." Allen turned back to his crew. "Keep it straight, damned yer eyes! The governor must have a straight line!"

Duncan, far up the slope, kept working, sharpening stakes for marking the supposed line.

"God's fire, boys! A traitor's on the prowl!" Allen shouted. "Keep a sharp eye to help our heroes on horseback! Looking for a varmint named—" He turned back to the officer.

"McCallum. Duncan McCallum. He left Fort Four two days ago. We believe he was using this road."

Allen looked back at his work crew and raised a finger, pointing at each in turn as he recited names. "I got Ben, Thomas, Rafe, Silas, Solomon, Asher, Levan, the boy Will, and Learned, though that's a hoot for such a dull fellow. Nope, no Duncan, though you're welcome to Rafe, he's an awful cook and snores like thunder." Allen wiped the sweat off his brow. "No concern of ours, boys!" Allen shouted up the hill. "Just another damned Scottish troublemaker!"

The dragoon officer rolled his eyes.

The burly frontiersman shrugged. "Only strangers we've seen was three we passed a day ago. But they was leaving the road."

The ensign leaned forward with great interest. "To where?"

"This be the only colonist road, to be sure. But the Injuns, they got paths aplenty. There's trails intersecting this road what'll take you all the way to Canada."

The ensign nodded vigorously. "He is reported to travel with an old savage," he confirmed.

"Those Scots are cunning bastards, to be sure. Put that McCallum with a savage or two and God knows what they be capable of. Might have walked right around us as we slept. That would be just like such a devil, to put us in mind they are going north, then sneak around us to the valley. That's where they would get food and supplies, the valley. So that's where they have to end up."

The officer studied the road that led west to the safety of the British forts in the Champlain Valley. He was clearly not comfortable with the idea of riding up Indian trails. He drew himself up and with a sharp command led his men at a trot up the westward road. Allen watched until they had crested the next hill, then stuffed his ledger back into his saddlebag, summoned his men, and broke out in laughter. "Lord, don't it give you comfort to know we got such sheep protecting us wolves?"

When they had repacked the equipment, Allen and all but one of his men remounted. The brawny man motioned Duncan to the riderless horse. "You're with me," he said in a voice that would brook no disagreement. He turned to the others. "There's a river in about ten miles, no deeper than your waist this time o' year. A couple miles beyond is a good campsite, on a flat by a stream. We'll be there. You can't miss it—by the big chimney rock."

Munro's head rose, and he met Duncan's gaze. A chimney had been prominently etched on Brandt's secret map of the Crown Point road.

"I take it this is not your first encounter with His Majesty's troops," Duncan said after they had been riding a few minutes.

"They be right handy when we're at war," Allen said, "but otherwise they want to nibble away at a man's lawful business."

"The business of land speculation."

"The business of opening these grand vistas to fruitful labor. Making it possible for honest men to raise new families in this forest paradise."

Ethan Allen had already shown that he was savvy about surviving on the frontier. He was also fluent in the language of the land huckster.

"A noble calling," Duncan observed. "I was impressed that you have a commission from the governor. These grants are hotly contested by New York and New Hampshire. So you've sided with New Hampshire, then?"

Allen gave another of his crowlike hoots of laugher. He patted his saddle bag. "Depends on who's asking. Got one from each!"

Duncan raised his brow in surprise. "That's quite an accomplishment."

His companion laughed again. "Hell, McCallum, we ain't so fastidious here on the frontier. They ain't exactly what a lawyer would call genuine, just close enough. And those soldiers didn't care. The king tends to dismiss what goes on in the Hampshire Grants as a dispute between two governors. That officer was on London business." Allen abruptly leaned over and grabbed the bridle of Duncan's horse. "And it's time you told me what that business is."

"Nothing that concerns the Hampshire Grants."

"I'll be the judge of that. Why do they call you a traitor?"

"Nothing that reaches into this land. Do not invent new troubles for yourself, Allen."

"I correspond with men in Boston. Mr. Hancock, Mr. Samuel Adams. You'd be surprised how long the arms of Boston can be."

"And those of New York," Duncan added.

Allen looked away for a moment. "Go too far west and you'll be forced to navigate a Livingston maze," he muttered. "Now, speak to me, Highlander!"

"You have business with the leaders of the Sons of Liberty?" Duncan asked as Allen's words sank in. What could this burly frontiersman have in common with the likes of Hancock, Sam Adams, and Livingston?

"Speak, damned you!" Allen insisted.

"There was a Livingston ship named the *Arcturus* returning from a voyage to England."

"I know her. I have a friend on her."

Duncan hesitated. "Then I am truly sorry. It called at Halifax, where two French agents cajoled their way on board. As the *Arcturus* approached Boston, they stole something that was of great importance to the Sons, a ledger of some kind, then blew up the ship and fled. Thirty-seven men died."

"Jesus bloody wept!" Allen groaned. "Thirty-seven? Please tell me not my friend Jonathan Pine!"

It was Duncan's turn to be stunned. "He was chosen for special punishment before the ship was destroyed. It was he who was protecting the ledger, secreting it on his person. They tortured him and left him to die. He saved the life of the boy Will, then died in the explosion."

"God Almighty," Allen murmured. "Poor Jonathan. A'fore Reverend Occom sunk in his claws, Jonathan was the best of traveling companions." They rode on for several minutes in grim silence before he spoke again. "Jonathan was with me when I got my first bear drunk," Allen recalled, as if beginning a eulogy. "It was he who set the rule we still abide by. No harm must ever come to the bear. Hell, that first night the bear finally crawled onto Pine's blanket and curled up around him to sleep it off. Damnest thing. Pine didn't budge, just stroked the bear's head and sang him some old tribal ditty." He sighed and looked at Duncan. "None of that explains a warrant on your head."

"The king had his own agents looking for that ledger. Without understanding the consequences, as a favor to the Sons, I led them to believe I had recovered it from the ship. Now I must find it to prove my innocence and avenge the dead. The spies who took it have killed two more men. Former rangers, both with Rogers on the St. Francis raid."

Allen looked away, as if trying to hide his reaction. "You encourage your imagination over much, I suspect."

Allen had not been surprised by Duncan's mention of St. Francis and had been quick to try to steer him elsewhere. Instead, Duncan explained his suspicions about the connection of the dead men to the famous raid. He watched Allen carefully as he offered his last suspicion. "I am not the only one accused of treason," he said.

"You be in good company, aye."

"So you know Rogers?"

"A good man. He did the suffering in the war, and the lace-collared generals got all the glory. By God, what he did at St. Francis was a miracle. It broke the back of the French Indians. No other man on God's earth could have done it."

"Command of the post at Michilimackinac seems a just reward."

"Nonsense! They just wanted him out of the way. It was an exile. Rogers reminded the generals of some unpleasant realities, so they dispatched him to oblivion and now want to tar him with conspiracy."

"Unpleasant realities?"

"That given the chance, the American colonials can fight as well as British regulars. That their way of discipline in battle may work in Europe, but not always here. That Americans think much of their own personal honor and have this perverse tendency toward independent thinking."

They were dangerous words. "Thinking about independence, you mean," Duncan said.

Allen threw up his hands in mock alarm. "I never said that. You be the traitor, McCallum, not me. I'm just talking about the honor of a free man."

Duncan rode on in silence, digesting Allen's words. In the British world, treason meant acts on behalf of a foreign king, almost always that of France. But in America there were new possibilities, acts against a king that would have been inconceivable, even impossible, in Europe. *The honor of a free man.* Surely that was not inconsistent with loyalty to a king.

They hurried up, then down a ridge, across the shallow river Allen had described to their party, then dismounted under a canopy of huge maples by a lazy stream. A hundred yards away, up a strangely barren hillside, stood a formation of huge, squarish stones stacked on one another by the hand of nature. It was, he had no doubt, the formation depicted on Brandt's powder horn, the image the old corporal kept trying to hide. As Allen led the horses to the water, he tossed Duncan a hand ax. "Firewood," he commanded, pointing to a circle of fire-blackened rocks.

Duncan chopped three armfuls of dead limbs, then headed up the slope to the chimney formation. The huge stacked stones reached nearly four times his height. Nothing grew within a hundred-foot radius except low shrubs and small flowering plants. It had the air of the stone circles Duncan had visited as a boy. The tribes, he knew, would show such a place special reverence, and as he neared it, he was not surprised to see strands of beads, animal skulls, crude carvings, and a few brilliantly colored bird wings laid on the protruding lip of the lowest stone. The bottom two stones bore patches of green and gold lichen, but the higher rock faces showed the work of humans. There were diamond and circle designs in rust-colored ochre, drawings of deer, birds, moose, wolves, and fish, even a small grouping of dancing stick-figure humans. Scattered around the stone faces were dozens of handprints, the hands of humans that had been covered with pigment and pressed to the rock, probably across a span of centuries.

"They call it the torch of the gods," came Allen's voice behind him, "because long ago there was a night when it burned bright at the top." He shrugged as he stepped to Duncan's side. "Lightning strike on some dried brush up there probably, though don't ever suggest that to a tribesman. It was, they say, the night after old Samuel de Champlain was first sighted on his great lake. The Christian Indians say it was a beacon of celebration. The others say it was a warning."

The bearded man stepped past Duncan and touched a hand against the rock, a sign of homage. Frontiersmen learned not to mock tribal traditions. Duncan approached the makeshift altars and studied the offerings. He pointed to a belt woven of white and purple beads. "That's Iroquois," he said in surprise. He counted the purple beads in the pattern along the bottom. "Mohawk," he declared then, wishing again for Conawago, struggling to understand the painted images. He pointed to the dancing stick figures, some of whom led captives by neck ropes. "That's about a victory in battle, though whose victory and whose defeat is lost to time." He lingered over the offerings, then turned to Allen. "Why would a Mohawk belt be here on a shrine so far from their lands?"

A small, melancholy smile rose on Allen's face. "His woman was a Mohawk. Formidable. She liked this place. When he was with her, he was always different, a softer, kinder man. But she took a fever and died before the war was over."

Duncan was about to ask whom he meant when it came to him that Allen was speaking of Robert Rogers. He paced around the rock, examining the other offerings on the narrow ledge around the chimney, then paused over a small rectangular wooden box stuffed into a horizontal crack in the granite. With a finger he pried it out into the sunlight.

"Abenaki, Mahican, Pennacook, Pocomtuc," Allen recited. "They all come here. Best not meddle with tribal offerings."

Duncan nodded, and pushed the box back into the narrow shadow. It was indeed tribal, but from the tribe of Israel. He knew such boxes from the Jewish ghetto he had lived near as a student. It was a mezuzah, one of the prayer boxes that was affixed to doorways of Jewish homes. There was only one person who could possibly have left it. In his quest to find his wife, the lonely Hebrew tinker tried to appeal to every god who might listen.

There were more offerings on the last side of the square. Little bone flutes, images of deer and bears skillfully woven into patches of soft doeskin, even two sashes with embroidered flowers and leaves, which Duncan now knew were worn by Abenaki women.

The talkative Allen had sunk into a contemplative silence. Duncan saw the mixture of wonder and discomfort on his countenance, a look that often settled over colonists who encountered tribal shrines. Their European upbringing taught them to be dismissive, even contemptuous of such altars, but those who had experienced the deep forest knew there was a power at such places that their own religion could not account for.

A tanager's lilting melody wafted through the woods behind them. Duncan walked about the rock again, then studied the landscape. The shrine sat in the middle of a long, open swath that ran all the way to the top of the mountain, widening as it descended. Spars of long-dead trees reached up from the undergrowth. It had been the site of another long-ago avalanche.

A little slice of blue appeared on the ground before him, a jay feather, and he bent to retrieve it, then dropped it on the stone ledge near the still-meditative Allen.

"My father was a devout follower of the faith," Allen said suddenly. "He made me study the Bible as a boy, and I was supposed to attend divinity school at the Yale College. But then I came here, to the mountains. The wildness cured me of those notions. How arrogant, to think we can be better men of God by becoming scholars. When you see what the hand of God has wrought here, you know that the affairs of mankind must be but a minor distraction to him."

Duncan had no reply.

"What always has puzzled me, McCallum, is how tribesmen like Occom and Noah take to the Scriptures. I asked Occom about it once. He said the Mysterious One wears many coats, and it is a great blessing to meet him wearing different ones." Allen reached out and touched the feather. "And I asked old Noah once why the Bible didn't prepare me for all this. He said Christianity is for crowds, for men dealing with other men. Then he pointed to the forest and said but walk into that wilderness and you are the first human who ever lived. They make me feel so damned small, talking like that. Just like this place makes me feel tiny. It's all backward, ain't it? I mean Occom and Noah's supposed to be the pagans and we're supposed to be the enlightened ones."

Duncan gestured at the handprints on the stone face. "At places like this I always feel that the people who left their mark are like old friends I should have met, forever lost to me."

Allen slowly nodded. "Like part of us is somehow in these stones, too," he said in a near whisper.

"Give me that expensive linen handkerchief I saw in your pocket," Duncan said.

Allen's brow knitted in confusion, but he complied.

Duncan flattened the linen cloth on the stone, laid the feather in the middle of it, folded the handkerchief around it, and stuffed it into a crack in the granite. He saw a patch of mud nearby, bent his hand into it, then pushed his hand onto the stone, leaving a muddy print. Allen solemnly did the same before they both turned away.

"You used the word *conspiracy* when you spoke of Rogers," Duncan said as they walked toward camp. "Why?"

"Stands to reason, don't it? Don't suppose treason is committed by just one man. It's what the major's enemies would suggest."

"The eagle, the squirrel, and the mouse," Duncan stated.

"Sorry?"

Duncan gestured to the nearest tree. "It's what Conawago says when we confront puzzles—about seeing things with different perspectives. The eagle, the squirrel, and the mouse might all look at the same tree, but none of them would see it the same way."

"You lost me," Allen confessed.

"Say Major Rogers had a second objective when he went to St. Francis. Not just to punish the Abenaki but also to take something, something that would guarantee that he would win the next battle, even the war."

Allen considered his words for several long breaths. "Can't imagine what that might be."

"Suppose it was a list of leaders of the French irregulars, the farmers and tradesmen of Quebec who formed the core of the French Army. By the time of the raid their morale was terrible. They hadn't received their promised pay, not to mention their promised supplies. King Louis was reluctant to send regular troops to America because he was fighting the British elsewhere. And he had no friends among the Quebec Jesuits by then."

"No need to bring the papists into it," Allen muttered.

"They have to be part of this. I understand that the Jesuit mission in St. Francis dominated the town. Jesuits had been accompanying the raiders for years, sometimes even leading them. The French king had begun suppressing the Jesuits in France. He dissolved the order back home. Even King George banned the immigration of new Jesuit priests to America. The Jesuits and their followers in Quebec were angry at the world. Still are, I imagine. What if Rogers thought he could turn them to his cause in 1759?"

"The war was all but over," Allen observed.

"Rogers didn't know that. It's all about perspectives. The eagle, the squirrel, and the mouse. Perspectives have shifted. What if Rogers has a new cause? That list becomes as explosive as a keg of powder. And the French haven't given up on America. They control some of the western lands still, where they could mass troops, then a rebel force in Canada could pound the English like a hammer on that anvil. If Rogers helped them achieve that, he would become a general at last, probably even a French count with his own chateau."

Allen produced a plug of tobacco and bit off the end. "Intrigue," he said with contempt in his voice. "Secret conspiracy. Those are things for kings and royal courts."

Duncan glanced at Allen, realizing the man wasn't exactly disagreeing with him. "And for those who oppose them. The French Jesuits of Quebec loathe King Louis. The French colonials have no love for King Louis or King George. Rogers has no love of King George. Maybe they instead seek a paradise without a king. This land"—Duncan swept his hand toward the horizon—"is wide-open. No settlers to speak of, no flag planted firmly in its soil."

Allen spat tobacco juice. "Lake George wasn't its original name."

"No," Duncan said. "Once, it belonged to Jesuit colonials. Lac du Saint Sacrement, they called it."

Allen bit off more tobacco, then pointed toward the camp, where the rest of the party was arriving. "The first name given to these mountains was Vert Monts. The inland sea is still called Champlain."

Duncan paused, watching Allen as the big man continued down the trail. His words sounded almost like an effort of persuasion. Allen had no love for the colonial governments, yet he kept surveying the mountains as if for the purpose of some government. Had Duncan just been speaking with one of the conspirators?

"Saguenay!" Duncan called to his back.

Although Duncan still did not know if the word signified a person, a place, or an object, it clearly meant something to Allen. The frontiersman halted so fast he almost stumbled, but he did not turn to face Duncan. After a moment, without replying, he continued down the mountain.

ETHAN ALLEN AND HIS MOUNTAIN boys, as he called them, were jovial campmates. They readily shared their ample food supply, and Will was soon being taught the fine art of flipping johnnycakes in a skillet as Corporal Brandt kept watch over a pot of molasses and beans. When they finished eating, Munro declared that he was not comfortable sleeping without a sentinel, and he volunteered to take the first watch.

"Thought the 'Naki that worried you was disabled," Allen observed.

"T'ain't the red-skinned savages I worry about," the sturdy Scot replied, "'tis the red-coated ones."

Allen puffed on his pipe, then slowly nodded and motioned with its long stem toward two of his men. "Silas and Thomas, two hours each after Mr. Munro's shift. Then rouse me for the dawn watch." He turned to the youngest of his men. "Ben," he said to the youth in his late teens, "early breakfast for ye. I want ye on the road, scouting ahead at dawn."

Duncan, exhausted from the long day, welcomed the moss pillow Will had collected for him, but sleep eluded him. More than ever he felt like a puppet, with invisible faces at the end of the long strings manipulating him. There was indeed a conspiracy by the French that somehow involved the Sons of Liberty, but he was also convinced that there was another in the north, involving the famous Major Rogers, these unclaimed lands, and the enigmatic Saguenay. It seemed impossible that the two conspiracies could be linked, but they had become so through French coins, dead rangers, and now Duncan himself. An owl hooted, mocking him. *Who*, it asked, *who, who wanted him dead?*

"Mind yer flippers, lad!" the grizzled old Scot called out to young Duncan, pointing to the pinnace that was gliding to a halt along the starboard rail where Duncan sat. Duncan swung his legs up just as the smaller boat nudged the hull of his grandfather's red-sailed sloop.

"Lively now, ye seahounds!" his grandfather yelled, and the two small crews quickly went to work, lashing the two boats together and forming a line to hand up the casks from the smaller boat to stow in the sloop's hold. The gray-haired captain lit his pipe and with a twinkle in his eyes raised it to salute the solitary old seal that often watched them; then he accepted the bottle presented by the kilted owner of the smaller vessel and pried out the cork. He sniffed the contents, took a drink, and swished the contents in his mouth before a deep swallow. "It'll do, McDuff," he told the whiskey maker, high praise indeed from the gruff Highlander, and called for Duncan to fetch the basket of horn cups they kept in the galley.

He poured each man a dram and had Duncan hold an extra to fill. "To the prince across the water," he proposed, and every man solemnly joined in the

Jacobite toast. When they were done, he took the cup from Duncan and threw its contents out in a long arc across the water. "Stay long and far away," he called after the spilled whiskey, and young Duncan finally gave voice to the question that rose to his tongue every time he witnessed the ritual.

"Why do you ask the bonny prince to stay far away?" he asked his grandfather.

The sailors and the captain laughed together, their amusement echoing across the bay, causing the old seal to raise its damp black eyes again. "The toast is for our bonny Stewart prince, lad," his grandfather said. "The whiskey in the water is a charm against the English king, to keep his long German nose out of our affairs. The whiskey in these casks is the fame and honor of the McDuffs, who have been making it for the clans since time began. For that distant king to pretend it is now a crime to do so does a dishonor to the McDuffs and all of us who rely on them. But the real dishonor, and the real sin, be on the king."

An hour later his grandfather tensed when a little cutter flying a Union Jack appeared around the point of one of the craggy islands in the Minch, the turbulent water off Skye. After several worried minutes in which he yelled at his crew to stand by the sails, he laughed once more, for the cutter had becalmed herself by sailing too close to the lee of the island.

"There ye go, Duncan lad," the wise old man had explained. "May the hand of the king ever fumble when he tries to smear yer honor."

Duncan stirred out of his deep sleep, smiling at the half-remembered scent of peat and heather that always clung to his grandfather's clothes. Then he awoke with the sense that something was amiss. The fire was burning low, and in its flickering light he saw Allen hovering beside him. The bearded man, on his dawn watch, nudged Duncan and gestured in the direction of the tribal shrine. A slight, shadowed figure was moving toward it.

The man had a head start, but he was proceeding so cautiously, so slowly, that Duncan had to pause frequently, hiding behind trees so as not to be spotted. The spidery, nervous aspect of the figure told him it must be Corporal Brandt, which he confirmed as the man emerged in the gray predawn light of the open swath around the sacred rocks.

Brandt placed something on the base stone of the chimney and bowed his head for a few words before continuing up the slope. Duncan paused only long enough to see that the old ranger had deposited a little strand of braided leather with feathers in its folds; then he followed. They climbed steadily for nearly half an hour before he spotted what he knew must be Brandt's destination, high up on a flat ledge near the top of the treeless avalanche run. Duncan slipped deeper into the woods, where he could make better time, so as to be close when Brandt arrived.

The forest of what Allen called his Vert Monts seemed somehow older than the woodlands Duncan knew on the west side of the Hudson. Every forest had its own character, and this patchwork of granite, maple, birch, spruce, and hemlock draped with hanging moss seemed unusually calm, as if patiently bracing for what were no doubt harsh winters ahead. Daylight was filtering through the heavy foliage, kindling birdsong that flowed over the slope. Ground squirrels appeared, scampering in search of breakfast. Above him in an aged spruce a porcupine took note of Duncan and shifted to the other side of the broad trunk. For an instant he saw a dog-size creature with rich brown fur as it leapt from one tree to another, a sleek fisher cat hunting the heights.

Brandt seemed shaken when he finally reached the ledge, nearly at the crest of the mountain, and stood motionless, staring at the six-foot-high platform that had been erected there years earlier. Duncan approached the old ranger, then halted as he noticed the sweeping vista opening before him. The view was one of the most remarkable he had ever seen. Ranks of long, green ridges, set apart by banks of low morning mist, rolled toward the eastern horizon. In the distant east he could see the lake where they had camped two nights before, flickering with the colors of dawn. His gaze settled on the northeast, where in the far distance he made out huge snowcapped mountains. Images from his youth leapt unbidden to his mind's eye. Working on fishing weirs with the snowcapped Cuillin behind them. Taking cattle to high pastures where he and his cousins would race from the nightly campsite to fill leather bags with snow for the whiskey and sugar treats their old Aunt Peg would concoct for the drovers.

Duncan stirred from his spell. As he reached the corporal, Brandt shrank back, then thrust a bony finger into Duncan's chest as if to confirm he was no ghost. He did not speak until he faced the platform again. "This was her favorite place, the major always said. Where they camped and first lay together as man and woman."

"It is one of the most beautiful places I have ever seen," Duncan acknowledged.

"Oh, the things I seen the major do, the things I seen him endure. The wounds, the hardships, not just battling against impossible odds, but also getting other men to do the same, which I reckon is even harder. I never saw him flinch, never saw him cower. But that night she died, he was all done in. I found him on his knees under the moon, weeping like a wee babe." Duncan, to his surprise, was glimpsing something noble under the surface of the unvarnished woodsman.

Brandt bravely looked up toward the top of the platform. Strands of tattered feathers fluttered from the corner posts. The weathered skull of a deer capped each post.

"He wouldn't let anyone come here with him," Brandt continued, "excepting one of his Mohawk sergeants, who knew the old ways of her tribe. They stayed up here all day and all night. They made a huge fire, like they was signaling the gods to come greet her eternal soul."

The platform itself was covered with a bearskin. At the near end, a braid of long black hair, tied with a faded red ribbon, dangled in the wind.

"Where is it, Corporal?" Duncan asked. "Where is what you are retrieving for Major Rogers?"

"Don't know, exactly," Brandt replied. "The place where no one would dare look," It meant, Duncan surmised, that Brandt did indeed know. He was uneasily watching the braid of hair.

"What was her name?" Duncan asked.

"Hahnowa."

"Turtle?"

Brandt nodded. "He called her Hannah."

"Do you have a flint and striker?" Duncan asked. When Brandt nodded, Duncan instructed him to light a fire and gather some cedar boughs. "There are words to be said," Duncan told him.

When the boughs were smoldering, Duncan lifted one and held it under each of the corner posts of Hahnowa's burial platform, then swept the fragrant smoke over the bearskin shroud. "*Jiyathontek*," he intoned toward the sky. "Here is the gentle Hahnowa of the Mohawk people, keepers of the eastern gate of the Haudenosaunee," he declared, referring to the role of the Mohawk in guarding the eastern border of the Iroquois League. He set the bough back on the small fire and raised the single strand of white wampum beads Conawago had given him in Boston, the signal for truth. He wiped the beads over his eyes to symbolically brush away his mourning tears, then at his throat to confirm he would speak truly and freely from his heart. Finally, he lifted the wampum and held it over the dead woman's skeletal remains. "*Enghsitskodake*," he said at last. *Thou shall be resting.* He repeated the prayer three times, then turned expectantly to Brandt.

The corporal held his hands in front of his chest, as if to push Duncan away. "Not me," Brandt protested. "Yer the one who discourses with Iroquois spirits."

Duncan steeled himself, then hesitated. "Saguenay," he said.

"Saguenay," Brandt repeated with a solemn nod.

"It's a place," Duncan suggested, lifting the beads toward the corporal.

Brandt clenched his jaw as he saw the beads, swallowing hard. "Ye talk about such things around campfires in the wilds. It was an old Oneida scout who first spoke to us of it. A beautiful place where all live in peace and harmony. No war, no famine, no disease. The major said you must mean heaven, and the Oneida said no, Saguenay is a real place in the north country that their ancestors often spoke of. A paradise where crops never fail and children are always laughing, he said, and everyone has thick fur robes for the long snow nights. A real place, he said, that no one has found yet."

"Saguenay," Duncan said again, feeling a sense a power in the word now. "Saguenay," he spoke toward the dead woman, as if to reassure her, then climbed onto the lower support of the platform. He clenched his jaw and pulled away the upper edge of the bearskin. It was far from the first time he had seen a dead Iroquois—he had once helped an entire village move all its dead when its elders had decided to relocate—but Hahnowa's desiccated face was somehow different. Another would have been repulsed by the shriveled, long-dead woman, but Duncan saw the vestiges of a strong, handsome countenance and felt an odd bond with the dead beauty, sensing the pain Robert Rogers must have felt over her loss.

She had died of a fever. In the tribes, that usually meant she had been killed by a disease brought by the Europeans, for which their bodies had no defenses. She had once been young and vibrant and in love. She had, he suspected, been the embodiment of the wild, joyful, and wise people of the tribes but had been cut down before bearing offspring, before aging, before knowing the fullness of life.

"*Bidh ainghlean da m'chaithris m'in cadal na huaigh,*" he whispered, not realizing he had spoken the Gaelic prayer until the words had left his tongue. *Angels shall guard ye in the sleep of the grave.* "Forgive me, Hahnowa," he added, and lifted her head. Her pillow was a rolled linen shirt, and in its center was a quillwork pouch the size of his open hand. He tossed the pouch down to Brandt, then rerolled the shirt and placed it under the woman's head, rearranging the black braids over the doeskin dress that adorned her skin and bones.

He whispered again in Mohawk, close to her ear. "*Kayanerenh.*" *Peace.* Then he covered the woman again with the weathered bearskin.

Corporal Brandt stood frozen, gazing at the pouch, when Duncan climbed down. As Duncan reached for it, however, the old ranger jerked it away. "It's the major's," he growled, backing away.

"You mean the pouch is what he wants in his cell in Montreal," Duncan said. The old Indian fighter nodded defiantly and pressed the pouch to his chest.

"First I need to see it."

"Not likely," Brandt said, stubbornly wrapping both arms around the pouch.

"If you refuse, it may do him no good at all." Duncan glanced at the embers beside them. "If you refuse," he added, "then I shall stack more cedar on this fire so all the Iroquois gods take notice of you. They know I have done this with the best of intentions, and she would have wished it. But if you hoard it, you may have defeated its purpose as surely as if that British patrol had taken it. I will tell the gods that Ebenezer Brandt has stolen a treasure from the spirit of this Iroquois princess."

Brandt stared wide-eyed at the top of Hahnowa's head, barely visible from under the bearskin shroud, then tossed the pouch to Duncan.

DUNCAN URGED HIS BORROWED HORSE forward, toward the long mountain that dominated the western horizon—the last mountain, Allen promised, before the inland sea. The first half of the morning had been spent listening to

Hayes and Allen debate the messages of Old Testament prophets, their talk often interrupted by the worried voice in Duncan's own head warning him that with every mile, he was getting closer to calamity. There was still too much he did not understand, but he felt compelled to run headlong toward the mysteries.

A two-toned whistle sounded from behind him. Allen was growing worried about Ben, the young scout he had sent ahead, and every few minutes he interrupted his debate with Hayes to signal for the teenage boy, to no avail. Duncan had begun ascending the final slope when his horse slowed, skewing its ears forward. He raised a hand to warn the others; then his horse gave a long, whickering cry as a riderless mount appeared, galloping toward them.

The frightened horse sped past him, then slowed enough for Allen to grab its reins. He flung them to one of his men and launched his own horse up the mountain at a full gallop. Duncan's mount, less sure-footed than Allen's nimble mountain horse, could not keep up, and Allen had disappeared from sight by the time Duncan reached the narrow pass over the crest of the mountain. He pushed his heels into the horse to urge him on, then just as urgently reined him in as the western lands opened before him.

Less than ten miles away, the shimmering blue mass of Champlain stretched toward the northern horizon. Low, compact ridges unrolled toward the west, pointing toward the slice of glassy blue in the southwest that had been christened Lac du Saint Sacrement by the early French explorers. Duncan's heart thrilled at the sight of the fertile, untamed landscape, unscarred by the hand of man.

His horse whinnied, and Duncan absently stroked its neck as he gazed toward the southwest at a shadow on the horizon that might have been the Catskills, where Sarah would be settling back into Edentown. He watched a great bird, probably an eagle, climbing into the sky and realized it was studying something below. He stared down the slope and in quick succession saw a stag standing on a ledge, a family of grazing hares, and Ethan Allen desperately bracing the legs of a hanged man.

"His arms, McCallum!" Allen shouted as Duncan galloped up to him. "Cut him down! By all that's holy, cut the rope!"

The young scout Ben had been hanged not by the neck, but by his arms, from a rope looped over an overhanging limb. His sleeves were soaked in blood from the open chafing at his wrists. A paper had been pinned to his shirt. Ben was moaning in agony, probably from the unnatural angle of his right shoulder. The youth gazed with a dull, unseeing expression as Duncan stood in his saddle to slice through the rope; then he fell into Duncan's arms, unconscious. As he fell, the paper blew away, snagging on a nearby blueberry bush.

Allen laid the youth on the ground, stroking his head as he knelt beside him. "Too young, too young for the perils of these trails. I told Ben's mother, but she insisted he ride with us, for she feared otherwise he would run away to the sea and she would never look on him again."

"He was beaten," Duncan explained as he examined the youth. "But he took no blade or ball in his body."

"But his arm," Allen groaned. "Look at the boy's arm!"

"The shoulder is dislocated," Duncan declared as he pulled away the boy's shirt.

As if to confirm, Allen pushed against the shoulder. The youth screamed in pain.

"Roll up the shirt and put it tight into his armpit," Duncan instructed Allen, who was watching their companions race down the slope now. "Now!" Duncan demanded. "The longer we leave it, the greater the pain."

Allen clumsily complied, then Duncan removed his own shoe, braced the bared foot against the youth's rib cage, and slowly, forcefully, pulled the arm. The youth's shout of pain abruptly stopped as with a loud pop the head of the humerus slid back into place. The scout gasped, more in surprise than pain now, then nodded his thanks to Duncan.

"Best keep it in a sling for a few days," Duncan advised, then opened his drinking gourd and began washing the scout's raw, bleeding wrists. "I need a fire," Duncan said to Allen. "I can make a brew to ease the discomfort."

Allen's alarm was quickly turning to anger as he studied the boy. "No need," he said, and retrieved a canteen draped over his saddle. Even from an arm's length Duncan could smell the potent liquor when he uncorked it. "Mountain tonic. We mix in a bit of maple sugar to give it the flavor of the hills," the frontiersman explained, then gently tipped the scout's head back to help him drink.

The youth gasped as the raw liquor hit his tongue, and his glazed eyes seemed to focus at last, acknowledging the worried faces that surrounded him. He grabbed the canteen and took a deep swallow. "Those dragoons," the youth spat as he recovered. "They rode on me out of the woods, surrounded me, and asked if I rode with the mountain militia. They pulled me off my horse and started kicking me. They were angry, as if they had decided we had deceived them, and they said if we brought any old rangers north, we'd all get the same treatment. Then they pinned the broadside to me and rode off toward the lake."

"The soldiers from yesterday?" Duncan asked as Allen retrieved the paper. "How would they have known to ask about old rangers?"

"The same, but with several others, newly arrived from one of the Champlain forts," Ben said, then sipped again at the canteen.

DUNCAN TURNED AS ALLEN CURSED under his breath. Duncan assumed that the broadside was about him, but then Allen held it up for him to see. *Robert Rogers,* it said at the top, under a row of skulls, *to be tried as a traitor before a Montreal court-martial. Traitor to the good people of New York and New Hampshire. Turn not your back on our blessed King George, father of our people. Conspirators be warned away from this foul path, or be dead.*

"Cowards hiding behind lies to intimidate free people!" Allen snarled, and crumpled the paper between his big hands. "Good for striking a fire," he growled, "no more."

The leader of the mountain boys left one of his men to tend the injured scout and escort him home, then urged their party on. In another two hours they had reached the flats along Lake Champlain, an hour later the little community at the landing place across the narrow strait from the fort at Crown Point, fifteen miles above Ticonderoga.

"Pointe à la Chevelure," Brandt declared as he reached Duncan's side. The corporal had lost much of his absentmindedness during their journey, as if he were slowly becoming a ranger again, though there were still moments when he drifted away to one of his past battles. "First time I come here, there was a couple dozen houses here, old French style, some even with thatched roofs. French families had been living here for thirty, forty years."

Duncan studied the settlement more closely, seeing now that some of the houses were indeed old and weathered. Brandt had a powder horn with the chimney rock etched on it. Chisholm had one with an outline of Lake Champlain on it, with only one location marked. Duncan had wondered why it would not show the forts at Crown Point or Ticonderoga, why it had shown only an X and the letters *Chev.* "You mean this was a French settlement?" he asked. The full name, Pointe à la Chevelure, meant Scalping Point, indicating that the early settlers had likely been visited by the Abenaki.

"Aye, farms built to support the old French Fort St. Frédéric, with its big stone castle tower." Brandt pointed across the strait to where a large stone ruin was clearly visible on the shoreline below the walls of the new British fort. "The major and I was here in '56, doing a secret scout. The war was on, and folks here had fled to Canada." He gave one of his dry, cackling laughs. "One of those terrible lake storms hit. We stayed snug and warm all night in an abandoned French barn while the boys across the water struggled to keep their tents from blowing away."

Half a dozen boats, some little dories, others wide shallops big enough for horses or even a cannon, were tied to the timber pier that jutted out into the lake. A drowsy man sitting on a keg near the dock stretched his arms lazily and stood. "Crown Point ferry," he invited.

Allen scanned the men working around the waterfront, then grabbed Duncan's arm. "No need to sail straight into that swarm of redcoats," he said, gesturing toward the opposite shore. "Best we sail down the lake direct to Fort Ti. Give me a minute."

Before Duncan could protest that he needed no further escort, Allen beckoned to one of his men and they disappeared into a squat log structure built into the side of the hill adjoining the water. They reappeared a moment later carrying an inert body by the arms and legs. Just as the man summoned his senses enough to protest, they swung him into the lake.

The man yelped as he hit the water, and he sank like a rock. Duncan had taken several worried steps toward the circle of ripples where he disappeared before the stranger emerged, spitting out water as he splashed to shore. He stopped while knee-deep in the lake to push his long brown hair up over his crown, and he shook his head with a stern expression. "Should've smelled ye from miles away, Ethan, considering how ye be the biggest turd ever dropped out of the ass end of a weasel." He broke into a loud laugh and splashed to shore, embracing Allen in an energetic bear hug. When Allen released him, he wrung water from his shirt and made a beeline for a jug by the cabin door. He shook it, cursed, then held it upside down in bitter confirmation that it was empty.

"Bring any of yer maple brandy?" he asked hopefully, rubbing the bristle on his chin.

"Looks like ye need some honest work, Rufus Powell," Allen suggested.

"Ferry's over there," the man replied, pointing to the pier.

"T'ain't Crown Point we seek, Rufe, it's Fort Ti."

The news seemed to surprise the boatman. Suddenly all business, he examined the low waves on the lake, the angle at which the breeze bent the nearby rushes, and the clouds overhead. "Can't make it back today. Ye got to pay my overnight expenses," he declared, holding up the empty jug.

"Two jugs and a shilling a head," Duncan put in, "provided we leave within the hour."

Allen muttered under his breath, casting a frustrated glance at Duncan. Rufus's eyes grew wide. He abruptly straightened and whistled at a gangly teenage boy who was talking to a girl with freckles and long blond hair. "Save yer French lesson for tomorrow, lad." The boy winced but gave a noble bow to the girl and darted toward one of the shallops tied to the dock.

As the boat was readied, most of their company reclined on the grassy sunlit bank. Will began tossing sticks into the water, each being retrieved by Molly to the cheerful hoots of onlookers. Duncan studied the little village, then left his rifle and pack with Munro and slipped between two buildings, reaching a large vegetable garden where the freckled girl was now attacking weeds with a hoe.

"*Bonjour*," he offered, and plucked a weed himself.

She glanced behind him, returned the greeting with a shy smile, and wiped her hands on her apron.

"Your garden looks fertile," he said, continuing in French as he motioned to the verdant rows of maize, beans, squash, and cabbage.

"The season is short, but the soil is rich."

"I hadn't realized any had stayed on from the old Chevelure," Duncan ventured.

"Not stay, came back. A handful after the war, half a dozen more families this past spring."

Duncan had marked a surprising number of oxen, new plows, and wagons. "Such a prosperous community."

"I lived here when I was very young. Now it is better. Now we will have our high windmill!" she said, and inclined her head toward the tallest hill behind the settlement, where a surprisingly tall, sturdy stone tower was being built. On the ground beside it men were assembling the frames for wind vanes.

Duncan indicated the rows of plants. "You are excellent farmers."

The girl smiled. "We worked just as hard in Quebec, but things are better here. We were able to get good seed, good teams, good tools. My papa says we owe our prosperous benefactors in the north. We pray for them at our evening meals."

"Thanks to the saint in the north, you mean," Duncan said. *"Merci a Saint François."*

The girl gave a cryptic smile. *"Grace au saint de Saint François, grace au saint de Montréal,"* she replied, and turned back to her cabbages.

UNABLE TO PUT WORDS TO the question that was nagging him, Duncan gazed at the little farming community as they sailed away. There was something about it that seemed off, but he could not name it. Why had Josiah Chisholm, the murdered ranger, received a powder horn marked with the town's location? Brandt's horn had shown chimney rock, which had been his mission. Had Chisholm been given a mission at Chevelure? Glancing about to assure that no one watched, he opened the stained pouch he had taken from the Mohawk woman's grave. He had already confirmed that it contained only a necklace of red and white beads with a quillwork pendant depicting a man and woman holding hands, and half of a dozen slips of paper. Not for the first time since leaving the burial platform he found himself saying a Mohawk prayer for Hahnowa, asking for forgiveness, then he extracted one of the papers.

All the other pages had been lists, all in the same elegant hand—lists of names, of supplies, of river mouths along the eastern shore of Lake Champlain—and, like the letters to the rangers, all in the same odd purple ink, even though the pages from Rogers's hidden pouch would have been written years earlier, in the months just after the St. Francis raid. This page held a drawing, a sketch he had recognized when approaching the boat landing that afternoon. The nine-year-old sketch was of Chevelure, with only a few differences from the village he was now looking at, including the huge windmill.

He hesitated, wondering for a moment if Brandt had played a ruse on him.

Now we will have our high windmill, the comely French maiden had boasted. He examined the paper more closely. The drawing hidden by Rogers and now sought by the imprisoned major had a windmill. But no windmill existed nine years earlier. He folded the paper back into Rogers's pouch and watched Chevelure until it was out of sight. It wasn't a drawing of the town that Rogers had hidden, it was a drawing of a plan, and underneath was a large, stylized S. It wasn't a signature, it was a symbol. The paper was part of the dream of Saguenay that Rogers shared with others. But it was no longer just a dream. Saguenay was being implemented, and its conspirators were in at least two towns in the north. When he suggested that the girl must give thanks to Saint Francis, she had corrected him, saying that they gave thanks to the saint of St. Francis, and to the saint of Montreal. They were giving thanks to specific men.

12

DUNCAN LONGED TO TAKE THE tiller of the little shallop as they sailed down the lake, though he had to admit the unshaven, malodorous Rufus was an accomplished sailor. The vessel was wide of beam for cargo but well built, with clean lines that responded to the steady lake wind. White, billowy clouds streamed across a cobalt sky, echoing the late spring snowcaps of peaks in the distant Adirondacks. He recognized on Molly's face the same anticipation he felt, and he knew that she too wanted to leap over the side and frolic in the clear waters. But as the high earthen walls of Crown Point disappeared from view, he pushed down the temptation, knowing that he was moving into enemy territory. There were answers to be found in Fort Ticonderoga, but there were also men who would clamp him in irons if they knew who he was.

As Duncan watched the wooded shoreline, his hand on a stay, Munro stood up from where he had been checking their weapons and approached. The Scot had been unusually withdrawn and now seemed to have difficulty finding words. "All this talk about turning our backs on the king unsettles my heart, Duncan," he finally said in a low, troubled voice. "I'm not here because I turned my back on the king, I ken this well, but if we are to pierce the cloud of these deaths, I feel that's where ye have to take us. Mother Munro raised no traitor."

Duncan followed the Scot's gaze back toward the hills, where a broadside had been pinned to the tortured young scout, and he realized that its words had triggered Munro's reflections. He wanted to argue with Munro, but his heart was not in it, for he felt much the same way. "We're not on some Boston liberty pole march that's going to end with a frolic at a tavern," he admitted. "We're here because of the debt we owe the dead."

"Yer here because Hancock and Adams and the governor of Massachusetts forced you," Munro replied.

"No. They don't own me, nor you," Duncan replied. "I confess the warrant has me looking over my shoulder sometimes, but we are not running, we are hunting. From the moment I saw all those dead on the beach, I knew I had to help them. In the Highlands and among the tribes a murdered man wanders aimlessly on the other side, never finding eternal peace until his death is put right."

A line formed between Munro's brows. "That's what the Deathspeaker does, then?"

Duncan looked back, studying the old soldier. Munro had never used that word with him.

"Git troubled souls into heaven?" the weathered Scot continued. "Like the ones called sin-eaters my grandfather spoke of when I was a bairn. They would free the dead or those consumed by sin by sitting all night at their side, absorbing their sins."

The words pressed down on Duncan's heart. "Something like that," he acknowledged in a whisper.

Munro nodded. "A thankless, lonely task, lad. Sineaters always became dark, burdened souls. My grandma had different words for them. The hounds of God. Is that what we are?" he asked. "Is that what a liberty man is?"

Duncan had no answer, and Munro stepped away.

An hour later a cold knot grew in Duncan's gut as the stone walls of the great northern fort came into view. Once again he was rushing headlong toward the enemy without having scouted its territory. His luck would not hold forever.

He realized that his companions were looking not at the fort, but at figures standing on a small overgrown landing on the eastern shore, used when Ticonderoga had been under siege in the French war.

"We bargained to go straight to the fort," Allen reminded Rufus as he nudged the tiller to investigate.

"And who be the captain of this ship, Ethan?" the waterman demanded in a surly tone. "I don't tell ye how to navigate the mountains, now do I?"

A deep voice hailed the boat from the landing. Duncan could see four or five men standing there, two of them waving energetically until a broad-shouldered figure stepped between them and raised a hand over his head as if giving a blessing. "What do ye make of them?" Rufus asked his young mate, who had climbed onto the rail, holding a stay.

"Not certain, sir, but the big man looks like—can it be?"

"By Christ, I know who the rogue is!" Rufus exclaimed, then whooped for joy as another figure raised a demijohn jug. "It be divine intervention, Ethan!" he declared, and swung the boat toward shore.

Molly soon recognized the newcomers, barking excitedly as two somber tribesmen wearing black waistcoats over their bare chests stepped into the water to guide the boat to the decrepit pier. Behind them stood Samson Occom and Conawago, still holding the demijohn, with Noah lingering at the rear. The old Nipmuc wore his hair in a trim blocked braid at the back of his head and wore his good green waistcoat over doe-colored britches.

"Heard ye took the fight to the devils in England, Reverend," Rufus called in greeting.

"I *was* in England, Rufus, you scoundrel, but as you can see, the prodigal has returned to more familiar devils," Occom answered cheerfully. "Still the unrepentant sinner?" The pastor was more relaxed than Duncan had ever seen him.

"As often I can, sir," the waterman cracked.

"My mission requires passage to the king's bastion on the far shore."

"Mission?"

Allen opened his mouth for what was no doubt a glib observation, but Occom caught his eye, cutting him off with a gesture that took in his own party and those in the boat. "Our mission," he repeated, "is to pound God's truth into men of the sword."

"Can we trust this sailor?" Conawago asked Occom with a bemused grin.

Occom climbed into the boat and approached its helmsman, giving an exaggerated wince at his odor. "Rufus fornicates with native women," the reverend loudly declared. "He comes to me and confesses each time because he grew up in the Romanish faith; then he believes he is free to repeat the act again. How many times has it been, Rufus? Ten? Fifteen?"

Rufus took off his tattered cap, scratched his head, and spoke in a humble voice. "Well, yer holiness, ye being in England and all, we got some catching up to do onc't ye can find a few hours. Still, I am most moderate in my affairs, the dusky ladies would all confirm. Never one to over-egg the pudding."

The men burst into loud guffaws. Even Occom managed a smile.

Conawago quieted the company as they cast off. "It is a short passage, and we must be ready to work together when we arrive. Reverend Occom is known to the colonel, who supports his efforts to build native churches. We are all his disciples, about to go into the wilderness to build a new chapel. There are a number of tribesmen living in the vicinity of the fort, army scouts and their families. We will be there to hold services with them and solicit their devotion."

"Where exactly are we building this blessed chapel?" one of Allen's men asked. "Did you bring good axes to cut the timber?"

"T'ain't no real church, ye fool," Rufus chided. "It's what we educated folks call a figment of the imagination."

The man's face clouded. "But he said there was to be a church."

Allen groaned. "Zeke, just stitch yer lip. Pray when the good reverend prays and sing when the good reverend sings."

"We have a quarter hour to practice," Noah declared with a grin. "We shall disembark with a hymn. A hymn shall be our passport inside the walls."

They spent much of their remaining time trying to identify any songs that might be known by all. After a few bawdy suggestions, they decided on two, "Old Hundred" and "When I Survey the Wondrous Cross." The reverend pushed for one more.

"'O for a Thousand Tongues to Sing'" one of Allen's men called out.

Occom stared at the man in mock horror. "Heavenly Father, protect us," he groaned, looking upward. "A Methodist is among us!" As he asked the man to teach the others the first verse, Duncan watched Conawago. The old Nipmuc could speak with silent expression better than any man he had ever known. He now offered Duncan a fleeting smile that said whatever damage may have existed in their relationship was now repaired. With a pointed set of his eyes and a nod toward Occom, he told Duncan to accept the charade. He had fled angrily into the night at the lake after pleading with Hayes, but he must have rushed back to Fort Number Four in a bid to help Duncan. It would have taken a headlong race to return to the settlement on the Connecticut and reach the landing in time to intercept him.

They sang "Old Hundred" as they docked at the long Ticonderoga pier, having threaded their way past a brig and several of the long rowing bateaux used for troop transport on the lake. When a sentry asked their business, they simply sang even louder: "'May God who made the earth and sky bestow his blessings from on high.'" Noah, more ebullient than Duncan had ever seen him, had brought two stripped willow limbs on board and during their short passage had managed to notch and lash them together to form a four-foot cross, which he now held like a battle standard as they approached the imposing stone walls.

"Goddamned mission Indians," a soldier groused as they passed him. There was contempt but also resignation in his voice. The authorities in London officially embraced the conversion of the tribes, having decided that the inconvenience it sometimes caused at its garrisons was far preferable to fighting the natives.

Another, less coarse voice came down from the ramparts. "It's the Reverend Occom, the Indian scholar!" the officer called out. "Colonel Hazlitt will want to greet him. Corporal, report to the colonel! Double time!"

A shudder ran down Duncan's spine as the heavy doors of Ticonderoga's gate opened and they marched through onto the parade ground. Not trusting Rogers's secret pouch to his own possession with so many hostiles nearby, just before docking he had returned it to Brandt, telling him to keep it well hidden. Duncan was never entirely trustful of the regular military, but here his fear seemed almost palpable, like a demon walking at his side. Allen and the mountain militiamen who had accompanied them had slipped away before reaching the gate, following Rufus toward the tavern by the docks. The men who had nearly killed his young scout were likely in the fort, and Allen was savvy enough not to confront them on their own ground.

Brandt, at Duncan's side, straightened and threw a knuckle to his forehead as the gate sentinels saluted, then missed a step as they emerged onto the broad, open yard and he saw the squad drilling there. "The Ladies from Hell," he gasped in surprise.

Duncan found himself smiling, forgetting his fears for a moment. Munro froze, a wide grin on his face and a hand pressed against his heart. "M' lads," he proclaimed.

The solidly built men marching in formation before them all wore black-and-green kilts, blue bonnets with black fur cockades, short red coats with no lapels, and red-and-white-diced stockings. They were from the famed 42nd Regiment of Foot, the British army's shock troops, the Black Watch. Duncan had never been sure whether the appellation Ladies from Hell had been coined by friend or foe, but the fierce men in kilts, always at the vanguard of battle, had left enemies shaking on three continents.

"Uncas!" The uneven singing died away as a tribesman in a scarlet uniform coat called down from the gun emplacement above them. He did not bother with the stairs, but with graceful ease lowered himself down the wall and dropped the last few feet.

"Reverend Occom," the minister sternly corrected, but his affectation was betrayed by a wide smile as the Indian trotted toward him. The man he greeted was a relic of another age. The open coat of the British infantry, sleeves cut off, which he wore over his tattooed chest was the only European influence in his attire. His loincloth was finely worked doeskin decorated with tribal images, the leggings laced with sinew were of heavier buckskin, and his moccasins were still heavier moose skin, adorned only with quillwork stripes. At his side was a treacherous-looking, well-used war ax. His thick black hair hung in two braids into which small seashells had been woven. The left side of his angular face was tattooed with a pattern of tiny squares.

"Mohegan," Conawago explained in a surprised whisper.

"Reverend Uncas," the Indian declared more loudly, as if the company needed an introduction to the true Occom. "Son of the son of the great Chief Uncas of the Mohegan people!"

The unshakable Occom actually seemed embarrassed. The Mohegan stranger seemed to enjoy ribbing the solemn missionary, but then the amusement left his face as he spotted Noah. He stepped to Occom's disciple and abruptly dropped to one knee, as if to pay homage. Clearly embarrassed, Noah quickly pulled the man to his feet as more Indian scouts appeared with enthusiastic greetings for Occom and his companions.

As the loud reunion continued, Duncan seized the confusion to slip away. Relying on his memory of the fort and Sergeant Mallory's description, he fixed on a window at the corner of the second floor of the old bastion and bounded up the stairs at the end of the building. The corridor was quiet, lit only by the sunlight that filtered through a few open doors. He quickly found the door marked REGIMENTAL CLERK, then, following Mallory's instructions, located the key behind the framed Roll of the Honored Dead that hung on the wall a few feet away.

His gut tightened as he unlocked the door. The chamber was indeed unoccupied and was much as the deserter had described—a dusty, stuffy chamber with a large trestle table on one side, holding candle lanterns and mounds of paper, and stacks of shelves on the other. The smell of candle tallow was heavy in the air. In the small hearth were the shavings of feather shafts where someone had recently shaped writing quills. The shelves were packed with ledgers, large parchment envelopes, and stacks of paper bound with red ribbons.

Duncan tried in vain to read the inscriptions on the ledgers in the dim light between the stacks, then reluctantly returned to the desk, pulled out his tinderbox, and quickly lit one of the candle lanterns. *Look on the back wall, past the files on reconstruction of Crown Point,* Mallory had carefully explained. Moments later Duncan stood in the bright light of the window with the file he sought. The broad parchment case was marked simply ST. FRANCIS OCTOBER 1759. He glanced out the window, where an officer was trying to hastily assemble the members of a company band near the entrance to the garrison offices.

There were two dozen documents in the case, each imprinted with a stamp in red ink stating *Garrison Clerk, Fort Ticonderoga.* Nearly all were written in the same neat clerical hand, no doubt transcriptions from other documents. Topmost was *Report of Major Robert Rogers,* followed by *Statement of Captain Joseph Wait, Statement of Captain Ogden, Statement of Lieutenant Dunbar, Statement of Captain M. Williams,* and similar accounts from half a dozen other members of the expeditionary force, then a list of dead from the expedition. Duncan quickly scanned Rogers's report. The major described a precisely co-ordinated attack on the Abenaki stronghold that began at 5:00 a.m. Rogers repeatedly praised the bravery of his men, stating that while the enemy had suffered two hundred casualties, he had lost only one man in the raid itself. He continued with a long explanation of the woodcraft and rangering skills that had brought most of his men back to safety.

The motley band began playing outside. Duncan knew he had to return to their party before the greeting ceremony was concluded, before they were led away to a campsite or quarters. He finished his quick perusal of the other reports from the expedition members, pausing only over two passages, the first in the report of Captain Williams, who recounted that he had gone into St. Francis the night before with Rogers. *I saw over six hundred scalps on poles*, he stated, then *I saw a score of enemy canoes on the river landing*. The second referred to Major Rogers disappearing in the heat of the battle by the large Jesuit mission church, then reappearing a quarter hour later on the far side of town, just before the church burst into flame. The final two reports were single-sheet accounts from others, one from the commander of the garrison that had occupied St. Francis for two years after the war, which offered little more than the comment that the biggest tension in the town was with the Jesuits, not the Abenaki, who were much subdued after the Rogers raid. The second sheet was from a report dated 1764 from a sheriff in New York town. Major Rogers had become an inveterate drunkard and gambler and in June of that year had been arrested for debt, only to be broken out by old ranger friends, who provided the fast horse on which he fled to Connecticut.

In the bottom of the parchment envelope were two sealed tubes, of the kind Duncan had seen used during the war for urgent dispatches. Each was about six inches long, its wooden cap fixed tight by a ring of the red wax used for official seals. The music outside seemed to be coming to a close. Duncan muttered a curse, then twisted open the first tube, breaking the seal. Inside was another statement, but not from a soldier. It was in a different hand, not the clerk's, and signed by Father Jean-Baptiste de LaBrosse, vicar of St. Francis. Duncan's heart leapt as he saw that it was inscribed in purple ink. He folded the statement and began to put it into his coin pouch, then reconsidered and folded it lengthwise and stuffed it under his belt. The second container held only a scrap of stained paper. It had a Christian cross at the top and a hastily sketched plan for a large building with several doors, windows, and altars. He stuffed the paper into his pouch, then as he returned the envelope to the shelf he noticed a large wooden candle box labeled ARTIFACTS and hastily slid open the lid. Inside were half a dozen powder horns, all etched with the usual scenes of battle or forest. Each was inscribed with a name. Samuel Gibson, he read, then Thomas Pickering and, to his surprise, Daniel Oliver. The drawing on Oliver's horn was of a simple church near a river, with a canoe beached in front of it. Duncan quickly surveyed the others, looking for names of rangers. There was Ogden, Jersey Blues, referring to the famed unit of the New Jersey militia, Ruggles of Massachusetts, Fitch of Connecticut, and finally, Williams, Pontius Pilate's Bodyguard. None were rangers, though Duncan had not heard of Williams's bizarrely named unit. In the bottom of the box someone had jammed a copy of the popular poem written about the raid, "The Ballad of Rogers Retreat." Duncan paused over one verse:

> *When ten days were spent in vain*
> *The Indians overtook them again*
> *Near thirty men as some do cry*
> *Now by the Indians they did dy.*

Suddenly he realized that the music had stopped and only a solitary drum-beat could be heard. He quickly held each tube to the candle flame, resealing the wax. Moments later he was back in the hallway, returning the key to its hiding place. As he walked down the stairs, touching the note in his belt, Occom's delegation, fortified by soldiers, burst into a loud hymn.

"By God, sir, I do so envy you!" the portly, ruddy-faced commander of Fort Ticonderoga exclaimed when Duncan explained that he had recently seen a fisher cat. "The great wolf cat of forest legend!" Colonel Hazlitt said. "Imagine when a trained natural philosopher gets his hands on one! Why, it may require a whole new branch of taxonomy!" The colonel was a genteel, learned man who had insisted on hosting his visitors at supper in his apartments. Conawago, Duncan, Occom, Munro, Noah, and Hayes sat at a long, lavishly set table with Hazlitt and three other officers, stewards hovering behind them. The colonel explained that he had twisted arms in Whitehall to obtain a posting in the New World so he might study its flora and fauna. He had earned the honors of Fort Ticonderoga by fighting the French in the fever isles, and had passed his long weeks on troop transports by reading the amazing zoological tracts of Harvey, Leeuwenhoek, and Linnaeus.

"I was skeptical about finding one-legged warriors who hopped into battle," Hazlitt confessed as he called for more claret, referring to some of the earliest accounts of the New World, "but that left the beaver as long as a house and the horse with the trunk of an elephant for me to find."

Conawago exchanged an amused glance with Duncan and added, "Not to mention the bird that bursts into flames and rises from its ashes."

The colonel's good nature was not offended by the gibe. "I am always open to suggestion, sir," he replied, his large eyes growing even more protuberant as he described encountering a bull moose by the lake shore. He turned to Duncan. "But the cat that flies, sir, what a thrill it must be to see one!"

"My friend Conawago calls it *ursus caelo*, the sky bear," Duncan offered with another uneasy glance at the stewards, all of whom were soldiers who had left their arms by the door. He had fervently hoped to avoid attending the dinner, but Conawago had convinced him that he would rouse suspicion in declining the honor. Their compromise was that Duncan would use a false name.

Hazlitt's face lit with excitement again. "Wonderful!" He searched his pockets and produced a writing lead, then, to his personal steward's obvious displeasure, recorded the name on the linen tablecloth. "So the bear that flies through the tops of trees is no myth!"

"More like a giant pine marten, but they do indeed exist," Conawago assured the officer. "They eat the dreaded porcupine," he added, prompting a long discussion of how this might be physically possible.

As Hazlett finally crossed his fork and knife on his plate, declaring their consumption of prodigious quantities of trout, venison, and potato-and-leek pie to be concluded, he leaned forward with a conspiratorial air. "Gentlemen," he proudly confided, "while my man fetches the port and cheese, I am going to show you something that will take your breath away!"

The colonel rose, straightened his lace-trimmed waistcoat, and disappeared into an adjoining room. One of the remaining infantry officers looked after him with a fond expression, but another, a scar-faced, sour-looking man was cocking his head toward the door through which they had entered. Heavy bootsteps and the clink of metal could be heard in the corridor.

"What a gentleman!" the colonel declared as he returned waving a tattered, much-read letter. "He may be a frog, but a more noble and intelligent chap you could never hope to encounter. Ironically, he was stationed in this very establishment during the unpleasantries here in 1758."

"When so many Highlanders were massacred," Duncan observed.

"Monsieur Bougainville went on to great success in his king's army," Hazlitt rejoined. "But he was a mere captain on that terrible day."

"Louis Antoine de Bougainville?" Duncan asked in surprise. "Who commanded part of the French army at Quebec?"

"By then he was a colonel, yes. And after the fall of New France, he went back to Paris to negotiate the treaty that yielded to King George all the lands east of the Mississippi. But that's not his real *célébrité*," Hazlitt said, using the French word. "He has become a renowned natural philosopher. King Louis has given him a charter, and two ships, to be the first Frenchman to circumnavigate the globe! And he sent me a letter from the coast of Brazil!"

The sullen officer, who had obviously heard the contents of the letter before, excused himself with thinly disguised impatience and disappeared into the corridor. Duncan and his friends listened respectfully as Hazlitt explained how he had sent a letter to Bougainville to congratulate him and to suggest that he pay special attention to the orchids on the remote isles he would visit. The colonel then energetically recounted the French officer's description of huge flocks of terns, pods of giant whales, and the amazing aviary of mangrove swamps along the mouth of the Amazon.

The door behind Colonel Hazlitt opened. The scar-faced officer, wearing an expression of smug amusement now, stepped through the doorway, which revealed a comfortable sitting room with a carpeted floor and a blazing hearth. A man sat in one of the armchairs in front of the fire, bent over a violin. He was feverishly playing a piece that sounded like Mozart.

Hazlitt lowered his glass of port and turned, his face reddening. "Lieutenant? What is the meaning of this?"

The dour lieutenant maintained a businesslike air, but his eyes were full of gloating, as if scoring a point in a personal match between himself and the commander. "Unexpected business, sir. Urgent business from Albany."

"In my personal study? You presume too much, sir!"

"The general's business, sir," the officer pointedly replied, as if it forgave all.

"And is that my violin—" the colonel sputtered as he struggled to his feet. "By God, sir, the insolence!"

The officer ignored his commander, and gestured them all toward the colonel's study. As Duncan and Conawago passed through the door, the entrance to the corridor opened behind them and two soldiers appeared, bayonets fixed on their muskets.

The violinist, ignoring them, played to a crescendo before turning to them with a victorious smile. An icy fist closed around Duncan's heart. It was Horatio Beck.

Beck rose and offered an exaggerated bow to the colonel, then extended the violin. "Imagine my surprise to find such a fine instrument here in the wilderness," he haughtily observed as Hazlitt grabbed it out of his hands. "Though I did have to tune it."

"What is the meaning of this, Lieutenant, you impertinent—"

"This impertinent officer works for the Ministry of War," the Englishman declared, acid dripping with every word. "Horatio Beck is my name. And allow me to correct that so we can avoid unnecessary delays. *I* work for the minister of war."

Duncan eyed the door Beck must have used to gain entry from the corridor and began to inch toward it.

"I so enjoyed your discussion of natural philosophy," Beck offered in a mocking tone. "There seems to be no end to the monsters inhabiting these wilds. Treacherous flying bears. Catamounts that swallow deer whole. Black-hearted Jacobites ravenous for the flesh of our precious sovereign."

Hazlitt's fury was quickly turning to confusion. "Sir?"

Beck extracted one of the bounty bills from a pocket, unfolded it, and extended it to the colonel. "The infamous traitor and murderer of over thirty men stands in this very room."

Hazlitt's face drained of color as he read the paper. Duncan took a quick step toward the door and grabbed the latch, only to find it locked.

"You are the infamous McCallum!" Hazlitt gasped. "How dare you sit at my table!"

Duncan darted toward the door to the dining chamber only to have the two soldiers level their bayonets at him.

"Seize him!" Beck snarled.

The two soldiers grabbed Duncan, each clamping a hand around one of his arms. Hazlitt fixed Duncan with a gaze that was as much disappointment as anger. "Do you have nothing to say, McCallum?"

"Don't trust everything you read, sir. Lieutenant Beck knows that the allegations of the broadside are false. He will use you as he is using me."

"Search him!" Beck ordered.

As one of the guards held him from behind, the other began piling Duncan's possessions on the little reading table between the chairs. His knife. His compass. His large belt pouch, which was emptied out to reveal coins, flints, buttons, and the folded drawing from the clerk's office.

Beck's eyes lit with pleasure as he straightened out the paper. "Stolen from your garrison archives," he stated to the colonel.

"What proof do you offer of that, sir?" Hazlitt inquired in a brittle voice.

Beck turned his triumphant smile toward the shadowed window, where Duncan now saw a man leaning against the frame.

"I am the proof, sir," the figure said as he stepped into the light, "because I am the one who put it there." It was Sergeant Mallory.

13

LONELY BIRDCALLS, THE PASSAGE OF a patch of sunlight on his wall, the rat-ta-tat of drumrolls from the parade ground. Duncan's world had become an incomplete mosaic of sound and light. Blessedly, the cells for the most desperate of prisoners had been built into the top floor of the tallest building, owing, an escorting guard had explained, to an embarrassing escape by a tunneling prisoner years earlier. This meant that through the small window seven feet above the floor a misshapen rectangle of sunlight traveled across the cell wall during the morning hours. That was when Duncan sat below the window, listening to the birdsong coming from the nearby orchard and woods. The drums rolled for morning and evening muster, and he learned to expect food after each, a bowl of glutinous porridge in the morning, when his piss pot was removed, and a plate of stale bread and hardened cheese at the end of the day.

As the sun finally rose after the first long night, he had extracted the Statement of Father Jean-Baptiste de LaBrosse from inside his belt. It was dated not 1759, but December 1764, years after the war in North America had ended and a year after the treaty of peace had finally been signed in Paris. Was it because only then—with his war officially lost and British authority established over Quebec—that the Jesuit LeBrosse was willing to speak? Or was it because someone had later begun to suspect Rogers and had interrogated the Jesuits, who had become reluctant subjects of King George? It was the same year Rogers had been arrested in New York for debt, and had escaped—as if something in the incident had triggered the Ministry of War's interest in Rogers. It hadn't been the minister of war exactly, Duncan reminded himself, but Horatio Beck, another inveterate gambler who was also deeply in debt.

The statement was disappointingly brief. It seemed almost an apology for Rogers, stating that the major had allowed the most cherished items of the church to be carried away before destruction of the town—and how, contrary to popular reports, Rogers had shown Christian charity to at least some of the women and children of the town, who owed their lives to him. The likely reason the statement was still in the file and hadn't been taken for evidence in Rogers's trial, he realized, was because it had nothing incriminating to say. Perhaps the most important clue lay on the surface of the paper, its purple ink. The ink itself had become like a signature. Had LaBrosse been Rogers's surrogate, had *he* been writing the letters to the rangers? It seemed unlikely that all the letters would have found their way from Rogers in the distant northwest, and certainly not directly from him in his prison cell.

Duncan repeatedly read the second paragraph of LaBrosse's statement.

There was no hidden treasure at St. Francis, now or in 1759, LaBrosse attested. There were no French nationals, only humble monks who had in fact been repudiated by the French king. LaBrosse could not attest to the where-abouts of the militant Jesuits, who were known, he admitted, to accompany Abenakis on their raids during the prior hostilities, and he suggested that such inquiries be referred to the Superintendent of Indian Affairs, Sir William Johnson. The first paragraph read like a general narrative, but the second one was written in response to specific questions. Five years after the raid, someone had asked about the lost treasure of King Louis, and now gold coins from St. Francis had been surfacing in New England. Duncan looked back at the date. December 1764. Rogers had been arrested for debt in June of that year. Surely it was no coincidence that the questions started being asked after his encounter with gambling and debt in New York.

Duncan's cell had originally been built to house soldiers, probably during the French war, when ranks had swollen for the northern campaigns, so it held a small hearth. Duncan had taken heart to see that the bars on the window were only wooden, but when he grabbed them to hoist himself up, he under-stood why. The window was just wide enough for a man to squeeze through but it was nearly thirty feet above the ground. No one could survive such a fall without broken bones, or worse.

In the back of the hearth he found a few charred sticks and used one to mark the arc of the moving sunlight; then, for a makeshift clock, he divided it into what he estimated were hours. At first he assumed he would be transported quickly to Boston, where he might at least reach out to friends. By the end of the second day, however, with no word and no contact with anyone but the solitary guards posted in four-hour shifts outside his cell, he began to despair. Surely Beck would not have waited to interrogate him. Surely his companions would have wanted to see him. Had Beck locked him up simply to get him out of the way?

The hatch cut into the heavy iron-studded door was eight by ten inches, big enough only to pass food through, but he discovered that if he sat on the floor at a certain angle from the hatch, he could often see the face of the sentry beside the door. During the first day, none would acknowledge him. One shoved his bayonet into the hole to discourage Duncan's attempt at dialogue. But on the second day the guard that came after the morning muster wore a kilt.

Duncan sat on the floor so he could see the man's stern, ruddy countenance and began softly whistling Highland songs. Beginning with "My Bonnie Highland Laddie," which caused the guard to turn in surprise toward the cell before returning to his sober vigilance, Duncan switched to "Charlie Is My Darling," then the doleful "Tears of Scotland." The guard did not react again, but his face softened with a faraway melancholy.

Duncan asked him, in Gaelic, what his clan was. The sentry's eyes flickered, but he would not reply. Duncan began relating tales of his own life as a boy. "My mother's people were boatwrights and sailors," he explained. "My father's people were mostly cattle drovers. My favorite day of summer was when we moved the herd to the high pastures in the mountains of Skye, the Cuillin. Do you ken them? My mother and her sister would wake me up in the wee hours and we would climb up through the blooming heather to a ledge that looked out over the waters to the east and north. She called it the Shining Place, for the way the sun lit the world from there, making everything glow at dawn. We'd get there in time to watch the sunrise and we'd eat a breakfast of bread and honey and dried herring. My aunt would break out in old songs about battles of fierce warriors of our clans against giants and witches. I wonder, is there anyone still alive in the Highlands who knows those songs? Sometimes," Duncan continued, "she'd stop in the middle of a verse and point out over the water and say, 'There's the old rogue his very self!' and I'd see my grandfather's trading sloop that he sailed among the islands. You could tell it from far away because he dyed his sails red. He told me he did that to hide all the pirate blood he had to spill, and I was young enough to believe him. I remember thinking what a grand world it was, what with me in the Shining Place and having warriors and drovers and pirate killers for kin. Once, I had a vivid dream about galloping on the back of a shaggy cow, sword in hand, charging to do battle with a pirate horde."

The sentry's posture relaxed and he cocked his head toward Duncan, who began to speak of cattle drives and long sails up the remote bays, where his grandfather would anchor so they could watch for selkies, the half-human, half-seal women. "If I'd misplace something when on his boat, my grandfather would say, 'See, your auntie selkie came up in the night and made off with it.' He would tie a ribbon to my wrist and say that was to let the selkies know I was already claimed by this branch of the family, because otherwise they'd take me to their undersea caves and I'd have naught but raw fish to eat the rest of my days."

Duncan quieted, drinking from the gourd of water that was provided each morning; then he watched the rectangle of light move across the wall.

"Buchanan," came a whisper. "My clan is Buchanan."

"Then Loch Lomand's your land," Duncan replied. "I had a cousin who married a Buchanan. *Clarior hinc honos,*" he added, remembering the clan motto. "*Brighter hence the honor.*"

The guard had a rich tenor voice. "I remember McCallums driving a herd of great hairy cows through the valley once. My father was in a bit of a tear over it, worried about damage to our own pastures, but when he rode off to complain, he came back with a smile on his face."

"My uncles always carried kegs of Highland whiskey to pay tolls along the way."

A tiny grin cracked the sentry's gruff countenance.

"Tell me, Corporal Buchanan, what a company of the Forty-Second is doing back at Ticonderoga. I thought you all had been ordered to Cork."

"Aye. All except us, on special detached service to the Northern Theater. The generals and colonels say we dress things up. Some days we go out and dig up Highland bones from the battlefield."

"Things?"

"Ceremonies with the tribes. Parades. Courts-martial and punishments."

"Courts-martial, here at the fort?"

"Aye. Lots of pomp and ceremony if it's a high crime. Escort the judges, roll the drums before sentencing. Full-dress uniform and solemn pipes for a hanging. Colonel Hazlitt will have us go up to Montreal with him soon when he goes to preside at an important trial."

"I was in Loch Lomand once as a boy," Duncan volunteered. "I remember little pockets of mist drifting over the lake, and my sister insisting they were all ghosts."

" 'As weel may I weep, o' yet dreams in my sleep,' " Buchanan said.

It took Duncan a moment to recognize the old ballad about forlorn lovers longing to meet at Loch Lomond. " 'But his arms and his breath were as cold as the earth and his heart's blood ran red in the heather,' " he continued, singing a verse not as well as known as the one about meeting on the bonny banks of the lake. "It was about Culloden," he ventured after a moment, knowing that the battle in which the English king had destroyed the Scottish rebels was a tender subject for many of the Highlanders who now fought for the son of that same king. "The one who wrote it was in a cell, condemned to the gallows after the battle."

"Aye, so I've heard," Buchanan stiffly acknowledged.

"After Culloden, it took over an hour for them to hang all the McCallum men who had survived the battle. Then they went over the mountains and finished the rest of my family. All the women. Then the children. Then the horses, the cows, and finally the dogs."

Buchanan had no reply.

"One of my companions was here with the Black Watch in '58," Duncan mentioned after several breaths.

"Oh, aye. Munro," the corporal acknowledged. "He took us to the field where so many died and spoke to us of that dark day. Later, he went off by himself to say a prayer where his friend Archibald died."

"So he is still here?"

Buchanan took a moment to collect his answer. "That Lieutenant Beck says he has authority from minister such-and-such in London. Says no one can see you, not even the colonel. Hazlitt's none too happy, but Beck says it's none of his affair. A rider came in with dispatches for Beck from Albany. He ordered that Indian reverend to leave, but the colonel says his authority does not extend so far and that order would have to come from the Indian superintendent. The reverend has set up a tent outside the gate and holds evening prayer meetings, inviting all the off-duty soldiers and giving each a mug of applejack for the trouble if they endure the whole service."

"You said you are going to Montreal?" Duncan asked after several minutes.

"Aye. The colonel is on the panel chosen to conduct the trial of the famous major."

"Major Rogers."

"The very one. The toast of the army during the war, but now—" The steps of the guard coming up the stairs to relieve Buchanan interrupted him. The corporal quickly opened his cartridge box and extracted a length of sausage, which he tossed to Duncan, then tapped his musket on the floor and returned to his vigilant posture.

LONG AFTER THE SUN HAD passed overhead and no longer lit the window, Duncan sat on the floor studying the arc he had drawn on the wall. An arc was a way of connecting things, he realized, then began writing pieces of his puzzle on the whitewashed wall above and below the arc. At its beginning, he wrote "sinking of the *Arcturus*," then reconsidered, rubbing out the letters and writing "St. Francis raid." After a moment he added "1759." It had been a year in which worlds had been turned upside down, a year in which Englishmen rushed to buy each new edition of their newspapers for fear of missing the news of still another English victory. Quebec had fallen on September 13. Duncan stepped back a moment, trying to remember the chronology of that all-important year and what he had read in the archive files. Rogers had left for St. Francis on September 13, the very same day. He wrote the date on the wall, and "Quebec falls" beside it. Rogers could not have known of the victory, but the French contact he had met at St. Francis before the raid would have known. Duncan stared at the date. *Quebec had fallen.* The French had known then that they could not prevail simply by holding on to Montreal, which they lost the next year. Any shrewd strategist would have known that all was lost in September, but Rogers had his orders—and his lust for punishing the Abenaki. St. Francis had been a sanctuary, a base for planning raids on New England, a stronghold built by Jesuits decades earlier, a place considered far from the reach of the English, where secrets and even military resources might be hidden. Someone had questioned Father LaBrosse years later, and his reply had been that there was no hidden treasure at St. Francis, then or now. It wasn't the denial that was meaningful, it was its implicit acknowledgment that the treasure existed.

By 1759 the Jesuits had begun to loathe King Louis for his jealous persecution of their order. Patriots of New France had begun to loathe the king in Paris for failing to send the promised soldiers and supplies and funds that could have won the war for them. Major Rogers made a connection with the French during the raid, as proved by Labrosse's statement that he had allowed religious valuables and women and children to escape. Now Rogers was accused of collaborating with the French against the British king. But which French? The spies who sank the *Arcturus* had come from Paris, but those in St. Francis were a different breed of French altogether. Yet the spies from Halifax had an Abenaki assassin.

"Damn!" Duncan threw his writing stick against the wall in frustration. He was unequal to the task of fitting the pieces together. Rogers, Beck, the French spies, the Abenaki, the Jesuits, and even Hancock and Livingston were caught up in some great game, and Duncan did not understand the rules.

He began putting new calibrations on his wall. "Rogers learns of Quebec" came next, for he was certain that although the news did not change Rogers's plan for the raid, it did change his mind about the secrets he had collected at St. Francis. Duncan added "Hahnowa dies." Rogers's wife had died just after his return from the raid. Like the seasoned woodsman who takes a kill only when necessary for survival, Rogers had decided to stand down after the raid, to lower his rifle, keep his powder dry, and cache his bounty for future use.

Next came "Crown Point road work," which had been a subterfuge used by Rogers to quietly take his wife's body to their favorite place, and hide more secrets with her at a place no one would disturb. Years passed. The French became more active. Horatio Beck and his handlers became active. French farmers came back to Chevelure. Beck visited Ticonderoga to study the St. Francis files. The French agents infiltrated Livingston's maritime operations and stalked a ledger to Boston harbor. Duncan paused, considering the sequence. There were secret offices in ministries in both Paris and London at work. Which had acted first?

He wrote "Henri Comtois and Philippe board *Arcturus* in Halifax," then "*Arcturus* sinks, ledger recovered, and Oliver, the first of the rangers, murdered." Then, "theft at Hancock warehouse" and "murder of Chisholm." He paused again, then wrote "Secret Ledger" and "King's Treasure" in bigger letters below the entries. The ledger had come from London, and he had the sense that it had been in the works for years. It was the keystone, the linchpin that held all together, but Duncan could not make it fit. He inserted new entries: "arrest of Rogers," "inquiries about treasure," then "warrant for D M," and "attempted kidnapping of Will Sterret." Below "Secret Ledger" he wrote two names: John Hancock and Robert Livingston. Below "Hidden Treasure" he wrote the name of the only man who had mentioned it, Father LaBrosse. In a separate column, near the corner of the wall, he recorded the names of those whose powder horns had been etched with secrets and their images. "Ebenezer Brandt," he wrote, and sketched the chimney rock beside the name. Daniel Oliver was next, with an image of a church and a canoe. Finally came Josiah Chisholm, with a map indicating Chevelure. After a moment, for no reason other than it nagged him, he wrote "Williams, Pontius Pilate's Bodyguard."

DUNCAN'S NIGHTMARES GREW WORSE. FOR years he had had visions of his father's long-dead corpse hanging from the gibbet by the tollhouse in Inverness, raising its shriveled arm to point at him, accusing him of not having died for the clan. Now there was another gibbet, from which the body of Conawago hung, and the old Nipmuc too pointed at him, but Duncan never understood what Conawago was accusing him of. Sometimes Conawago was on a mountain trail, and he looked up, weeping, as he held the dead body of Ishmael. Then there was the worst dream, repeated over and over. Sarah and a strange man whom Duncan somehow knew to be her husband were being hacked to death by British bayonets.

With a groping hand blindly exploring the narrow chimney, he found a long edge of stone and with bloody knuckles kept hitting it until it broke away. He jammed it into a seam between wall planks below the window and used it as a step so that he could stare outside for extended periods, sometimes watching stars, sometimes clawing futilely at the base of the oaken bars with his fingernails. By diffuse moonlight he went back to the chimney, and though he paid the price of a painful spider bite that kept his hand numb and swollen for an hour, he finally pulled away another stone lip that he sharpened on the hearth-stone, and he went back to work on the base of the bars. Even if he did manage to knock them away so he could fit through the window, he doubted he could survive the fall on the other side. He wasn't doing it for his freedom, he realized, he was doing it for the defiance, for the honor of the prisoner he had become.

Corporal Buchanan, who had opened the door to retrieve Duncan's slop pot and deliver his breakfast, paused with the bowl of porridge in one hand. Duncan, ravenous, took the bowl while Buchanan gazed at his decoration of the white plaster wall. "Ye been busy, McCallum."

"Tracing the mysteries that would stretch my neck," Duncan said between mouthfuls.

"Rogers," Buchanan said. "St. Francis," he added, apparently mouthing the words he recognized. "And more Scots in your puzzle, I see."

Duncan lowed his wooden spoon. "Sorry?"

Buchanan pointed to the last line of the column in the corner. "Pontius Pilate's Bodyguard," he said. "Now there's some wild *Ghaidheil*."

"They're Scots? With that name?"

"Aye, because the lineage of the regiment goes back centuries, through the mists of time, as they say." He saw Duncan's confusion. "The Royal Scots, McCallum. Pontius Pilate's Bodyguards, they call them, like they call us the Ladies from Hell, as if they were so old they were there at Jerusalem. Williams, he was their captain. Thought ye had him there 'cause he was a close friend of Major Rogers, went to St. Francis with him and all."

Duncan stepped to the wall and underlined the name of the Scottish unit, then eyed Buchanan with new curiosity. "Are you up to a little mischief, Corporal?"

Buchanan grinned. "Life can be mighty boring here."

Duncan proceeded to tell him how to find the box of powder horns.

On the fourth day, the lock on the door rattled and Corporal Buchanan and another kilted soldier stepped in, then halted and pounded the butts of their muskets on the floor as Colonel Hazlitt appeared in the space between them. Duncan found himself standing as erect as the soldiers.

The colonel made a fluttering motion with his hand. "At ease, son, at ease." The colonel, appearing oddly uncomfortable, surveyed the room, then leaned into Buchanan's ear, and the corporal backed out of the cell. "I don't know whom to believe, McCallum," Hazlitt began. "I have been beseeched almost hourly by your friends. I accept that you have done works of justice and compassion for settler and Indian alike in this inhospitable frontier, that you even gave valuable service in the war, but . . . damnit, man, you have made enemies in very high places. I may control this fort, but Beck has letters from London. There is only so much I can do."

"Letters from what high places?"

Hazlitt sighed. "From the civilians the generals are beholden to. Members of Parliament, men who have the king's ear."

"Men whom you would trust, Colonel?" Duncan asked.

Hazlitt winced without reply.

"Was it Horatio Beck who had Rogers arrested? Did you know that Beck lost a great sum of money to Rogers and has barely escaped being committed to debtors' prison more than once?" Duncan had recalled the words Hayes had spoken in Agawam. Could it be true, could Beck himself be the fulcrum, the hinge on which all the events turned?

The colonel eyed him with new interest. "You have proof of this?"

Duncan reached into the waist of his britches and produced the letter from Hancock, worse for wear but still readable.

Hazlitt read it twice. "Hancock?" he asked. "John Hancock of Boston?"

"The same. He and Robert Livingston asked me to find those who sank the *Arcturus*. Beck wants the glory for himself. And if Rogers hangs, Beck's debt to him is extinguished."

Hazlitt stared at the letter for several heartbeats. "I am not sure a mere letter can be taken into evidence."

"Send for Hancock. Send for Livingston."

"There's no time, McCallum. For you or Rogers. Beck now says you were in alliance with Rogers, who is accused of conspiring with the French to help them take back the western lands."

"Based on what? Beck's accusations?"

"Apparently there is evidence of a secret meeting between Rogers and the French in the west somewhere."

"Meeting with the French, or meeting with some Jesuits?"

"Is there a difference?"

"I think there may be. The Jesuits have no love for King Louis after he suppressed their order."

"We would have to have witnesses, McCallum."

"We?"

Hazlitt sighed. "I am the president of the tribunal. Three of us, charged with conducting Rogers's trial in Montreal."

"You would hang us both on the word of Beck?"

"On the word of the men Beck represents, who speak for the king. In the war, such things happened."

"If this is to be a new war, would you let a man like Beck start it? Beck has no honor. Finding me guilty will just bolster his case against Rogers."

The colonel frowned. "Innuendos. I can do nothing with them." He noticed Duncan's writing on the wall and paced along it in careful contemplation. He pointed to Duncan's most recent inscription, "*louis d'or.*" "King Louis's gold?" he asked.

"A successful prosecution of Rogers may win Beck accolades in London and relieve him of a large debt," Duncan said. "But finding the missing gold, more importantly, would make him one of the wealthiest men in London."

"It's a myth!"

Duncan shrugged. "The gold existed. It didn't just evaporate. Beck started asking about it years ago, after he gambled with Rogers in New York."

"If it exists, it belongs to King George."

"But I wager Beck has not reported that he has caught a scent of it."

Hazlitt stared silently at Duncan, then called to Buchanan, waiting at the door. The corporal entered carrying a small writing table, followed by the second soldier with a chair. "There are empty quarters on this floor," the colonel explained with a shrug. "This furniture is unused. I will have a fresh straw pallet brought." He glanced up at Duncan and quickly looked away, instructing Buchanan on placement of the furniture. "I will send paper, ink, and a candle lantern," he added. He took a step toward the door, then halted and extracted a small volume from a pocket and set it on the table. "Meditations in poetry," he said. "I sometimes find them comforting." He turned to the door.

Duncan spoke to his back. "You would hang Rogers on the word of Beck and some faceless men in London? The ones who would have me dragged back to Boston in chains, just as they dragged Rogers in chains from Michilimakinac?"

Hazlitt spoke over his shoulder. "No one is intending to take you to Boston," he declared in a thick voice, then disappeared down the dark corridor.

Left on the table was a slip of paper. Buchanan had inscribed the images from the powder horn of the officer from the Royal Scots. The corporal had helped by adding under the sketched fortress walls the scrawled word *Montreal*. Beside the walls he had drawn the graveyard from the horn, with several nondescript tombstones on either side of a much-larger one. It was a Scottish cross, a traditional cross intersected at its center by a circle, or nimbus, as the church called it. Duncan lifted his charred stick and drew a similar cross at the bottom of the column in the corner, by Williams's name. He considered the images on the horns of Rogers's confidants. The chimney rock, marking the location of Hahnowa's grave. Chevelure, where new settlers from Quebec were building a tower. The church with the canoe, which he suspected was at St. Francis. The nimbus cross in Montreal. It was a geographic sequence, a listing, he suspected, of missions or assignments for four stealthy rangers. There had been another ranger, Branscomb, who had died in Boston of natural causes. He must have had a horn as well, and Duncan suspected it would have depicted Fort Number Four or perhaps a ship on Lake Champlain.

Minutes later the door opened again and Buchanan gestured in a new visitor. Conawago brought his own stool, which he set in front of the table. His face was haggard and heavily lined, as if he had been sleeping no more than Duncan himself. He silently reached inside his waistcoat and in quick succession extracted a sausage, a small fresh-baked loaf, two apples, and half a dozen hard-boiled eggs.

Duncan sat opposite the old Nipmuc and ravenously consumed half the sausage, then slowed, breaking off a piece of bread. "You look terrible," Duncan said to his old friend.

"I never sleep well at military establishments," Conawago replied in a weary voice. "Are you comfortable here?"

"I am dry, and what bedding there is isn't infested with lice. Why haven't you come?"

"I tried, from that very first hour. Horatio Beck lords over everyone in this fort and placed guards not only at the cell but at the base of the stairs as well.

At every change of the guard for the first two days I tried again, the last time coming with Will and Molly. That despicable Sergeant Mallory stopped us, and when Molly growled, he kicked her so hard we feared he broke a rib. He said next time the beast tries to interfere with him, he will put a bullet in her head."

"But you're here now."

"I'm afraid Beck has gone. That's why we've been able to come at last."

"Afraid?"

Conawago looked down at the table as he spoke. "Beck said he had the authority to hang you, right here, that summary execution was authorized to prevent the active spread of treason. The colonel refused, said he would use force to stop such a travesty. So Beck has gone to Albany to get a tame general to sign."

Duncan felt a tightness in his throat. "Sign?"

Conawago seemed to have trouble speaking. "A warrant, Duncan. When he returns in two days, he intends to hang you."

STANDING ON THE TABLE NOW, Duncan stared out the window, watching the moon rise over Champlain. In two days, Beck meant to hang him. He would never let an English noose choke away his life. He tested the bars. With a little more work with his shaped stone they would be ready for a blow that would break their fittings. Tomorrow at midnight, with the moon high over the water, he would knock them away and drop to the ground. If the fall didn't kill him, they would find him dragging his broken body toward the forest, and he would resist enough for them to use their bayonets. His death, like his life, would be measured by the smallest of victories.

A new ship had arrived that day, a two-masted sloop of eight small guns, with a square-rigged mainmast and a rear mast rigged fore and aft. She was smaller than the brig anchored nearby, but both were no doubt part of the Champlain fleet that patrolled between the Rideau River at the far north end of the lake and Ticonderoga. For a moment Duncan saw the lined, weathered face of his grandfather standing behind the wheel and laughing as wind-driven rain slashed his face, and he realized that the sleek lines of the sloop were much the same as those of his grandfather's favorite vessel. Earlier, he had heard his mother's voice coming down the chimney, singing one of her waulking songs used when softening the wool before weaving. Was this the way the soul prepared for the end, summoning images and sounds from earlier in life? The bones of his body would break the next day, but the bones of his soul felt like they were already breaking. Had he begun to die?

He had dozed off, his head cradled in his arms on the table, when the sound of the shutting door stirred him. Solomon Hayes stood before him. It was past dawn, and Hayes put his porridge bowl on the table, along with a small piece of ham.

"You are looking much recovered," Duncan said to the Jewish tinker after drinking from the jar of barley water offered by Hayes.

"Fully so, thanks to your assistance."

Duncan knew he did not deserve the tinker's gratitude, and he did not reply.

Hayes looked at him with an awkward expression. "The guard at the stairs finally took a shilling to give me a few minutes. The big Scot at the door declined my offer."

"You bribed a guard?"

"An accommodation, they call it. The sutler by the gate explained that they accept accommodations to allow small favors to prisoners."

"The favor of your company?"

To Duncan's surprise, Hayes laughed. "More in the nature of a mutual favor," he said, glancing nervously toward the corridor. "I sell my beads and tin cups and buttons up and down the frontier, and I actually have become quite adept at repairing broken pots. But my real business is paying coin for information."

Duncan, careful not to give offense, took a moment to weigh his words. "About your wife, you mean."

"My first year on the trails it was always about my wife. Have you seen a woman with reddish-brown hair, my height, with hazel eyes? But then I realized that direct questions made most tribesman uncomfortable, as if I would think them complicit if they knew something. So I became more subtle. I would ask if business for my wares would be good at the slave markets in the north, for example, and what kinds of things might sell. I ask if silver brooches or yellow ribbon would sell in the north, for my Rebecca liked both, on the off chance she had a generous owner. Over time, my informants became something of a network," Hayes confessed. "They would seek out information knowing I would pay for it. Sometimes they offer secrets that seem to have nothing to do with European captives."

"And?"

"One of those informants is here. He's been looking for me these past weeks, up and down the lake. He thought I should know about movements in the Champlain Valley."

"Movements. You make it sound like military intelligence."

"Judge for yourself. Movements of farmers, all from the old New France colony, several to Chevelure but also along other strategic points where rivers enter the lake." Duncan recalled that one of the lists in Rogers's secret pouch from 1759 had been of rivers that flowed into the eastern shore of Lake Champlain. "The farmers are receiving plentiful deliveries of supplies, and they've been given credit with certain French merchants in Montreal who commit that the debt will be forgiven if they stay on their land for a year."

Duncan's brow narrowed. The girl at Chevelure had mentioned benefactors in the north, saints in St. Francis and Montreal.

"Credit to buy supplies, even wagons and horses. They are moving south." Hayes looked back at the door and leaned closer. "I try to keep eyes at those places, watching for signs of captives being moved. There's a report from a river at the north of the lake, of barges being loaded with supplies. There's a word they speak, like a secret password."

"Saguenay," Duncan suggested.

Hayes nodded. "Exactly. And then there's this." He reached into his waistcoat and produced a large golden coin. "My informant had worked for a month for them, and this was his pay. He asked me to change it." He pushed the coin across the table to Duncan. It was a gold louis from France, with a mint date of 1756, identical to the one Will had received from the dead ranger. If the French treasure existed, its coins would have been minted no later than 1759.

"He also reported that Abenaki from all the mountains and valleys are being summoned to St. Francis to speak of migrating to the west. They would travel with their captives."

Duncan eyed Hayes with alarm. "Surely you don't mean to go to St. Francis?"

"I do. I must. If Rebecca is a slave to one of those families bound for the west, she may be put forever out of my reach."

"You could become a slave yourself, or sliced into a stewpot."

"I don't think so. That's part of it, you see. This is being organized by a Christian, by a Jesuit."

Duncan's hand went to the folded statement, hidden again inside his belt. "Tell me, Hayes," he asked urgently, "do you know his name?"

"Of course, for I mean to speak with him. Father Jean-Baptiste de LaBrosse."

For an hour after Hayes left, Duncan paced along his arc, once more trying to fit his fragments together. Every time he felt close to finding answers, it seemed the pieces were tossed into the air again, coming down in new patterns. He stared at his jumble of words on the wall, then wrote one more, *Saguenay*. He began drawing lines connecting to Oliver and Father LaBrosse, then Chevelure, the village whose tall windmill had been foreseen years earlier. He drew another line, connecting Robert Rogers to Saguenay. *Saguenay?* It was the word that linked everything together, though he could not cipher how. He paced along the wall, then gave up and climbed to the window, watching the birds and the small boats moving on the lake. Perhaps if he watched long enough, the fabled beast of the lake would rise up and free him.

The door latch rattled, and Duncan jumped down, sitting on the table as Corporal Buchanan appeared. The big Scot stepped aside for Conawago, then returned to the corridor, locking the door behind him.

The old Nipmuc had not taken notice of Duncan's notes on the wall during his first visit, but he lingered over them now, finishing with a new inscription Duncan had borrowed from Hazlitt's volume of poetry:

Early or late,
They stoop to fate
And must give up their murmuring breath
When they, pale captives, creep to death.

"James Shirley, if I am not mistaken," Conawago said with a sigh. "Not particularly profound, Duncan."

"Nothing about this feels profound. Ironic, no doubt. Tragic. Morbid, even. Perhaps I should have chosen that most Scottish of complainers, Macbeth. 'Life's but a walking shadow, a poor player that struts and frets his hour upon the stage and then is heard no more.'" Conawago seemed about to protest, but Duncan cut him off by raising his voice. "'A tale told by an idiot, full of sound and fury, signifying nothing.' That's more like it, though I'm the idiot, dying as a pawn without even knowing who is playing me."

The Nipmuc stared impassively at him.

Duncan felt shamed. He had been terrified of this moment. He did not know how to say goodbye to the gentle old man.

Conawago's gaze turned to the crumpled papers in the hearth.

"Letters to Sarah," Duncan explained. He had sat for hours, his heart leaden, trying to find the right words. "I decided none is best."

"Surely you must write."

Duncan's voice was becoming hoarse. "Write what? An apology for disappointing her on the journey? A diatribe against an unjust king? My regrets that our impossible dream could never happen? Instructions for planting the apple trees?"

"To speak the words of your heart, of course. Those are not from your heart. She deserves better."

Duncan knew there no words left in the cavern of his heart. "Best for her to just continue on the course she chose in Boston."

"Boston? I am not sure I follow."

"There's no point in shielding me anymore, old friend."

"Duncan, I am at a loss."

"She wouldn't say goodbye to me when we parted. She thought she was coming to Boston to marry me, and I ruined that. You and I both know there is another man in her life now. The brightest man in Boston, she calls him, barely able to contain her enthusiasm. The one she met at Mrs. Pope's on more than one occasion, though very carefully orchestrated so I was never there. The one she writes secret letters to. I may have been slow to ken it, but I am not blind. John Adams is his name. She said that if I am arrested, she can always go back to Boston, to Mr. Adams. There is no point in my standing in the way of her feelings for him, no point in pretending any longer."

Conawago's jaw dropped. He stared in disbelief; then a grin slowly creased his weathered face. A sound of surprise escaped his throat, then another, until finally the sounds congealed into laughter. He laughed so hard he had to put a hand on his belly to catch his breath. "Perhaps not completely blind, but completely the fool. John Adams is a lawyer, Duncan."

"Another reason to loathe him."

Conawago still chuckled. "Sarah retained him for his counsel, to file a writ. She made me promise to keep it secret because she wanted to surprise you. She hired him to set aside the order extending your indenture. Adams said that you never left British territory because you were serving under obligation on a British ship, Mr. Hancock's ship. So the extension to your indenture ordered because you left British territory is mistaken. He told her he is confident he will prevail once the magistrate takes up the case."

The words did not fully penetrate Duncan's gloom. "Set aside the order?" he asked.

"Establishing officially that your indenture is finished despite the devious efforts of Lord Ramsey. She's doing it because she says you are a stubborn Scot who puts too much reliance on pieces of paper and she has to teach you the Mohawk way of the heart. It's her way of fighting for you, of being the warrior for the two of you."

Duncan was having difficulty breaking through the chaos of his grief and anger. "I am her indentured servant."

"No, you will not be when Adams is finished. You will have been free for weeks. You will be free to take the marriage bonds."

Duncan sensed something like a dim light shining through the fog of his torment. "But surely after what I did to Hayes . . . I had never seen her so angry."

Conawago held up an interrupting hand. "That very night, at the little farm, she asked for a candle and stayed up long after the others to write a letter to Mr. Adams, asking him to speed up the process at whatever the cost, for she feared you were getting frustrated with her. She is prideful, Duncan, like you, but her heart has never strayed."

Duncan's head seemed to spin. From outside came the echoing boom of the evening gun. He looked back at the wall, then down at the paper and quill on the desk. "Then what a terrible letter I must write her," he said with a strangled voice. For a moment his heart had soared, but the gun had brought him back to his senses. Everything in his heart had changed, but nothing about his death had changed.

Conawago quickly sobered. "There is still another day, Duncan."

"Is there word from Ishmael?"

"I fear not. We cannot confirm that our messages intercepted him. But I hope for him every hour."

Despair crept back into Duncan's heart. "Could Munro visit?" he asked.

"I will see. He has been busy. Spends much of his time with the Highlanders."

The explanation hurt. Duncan thought his friendship with the old Scot had been stronger. Had Munro's discomfort over the talk against kings indeed come between them? "Then you can tell him for me. There is a burial field at the edge of the plain where all those Highlanders died back in '58. They were brave men, men who knew Clan McCallum. I would like to rest with them."

Conawago looked down into his hands, one of which was desperately squeezing the other, and silently nodded. "There is still another day," he repeated in a whisper.

Duncan fingered Hazlitt's little volume. "Then I can finish my reading," he replied.

IN THE NIGHT, ONE OF the lake's frequent summer storms raged over Ticonderoga, casting angry thunderbolts down upon the surrounding mountains. Despite getting soaked, Duncan stayed at the high window of his dungeon, watching as the flashes illuminated whitecaps on the lake and the wind tore away a small tent pitched near the pier. The anchored ships strained at their cables. Someone appeared on the dock, and in the next flash Duncan made out the long, braided hair and green waistcoat and realized it was Conawago. In another flash the old Nipmuc stood at the end of the dock, his face uplifted into the pelting rain and his fists raised overhead, raging against the heavens.

The blackness that followed the tempest was so complete, Duncan could barely see his hand before his face. There were no stars, no moon, no hope, no sense to be made of his death. A general in Albany would sign his life away at Beck's request, probably already had done so, just a quick scrawl between sips of tea. Duncan's joyful childhood embrace of his clan, his education in Holland and Edinburgh, his years helping tribesmen and settlers on the frontier mattered not at all. He had nothing left but the small, bright gem of his love for Sarah, and soon he would leave her weeping and shaking in Edentown.

He surrendered to his fatigue, then woke abruptly, gasping, from a dream in which his father pointed at him from the gibbet again, but this time he was laughing at his son. Duncan quickly grasped the message from the other side. He was going to die as they had, useless deaths at the hands of a tyrant. He understood the blackness now. It was the blackness of his heart spreading into his world. That world would never know light again.

Sometime before dawn a monkey dropped a coin by his head.

14

DUNCAN HAD LIT THE LANTERN in the middle of the night and tried to begin a letter to Sarah, but he finally succumbed to sleep, his head on the table. He woke with a shudder, this time to the gaze of two inquisitive eyes set on his, inches from his face. Fogged as he was with sleep, he did not immediately recognize his visitor. Then a familiar whistle came from below, and she shot away, leaving a large metal disk spinning on the table beside him.

Suddenly he was alert, leaping up to catch a glimpse of Sadie and Hayes as they ran toward the forest. A gray fog hung over the fort, and the candle had gone out, but enough light filtered in for him to recognize the disk. It was a ranger token, a forest coin some called it, inscribed with a large tree on one side and on the other a long rifle crossed with a war ax. Patrick Woolford, deputy superintendent of Indian affairs, had issued this particular coin to his small elite band, and the handful of stealthy scouts who served him still carried them.

Duncan watched, trying to will the fog to disappear, until finally he could make out the trees at the end of the cleared field to the southeast of the fort. A figure stood on a limb halfway up the trunk of the largest tree. Even at that distance Duncan could recognize his friend. Ishmael had succeeded in his mission. The deputy superintendent had arrived.

Duncan pressed his face against the bars in the hope of being seen. As he watched, the former ranger officer cocked his head, raised his arm to shoulder height, and opened his palm in a Mohawk greeting. Then he spun his fingers in an upward spiral and brought his hand down fast. It was one of the silent signals used by rangers going to battle. *Remain in position and await orders.*

A bank of mist blew in from the lake and obscured the tree. When it cleared, Woolford was gone.

The flood of hope that had risen at the sight of his old friend began to fade as the morning progressed. If caught aiding a traitor's escape, his companions too would face the hangman's noose. Duncan could not bear the thought of bringing a death warrant to any of them. He would be surrendering to the worst kind of weakness if he allowed it. To his forebears such dishonor would mean eternal damnation. To the Iroquois, whose warriors' code he lived by, it would mean an eternity spent wandering in a fogbound forest. It would mean dishonor, and Duncan had nothing left but his honor. He was heartened by the efforts of his friends, but despite their best intentions, they could not magically convey him thirty feet down the wall. If they tried a ladder, they would be shot by the wall sentries. If they tried to rush the cell, they would have to fight the entire garrison. He would not wait for them and their inevitable, bloody failure. At dusk, he would break the bars and drop to the ground. It was the slimmest of hopes, but the only one that preserved his honor. Then he heard shouts from the ramparts and looked out the window, and even that thin reed was shattered. A small company of soldiers was galloping up the Albany road, Horatio Beck at their head.

BECK SAID NOTHING AS HE entered the cell, just cast a lightless smile at Duncan and stepped aside for Sergeant Mallory and a misshapen Indian in a scarlet waistcoat. The tribesman's head was unnaturally long and ovoid, as if it had been compressed when he was a child. His horselike appearance was accentuated by a severe hunchback. His arms and hands were disproportionately large, with bulging muscles. Three fingers were fused together, giving the appendage the appearance of a claw. The man's eyes were dull but expectant, like a subdued predator waiting for a blood-soaked meal.

Mallory paced a circle around Duncan, then, without warning, slammed a fist into Duncan's belly. As Duncan gasped, the Indian shoved him into the chair and slapped him with a backhanded blow that rendered him senseless for several seconds. When he recovered, the Indian had tied his ankles to the chair.

Beck dragged the table so that it was two feet in front of Duncan, then sat on the stool a few feet away, watching in silent amusement. Mallory gestured to the grotesque-looking Indian, who began extracting objects from his person and arranging them in front of Duncan. A crumpled piece of thick leather with two holes in it that had been hanging from his cartridge box. From inside the box, a wrinkled brown object that looked like a thin, desiccated sausage. From inside his waistcoat a strand holding several thick leather loops. Finally, unbuttoning the top of his coat, he removed a necklace of shriveled leather scraps, each roughly the same oval shape. He set everything in a neat row and smiled hungrily.

Beck stood, lifted the writing quill, and with its tip separated some of the objects so Duncan might see them better, starting by moving the ovals on the necklace. Some had small silver rings attached to them. With a lurch of his gut, Duncan recognized them and then, to his horror, recognized each of the other objects. Paralyzed by the discovery, he did not react as the sergeant tied his hands behind the chair. He was looking at a necklace of human ears, a human nose, a finger, and a strand of carefully excised human lips. Most, but not all, the parts seemed to be from Europeans.

Beck broke the silence. "Sergeant Mallory and I met during the war," he declared in a conversational tone. "Two of a kind, though not in techniques. Mine are subtle in the extreme, his much more direct, made more so with the help of his friend Wolf here, another wartime acquaintance. An Ottawa, we understand, though no tribe has allowed him to stay long in their lodges, for they would call him a witch, a monster, a demon. But he found his place with us. Now he is a professional allowed to pursue his art to perfection. With Wolf's capable assistance, our interrogations have always been most efficient. As you can see, Wolf likes to wear his trophies. I prefer ones that are more ethereal."

Mallory gestured to the sack Wolf had dropped on the floor. "There's more specimens, McCallum," the sergeant pointed out in a casual tone. "Do we need to show you? You wouldn't credit the collection of female parts he has."

"I saved your life, Mallory," Duncan spat.

Mallory sighed. "I never thought Hancock would let that fool with the pitchfork get close enough."

"I trusted you! Sarah trusted you!" Duncan was seized with a black thought. "Where is she? What did you do to her?"

"I got the lovely creature safely across the Hudson and bid farewell, though what a tempting blossom to pluck, eh? Mr. Beck was waiting in Albany, and we had to get here before you, to make sure you did exactly what I suggested in the archives. You made it so easy, McCallum. And I shall return to Miss Ramsey. There is a warrant that will allow me to seize her. And seize her, and seize her," the sergeant said with a gloating laugh.

Duncan fought to keep his voice level. "You're not really a lieutenant. Why bother with the uniform?" he asked Beck.

"Actually I am paid at the rate of naval captain," Reck replied in a bored, airy voice. "I have been given papers as a major, a commander, even a naval surgeon, though I learned I am not nearly as adept with surgical instruments as Mallory and Wolf. But on this mission the rank of army lieutenant serves me well. More inconspicuous. Enough authority to order up resources, but not so much as to attract undue attention. I wore a major's gorget in Halifax, but everyone wanted to pamper me so."

"I am not your enemy, Beck."

"But you must be! I have a warrant for your arrest. And even a warrant to hang you, signed just hours ago! The king only hangs his enemies."

"I had no trial. You have no authority."

"There is authority from the king to hang those who constitute a clear and present danger to the empire. I have letters from London making me the king's agent. You have been found guilty of treason in absentia, by a hearing in Albany. Your life is mine. I can hang you tomorrow."

Duncan heard the shift in his tone. "Is that an invitation?"

"There are only two possibilities you need to concern yourself with now, McCallum," Beck continued in his oily voice. "Tell me what I need to know now. Or tell me after Wolf and Sergeant Mallory take some trophies from you. Did you know those lips actually came off living humans? When he was young, Wolf's people practiced cannibalism. An acquired taste, I take it, but one that apparently stays with you."

Beck bowed his head to Wolf, who acknowledged him with a low, impatient growl before reaching into the sack he had dropped by the table. Mallory began rolling up Duncan's sleeve.

Duncan closed his eyes. He saw his father on the gibbet again, but this time he was staring at Duncan with curiosity, not accusation. Duncan fixed Beck with a baleful stare. "Did you kill the captain of Hancock's sloop the *Liberty* in Boston harbor?"

Beck gave an exaggerated grimace. "So ironic, a ship called the *Liberty*." He shrugged. "I had to search the boat, didn't I? It had just arrived. I had to be sure Hancock hadn't tricked me and placed it on her instead of on the *Arcturus*. The fool captain kept protesting, saying I didn't have the proper papers. I hit him on the back with a timber to shut him up. Later the army doctor said the blow had burst a kidney. How was I to know?"

"He was innocent," Duncan said.

"He was nobody."

"I think I am not the traitor in this room, Beck."

Beck sighed and made a gesture to the sergeant, who nodded to Wolf.

Before Duncan could react, the Ottawa clamped his hand around Duncan's left arm. Duncan gasped as his flesh exploded in pain. When Wolf pulled his hand away, a dozen small porcupine quills were impaled in his arm.

"So inventive, no? The true genius always seems to find new uses for old things." Duncan saw that Wolf's hand held a pincushion fixed by a strap, made for a seamstress's wrist. But he was inserting into it several more short quills from a porcupine's tail, the barbed ends sticking out for another blow.

"Surely a frontiersman like yourself knows about the amazing spiny pig," Mallory said. "Its quills are barbed so you can't easily pull them out, and left on their own, they will work themselves deeper and deeper until they just disappear into your body. We experimented in the war. Wolf drove quills into a captive's spine. After two weeks he was completely paralyzed."

Duncan spoke through his agony. "I am just doing a favor for friends in Boston. You know their names. They gave you my name out in the harbor. Hancock and Livingston."

Beck slowly clapped his hands. "See. Cooperation is not so arduous. You admit you work for the insidious Sons of Liberty, then."

"Every man I know is a son," Duncan said, ending his words with a groan. His arm felt as if a dozen red-hot needles had been thrust into it. Blood began dripping from his arm onto the floor.

Beck sighed. "I fail to comprehend this obsession with liberty. A man has no liberty except that granted by his king. You think you can seize liberty from our blessed George? You will find only enough liberty to hang yourself."

Sergeant Mallory grinned at Duncan, then produced a small metal hammer with a ball on one end that looked like a tool from a gunsmith's shop. In one quick motion, he flattened Duncan's hand on the table and slammed the ball down on it.

"I keep wondering where that journal is," Beck said in his casual voice as Duncan painfully moved his fingers. Nothing was broken yet. "Did you ever actually have it?"

"You should have done a better job in Halifax, Lieutenant," Duncan said, gasping between words. "The French were always going to leave the ship that night, but you made them so desperate they had to destroy the *Arcturus* to throw you off the trail."

"It would have been so much simpler if I could have arrested them in Halifax," Beck agreed, "but they didn't have the ledger yet. And it would have been far less of a nuisance if they had just let me overtake them in the harbor. I could have been back enjoying long dinners at my club in London." He returned Duncan's furious stare.

"A nuisance?" Duncan spat. "Thirty-seven men died."

"What a spectacle! But the explosion only confirmed that I was on the right track—not who had the ledger."

"You knew they were responsible for the *Arcturus*," Duncan hissed. "But you issued a warrant for my arrest for killing those innocent men."

"*Treason* is such a slippery word for the people of Boston. Out in the countryside it works wonders. In Boston they might hail as a hero someone we branded a traitor, but they would always loathe the man who sank a ship." Beck shrugged. "I couldn't very well charge Hancock and Livingston, not yet. But you have admitted you are their agent. They will be stopped before they do real damage to the king, if I have to hang a score of their surrogates."

"It gets you no closer to the French spies." Blood continued oozing out of the punctures in Duncan's arm. "No closer to the ledger."

"You are a strategist, McCallum, I grant you that. Someone who understands feigns and hidden thrusts. It is still possible that you have the ledger in your control. We will know that in an hour or two, I assure you."

"If you were truly after the enemies of the king, you would be on the trail of the French spies, not setting a trap for me in Ticonderoga. You know they sank a British ship. But maybe the odor of gold has clouded your judgment, Beck."

Beck raised a hand to forestall Wolf, who had lifted a long corkscrew out of his bag. "Not the ear, Wolf, not yet. So very messy." The king's agent considered Duncan in silence for several heartbeats, then followed Mallory's gaze toward the writing on the wall. His eyes brightened, and he paced along the arc with great interest. "You are good, McCallum. Your talents are wasted. You perceived how the two paths converged." He halted at the corner, staring at the column of powder horn names, then pointed at the Celtic cross. "My God! Remarkable! You did pick up the scent!" He stepped to Duncan's side and picked up the corkscrew himself. "Where?" Beck demanded. "Where is that graveyard?"

Duncan tried not to look at the long, twisting piece of steel. "I won't be able to tell you if you scramble my brains."

Beck pushed the corkscrew under Duncan's nose, as if considering a new use. "The trail of dead rangers leads ever northward. Who would have thought it would be paved with gold? I gave up on that treasure years ago, thinking it was sitting in a French chateau by now. But now I know it never left American shores. Sergeant Mallory and I would very much like to find that particular chest. Tell us where that lonely grave is, and I don't have to hang you."

"Ask Comtois and his friend Philippe."

This time Beck struck Duncan himself, a painful backhanded slap that left Duncan blinking. Beck motioned to Mallory, who was extracting an assortment of medical instruments and Indian tools from the sack. Long, scissorslike forceps. A small, treacherous tomahawk. A tourniquet with a metal tightening clamp. A bone saw and a small bloodstained cutting board.

"The French fools didn't know about its sudden appearance themselves until they arrived in Boston," Beck explained. "It was just distant history for all of us, until Rogers spoke of it one night while he drank too much brandy at our gaming table in New York. He was down for the moment, with no backing, and he asked for credit, said he could always bring a sack of gold louis from the north if he had to. Then his cursed luck changed and he seemed to forget it. But I didn't. I got him arrested, but the cunning bastard escaped before Wolf could work on him."

"And so all those years ago you came up here," Duncan said, "to investigate Rogers."

A thin, icy grin rose on Beck's face. "I think Rogers was going to meet with Comtois to offer the gold as his dowry for marrying himself to the French cause. For fulfilling the legacy of King Louis."

Duncan looked past Beck to his arc on the wall and saw all the pieces again, once more having been disassembled and thrown into the air. Beck did not know about the secret movement of French colonists, about Chevelure, about Saguenay. He thought Rogers had the gold, or soon would, for his own greedy purpose.

Beck angrily threw a coin onto the table. It was a gold louis. "There's thousands more. Where is that grave?" he shouted at Duncan.

"Ask Captain Williams. It was his powder horn."

"Died months ago of consumption, the cheeky bastard, just a day before we went to interrogate him. I discovered he had led the gang who broke Rogers out of debtors' prison. I found a letter from Rogers in his hearth, mostly in ashes. But that coin was in his pocket, and two powder horns on his table."

Beck was so jealously guarding his secret that he had not inquired more broadly about the fortress etched on the horn, Duncan realized, had not learned where the Celtic cross was. "Two powder horns?" he asked, then understood. "He had Oliver's horn."

Beck spoke impatiently, inching toward the instruments of torture. "And on a slip of paper beside it the words *Arcturus*, due Boston harbor May."

"He was going to deliver the horn to Oliver when the *Arcturus* docked."

Beck's sneer was the only confirmation Duncan needed.

The sergeant looked at Beck expectantly, and the lieutenant pointed to an instrument Duncan hadn't seen, a long sailmaker's needle, which Wolf now lifted with a moan of satisfaction. "When you hang, no one will care if you still have your eyes or your fingers. Where," he shouted again, "where is the king's treasure that disappeared into Quebec in 1759?"

Duncan roared a protest and tried to twist his body as Mallory moved behind him to pin his head. Wolf was going to pierce an eye.

"London doesn't know about the gold, does it?" Duncan tried. "Everyone there has forgotten it, given up on it. You didn't tell them. You and Sergeant Mallory mean to keep it for yourselves."

Beck sighed. "Recovery of the ledger in itself will make us heroes. Surely a man is entitled to some recompense for putting up with this filthy wilderness. Enough! Sergeant, time to show McCallum the point of the—"

Duncan found purchase with the ball of one foot and shoved hard, jerking the chair so that it tipped over.

Beck's temper erupted. He kicked Duncan in the belly. "One eye, Sergeant," Beck instructed in a boiling voice, "then some fingers."

Duncan struggled helplessly as Sergeant Mallory righted the chair and dragged it closer to the table, where Wolf impatiently extended the long needle.

Duncan was about to twist again when cold metal pressed against his temple. Beck cocked the little pistol. "Lose your brains or lose an eye. Your choice, McCallum. Decide. I haven't all day, damned you!"

The door slammed open. Colonel Hazlitt appeared with four kilted guards. Corporal Buchanan leapt forward, knocking the needle from Wolf's hand. The Ottawa roared with anger and was crouching for an attack when another Scottish trooper slammed his musket into his neck, knocking him to the floor. Beck did not lower the pistol.

"Stand down, Lieutenant," the commander of Ticonderoga growled. "You have a warrant to hang him, not to butcher him."

"You interfere with the king's business!" Beck hissed.

"You interfere with the honor of the army, sir!" Hazlitt shot back. "This is my fort, my garrison! You will conduct yourself as a gentleman or you may leave Ticonderoga."

As Beck lowered the pistol, the fire went out of his face. He shrugged. "McCallum keeps getting in my way. He has become the biggest threat to my mission." He stared at the image of the Celtic cross on the wall, then fixed the colonel with one of his thin smiles. "The king has decreed that he dies tomorrow."

Hazlitt briefly met Duncan's eyes, then looked away. When he spoke, his voice cracked. His reply was a whisper. "The general was most clear. McCallum dies tomorrow."

CORPORAL BUCHANAN RELIEVED DUNCAN'S GUARD an hour after sundown, looking in as Duncan stared forlornly at the paper before him on the table, which contained one word, *Sarah*. The Highlander changed the bandage on Duncan's arm, where Duncan had extracted most of the barbed quills, then assumed his post. After a few minutes, he began to whistle, one of the Scottish songs Duncan had first tried on him. Dinner came, a fresh loaf, half a roasted chicken, and a jar of ale, the condemned man's last meal. As he finished eating, a new sound arose from outside, a chorus of singing men.

Buchanan opened the door and listened at the window, nodding, as if it were an expected signal. "The good Reverend Occom is holding a service on the parade ground," he announced, "with the colonel and his officers attending. Look lively now." Strangely, the corporal began laying the accoutrements of his uniform on the table. "There be people who await ye."

"Await me?"

"On the ground. Be quick, McCallum. The moon rises soon, and the singing won't last forever. Occom and Munro assembled a chorus of soldiers for the colonel's entertainment. They have been practicing for days, but they keep forgetting the words. Now get up there and knock out those bars ye've been cutting at, lad."

"It's thirty feet to the ground, Corporal."

Buchanan plucked away the pin that secured his plaid. "Twenty-eight if you credit Mr. Munro's scouting abilities."

"It may as well be fifty, unless you have a rope hidden about you?"

"Don't be dense. The Forty-Second wears a full *feileadh mor*," Buchanan said.

Realization finally pierced Duncan's confusion. A *feileadh mor* was a full traditional kilt, which was simply twelve yards of tartan wool cleverly wrapped around the body. Buchanan was indeed wearing Duncan's rope. He sprang to the corporal's side, helping him unwind the heavy fabric. When Buchanan was reduced to nothing but his long-tailed shirt and his red-checked stockings, Duncan leapt onto the table and with two hammerlike blows knocked away the weakened bars. As he turned, ready to fish the end of the plaid out the window, Buchanan was tying the last two yards around his waist.

"They'll save the gallows for you if they find out," Duncan said to the grinning Highlander.

"T'is a miracle, I'll report. I never left my post, never unlocked the door, and no sign of a rope. No doubt something left by that disgraceful Lieutenant Beck, who brought in so many tools to entertain ye with. Now on with ye. The good reverend couldn't promise more than half an hour of loud song."

Duncan hesitated and extended his hand. "Thank you, Buchanan."

"Thank yer Mr. Munro," the corporal said as he gripped Duncan's hand. "He set me right, speaking of the clans when he took me out to the graves of the Forty-Second. I'll not help kill more Highlanders at Ticonderoga. And the colonel will be happy not to use his gallows. Now, swift passage, lad, and may God watch over ye." Buchanan set himself sideways and bent to bear Duncan's weight.

Duncan wormed his way out the window headfirst, then pulled his legs out and twisted upright, hearing Buchanan's grunt as he took the full load. He dropped quickly, hand over hand, feet channeling the fabric, until suddenly hands were grabbing him.

"McCallum," came a quiet acknowledgment.

Duncan took a moment to recognize the voice of one of Woolford's rangers. More of his Mohawks appeared out of the gloom. "Corporal Longtree," he said, "I cannot tell you what a pleasure it is to see you again."

"*Yoyanere*," came the Mohawk reply. *It is good.* The ranger took Duncan's arm and led him into the darkness.

They ran not to the forest as Duncan expected, but on a diagonal line that quickly took them to the lakeshore a quarter mile below the fort. The call of a nighthawk split the stillness. Longtree answered, stepping knee-deep into the water, and extended an arm to catch a rope. A long dinghy appeared, rowed by Ishmael and Munro. No one spoke as Duncan and the Mohawks quickly climbed in, the sound of Occom's hymns echoing behind them. Soon, Duncan assumed, they would be on the far shore, escaping into the dense wilds of the Hampshire Grants.

Duncan was watching the lights of the fort recede, already calculating how he might complete the long journey to St. Francis, when suddenly the boat shifted course, running parallel to the shoreline.

"No!" came his urgent whisper. "You'll put us right under the guns of the ships!"

Munro laughed. "I certainly hope so." A moment later, as Duncan watched in confusion, their boat nudged against the side of the two-masted sloop and a boarding ladder was thrown down. On the deck, a familiar figure grinned in greeting. His warm, crooked smile was better than any words. "I do hope you're up to a nautical task, Duncan," Patrick Woolford said. "The Department of Indian Affairs has requisitioned this vessel, but damned if my Iroquois know how to sail her."

15

WHEN HE CLOSED HIS EYES and set his head into the wind, Duncan was back in his beloved Hebrides, cruising with his grandfather. He had not realized how much he missed being on the open water, had never imagined that he would feel the pleasure of deepwater sailing again. The wind and spray slowly scoured away his despair, and he jumped so thoroughly into the work of sailing the ship with Munro that it was dawn before he collected himself enough to ask about the unlikely events that had allowed his escape.

The small sailing crew of the sloop, named the *Osprey*, were all Scots, and Munro had made a point of befriending them from the first hour they had reached the pier. He had been generous in buying them ale at the tavern near the fort's gate, and they soon wanted to show off their sloop to their fellow Scot after he boasted of his own Atlantic sailing adventures.

"Full set of charts," Munro explained as he held the long handle of the tiller. "Most of the bays in the north have not been closely surveyed, so we brought a pilot vouchsafed by Ethan Allen," he added, nodding toward the foot of the mainmast. What Duncan had taken for a pile of blankets held down by a demijohn began to move, revealing the unshaven, gaunt, and drunken form of Rufus, the ferryman.

"And the crew?"

Munro's face clouded. "The marines stationed on her were all ordered by Colonel Hazlitt to attend Reverend Occom's service, at the good reverend's request. We couldn't be sure if her sailors wouldn't call out to shore once they smoked our intentions, so for now, they're locked up in the galley."

Woolford had not flinched when Duncan suggested that he could be arrested, and worse, for taking the sloop. Duncan had never heard of the Department of Indian Affairs taking over a vessel larger than a canoe.

"Borrow, only borrow. She was slated to sail today for a few days of survey work." Woolford winked at a grinning Conawago. "We made up a contract of charter on a napkin at the tavern, all formal and proper, and left it for the colonel. I arranged for one of my scouts to conspicuously deliver a dispatch bag with an urgent message to me. As far as everyone in Fort Ti knows, the Department of Indian Affairs is pressed to pursue a report of a possible rebellion in the north country. Official business." He grinned. "Official enough."

Duncan shook his head in wonder. Did Woolford know how close his fictional excuse could be to the truth? "Horatio Beck will know what happened."

"You were his business. His business no longer concerns Ticonderoga, meaning the colonel will not tolerate his presence much longer. If he wants to pursue, he can return to Albany for assistance."

Duncan was by no means confident that Beck would wait for orders to pursue him, not after Duncan let him believe he too was pursuing the treasure. "I pray you are right. It won't go well if we are intercepted by that brig."

Woolford frowned, looking back toward their wake, then conspicuously pushed down his worry and pounded Duncan on his back. "Don't darken this magnificent day with thoughts of what lies behind," he said, gesturing at the dawn landscape. The Adirondacks rose majestically along the western horizon, reflected in waters that glowed with the blush of sunrise. The lower, verdant mountains of the Hampshire Grants rolled toward the east, and in between, stretching to the north, lay the vast inland sea.

Duncan slowly nodded. The torment of his imprisonment still hung over him like a cloud, and his arm throbbed from where Conawago had carefully excised each of the quills that had broken off in his flesh, but he knew he would never find true release from his agony until he discovered the truth. It was a debt he owed to the dead, and he would not stop until it was paid, whatever the cost. "I don't even know how to find St. Francis from the lake," he confessed to Woolford.

"Rufus will land us as far northeast as is safe, and Brandt will find the route," Woolford stated. "There's still a ranger inside that grizzled shell of a man. How far by your reckoning?"

Duncan did a quick calculation. They had passed the narrows at Crown Point in the night. "Not much more than a hundred miles. Surely sometime tomorrow morning, if the wind holds. I won't want to navigate the northern isles in the dark." Duncan felt a thrill in his bones as he realized he would have a long day of sailing along one of the most magnificent lochs he had ever seen.

"Your friend Hayes seems to be urging her along on sheer willpower," Woolford said, nodding toward the bow.

The tinker leaned out over the slanted prow, staring northward. What had Hayes said? He felt a sense of destiny, as if his Jehovah were finally playing a hand in leading him to his lost wife. What will you tell her owners when you find her, Duncan had asked. Hayes had touched his belt. "Show them my purse. They sell their slaves as readily as skins and furs."

Standing a few feet from Hayes, holding a stay and awash in the spray, was the tall lean figure of Noah, who watched the water with a faraway expression.

Duncan had not known such a glorious day since his voyage to Bermuda. It was as if he were cruising into an entirely new world, a bright, clean world where a comforting sun raised diamonds on the water. A pair of mergansers watched them glide by. As he took the tiller from Munro, the wind freshened, stretching the canvas, and the sloop leaned her shoulder into the water. The tiller became like a living thing in his hand, and he thrilled as the rigging groaned and a long plume of spray shot up from the bow, leaving Hayes soaked but uncomplaining.

Rufus revived and walked along the rail, grinning with delight as the *Osprey* plowed through Champlain's waters. After a few minutes he wandered over to the Mohawks, who had been trying to use a spare line to tie the knots they saw in the rigging overhead. Rufus helped them, good-naturedly laughing at their frequent mistakes, then approached Duncan and Munro at the stern. "If we have a blow, we'll need more than those dusky landlubbers," he suggested. "No doubt they be true Vikings of the forest when they raise their war axes, but on water they don't know chalk from cheese."

Munro considered the words, caught Duncan's approving glance, then disappeared down the hatch. Minutes later he led a line of six worried men onto the deck. "The crew says they want no trouble," he declared.

The compact man at the front of the line spoke in a tentative voice. "It's our little lady, sir—the *Osprey*, I mean, sir. She deserves to be well tended."

Duncan smiled at the thick burr in the man's voice. Munro had said they were Scots, but he assumed they would be lowlanders, like most he met in America. "*Ghaidhealach?*" he asked in surprise.

The man tapped a knuckle to his forehead. "First Mate Sinclair, sir, of Caithness. We all be of the Highlands, sir, took the bounty to stay in America after the war."

"Where's your captain?"

"Likely lying passed out in the tavern at Ti. He ain't much of a sailor, just an infantry officer who thought he found a cush way to avoid long marches."

"And, First Mate Sinclair, what would you say of the set of our sail if you returned to duty?"

Sinclair studied the canvas with a thoughtful eye. "Trim the topsail a might, sir, and it wouldn't hurt to tighten the jibstay."

Duncan grinned. "Make it so, Mr. Sinclair." A smile creased the first mate's square, windburned face and his men sprang into action. Will and Molly ran onto the deck and joined Hayes and Noah at the prow.

Several minutes later Duncan became aware of Munro lingering at the stern rail, anticipation on his sturdy countenance.

"Fort Ti had a postmaster," the Scot said abruptly. "I sent a letter to Mr. Hancock."

"A generous thought, Munro, but John would not have been able to help with the army."

"No, not that. I wrote to say I was done, that I was no longer in his pay."

Duncan looked at him in surprise. "You quit?"

Munro gave only a curt nod in reply.

An empty place seemed to grow inside Duncan. He had come to rely on Munro's steadying presence. He recalled now their conversation on the shallop, and he grasped why Munro had not come to his cell. "I understand," he said. "It's too much to ask of a man. I never wanted to taint you with the charges against me. Perhaps a man needs his king, like he needs his God." He hesitated, wondering why Munro was still with him. "But you should have stayed at the fort, my friend."

"Ye nay ken me. I meant I didn't want anyone, including ye, to think I was doing this for coin. We owe justice to those dead, like ye said, Duncan. I want them to understand clear that I do this for them. And for ye."

"For me?"

"Mr. Noah, he said to me that we are all moving toward a battle that we are destined to fight. But it came to me, sitting out on the pier under the moon as I watched yer cell window, that maybe we don't have to do battle because of what ye are doing. I mean, well . . . I'm nay so good with putting grand thoughts in words, mind—"

"Just say what is in your heart, my friend."

"Well, if ye ken my drift, I believe ye be correcting mistakes made by the king. I think ye be a sin-eater for the king."

An hour later the big dog barked and one of the Iroquois gave an astonished cry. An older sailor leaned over the rail, following the ranger's outstretched arm, then staggered backward and dropped to his knees, crossing himself. Duncan looked at Conawago, who had risen to investigate, and he watched as the old man's face filled with excitement. The kneeling man found his voice. "T'is herself! The monster of the lake!"

The sloop canted to starboard as every man ran to look over the side; then it began to level as several backed away, three of them crossing themselves and another clasping his hands in prayer. Will leapt up in the shrouds for a better view, followed an instant later by Ishmael.

"Leviathan!" the young Nipmuc whooped.

Everyone who lived near Champlain, European and Indian alike, had some tale of the great creature that lurked in the lake. "Water horse!" one of the Scots called out, evoking the myths from the lochs of Scotland. Champlain himself had reported seeing a water beast with the head of a horse more than a century and a half earlier.

"*Tatoskok!*" one of the Iroquois called with awe in his voice. The tribesmen had their own name for the legendary creature.

Woolford, his face alive with delight, stepped from the rail to the helm and extended his hand. Duncan gave him the tiller and darted to the rail. His heart leapt as he saw the *Osprey*'s escort. Its sleek gray body was as thick as a barrel and at least fifteen feet long, with a sharply tapering head that held two huge black, inquisitive eyes.

"*Tatoskok!*" Corporal Longtree repeated, but with reverence, not fear. Noah touched his totem bag and began urgently whispering in a native tongue as he watched the animal with awed joy. The tales of the mysterious creature varied from campfire to campfire. Many called it the king of the water world, others the guardian of drowned souls, still others the storm-demon that conjured Champlain's violent squalls. But almost always there was an ancient, timeless element to the tales, a connection to the primordial powers that occupied the land before man.

Duncan sensed an unexpected resonance rising within him. There had been water beasts that shadowed boats of the Hebrides, and sometimes a McCallum would affirm an ancient tie with them. He grabbed a coil of line and tossed it to Ishmael. "Tie it to the starboard sternpost and let it trail behind," he instructed the young Nipmuc.

He had seen his grandfather embrace such creatures, renewing the ancient ties, and now from some distant chamber in his mind he heard the old man's ebullient laugh. He reached for the buttons of his waistcoat.

"Duncan! No!" Munro shouted as he saw that Duncan had stripped to the waist. All the Iroquois stared wide-eyed. Conawago's face lit with excitement again. Noah's jaw dropped, and he clutched the totem bag that hung from his neck with both hands.

"Keep her steady," Duncan shouted at Munro, then leapt onto the creature's back.

Taming the berserker, is what some of the Skye fishermen had called his grandfather's wild bonding with the beasts of the Hebrides. What most didn't know was that the massive creatures he rode were docile whales or basking sharks, and Duncan always had the impression that they enjoyed having the old man scratch their backs.

There were no whales or sharks in this freshwater sea, and Duncan knew instinctively that this creature had no interest in digesting humans. It seemed to take no notice of him as he settled onto its long, protruding spine, but then, as he wrapped his legs around the thick body, it shook its back slightly, as if to make sure Duncan had his seat. Suddenly, to terrified shouts from the deck, it dove. They were under for no more than twenty seconds, and the great fish, which he suspected to be an aged sturgeon, surfaced again alongside the sloop.

Duncan realized he was shouting in Gaelic, the battle cries of the Highlands his grandfather shouted when taming his own berserker. The great fish made a leap that brought Duncan's head almost to the height of the deck, and it dove again, much deeper this time. He released his legs, and the creature disappeared into the murk below. He surfaced, treaded water for a moment, then caught the trailing line. As the crew pulled him in, he recalled one of the dreams Sarah had worried about. *I see a great, long beast lying in wait for you,* she had said.

The Scots cheered as he came on board. The Iroquois gazed at him in astonishment. Rufus, to Duncan's momentary discomfort, grabbed his head and kissed both cheeks. Noah approached him and bent, lifting Duncan's dripping totem pouch and solemnly touching it to his forehead.

"*Tatoskok* is our protector," Noah declared, his voice thick with emotion. "He has not been seen for many years, and we feared he had abandoned us. A brother of *Tatoskok* is a brother of mine."

Duncan looked to Conawago but found only surprise on his friend's countenance. "Your protector?" he asked Noah.

As if in answer, Noah stripped off his black waistcoat, revealing a torso covered in tattoos. He made a gesture that took in the vast country to the northeast. "Of my people. You are taking me back to them, brother. My blood is Abenaki."

IN THE CRAMPED STERN CABIN, Duncan and Woolford examined a chart of the northern half of the lake. They had made good time, covering at least fifty miles, but the wind had slackened and the *Osprey's* regular crew, fearful of uncharted rocks in the night, had recommended that they put into one of the bays until dawn.

"If Beck comes," Duncan said, "he will bring the brig and won't hesitate to shoot us out of the water."

"Nonsense. He's back in Albany licking his wounds, probably telling the general to send for the superintendent to complain about me," Woolford said. "But Sir William loathes the general. He'll defend me just to spite him."

"We'll reduce sail and keep a sharp lookout, with men holding poles to fend off rocks. There should be enough of a moon to spy them."

Woolford shrugged. "You're the captain of this boat," he said. "I'm the one charged with addressing the little fires in the frontier before they become conflagrations."

Duncan studied his friend. "You didn't want to review the charts—you wanted me in the only private space on the sloop. You wanted to talk about New France."

"I wanted to talk about the other side of that particular coin. Major Rogers."

"I am apparently his coconspirator."

"Beck named you because he doesn't know enough to find any real ones."

"You mean the French colonials," Duncan suggested.

"Not only them. It took years for Rogers to get what he thought he deserved for his service in the war. He performed miracles, and not just at St. Francis. Without him there would have been no effective ranger force. And without the rangers the war could easily have gone the other way. London slighted him, without question. They have disdain for heroes with no pedigree, and by the end of the war he had no friends left in positions of command. He is bitterly resentful of London."

"Resentful of the king."

Woolford winced, as if he had bitten something sour. "Years ago, Rogers and I spent a night in a tavern when he returned from his amazing voyage to Detroit." Seeking to avoid unnecessary bloodshed after the surrender of the French at Montreal, Rogers had raced to the fort there with the news, repelling ambush and reaching the fort in half the time others would have taken. "He saved dozens, probably hundreds of lives by doing so. All the colonials knew that, but when he returned, his colonel just said well done and with the next breath chastised him for erecting his tents in a crooked line. Rogers raised his glass for a toast. 'Bugger the king and long live this great land,' he said."

"You returned the toast?"

Woolford winced again. "I repeated 'this great land' and drank."

"He had spies in New France during the war—" Duncan stated.

"Doubtlessly. At least some would call them spies. He would call them old friends with common interests, from his early days in the frontier. You've seen his *Rules of Rangering*," Woolford said, referring to the short pamphlet that had become a second Bible for the rangers. "One of the most fundamental is to know the lay of the land before you attack. Know the land, know your enemy, know your enemy's other enemies. 'Put on your enemy's skin,' he used to tell us."

"Many of those in Quebec were trained by Jesuits, colonials and tribesmen alike."

Woolford cocked his head. "I'm glad you appreciate the point."

"They hate the French king now."

"*Hate* isn't a strong enough word. He tried to banish them from their God. 'An instrument of Satan' is what some of the priests call King Louis. The famous Father Roubaud, warrior priest and once our great enemy, now pays regular calls to Sir William, reporting on French activity in the west. There's no sign of Rogers conspiring with the French there."

"Which leaves the east," Duncan said. "There are still many from Quebec who are voyageurs in the fur trade, who would make regular calls in the northwest, where Rogers commands. The makings of a secret network."

"You sound as if you think he should hang," Woolford observed.

Duncan looked down at his hands folded on the little table. "No. I would have raised my glass to his toast. It was the British king who butchered my clan."

"That was a different George."

"George the Second, George the Third. They both washed their hands in blood of the innocent."

"Steady," Woolford cautioned, lowering his voice. "These walls may not be as thick as you think. And I know you better than to think it is vengeance that is driving you north."

"Rogers is a shrewd warrior," Duncan observed. "He would not have pursued a new country populated by free Frenchmen unless he knew the resources were in place. Gold louis are beginning to appear among the colonists."

The deputy superintendent looked out the stern window. He seemed to be deciding what to share with Duncan. "The *Joan of Arc*," he said. "That was the name of a little sloop favored by the French general for special missions along the St. Lawrence. Near the end of the war, harvests had failed for two straight years in Quebec. The French soldiers were mostly militia. They began deserting in large numbers, going home to hunt and fish to feed their starving families. The governor of New France decided to divert the funds sent to pay the regular troops and buy supplies—to use it instead to pay the militia. At least twenty thousand pounds sterling, maybe more. While Quebec was falling, we think the *Joan* was sent with the chest of coins to one of the forts on the south side of the St. Lawrence, but she was never seen again. There was talk about monks in black robes carrying a chest in the middle of the night, but only rumors."

Duncan weighed his words. "That kind of money could fund a new government. French farmers have been moving down into the Grants. But is it a free New France they seek? Or a new royal colony ruled from Paris?"

"We keep asking ourselves that very question. There are still ships that sail from Quebec to Normandy. If word arrived in Paris of the missing treasure, some would see it as an opportunity for the king to reverse his fortunes in America. Maybe Noah's right."

"I'm sorry?" Duncan asked.

"We were speaking of St. Francis. He said the Abenaki war chiefs always did the French king's dirty work. Now the Abenaki are gathering. During the war, one named Mog had a whole pole of ranger scalps at St. Francis," Woolford said in a tight voice, "right outside the Jesuit church. He had a special ritual during the war, just for rangers. We rescued a prisoner who witnessed it. He would cut their hearts out and eat them, usually while they were still beating."

"He hasn't stopped," Duncan said, his voice hollow. "He cut two more out in Massachusetts." He explained their experience with Chief Mog in Boston and on the western road.

"God help us," Woolford muttered. "We are going into the jaws of the beast."

THE *OSPREY* GLIDED OVER THE still waters, chasing the reflection of the gibbous moon in her northward passage. One of the Scottish crew kept watch at the prow, another stayed close with a long pole. Several of the company lay on the deck, some snoring, some watching the stars.

Munro stood beside Duncan at the helm. "Gonna storm," the old Scot said.

"The sky is clear," Duncan pointed out.

Munro just shook his head. "Gonna storm, my bones know it," he replied, then yawned and curled up with a blanket by the stern rail.

Much later Duncan became aware of Sinclair, the first mate, standing nearby awkwardly, holding a soiled sack in his hand. "The owner died in the war, sir. We carry them with us, just in case. Last time we found someone was nearly two years ago."

"I don't follow, Mr. Sinclair—"

"Mr. Munro, he's the one who told us. He said you did it most nights when you sailed to Bermuda. Even just a few minutes would mean the world to us."

Duncan gazed at the lumpy bag and felt a spark flash in his Highland soul. "Can you handle the helm, Mr. Sinclair?"

The sailor smiled, put a knuckle to his forehead, and extended the sack as he grabbed the helm.

"Keep Polaris true over the bow," Duncan advised, then knelt by a lantern and extracted the contents of the dusty muslin sack.

It had been a fine instrument once, and though it had seen much abuse, its cherrywood chanter and drones still retained a polished sheen, and the leather bag, though much scoffed and patched, seemed intact. He put the reed in his mouth to moisten it, then reinserted it in the chanter before he tested the blow-pipe. It leaked slightly, but Duncan knew it would likely seal itself after a few minutes.

He filled the bag and then, his heart thumping, adjusted the drones. The high-pitched notes echoed out over the lake. One of the Scottish crew sat up, a huge grin on his face. A Mohawk shot up from his sleep, a hand on his ax. Others of the exhausted men stirred at the sound, then rolled over for more slumber. Duncan piped a romantic ballad at first, getting the balance of the chanter as he faced the stern. When he turned, every man on the desk was up and watching him. He offered a jaunty song of the Highland drovers, his heart pushing up into his throat as he remembered his sisters singing to it. Men began calling out suggested tunes, many of them odes to Bonnie Prince Charlie or ballads of the lost Jacobite cause. Sadie, on Hayes's shoulder, swayed to the music. Between songs, loons responded from across the dark water with long, questioning wails, sometimes answered by a single bark from Molly.

The Iroquois and Noah watched with intense expressions, and as he began a series of *ceol mor*, ancient ceremonial music, they kept searching the skies. They thought he was calling down spirits. An old Scot sobbed, and another patted the man's back, comforting him in Gaelic. Was he weeping just from the memories, Duncan wondered, or because he knew the Highland world was gone?

"Killiecrankie," someone called out, and later "Maggie Lauder," then "The Hills of Glenorchy." Duncan's fingers knew the tunes, and as they worked, his mind drifted to scenes of his youth, to the great festivals of his clan when his grandfather and uncles competed with pipes and fiddles, engaging in playful musical duels. His sisters danced, and sometimes all would stop as his mother entranced them with songs of selkies and the king of the sea. Once, a flaming stick had arced through the night sky, landing in their circle, and an uncle had run out of the darkness gasping, insisting to Duncan and the other children that he had been chased by the fairies who had gathered to listen.

The *Osprey* coasted along, followed by the echoes of the pipes, until the lookout shouted and everyone turned to see black clouds close ahead, stabbing the lake with daggers of fire.

"THERE!" SINCLAIR SHOUTED, "I SWEAR she's there, port bow five points!" He pointed through the frenzy of water so thick it was hard to tell where the lake began and the storm-driven downpour ended.

Duncan desperately fought the tiller as the ship scudded down the lake with only her top square sail set. His heart sank as he finally saw what Sinclair had been shouting about for the past ten minutes. Between the drifting torrents, he glimpsed the brig from Ticonderoga.

The *Osprey*'s prow lunged into the lake, and one of the Mohawks, desperately clinging to the main mast, began a prayer toward the heavens. The ship lurched again and the man was thrown off his feet. He did not resist when Woolford grabbed him, half dragged him to the hatch, and pointed below deck, where the others huddled, including Will, who had dragged the seabear Molly from the deck.

They had had no choice but to turn before the heavy wind, backtracking into the widest part of the lake, where they had the best chance of avoiding the rocky shores.

Woolford struggled to Duncan's side, holding one of the manropes they had rigged, and peered into the pelting rain. "She may just be taking Hazlitt up north for his Montreal trial," Woolford suggested, shouting to be heard.

"It's Beck!" Duncan shouted as the rain slashed his face. "Only he would be fool enough to take her out in this."

"But we're faster," Woolford pointed out.

"Not necessarily our advantage now," Duncan said. "She's heavier, more stable, and we are speeding right to where he wants us." Beck was desperate to learn the location of a certain cross. Duncan was desperate to find the men who sank the *Arcturus*. Here, on Lake Champlain, their paths were violently converging. "We have to wear round, to come about and start tacking north again, but she will pass close by while we do, and then it will be a race on short sail, beating into the wind."

"Unless she blasts us," Sinclair suggested.

"We have guns as well," Woolford said.

The Scottish seaman looked much taken aback. As the wind ebbed for an instant, he chastised Woolford. "We would ne'r fire on a king's ship, sir."

Woolford took a long moment to answer. "No, of course not. But Beck's hell-bent on stopping us." He turned to Duncan, who had never seen his friend so worried. "So it is up to you and your storm-demon friend." As if the spirit in the lake had heard, the sloop pitched violently, knocking Woolford into Sinclair's arms.

"You saw the beast as sure as we did, sir," Sinclair reminded Woolford as he untangled himself from the deputy superintendent and carefully placed Woolford's hands on the manrope. "Mustn't make light of him. He summoned Mr. Duncan for a reason."

BUT THE STORM-DEMON'S LAKE WAS not the broad ocean, only a narrow chute of furious whitecaps. There was nothing to do but continue beating down and wearing before the rapidly approaching narrows. They had lost most of the progress made during the day.

Suddenly the brig was before them, adjusting course and coming directly at the *Osprey*.

"The bastard's opening his gun ports!" Sinclair shouted.

"He'll aim high," Duncan explained. "He won't try to sink us at first, just disable us." He exchanged a worried glance with Sinclair. They both knew that being disabled in such a gale would likely mean the end of the sloop.

Both ships lurched violently, and as they recovered, lightning flashed, illuminating a solitary figure gripping the shrouds of the brig, watching them. Horatio Beck seemed to take no notice of the storm as he shouted at the men on his deck. Behind him, clutching a stay, was Sergeant Mallory.

The ships were a hundred yards apart, then fifty, and as Duncan turned the tiller to momentarily confuse the enemy helmsman, the eight guns on the brig's port side fired. Sinclair shouted a desperate warning, then paused and laughed. All but one of the guns offered only a puff a smoke. The last gun sputtered, and her ball flew out a few yards. "Damp powder!" Sinclair shouted in glee, then faced Duncan. "The storm-demon chooses sides! He's spiked those guns with nails of rain. There'll be no cannon play this day."

Beck was screaming at his crew, so loud they could hear him above the din of the storm. Mallory had a musket now but was having difficulty priming it in the heavy weather.

"Now, Mr. Sinclair," Duncan said with a bitter grin, "let us come about while they are confused." Perhaps indeed the storm-demon would see them through.

Minutes later, after a flurry of action by the *Osprey*'s steadfast crew, they left the brig in their wake as they angled northward. Duncan's hope was to make enough progress in what remained of the night to be able to lose the brig among the northern islands.

Duncan gave Sinclair the difficult task of raising enough of the fore and aft canvas to give them maximum speed without capsizing. In all his experience on the open sea, Duncan had never known such a nightmare. The prudent course for the brig would have been to reduce its straining load of canvas and ride out the weather. But Beck had made clear his intentions to brig and sloop alike. As his brig heaved away after misfiring her guns, Beck had aimed a pistol at the man at the wheel. "Ram her, damn you!" he had screamed. "Ram her!"

Duncan was left to navigate the *Osprey* along what was by nautical standards a long alley between two treacherous shores, through violently rolling waves and torrents so thick he could sometimes barely see the bow of the sloop. All the while, lookouts kept watch for the brig, which could materialize out of the gloom at any moment to run them down.

They were in the widest part of the lake, but even that was less than fifteen miles, and Duncan's breath caught as a great lightning burst illuminated the jagged, ship-killing rocks of the shore only a few cable lengths away. It became impossible to measure the passage of time, nearly impossible to measure their passage back up the lake, though more than once a flash from the skies showed a landmark they had passed the day before.

Finally—it may have been midnight or it may have been four in the morning, Duncan could not tell—he became aware of Sinclair and Woolford speaking to him. Woolford pried away his fingers, which were clenched around the helm, and led him to the aft cabin. His friend produced a horn cup filled with an amber liquid and ordered Duncan to drink.

Duncan jerked upright as the liquor inflamed his throat, slamming his head against a low ceiling beam. "Mother Mary!" he spat, suddenly much revived.

"Sinclair says he has been saving the whiskey for a special occasion," Woolford said. "Corporal Longtree says to give you this," he added, dropping a small bundle of scarlet and blue feathers on the table. It was a Mohawk token, given to victorious warriors.

"We haven't won anything yet," Duncan said as tendrils of warmth crept into his limbs. He felt as if he had been waging a running battle for hours.

"You kept us alive. The storm lessens. Noah said it was the storm-demon's gift to you."

"Felt more like a curse."

Woolford turned the feathered bundle over, studying it. He, like Duncan, had deep respect for the words of the natives when they spoke of nature. "But for the maelstrom, we would have been at the mercy of those guns, and the storm made possible our escape. Noah says it was your baptism, that now you are bonded to the ancient one of the lake."

Duncan had trouble moving his stiff fingers as he lifted the feathers. His entire body was shaking. Woolford stepped into the gangway and returned with a plate of bread and cheese. "Eat and sleep. Rufus and Sinclair have the sloop now. We'll be threading the islands soon. We'll wake you when we need you."

It wasn't a crewmember that woke him, but the call of a gull. Soft, diffused light came through the stern window. The ship had stopped rolling but seemed to be making little headway.

The pearl-white fog was so thick he could not see the far end of the sloop. He stepped around sleeping bodies on the deck to find Noah and Conawago at the bow, keeping watch. They nodded their greetings and turned back toward the fog with worried expressions.

"We should anchor," Duncan said when he reached the helm. "I'd hate to have saved the sloop from the storm only to lose her to a fog."

Sinclair looked at his gaunt companion, Rufus—who seemed shaken and soberer than Duncan had ever seen him—and shook his head. "That bastard will catch us if we do, sure as eggs. If I can just get us into the passage between the last islands and drop you in Massaquoit Bay by noon, you'll be set for St. Francis and I'll still have a chance to go back up to the fort at the north end of the lake. There I will report that Mr. Woolford had to have a rapid transport to the Montreal road for secret Indian business."

"If you don't make it there before Beck?" Duncan asked.

"Then he'll catch out the lie. Won't be enough rope in Ticonderoga to hang us all."

They moved with agonizing slowness through water as still as glass, the eerie silence sometimes as nerve-racking as the gale they had endured the night before. A gull called from somewhere in the gloom. A large fish twisted the surface and was gone. Sinclair watched Rufus, who seemed to navigate by some sixth sense, following marks that were invisible to Duncan. The land was seldom seen, the sun indicated only by an occasional brighter smudge in the fog. At times the lake itself was so obscured that they glided along as if in some sky-bound cloud. Only once did Sinclair or Rufus show alarm, when for a few heartbeats the shroud thinned to show a rocky shore a cable length away. Sinclair muttered a Gaelic curse and leaned hard into the helm.

Conawago beckoned Duncan forward and continued his lookout as Noah sketched a crude map on the blank frontispiece of his pocket Bible. "No swamp this time," the old Abenaki said, referring to the ordeal Robert Rogers and his men endured when they had eluded pursuers in 1759 by hiking through a massive miles-wide swamp to reach St. Francis. "We'll go around," he explained, penciling a short arc, "and should reach the river above town by dawn on the third day." It was beginning to sound like a ranger raid.

Duncan studied the tribal elder, trying to decide if he felt more or less comfortable with the man now that he knew he was an Abenaki. "You told Munro that this was the battle that was destined to take place. What did you mean?"

Noah touched the spirit pouch that hung beside his cross. "The struggle between king's men and"—he paused to carefully choose his words—"those who are not king's men."

Duncan was tempted to ask if Noah himself had received a letter from

Rogers, but he worried that the question might offend the enigmatic elder. "I'm just helping the men who died in Boston," Duncan said.

"No," Noah replied with conviction, and he fixed Duncan with one of the stares that seemed to belong uniquely to tribal elders, a gaze at once searching and challenging, wise, and somehow lonely. "You are shaping the war that is to come."

"Not so," Duncan insisted. "I am all done with war. I am just helping some murdered souls find peace."

A sad, apologetic grin twisted Noah's mouth. "You will have no choice, McCallum. It will come to all the land, to all the known world."

Before Duncan could press him for an explanation, Conawago and Hayes frantically extended poles to fend the sloop off a boulder, and Noah leapt forward to join them at the bowsprit.

16

THE *OSPREY*'S LITTLE BOAT HAD to make three trips to ferry their party and its supplies to the north shore of the bay the natives called Massaquoit. Rufus, Sinclair, and the crew seemed forlorn to see their new friends leave. Rufus leaned closer to whisper in Duncan's ear.

"Yes, Rufus," Duncan replied, trying to match the solemnity of the request, "if the beast of Champlain ever approaches you, you may assure it you are a friend of mine." He hesitated, then added, "But never again call him the beast. Call him the keeper of the lake." Rufus pumped his head and nodded energetically.

"I'd gladly take such a maelstrom to hear ye play the pipes, McCallum," the mate from Caithness declared with a wide grin. "I'll be hearing those echoes for months." Sinclair extended his hand. "Fare thee well, lad. Try to keep a step ahead of the king's rope."

They ran hard, at the woodsman's pace, letting Noah lead them along moose trails at the edge of the great bog, sometimes taking turns carrying Will on their backs. The sun had set, the light of day nearly extinguished before they finally collapsed in a grove of hemlocks. As Duncan sat against a thick trunk, sapped of energy, he marveled at the energy of the two old tribesman as they collected wood and lit a fire. Noah and Conawago had grown much closer since Ticonderoga, and sometimes it seemed to him that they shared great secrets, like two old wizards who watched the world from afar. His admiration for them, however, was marred by an increasing sense that both men had begun to devalue their long, rich lives, that they were becoming resigned to finishing their days without fulfilling their lives. He saw Woolford studying them as well and realized that his friend shared the same worry. They had both seen it happen to too many tribal elders, had seen the light gradually fade from their eyes. A pain rose in his chest to think of it. For reasons he knew he could not put into words, he suspected that of all the people he had ever known, these two lives might be the most valuable of all. He despaired over it, not just because he felt powerless to change the fate of the old tribesmen, but also because in this, the most vulnerable of times, he had dragged them into the treachery that had stalked him from Boston.

They ate their meal of corn mush and ham with little conversation, for everyone in their party was exhausted, and they had to wake Will, who had collapsed onto Molly, to force him to eat. Munro insisted on keeping watch, and Duncan volunteered to relieve him in two hours.

He woke abruptly, jabbed by some inner alarm. Sitting upright in the darkness, he surveyed their camp. The fire had ebbed to glowing embers. Will and Molly lay curled up together beside it, with Hayes lying an arm's length away. There was no sound but that of the water in the nearby creek and the chatter of night insects. Duncan could smell tobacco mixed with the sharp, sweet scent of spicebush and sassafras. It was a mixture Conawago used at council fires.

Duncan followed the scent to a ledge that opened onto a long view of rolling hills glowing under a brilliant moon. The two old tribesmen were on the ledge, nursing long-stemmed clay pipes. As Duncan approached, they made room for him, forming a small half circle, in the center of which more tobacco smoldered, stacked over coals brought from the campfire. The spiraling smoke was an invitation to the spirits.

As was the custom in councils, Duncan would not speak until he was asked to do so. He watched the silvery thread rise to the stars. A barred owl called in the distance, answered by one in the trees below them. Noah began a rhythmic chant, so low that Duncan could not understand the words, if indeed there were words. Conawago did not join in, only watched the Abenaki with what seemed a worried curiosity; then he finally nodded and shifted his gaze to the immense sweep of country before them, puffing on his pipe.

Gradually Duncan comprehended that Noah was speaking to the gods of his people. He was an Abenaki medicine man, a sachem, and he wanted them to know that he was returning from his long self-exile, if they would permit it. How long had it been, Duncan wondered. Twenty years? Thirty? Even more? Would his tribe welcome him? Would they shun him? Would any still know him?

Stars had shifted in the sky before Noah finally stopped. He renewed the tobacco in his pipe, relit it, and handed it to Duncan. The Abenaki elder waited for Duncan to take several puffs before he spoke. "You do not know the place you seek, McCallum."

Duncan was not sure how to answer. "All I know is a map in a Bible," he offered, and saw the slight uplift of Noah's lips.

"The St. Francis I knew was like an oasis," Noah recalled. "A sanctuary town where the living came easy. Always fish in the river, always venison in the forest. But that was a long time ago. Now many have moved away to the far western country, more going every few months, I hear. It's different, has been different for many years because of the wars. It's a place divided—between those who yearn for the peaceful days and those who stand with the war chiefs, with the Jesuits in between."

"Did you leave as a boy?" Duncan asked.

Noah looked out over the landscape for several breaths before answering. "I was the son of a great chieftain who wore the feathered robe of our ancestors and kept our people proud to be Abenaki, not because we were feared warriors, but because we were a noble tribe. I was young and strong, and my parents had accepted that I should be a war chief in my early years, as a way of learning the responsibilities of the feathered robe. I was on a raid in the eastern lands that you call Maine. One day the sun suddenly went black. It lasted only minutes, but we were terrified. The Jesuit with us explained that it was an eclipse. No one was interested except me, the others just said the spirits were telling the English to go home, but the priest used round stones to show me what had happened with the earth and the moon. I thought he must be the wisest man in all the world, and after that I studied in his classroom whenever I could. The priests sent me to Quebec to study, though I returned every few months to St. Francis.

"After two years they insisted that I go to France, even Rome, to learn more. I was so intoxicated with the learning that of course I went. Two years became four years, then seven. By the time I sailed back up the St. Lawrence, all of my family had died of fever. My teachers consoled me by putting the black robe of a monk on me and sending me to the western lands, where we built missions, even traveling down to the Mississippi River settlements of the Acadians who had been evicted from Nova Scotia. But I kept asking myself why I was helping other people when the tribesmen of the north needed so much help. And I began to perceive the intolerance of the priests, who thought that gods spoke only to Christians. One day I went to get firewood, and I never went back. I just walked. For over a year I walked." The old Abenaki's voice faded away, and he seemed to have drifted into memories of those long-ago years. "Eventually I found an aged woman of the tribes who was living alone in a cave, one of the wise ones who knew the old ways. I stayed with her for a few years, until she died, and then I found Reverend Wheelock and Occom. They gave me a place where I could still learn about the spirits but keep my own counsel."

Duncan looked at Conawago, who nursed his pipe and watched the horizon. The tale perhaps too painfully reflected Conawago's own life.

Noah looked up and spread his arms. "Here is *Totokanay*!" he shouted to the stars.

A chill ran down Duncan's spine. The man he had known as Noah had called in the spirits and was revealing himself after so many years of wearing another face. It was a solemn moment, a moment when hard and terrible truths might be revealed. The Abenaki elder would likely not want Duncan to use his tribal name, but he had decided to share this deep, vital secret.

Totokanay turned so that he faced Conawago and Duncan across the little smoldering pile. "There is death ahead," he declared.

"There is a reckoning ahead," Duncan replied.

"You don't understand the place you go to."

"I don't understand the place I have been."

"St. Francis is a place of old hatreds, old faiths, old hunts."

Duncan hesitated over the Abenaki's choice of words. "Old hunts?"

"Warriors who hate all English, who once would bring back captives so women and children could kill them slowly with sharp sticks and hot coals. And another kind of warrior, who hates the French king. St. Francis is as much a Jesuit town as an Abenaki one. A Jesuit hermitage, in a way. When the French King Louis outlawed them, several more came to evade his long arm. Montreal and St. Francis have become havens for broken priests."

"The Jesuits," Duncan repeated. "You said Jesuits were with you on that raid in Maine many years ago. Why?"

"The raids were their idea. My people were growing weary of war, but some—not all—of the Jesuits kept the bloodlust alive."

Duncan weighed the words in silence. "Tell me something. Did the Jesuits befriend Major Rogers?"

"They were sworn enemies in the last war, but today—" The Abenaki shrugged. "Call them allies. There was too much bad blood between the militant Jesuits and Rogers for them to reconcile, but there is another Jesuit at St. Francis whom Rogers has known for years."

"You mean Father LaBrosse?"

It did not seem that Totokanay had heard him. The Abenaki watched the glowing twists of smoke that connected them to the spirits. "They are all beginning to understand something in St. Francis. It makes them very dangerous."

"Understand what, exactly?" Duncan asked.

The old Abenaki looked at Conawago before replying. His voice cracked when he finally spoke. "There are no clear words for it. How does an animal feel when it is caught in a trap and bleeding to death, knowing it can do nothing to change its fate? They have all seen that they are in their ending times."

The words lingered in the silence. A spark of light shot across the sky and died. The owl called but had no answer.

This was the world the two old men lived in, a world in which their bloodlines and their rich, centuries-old tribal cultures were being extinguished. What made it acutely painful for Conawago and Totokanay, Duncan realized, was that they now understood that, having been taken away by Europeans for education and conversion, they had become unintended agents of the forces that crushed their people. They had thought to help their tribes with their knowledge, becoming bridges between cultures, but all their training had done was make them more aware of the slow, grinding annihilation of all they held dear. For decades they had borne witness to the inexorable destruction of all they and their forebears had been, knowing they could not change it.

Duncan felt small, inadequate, like an intruder at the death of someone else's loved one. "They will be desperate there," he said at last.

"You understand nothing," came Conawago's voice, surprisingly impatient. "You do not understand your part, Duncan, because, like so many others, you do not grasp the stage you perform on." For a moment, apology lingered in the old man's eyes. It wasn't like him to speak so harshly to Duncan. He dropped more of his fragrant tobacco onto the smoldering mound. "*Jiyathon-tek*," he whispered to the heavens before turning back to Duncan. "We are lost if we don't recognize that everyone in this drama is in their ending times. All of us here. You try to convince yourself that you are different from us, but you are not. The life of your Highland tribe is gone, as is that of the Nipmuc and the Abenaki, and soon the Iroquois. But it doesn't stop there. The Jesuits have glimpsed their ending. They may be desperate, but they have more power than people think."

"Only the kings survive," Duncan said after listening to the owl again.

"No. You are wrong," his old friend replied. "There is an ending time for them too. King George has America. King Louis thinks he can get much of it back. But they don't know the people who have taken root here. Those people are beginning to grasp the truth that the tribes have always known. Nothing important in life has ever been granted by a king."

Conawago shifted his gaze back over the silver-gilded mountains. Minutes passed before he spoke again, in a slow, reverent voice. "There is no land like this land," declared the old Nipmuc, who had seen more of the world than anyone Duncan knew. "There is no freedom like this freedom."

17

THEY DROVE HARD THE NEXT day, ranger style, running for an hour, then stopping for a few minutes' rest, taking turns with the heavier loads. Munro cleverly rigged a pack for Molly out of belts and pouches, and the big Newfoundland carried twenty pounds at Will's side without ever breaking stride.

Duncan found himself drifting to the back of the line, and more than once, Brandt, running on a flanking path as rangers were taught to do in enemy territory, had to throw a pebble at him to force his attention back to the trail. He found himself revisiting his time with the old tribesmen the night before, which had strangely disturbed him. *There is no freedom like this freedom,* Conawago had said. Duncan had not understood, protesting that he could not escape the bounty hunters and magistrates forever.

"Not you. Everyone," Noah had said, as if to correct him.

Were they suggesting that the entire world was adrift? They seemed to think men were drifting away from kings, but surely that wasn't possible. Duncan may have hated what the government did, but the king was the king, the head of the nation. The Jacobites hadn't rebelled against kings, they had rebelled for their own Scottish king. He recalled the words of Josiah Chisholm, who said he could not get his mind around the notion of not having a king. There was no such thing as a country without a king. It was the old men's tribal blood talking, the part of them that walked the forest in freedom. But the forest was not a country. No civilized nation had ever not had a king.

He slowed, looking at the native rangers who ran with Woolford. The Iroquois had a civilization, and they had no king, only a council of wise chieftains and the matriarchs who counseled them. There were those who called the Iroquois the Romans of the New World, and he recalled too that for a time, ancient Romans, and Greeks, had lived without kings. What had Conawago said? *Nothing important in life has ever been granted by a king.*

A pebble hit his shoulder again, followed quickly by the whistle of a warbler. He looked up from his musing to see Munro, silently pointing him up the trail. Duncan had fallen behind again. He had to stop worrying about freedom and honor and focus on murderers and traitors.

"THE CHURCH IS HERE," BRANDT explained in the last light of day, making the sign of a cross in wet sand by the riverbank, "facing the square that adjoins the river on its western side." He was drawing a map of St. Francis, which lay only three miles downriver now. "Rows of houses here and here," the old ranger said, drawing lines radiating north and south from both sides of the square, where the Christian Indians lived.

"We must split at the river's edge," Woolford advised. "One party around to the south, the other straight in from the north."

"Sounds like a military operation," Conawago observed. "We are not trying to relive the St. Francis massacre."

"At least not the bloody parts," Duncan rejoined. "Something else happened during that raid, and we must discover what it was."

Noah frowned. "Conawago and I will just walk into town. No one will suspect two old wanderers."

In the end, they agreed that Woolford and his rangers would flank the town and enter from the south while Duncan would lead his party along the bank to the riverfront landing. Hayes had announced that he would speak with the town leaders about European captives once Duncan had completed his business. The tinker, however, refused to stay in their camp with Will, Molly, and Sadie, insisting that he would carry his weight. "Jehovah has not brought me this far to have me linger behind," Hayes stated, his face set in fierce determination.

It did indeed feel like a wartime raid as they used hand signals to finally advance into St. Francis. It was an hour after dawn, and the town was still rising. If they met no resistance, they would meet at the church and seek the Jesuit priests.

Duncan's heart pounded as they cleared a little spit of land and the town came into view. Smoke rose skyward from more than four dozen buildings, some crude timber cabins but others substantial clapboard houses, beyond which were five or six more traditional bark longhouses. The big white planked church at the center of the town was flanked by a cemetery on the far side of the square, just as depicted on Daniel Oliver's powder horn. Three or four women were already at the wide landing place below the town square, where canoes and dugouts were pulled up on the pebble beach.

They stayed in cover, stealthily advancing, hands on the weapons they prayed they would not have to use. Munro softly whistled, indicating two men who emerged from a log house fifty yards away, one of whom pushed aside a loincloth to urinate on a tree. They kept up their approach.

A woman in a long, dark dress dumped a basket of laundry on the pebbles, then took a shirt into calf-deep water and bent to soak it. She had her back to them, and as the sun emerged from a cloud, it lit the auburn hues in her carefully combed and ribboned hair.

A choked cry rose from behind Duncan, and Hayes suddenly stood up from the alder he had knelt behind and took a staggering step forward. "Blessed God!" he murmured as he splashed into the water. "Rebecca!"

The woman turned in surprise. Her European features lost all color as Hayes rushed to her. "It's you!" Hayes cried. "My darling wife at last!" he called, sobbing as he wrapped his arms around her. She did not speak. She did not return his embrace. "It's me! It's Solomon!" Hayes cried as he tightened his embrace.

"*Va t'en!*" a child shouted. Two small Indian boys, perhaps three and five years of age, burst from the shadow of a tree, shouting as they ran into the water. The oldest leapt onto Hayes's back and violently pounded his head. "*Arrêtez! Arrêtez!*" the younger cried as he grabbed a leg and desperately tried to separate the woman from Hayes.

Duncan and his companions stared transfixed at Hayes and his long-lost wife. As Duncan stirred from his trance to help the tinker, Munro grabbed his arm. "No!" the Scot warned. Duncan followed his gaze toward the bank. An Abenaki warrior wearing a bandage around his thigh stood grinning at them. With one hand he gripped Conawago, whose arm was covered with blood. With the other he pressed a bloody blade to the Nipmuc's throat.

The boy on Hayes's back scratched at an ear, drawing blood. "Leave my mother alone!" he screamed.

CONAWAGO WINCED AS DUNCAN PUSHED a needle into the skin of his arm. Mog had stabbed deep into his bicep when he ambushed the old man, leaping out of the shadows with a blow aimed between the shoulder blades. Noah had shoved Conawago an instant before the blade struck, saving him from the fatal blow the warrior had intended. Mog, hearing the shouts from the riverfront, had changed his mind and quickly dragged his victim toward the water.

When, an hour after their capture, Duncan and his friends had been marched at gunpoint into their makeshift prison chamber, the old Nipmuc was already there, being tended by a young priest. The Jesuit had been alarmed, if not outright frightened, by the arrival of the new prisoners and had fled without responding to any of Duncan's urgent questions. The basket he left on the bench, however, contained additional bandages and even a needle and silken thread, which Duncan was using to close up the wound.

"His name is Father Tremblay," Conawago explained with another grunt as the needle pierced his skin again. "Arrived here a few months ago, he says."

"More talkative with you than with us," Munro observed.

"Because Mog told everyone you were rangers who had come back to finish the job they started nine years ago. Tremblay says the old ones tell him they spent days digging graves the last time rangers came to St. Francis."

The long, narrow chamber they had been locked in seemed to have once been a sacristy, where priests stored vestments and changed into them before services, though apparently for a larger church than the one they had been led to. The narrow loophole windows illuminated a long row of pegs and, bolted to the wall, an old armoire that had been scorched in a fire, in which discarded moth-eaten cassock robes hung. More recently, the room seemed to have been used as a small classroom. Four benches were pushed against the inner wall, with half a dozen small writing slates stacked on one. On the plaster walls were drawings in pencil lead or chalk, some crude renderings of animals and trees but others expertly drawn images of religious symbols and events in the town.

Munro seemed unshaken by their captivity and spent his time studying the drawings, pointing out what he recognized, including christenings, weddings, meetings with visitors, harvest festivals, and even an Easter crucifixion scene. Corporal Brandt's eyes had lighted with a disturbing gleam, and he claimed one of the narrow windows, staring out onto the St. Francis square and the river beyond, muttering to himself as he pointed at the poles along the perimeter of the square that were mounted with human scalps. Sometimes he pretended to shoot passersby, emitting one of his roosterlike laughs each time he pulled his make-believe trigger.

Hayes sat in the darkest corner of the room, his hollow, unfocused expression resembling that of a soldier who had been rendered senseless by the explosions of battlefield artillery. Duncan repeatedly tried to speak with him, but the tinker showed no sign of hearing. His despair was a horrid black serpent that was slowly strangling his soul. Duncan would never forget the forlorn confusion, then the desolation on his face as a mob of furious Abenaki women had dragged him away from the woman he had sought for so many years. He had committed his fortune, his hopes, his entire life to finding Rebecca. But she had just stood in the water and stared at him, her only acknowledgment the tears that welled in her eyes.

It was midday when the heavy door opened. Two Abenaki guards armed with muskets stepped aside to let in Father Tremblay and another Jesuit, a compact middle-aged man whose round face was lined with worry and marked with deep bruises along one side. Behind them came a native woman with a massively wrinkled face, carrying a basket of food.

"Maria has water, bread, and dried fish," the older Jesuit explained. "And two bottles of disappointing wine. Not our usual hospitality, I fear."

"Very generous," Duncan said as Ishmael enthusiastically helped the woman distribute the food. "Father—"

"LaBrosse. I am trying to convince the elders to release you. But our war chief Mog is most insistent." He seemed not to notice the intense way Duncan stared at him. Here at last was Jean-Baptiste de LaBrosse, who sent purple-inked letters and gold coins to rangers. "Seeing armed English stealing into our town revives old anguish. It's a bad business, trying to recover a captive. The Rebecca you seek exists no longer. She is married to one of our chieftains."

Without waiting for a reply, LaBrosse bent to examine Conawago's bandage with an approving eye, then experimented with the Nipmuc's hand, asking him to squeeze and extend his fingers. When he finished, he walked among the prisoners as they ate, asking if any were injured, shaking his head over the unresponsive Hayes, who showed no evidence of even being aware of the Jesuit. The priest's gaze shifted, and he cocked his head at the wall, then quickly produced a writing lead from inside the folds of his robe to finish the sketch of a tree on the wall. The old woman watched for a moment, then shook her head as if in frustration over his absentmindedness and left the chamber.

"We are not here for Rebecca," Duncan said to the priest's back. "We came because of men who were murdered in Massachusetts."

The lead froze in midair for a second, but then LaBrosse continued his drawing. "Massachusetts is a long way away. Another world. Not our world."

"I am afraid it has become your world, Father. St. Francis is involved in the crimes."

LaBrosse, still facing the wall, made a dismissive gesture. "That was always one of your sins, you English. Exaggeration is but the shadow of a lie."

"Thirty-seven men were lost on a ship. I saw the bodies. They were killed by two Frenchman allied with your war chief. Two more men were scalped and murdered by the same man who stabbed my friend Conawago. And don't accuse me of being English. I am Scottish."

The writing lead in LaBrosse's hand snapped against the wall. "You don't know it was Mog," he whispered, still facing the drawing.

"We do. I saw him, twice, once in Boston and then when we wounded him in his thigh as he tried to kidnap a boy."

From his waistcoat pocket Duncan withdrew the swatches of cloth he had been carrying for weeks and dropped them on the bench beside Father LaBrosse. "I took these from the mouths of those two dead men. They were both rangers with Rogers. In October of '59."

Brandt, listening, gave another of his unsettling laughs. The old ranger's mind seemed to be unhinging again since arriving in St. Francis.

The Jesuit picked up the swatches and lowered himself onto the bench. He stared at them with an anguished expression, then studied his prisoners as if seeing them for the first time. "Please, I beg you, just tell them you came for news of that man's lost wife," he said with a nod to Hayes.

"Too late for that, Father," Duncan replied.

LaBrosse seemed to sag, fixing Duncan with a mournful, apologetic expression that Duncan tried to ignore.

"Tell me, Father, how long have you been here?"

LaBrosse sighed. "Long enough." He looked down at the embroidered leaves and fish stained with blood. "Mogephra was a great war chief, famous among all our people. They would sing all night when Mog returned from raids, parading with long poles adorned with English and Iroquois scalps. When the children draw him"—the priest pointed to an image on the wall opposite him—"he is always bigger than the other figures."

Ishmael studied the scene, then glanced nervously at Duncan. Duncan looked closer and saw women carrying torches. It wasn't the crucifixion scene Munro had thought it to be. It was a scene of three men tied to T-shaped posts, about to be burned alive.

"The Abenaki had always known war," LaBrosse continued, "but it had always been far removed from here. Rogers changed that. The Abenaki coined a special term just for him. *Wobomagonda*. It means *white devil*. Our people still have nightmares about the raid of the Wobomagonda." LaBrosse reached out and pulled Duncan away, as if he didn't want him looking at the scene. "Mog's family died in that October dawn," the priest continued in a brittle voice. "His heart shriveled into a dark, black thing. If a cause allows him to keep killing English, whatever it may be, that cause will be his."

"You speak of him as if from a distance," Duncan observed.

"I am not one of those priests who put on war paint. They all left St. Francis after the war, thank God."

"There are Frenchmen who would start the last war all over if they could."

"I am not one of those," the Jesuit said again.

"Yet here we are, locked in your church. The Jesuit church that was the center for Abenaki war making. When was it used first? Nearly fifty years ago, St. Francis war parties were raiding the Maine coast. Twenty years ago it was Western Massachusetts and New Hampshire. Then there was the battle at Lake George. The massacre at Fort William Henry. How many scalps did your good Christian Indians bring back from that one? Fifty? A hundred?"

LaBrosse stared into his folded hands. "That was a different church, not my church. Rangers burned it down in 1759."

"Most of it," Duncan corrected.

"Most of it." LaBrosse sighed and looked up. "This sacristy survived. I used it as something of a cornerstone for our new one."

Conawago sat beside the priest. "Tell me something, Father. The Abenaki began to call Major Rogers the White Devil. But what do you call him today?"

LaBrosse, Duncan had decided, was a complicated, even cunning man despite his simple appearance. But he was also an honest one. "Liberator," the Jesuit said. "Proof that compassion and mercy can transform a savage enemy into a savage friend."

"A friend of the Abenaki or a friend of the Jesuits?" Conawago asked.

LaBrosse returned his steady gaze. "A friend of the downtrodden. A friend of freedom."

A chill ran down Duncan's spine.

"Freedom," Munro repeated. "A bold word in such a small cell. Freedom from what? I've heard priests speak of the eternal freedom of souls, of becoming free from sin, of earning the freedom of redemption through confession."

The priest's reply held none of that biblical pretense. Defiance seemed to enter LaBrosse's eyes. "Freedom for the Society of Jesus to worship the Lord as it sees fit," he declared. "Freedom from the chains of kings."

The words cast a new silence over the chamber. Every man in the cell stared at the priest, all except the despondent Hayes, who had retreated so far into himself that Duncan feared he would never find his way out.

Duncan paced, staring at the scenes on the wall, pausing for a moment over one of two bearded men, one very large, the other much smaller. The big man was extending a letter, the smaller held the hand of an Indian woman as they conferred with a priest. Duncan moved on to the drawing nearest the battered armoire. It was an intricate depiction of burning buildings, men firing muskets, complete with puffs of powder smoke, and dead men and women. Right above the burning church, in what appeared to be the forested slope above the town, was a line of more than twenty women and children holding hands, led by a robed man holding a vizier, a cross mounted on a staff. At the end of the line were two warriors carrying a heavy box or chest. Duncan pointed to the monk. "That is you. You saved those women and children."

"It was a blessing to have that opportunity. With the help of merciful God."

"No," Duncan disagreed. "You mean with the help of merciful Major Rogers, as you described in a statement to the British army five years later."

LaBrosse's eyes narrowed. "A statement to a contemptible man named Beck," LaBrosse said in a near whisper. "An arrogant bully. I was never sure whom he served."

Corporal Brandt appeared at Duncan's side. He ran a bony finger along the line of figures fleeing through the trees. "Oh, aye," he murmured. "On the trail above the church I saw them plain."

Duncan tried to recall what he had read in the official reports of the raid. "Rogers was in the town the night before," he recalled. "He came with Captain Williams, but Williams's report said, 'I saw over six hundred scalps, I saw a score of canoes on the landing.' Not *we* saw. He was alone then because Rogers had left him to go meet you."

As if wondering who was the prisoner and who the captor, LaBrosse nervously looked at the men gathered around him. "My first mission, years earlier, had been traveling among Indian villages in what is now the New Hampshire colony. Rogers was working to map the frontier. I was traveling in a canoe on the Merrimack River when I lost control in some rapids. I capsized, and in my heavy robe I was certain to drown. But Robert Rogers saw me and pulled me to safety. We were much the same age and both much taken with the natural power of the wilderness. We visited waterfalls and treeless mountaintops just for the beauty of them. We became friends and corresponded from time to time."

"Even when the war broke out," Duncan suggested.

"Like he said, what's a little war between friends," the priest replied.

"Half the rangers with him that night had family killed by the 'Nakis," Munro inserted.

It took a moment for Duncan to understand the Scot's words. "He had to kill the Abenaki to give them a dose of their own medicine. But Rogers gave you a chance to save as many women and children as you could."

LaBrosse nodded. "He is an honorable man."

"He gave you that warning the night before. And you agreed to give him a list of names the next day. Potential allies, French colonists who were weary of the war, weary of their king."

"The king had sent no support for over two years but kept ordering us to fight. We were just his puppets. He had no regard for our lives and livelihood."

"Or for Jesuits."

LaBrosse did not disagree. "Then he gave us all away in the Treaty of Paris.

Every colonist here was French, ever since Champlain and Cartier set foot on these shores. Most did not even speak English. But with a few strokes of the pen he decreed that we were English. Just as he later decreed that Jesuit brothers were no longer priests, that our very vows were acts of sin." The fiery light returned to LaBrosse's eyes. "That wasn't just wrong, it was against the will of God. My vow is between me and my God, not between me and the frivolous Sun King."

Conawago, Duncan realized, was smiling.

"Some fat king in Paris cannot tell me I am not a Jesuit or not French, just as some fat king in London cannot tell you that you are not Scottish."

Duncan glanced at Munro, who was also grinning now. They were warming to the priest. "Rogers is not French," he observed. "Nor is he a Jesuit."

"We are both free men of the frontier lands. That is our bond."

Duncan saw that Conawago was gazing expectantly at him. He remembered once more their conversation in the moonlit mountains. It was as if the Nipmuc and Noah had anticipated this very conversation.

"Free men of the frontier lands," Ishmael, behind Duncan, repeated in a pointed tone. He was gesturing at the scene of the two bearded men and the priest.

"When was this?" Ishmael asked LaBrosse.

LaBrosse sighed. "Last year. It's nothing."

"Just friends of ours. Were they delivering a letter to you?"

When the Jesuit did not answer, Duncan stepped to Ishmael's side. "It's Ethan Allen," Ishmael explained, "and Rufus with one of his Indian paramours."

Duncan stared in surprise at the drawing, recalling how Allen had reacted to his mention of Saguenay. "He isn't delivering a message," Duncan suggested. "He's receiving a message. It's how the letters were delivered to the rangers in Massachusetts." He turned to Brandt. "And to you, Corporal."

"Mountain postmaster, Allen calls himself sometimes," Brandt confirmed with a grin that showed his missing teeth.

Duncan watched as LaBrosse retrieved the basket, ready to leave, and he realized that he had one more question. He was pointing to the chest being carried in the last drawing when Conawago interrupted. "Who was it, Father," the old Nipmuc asked, "who did you marry that night before the raid?"

Duncan cocked his head, not sure if he had heard correctly. Why speak of a wedding at such a desperate time?

The priest grimaced, then glanced at Hayes. He seemed about to reply when Ishmael gasped and pointed out one of the narrow windows. Outside, along the nearest edge of the square, Mog was directing the erection of three of the T-shaped posts used for burning captives alive.

ISHMAEL STAYED BY ONE OF the windows, unable to take his eyes off the posts. He had spent time among the violent western tribes and perhaps knew better than any of them the horrors of such deaths by fire. Mog, adorned with fresh paint, noticed the prisoners watching and dispatched one of his men to bring a bag out of one of the cabins. From it Mog extracted three human skulls and, laughing, placed one on top of each post, facing the prisoners.

"Oh, that unholy sonofabitch," Brandt cackled, slurring the last syllables as if one word, then shot his imaginary rifle at the war chief and leaned close to the window. "Who comes to kill? Who comes to kill?" he called, the ranger owl chant. He seemed excited, not fearful, at the sight of the posts.

When his uncle finally pulled him away from the window, Ishmael looked up with a hollow expression and just said, "Three," then gestured to his companions. There were six prisoners.

Brandt had wandered to the drawing of the burning town again and was studying it with intense interest when the door opened to admit Maria, the old woman who had first appeared with LaBrosse, carrying a basket of apples and water gourds. A guard shoved her as she crossed the threshold, and Munro caught her as she fell, sending several gourds tumbling across the floor.

"Merci, merci," she said as she recovered her basket, then unfolded a linen cloth at the bottom, releasing the fragrant scent of fresh-baked corn cakes. "S'il vous plaît," she said, inviting them to eat, and spread the cakes on the bench beside a long sausage. She glanced at the door, then, from within the folds of her dress, produced a small knife and laid it beside the sausage.

Brandt made no move to join, but instead ran his finger over the line of fleeing figures in the drawing. One of his odd, gobbling laughs escaped his throat, and he turned, extending the same finger toward the Abenaki matron.

My God, thought Duncan, surely the old ranger didn't recognize the woman he had seen with LaBrosse so many years ago. He pushed Brandt's arm down and was about to approach the woman when Conawago began speaking with her in his fluent French. Her back was bent, and she had more gray in her hair than most native women, with traces of a white strip of hair over her crown. Her eyes spoke of long knowledge of sadness and disappointment. Duncan recalled Brandt's earlier description of a woman with hair like a polecat who had helped with the rescue of children during the raid.

Conawago spoke of the fine church that had been built on the ruins of the old.

"The king in Paris was generous," she observed, then counted out the bottle gourds, making sure there was one for each prisoner. Conawago and Duncan exchanged a perplexed glance. The king in Paris wouldn't pay a *sou* to restore a Jesuit mission church.

The old Nipmuc made a show of admiring the drawings near the woman, then pointed to the one of a wedding. "They say there was a wedding the night before," he casually mentioned. "Was this the one?"

The woman's eyes seemed to look toward some distant point, as if she could see beyond the walls. "Pere LaBrosse came for it. She was such a sweet thing, had put off the wedding for two years because her father was going blind and her mother had a bad leg and she said they needed her." The old matron sighed and made the sign of the cross on her breast.

"A big affair," Conawago suggested. "Who were they?"

"We had such great hopes. He was from the warriors, the ones who kept pushing our young ones to go and bleed on distant trails, but his love for her was slaking his ardor for violence. She was from a good church family. We thought the union might ease the tension, cool the blood of both her husband and his brother, so some of our boys might be saved." She motioned Conawago closer so she could examine his bandage.

"You mean warriors under Mog the war chieftain."

"Yes, yes," the woman said distractedly as she lifted the linen over the Nipmuc's wound. "Mog's brother was the groom. I think it was the only time that devil Mog entered our church."

Conawago cast another pointed glance at Duncan, but Duncan did not understand. Why was the Nipmuc so interested in a wedding that took place nearly ten years before? He was about to ask when angry voices rose outside. The old woman stepped to a window, then abruptly began a low chant. *"Je vous salue Marie, pleine de grâce, le Seigneur est avec vous. Vous êtes bênie entre toutes les femmes."* He saw her fingers working at her wrist, and as she repeated the words, he realized she was reciting her rosary as she watched something on the town square.

Father LaBrosse was standing in front of one of the death posts as Mog directed the stacking of dried brush around it. The war chief was shouting furiously. LaBrosse was speaking in a low voice, his hand on his crucifix, in what sounded like a prayer. As Duncan watched, Mog slapped LaBrosse so hard the Jesuit staggered and fell to one knee.

When the old woman turned back, tears filled her eyes. "He came back five days ago, and suddenly it was like the old godless times again."

"Was he alone, grandmother?" Duncan asked.

"Not alone. Two angry Frenchmen were with him. They met with Pere LaBrosse and shouted at him. They questioned him and hit him, hit our blessed priest, and almost killed a lay brother. When we objected, Mog laid one of those trophy poles with scalps across the doorway of the church, as if declaring war on us. We have members of the tribe arriving from distant villages for the migration west, and we fear he will win some over." The Abenaki woman fought a silent sob, then collected herself. "Those Frenchmen left for Montreal two days ago." She straightened and spoke more loudly, to all the prisoners. "I am sorry. I will pray for a miracle, but God seems far away these days. Prepare your souls. Three of you will die tonight."

THEY KEPT A SILENT VIGIL at the loopholes, watching as brush and branches were stacked around the posts while two of Mog's fierce warriors kept shoving Father LaBrosse and three older women as they tried to pull away the fuel. Two women in long black dresses knelt a stone's throw away, fervently reciting their rosaries. Another, the man's mother or aunt, Duncan guessed, arrived to harangue one of the guards, who stared stoically ahead without responding. Duncan more than once thought he saw Noah in the shadows by the houses, watching and speaking with some of the onlookers, and when Conawago took a turn at the watch, he nodded and whispered "Totokanay," as if acknowledging the old Abenaki. There was no sign of Woolford and his rangers, and Duncan, finding himself looking at the trophy poles to see if any scalps dripped fresh blood, was beginning to worry that Mog's warriors had attacked them. More wood was being stacked for a bonfire in the center of the square. Mog's ceremony would not start until an hour or two after sunset, Conawago explained, when the full moon would rise above the trees to light the square by the river.

Hayes, still morose and silent, took a turn at the windows, gazing without expression at the preparations for death. "Only two of you," he finally declared when he turned from the window. He began straightening his clothes, brushing away the dirt on his waistcoat. "I will take a post," he announced. "I think Mog will mean to burn me in any event. More the honor in volunteering. My life is over."

"More the honor in finding a way to live!" Duncan snapped, feeling an unexpected anger at the tinker's words.

Hayes reacted with a hollow smile, then bent to brush off his legs, as if he wanted to look his best for the death post.

"You would do this to Sadie?" Ishmael asked.

The tinker's breath caught a moment, and his voice cracked. "I am no good for her anymore. Young Will can watch over her."

"Is this how you would repay your debt?" Conawago demanded.

The tinker continued to clean himself for his death. "Debt?" he asked in a disinterested voice.

"To your God, Solomon. He took you to the end of your quest. He gave you strength all these years. He brought you to new friends. He brought you to the truth, as bitter as it may be."

Hayes sobered and surveyed the faces of his companions. "Yes," he defiantly declared, "this *is* how I repay you, by giving one of you his life." He retreated to his corner and slumped against the corner again, speaking no more.

THEIR CELL WAS LIT BY the dull orange glow of dusk when the door latch rattled again. The tall figure who entered wore a cloak fashioned from an old blanket embroidered with flowers and six-pointed stars. When she lowered the hood, Hayes uttered a small moan and struggled to his feet. "Rebecca!"

Duncan had only glimpsed her face in the chaos of that morning, but now he saw that Hayes's former wife was strikingly beautiful. The Jewess from Rhode Island had braided her brunette hair, weaving beads and small feathers into the plaits. The braids set off her long, graceful countenance and the tattoos along one cheek. Her eyes were filled with a deep melancholy. She seemed to have trouble speaking.

"Tetwanay. My name is Tetwanay, Solomon," she finally said, then glanced at her onlookers. "I was hoping we could speak."

"These are my friends," Hayes said. His voice was hoarse. "I keep no more secrets from them."

Ishmael pulled a bench away from the wall, then helped her remove her cloak so she could sit. Her eyes brimmed with moisture. "I wanted to die when they killed our darling Ezra in front of me." Her gaze was fixed on the floor as she spoke, as if she could not bear to look at Solomon. "I tried to die. Part of me did die. I begged them to kill me." She pressed a fist against her lips to stifle a sob. "I jumped in a river to drown, but Mog pulled me out. I pestered a rattlesnake to bite me, but as it sprang, his war ax split its head. I ran away, but each time, a warrior tracked me down within an hour or two and beat me. I became a slave. The women and children spat on me, flung filth on me. I lived on nothing but the scrapings of pots after they ate, fighting with dogs for the leavings. They would not let me keep the Holy Day. If I hesitated at any task, they hit me with switches." She glanced up as Hayes rose, then she spoke to the floor again. "For the first few months I prayed every night that you would come. They were so angry over the raid by the rangers, sometimes they would come and hit me just for being what they called English. I began to learn their language, and one day a group of women came to me and said I was very fortunate, that now I would be a real person, an Abenaki. I said I was of the Jewish faith, of the Hebrew tribe, and they just laughed and said that person was dead.

"They stated that a great man wanted me for a wife, the man who had been married the night before the raid. His new wife had lingered behind in the raid to help her parents and the rangers killed them all. I said I was already married, and they said no, that person was dead, that I was now Tetwanay of the Abenaki. Then, that night, Mog's brother came and an old man spoke words over us and washed smoke over us and declared us married. They pushed us into a lodge. I would not let him touch me that first night. But the second night Mog came into our lodge." The woman's voice lowered to a near whisper. "He ripped off all my clothes and said if I did not lie with his brother, he would go south the very next day and bring back your head, Solomon." Tears flowed down her cheeks. "He knew your name from the papers in the packs they stole when they attacked us, knew that you lived in Rhode Island. He said you would die slow and then he would rip off your head the way he had ripped off our son's head."

Solomon slowly stepped forward to embrace the woman, but she raised a hand to stop him. "I have new sons, Solomon. Good boys."

"Abenaki boys," Hayes protested.

"Tetwanay's boys."

The tinker's heart had risen at her appearance in the cell, but now, as Duncan watched, it seemed to shatter, to break into a hundred pieces that could never be joined again. It would have been easier if Hayes had found Rebecca's body or her grave. But now he had found his beloved Rebecca and she was no longer the woman he sought, no longer his. He had struggled through storm, Indian attack, blizzards, derision, and terrible wounds only to find another man's wife.

"Is he . . ." Hayes's words were choked. He scrubbed tears from his gaunt cheek. "Is he a good man?"

"He is a good father. He keeps us fed. Tomorrow we are leaving for the west, fifty of us, up the St. Lawrence to the sea of the Hurons, where they say no white—" She stopped. "To a land that knows no strife, they say. I had to see you once, to make you understand. You must stop your searching. You must forget me, Solomon."

Hayes still loved her. Duncan could see it in his tormented eyes.

She rose, unable to raise her face to him, then reached around her neck. She pulled away a leather strap with a shiny medallion on it. To his great surprise, she turned and gave it to Duncan, then stepped to the door.

Hayes darted forward. He pressed his hand to the wound on his scalp and with a bloody finger drew a sign on the wall by the door, a Hebrew sign. Tetwanay paused, then wetted her own finger in the blood of the letter and drew another sign beside it. Then she wiped away both signs. "The night is not over," she said to Conawago, who stood closest to her; then she rapped for the door to be opened and was gone.

HAYES STARED IN ANGUISH AT the smear of blood on the wall for several minutes until Munro led him away. He was but a hollow scarecrow of a man. There was no life left in his eyes. His soul had been drained. His body simply complied with Munro, walking stiffly, then dropping to the floor again in his corner.

"You weren't surprised," Duncan whispered to Conawago.

"No. He should have been told this was possible. But none of us who expected this had the courage to explain. Young women are not captured to be killed. And if they are strong and fertile, they won't be kept as slaves for long." He gazed wordlessly at Hayes and sighed. "The greatest enemy of the tribes isn't the Europeans as such, it is the arithmetic. For two generations and more, they have failed to breed enough babies to replace those who die. With enough study, I suppose someone could calculate how long each tribe has until extinction."

The words tied a cold knot in Duncan's belly. He had grown to think of the tribes much as he thought of the Highland clans, many of which faced the same devastating math. *They were all in the ending times.*

"Did you recognize the symbols they drew?" he asked his old friend.

"Solomon drew *achat*, the number one, which also means unity or one hope. She drew *shalosh*, three, which can also mean resurrection or a new life."

The smear of blood was painful to look at. They had just witnessed another ending.

Conawago had his hand out, and Duncan realized that he wanted to see the medallion Tetwaney had given him. The old Nipmuc took it to the nearest window. "She wanted you to have this," he said. "You, not Hayes."

"A remembrance. She knew he was in no condition to receive it. I will give it to him later."

"No. Not a remembrance. A clue. It's a coin, Duncan." He held the gold piece up in the dying light. A *demi-louis d'or*, the French call it. A half louis. She's telling us about that chest, about why the old woman says the king paid for the new church."

Duncan stepped to the drawing of the raid and pointed to the chest being carried by those escaping into the woods. "The French treasure was here."

Conawago nodded. "St. Francis was a bastion, a distant place of safety. I suspect that somehow they kept it concealed after the war. From the French king. From the British king. They must have taken some of it to rebuild the church, and then it was probably hidden far away, where none are likely to find it."

Duncan took the coin back, hefting it in his palm. Twenty thousand pounds had gone missing. It was a king's ransom. "Rogers knew and never said a word," he stated.

"And LaBrosse, who sent the letters with the coins. The French must have assumed that the British took it, were probably told that Rogers took it in the raid. But it had been concealed here, in this remote sanctuary in the wilderness. LaBrosse lied in his statement to Beck."

Duncan held the coin up in the fading light. "Is this why men have been dying? A chest of metal?"

"No," his old friend replied. "Men have been dying over dreams and strategies for empire. The gold adds power to their dreams and strategies." He nodded to the coin. "To Rogers and his friends, this is wagons and oxen and seed for new farms along Lake Champlain."

"Saguenay," Duncan said.

"Yes, for Saguenay. But for spies from Paris this is the means to a new campaign in America by King Louis."

"Or a private estate for Horatio Beck, if he finds it first. It was why he was so desperate to kill us all on the lake that night. At Ticonderoga he realized we too knew about the treasure, and he couldn't have us interfering, couldn't have us reach it first. By now he knows it is in Montreal, where the French spies have gone. It's not about treason anymore. He could settle his debt, buy a title even."

Conawago turned his head toward Ishmael, then Munro, whom the young Nipmuc was staring at. Munro was standing with his back to the window, where he had been watching with a cool, determined glint in his eyes, his hands folded before him. Ishmael, then Conawago, Duncan, and Brandt did likewise.

"Michael, Archangel, defend us in battle," the old Scot intoned. "Be our protector against this wickedness and strengthen our arms. Amen."

"Amen," Duncan repeated. It was the Blessing of the Red Sword, an ancient blessing of Scottish soldiers about to enter battle.

"Amen," the others echoed.

The door opened abruptly, and Father Tremblay, the young priest, appeared with a bright candle lantern. "There is to be an exodus," he announced. "At least that's what I call it. A migration of a dozen families to the safety of the Huron lands."

"So Tetwanay told us," Conawago acknowledged.

"They need a man who knows the western lands. A guide, as it were. If one of you has had the experience—have indeed any of you made that journey?"

Conawago, Ishmael, and Munro exchanged glances. "Three of us," Conawago confirmed. Duncan stepped away. This was no longer his business.

"Splendid! Then one of you is saved! Perhaps I could convince them to take two!" Tremblay hesitated, his round face pinched in confusion over the lack of interest in his words. "You do know what those stakes out there are for?" he asked. "St. Francis is a complicated place, my friends," he said. "Many are Christians, but the others remain fiercely otherwise. The Christians are reluctant to oppose them for fear of being accused, as they often are, of being unfaithful to the tribe. I am told that prisoners burned frequently during the old wars. Mog is telling his followers that the flames are hungry and need to be fed, that the old spirits need to be shown that the tribe still believes in them."

Conawago took two steps back to stand at Duncan's side.

Tremblay reached out and put a hand on Ishmael's arm. "They will tie you to the post and light the fire! I beg you, allow me to help you! You don't understand!"

Ishmael shook off his hand and stepped to Duncan's other side.

Tremblay put both hands on Munro's arm, pulling him. "Please!" he beseeched. "You need not be a martyr!"

Munro had to pry off each of Tremblay's fingers. The old Scot had been polishing the brass emblem of the 42nd Regiment he had been wearing on his waistcoat. "I made a vow in Boston to stand by McCallum," he explained. "If a man can't die for his word, his life ain't worth a groat." He retreated to stand beside Conawago.

"Do you think this is playacting? Mog will do it! He is the devil in buckskin! I beg you! He will laugh as you scream your life's breath away!" Tremblay cried. "Has your fear deprived you of your wits?"

"I have a question," Conawago interjected.

Tremblay brightened, misunderstanding.

"Where are Comtois and his friend Philippe?"

Tremblay jerked backward as if physically struck. "Not—not here," he said. The priest looked at the door as if thinking of bolting.

"But they did come on urgent business," Conawago pressed, "and left as urgently. Why?"

"I am just a simple priest. How would I know such things? Please listen to me. Not all have to die!"

The old Nipmuc fixed Tremblay with an intense stare. "*Qui est rese vester?*" he asked.

Tremblay hesitated, obviously not understanding.

Conawago switched from Latin to French. "*Louis va-t'il vraiment sauver les jésuites?*"

The priest brightened. "*Oui! Oui! Il nous a fait la promesse!*"

Conawago nodded good-naturedly. "*Et les amis français de Mog. Sont ils allons a Montréal pour l'or? Pourquois Montréal?*"

The color slowly faded from Tremblay's face as he recognized the trap Conawago had laid for him. He backed away and rapped on the door, then turned before leaving. "*Pour assister à la naissance du nouvel âge!*" he snapped triumphantly.

Munro and Ishmael looked expectantly at the old Nipmuc. "I asked if the French spies went to Montreal for the gold, and why Montreal," Conawago explained. "And he said they are going to Montreal to witness the birth of the new age."

"So you suspect he is not a true Jesuit?" Duncan asked as the lock rattled shut on the door.

"He would never be given the robe by the order without knowledge of Latin. He does not speak the tongue of the Vatican."

They gazed at the cell door, then turned at the sound of axes chopping more fuel for the posts. "You were watching Noah earlier," Ishmael said to his uncle. "Did he signal something?"

"All he did," Conawago said with a grin, "was hold a cross upside down."

"Tremblay is the link," Duncan suggested. "He came from France on Comtois's original business but caught a fresh scent of the gold and was sent here."

"But why?" Munro asked. "Why did Tremblay try to save one or two of us?"

Duncan shrugged. "Perhaps he has enough of the Jesuit in him to feel guilty. Or perhaps he wants to be sure of who dies. If he could take two of you as guides for the west, that would narrow the choices considerably. They will want Hayes, and me. And an old ranger from the raid," he said, nodding to Brandt.

Brandt puffed up at the announcement and slipped a hand inside his shirt, extracting a short blade. He had kept the knife the old woman had brought with their meal. "T'ain't the first time I fought 'Nakis," he declared with a dangerous, almost maniacal gleam. "Let that damned Mog lay his hand on my hair, and I'll—" The ranger halted to listen to a curious scratching coming from somewhere in the room.

"The cabinet?" Munro declared. Brandt aimed his knife toward the noise as Munro eased open the door of the old armoire. A small, furry shape darted out and leapt onto Hayes shoulder with a chattering cry of greeting. The tinker, still numb from Rebecca's visit, took a moment to notice the effort of the monkey to put her arms around his neck; then, with a sob, he returned her embrace.

A moment later the old cassocks inside the armoire shook, and a small, familiar head appeared between them. "Do I need an invitation to this party?" Will Sterret asked with an impish smile.

Their shocked silence lasted only an instant. Munro reached in and pulled the boy out. As Duncan brought the candle lantern closer, Father LeBrosse's head appeared at the back of the armoire. "No time to explain!" the priest exclaimed. "Follow me!" he instructed, then disappeared into the shadows at the back of the cabinet.

"It's a secret passage!" Will explained unnecessarily.

Duncan had not forgotten how a score of inhabitants had gone into the old church and escaped its fire. It could only have been through a tunnel, he had concluded, but he also assumed the tunnel would have collapsed in the fire. He saw now that the passage had been built into the thick stone wall of the old building, this entry cut into the back of the battered armoire after it had been fastened to the wall.

The slender hole opened into a narrow landing that led down a flight of steep stone steps. The musty air of the hall at the bottom of the stairs was cut by the acrid scent of the incense used in Catholic censures, a smell that increased as they stepped into a surprisingly large chamber that had been shaped by setting heavy timbers over the tops of buried granite ledges. The irregularly shaped room, easily twenty feet wide and twice that long, held several large tables, a few narrow cots, and a rack of casks labeled BRANDY, ARMAGNAC, and SHERRY. The Jesuit order had, after all, been founded in Paris and was not inclined to deny its members at least some of the simpler pleasures of life. A timbered wall was covered with dusty maps inscribed with notes explaining movements of troops and supplies. It had been a room used for planning military campaigns during the war.

On a table lay another, more recent map showing the Champlain region, including recent marks made at Chevelure, across from Crown Point, where new French farmers had been dispatched like advance troops. Along the margins of the map were tallies, not of soldiers but of horses, cows, oxen, barrels, wagons, and tools, with a separate column reserved for muskets and gunpowder. At the bottom were calculations of sums of money.

Duncan picked up a paper and held it to the nearest candle. "This is purple ink," he observed.

"Yes, yes!" LaBrosse said. "During the war when there were shortages, we got into the habit of making our ink from berries. But there's no time! Hurry!" LaBrosse chided as Duncan lingered at another, larger-scale map that included the far west. Someone had circled a cross at the intersection of the two inland seas called Huron and Michigan. *Michilimackinac*, it said. It was Rogers's outpost.

"You correspond with Rogers," Duncan stated.

"Of course! Now—" LaBrosse hesitated as Duncan pulled back a curtain that walled off a small alcove between the rock walls. A heavily bandaged grayhaired tribesman lay on a cot, sleeping. Duncan recalled the old woman saying that the French had almost killed a lay brother.

"Comtois and Philippe did this," Duncan said as LaBrosse pulled on his arm. "To learn where the gold is. The bruises on your face are recent. They beat you."

"Yes, yes. But they gave up when they realized we do not know. All I know is that I surrendered it to men from Montreal, nothing else. The major insisted on secrets, on blind layers between secrets, as he would say." LaBrosse pulled his cassock up over his ankles. "Now, run!"

The priest led the fugitives, with Ishmael bracing the unsteady Hayes, out of the chamber and into an earthen-walled passage that slanted upward. They passed through a narrow maze of tentacle-like roots to reach a natural cavern with a moist earthen floor. Moments later they emerged in a moonlit clearing. Through the trees they could see the white steeple of the church below. The old Abenaki woman waited for them beside their packs, brought from their campsite. LaBrosse halted, gasping for breath as he scanned the shadows. "Marie," he said to the woman, "where are their weapons? I had stacked them by—"

His words died as Mog emerged from the shadows. The war chief slammed the side of his war ax into the priest's head, and LaBrosse collapsed, unconscious. With a click of Mog's tongue, half a dozen warriors appeared, all cocking muskets as they trained them on the fugitives.

18

CHAIRS, TABLES, AND BED PLATFORMS lit the town as Duncan and his companions were shoved onto the square. A huge bonfire was being fed by furniture. Warriors with painted faces were gutting the houses of those abandoning St. Francis for the west the next day. Duncan realized that this was Mog's way of telling them good riddance.

The captives were arranged in a row before the death posts, positioned with kicks and then, with sharp blows to the backs of their legs, forced to kneel. A rivulet of blood ran down Duncan's forehead where a club had hit him. A much-worse cut had been inflicted on Munro's arm, which had deflected the spike of a war ax that had been aimed at Duncan's shoulder.

Mog had all night to kill his prisoners. First he would perform for his audience, the crowd of more than a hundred Abenaki who had gathered, backs to the riverfront, by the bonfire. Some, probably those who were migrating west, looked at him defiantly as their belongings were flung into the flames. A few others stared not at Mog, but at LaBrosse, now gagged and tied to a nearby tree. But most seemed excited by Mog's ceremony and listened attentively as he spoke of how the old gods would remember the glorious Abenaki nation that night.

Brandt had his own chants and was interrupting the war chief as he spoke. "The rangers are coming!" he shouted in his high-pitched voice, then intoned the rangers' owl call: "Who comes to kill! Who comes to kill!"

Mog snarled, and one of his men knocked Brandt to the ground and hovered over him with a threatening war ax.

"There is no second raid of rangers coming," Mog loudly declared in French, indicating his captives. "You think these cowards who came to steal my brother's wife are capable of a raid?"

Duncan shook the blood from his eyes and studied the crowd, realizing the implications of Mog's words. Before Brandt's cry, there had been a rumor that rangers were coming.

"There will be no raid tonight or any other night, for the rangers are broken! Let them come, and I will taste the sweet flesh of their hearts," Mog declared with a wild laugh. "Tonight we will send a message that will be heard throughout the colonies! The Abenaki bear still has his claws, his teeth can still tear flesh, and his growl can tumble mountains!"

Mog seemed to glow in the moonlight, an otherworldly demon in his warrior's garb and paint that colored half of his face and his bared torso red, the other half white. He lifted a thin leather strap, the end of which had been shredded into narrow strips like a cat-o'-nine-tails. When he reached Conawago at the end of the row, he abruptly swung it at the Nipmuc's face, leaving long red slashes that began seeping blood. He quickly administered the same violent blow to Munro, but when he raised the whip over Ishmael's head, a black fury lunged out of the shadows, grabbing Mog's arm in her jaws. Molly dragged the surprised chieftain to the ground, but Mog's warriors swarmed over her, kicking and pounding their clubs into her, raising yelps from the big dog and anguished cries from Ishmael; then she limped away, uttering low cries with each step.

Mog slashed at Ishmael's face, but as he turned his whip to Corporal Brandt, the wiry ranger twisted and caught the strap in his teeth, yanking it from Mog's hand and spitting it onto the ground, which earned him two furious blows when Mog recovered it. Duncan returned Mog's glare and did not flinch when the lash struck him. More rivulets of blood streamed down his cheeks, dripping onto his waistcoat.

The chieftain had struck Hayes once and was about to hit the tinker again when a banshee shrieked and something small and brown launched itself at Mog, landing on his back. Sadie scrambled onto his shoulders and savagely bit the war chief's ear, then shrieked again. Mog seemed confused, even frightened for a moment, and Duncan recalled the night in Hancock's warehouse when Munro had reported that the Abenaki intruder had not seemed intimidated at all by the human defenders and had fled only when the monkey screamed at him.

A flicker of shame appeared on the war chief's countenance, which only enraged him more. He seized the capuchin in his hands and squeezed it violently, apparently trying to choke it to death, but then Sadie twisted, bit his hand, and squirmed out of his grip. "Take it!" Mog shouted to his warriors. "I will roast it on a stick for my supper!"

As the crowd breathlessly watched, Sadie squirmed and swerved around the outstretched hands, then raced up a tree that leaned far out over the water. She crept out on a long, thin branch and began screeching at Mog again.

"No!" Hayes moaned as Mog grabbed a musket, and threw himself toward the Abenaki. Mog kicked him to the ground, aimed, and fired at the capuchin. The bullet missed Sadie but severed the thin branch. With a strangled groan from Hayes, she tumbled head over tail into the river, screaming now in fear.

"Sadie!" Hayes moaned. He had lost his wife and now lost all he had left of a family.

A murmur rose from the crowd, and it parted to reveal the suffering Molly struggling to her feet. The big dog limped at first as she headed toward the riverbank, but as she neared it, she seemed to gain strength, running at a crooked gait.

"Molly girl, no!" Ishmael cried in torment as he realized what she was doing. As he spoke, she leapt off the bank and with a huge splash disappeared into the dark, fast-moving waters. From somewhere midstream came a small, terrified cry.

Mog gave a satisfied laugh, then turned with a gloating expression to his captives. "First your beasts die, then you!" he shouted, stepping to a basket filled with slender, stripped willow branches, and he offered a short speech about the glory of Abenaki warriors before inviting children to take up the switches. Duncan saw him pause for a moment, distracted by something in the shadows between two houses; then he released the assembled children to badger the captives. Although three of the children were pulled back into the crowd by their parents, the rest uttered squeals of delight as they energetically applied the switches to the arms, backs, and faces of the prisoners.

Duncan shook at the first blow but remained still as two girls struck him repeatedly with their stinging canes. He ignored the blows, instead watching

Mog approach two men in the shadows, urgently motioning them toward the river, where canoes waited. As they hurried away, they passed through a pool of moonlight, giving Duncan a glimpse of their faces. Father Tremblay was rushing away with a warrior escort.

As Mog returned, he muttered an order, and one of his painted men ran to each of the death posts. Before each prisoner he swung his war ax, a treacherous weapon that ended with a skull-crushing knob of wood on one side of the head and a skull-piercing iron spike on the other.

"You always know the greatest cowards among the tribes," he announced to his onlookers, "because it is their tribes that are extinguished first. The worst are those who pretend to be like Europeans, for they deny their true blood!" He spun about and with a catlike leap landed in front of Conawago, tapping his head with the side of his ax as his feet hit the ground. It was a carefully placed blow, intended to stun. As Conawago sagged, Mog threw dirt at him; then, with another word from the war chief, the children ran to other baskets and began throwing eggs and horse manure at the old Nipmuc.

A roar of protest escaped Duncan's throat, and he tried to stand, only to be clubbed down by the warrior behind him.

"The rangers are coming!" someone shouted from the crowd. The words caused the children to abandon their baskets and run to their parents.

"Who comes to kill! Who comes to kill!" crowed Brandt, earning himself another blow.

"Who comes to kill! Who comes to kill!" came an echoing cry from the shadows. Duncan recognized with a shudder the voice of Will Sterret. If Mog discovered the boy, he would not hesitate to kill him.

Mog shouted what sounded like an Abenaki curse, then lifted the strap that hung from his waist and extended it toward the moon. "*Est-ce que je ne prends pas les cheveux des gardes-frontières?*" he screamed.

Despite the hot pain on his back and shoulders, something icy seemed to grip Duncan's spine. *Do I not take the hair of rangers?* Mog was displaying the scalps of the rangers he had killed in Massachusetts. Duncan watched in agony as the war chief shook the scalps toward his captives, then ordered his men to begin the final act of his ceremony. Conawago, unconscious now, was dragged to the first post and tied to it. The old man had survived more than eighty years only to be burned alive by an Abenaki madman.

"It is you who must burn, Mogephra!" a voice boomed from the crowd. "It is you who betray the Abenaki by your unholy alliance with the French king! It is you who is the coward, killing men in the night from ambush!" The speaker stepped forward into the light of the bonfire. It was Noah, Totokanay of the Abenaki. He wore a long ceremonial robe of feathers, a robe he had said his father once wore. "You do not have the wisdom to lead our people. You are nothing but a vessel of hate! You are lost to the ancient gods."

"I spit on your words, old man!" Mog shot back, but he did not race toward Noah with his weapon raised, as Duncan expected. He was wary of the newly arrived elder. "Anger me further and you will be tied to a post."

"No," came a woman's stern voice. An old woman in tribal dress appeared at Noah's side.

"No," repeated another woman, then a third and a fourth. They all stood at Noah's side, all of them old and weary but all fiercely determined. The true leaders of most woodland tribes were the matriarchs.

Mog hesitated for a moment, then spat in their direction and turned his back on them. He stepped to Duncan with a businesslike air. "You will die after the burnings, McCallum," he hissed. "You will die for many hours after listening to your friends scream as their blood boils!" He moved on to Munro, hesitating as he spotted the shining brass 42 on his breast, then roughly seized the Scot's hair and pulled it back to reveal the wide scar he had received on the battlefield of Ticonderoga. "I love these English farmers," he called mockingly. "They learned how to grow a second crop of hair for my pole!"

His men replied with jubilant war cries, waving their axes in the air. Munro's struggles against the men who seized him lasted only moments, and they soon had him tied to the second post. It came to Duncan that Sarah, daughter of an Iroquois prophet, had seen this in her dreams. *I see you beaten and bleeding before a fire of death*, she had said. *I see men bathed in blood and men burning.*

"Before they burn," Mog ordered the men who were stacking more brush around the first two poles, "take their hair."

"The rangers are coming!" another voice called from the crowd. Mog pretended not to hear. He was growing tired, Duncan saw, limping more noticeably. He stepped to Ishmael, who raised his lashed and bloody face in defiance.

Mog was about to strike him again when Duncan called out, loud enough for the crowd to hear. "Who put that ax in your leg? I was there. It was a Mohawk woman!" he shouted. Mog spun about, his fury as hot as the bonfire now. "The great Mog was maimed by a woman!" Duncan shouted. "And you ran from her!" he taunted. "Who are you calling a coward?"

The war chief sprang to Duncan, whirling his ax overhead. "The Mohawks are rangers too," Duncan shouted defiantly. "Is that why you fear a Mohawk woman?"

The ax blow that came down on Duncan would have split his skull, but at the last instant Mog twisted his arm, and the spike slammed into the moist earth.

"Who comes to kill? Who comes to kill?" Brandt hooted. "Burn it, burn it all, boys!" he shouted, as if back in the October dawn nine years earlier.

Mog shrieked and struck a blow to Brandt's head that stunned the old ranger. Straddling him, Mog slapped him viciously and began ripping away his clothes. He paused as he lifted Brandt's powder horn. For a moment Duncan wondered how well Mog could read, but the inscription was simple enough. ST. FRANCIS OCTOBER 9, 1759.

The war chief's eyes flared with bloodlust. "Loosen him!" he ordered his men. "Before he burns, we will take his fingers; then I will eat his heart!" His words were lost in an outcry from the crowd.

"They are here!" someone screamed as everyone pointed toward the edge of town. A house was in flames.

"Burn it, burn it all!" Brandt crowed.

With blinding speed Mog spun about and buried the spike of his ax in Brandt's arm. In the same instant, the crisp crack of long rifles split the night air. Two of Mog's men collapsed to the ground. A man marched past the burning house, a rifle in one hand and a tomahawk in the other. He wore the green uniform of a ranger. Woolford had not abandoned them. Mog shouted, pointing to figures running from tree to tree toward them. Woolford's Mohawk rangers had old blood scores to settle with the Abenaki.

The chieftain raised his arms as if in celebration and uttered a long, ululating shriek of war. As he took a step forward, a wiry figure sprang onto his back. Blood streamed down Brandt's arm, but he seemed to take no notice of his wound. "'Tis Mog the war chief, Major!" he shouted in his high-pitched voice as his hands gripped Mog's neck. "Who comes to kill, who comes to kill?" he repeated, laughing, then gave a piercing cry that almost matched that of the war chief.

Duncan, his hands still bound at his back, struggled to his feet and slammed into Mog, trying to knock him down, but the Abenaki slammed an elbow into his belly, causing Duncan to stagger backward. With a great twisting jump, the war chief threw the still-laughing Brandt onto the ground, then buried his ax spike into his chest. The old ranger groaned as he took the blow, but laughed again even as blood welled up out of his mouth, and he held up his little knife. Mog saw the blood on the blade and hesitated, then put a hand to his neck. It came away soaked with blood, which now began sheeting down his painted chest. Brandt had sliced open his throat. Mog slammed the spike of his ax into Brandt again. Still the old ranger laughed. The ax struck again, and this time the old ranger gasped and looked up into the night sky. "Corporal Brandt, First Company, reporting!" he called out before his mouth filled with blood and he spoke no more.

Mog staggered and dropped to his knees. He raised his ax with great effort; then it fell from his hand and he collapsed onto Brandt.

Duncan, sobbing, struggled with his bindings, twisting, trying to reach the old ranger. A hand closed around his arm.

"They're done, Duncan," Patrick Woolford said as he unsheathed his knife to cut the bindings. "The Abenaki fight no more."

Duncan knelt at the corporal's body. Brandt had sensed it from the beginning, Duncan knew. He believed that his destiny was tied to St. Francis. The death of the infamous war chief completed the mission Robert Rogers had started nine years earlier.

Two of Mog's warriors were dead. The others had laid down their weapons. One was being led away by an old woman who was pummeling him with one of the willow switches.

"You burned someone's house, Patrick," Duncan pointed out. It wasn't like his friend to be so callous to tribal families.

"Actually, no. She did it. She said they could not turn back, so we should use it to frighten Mog."

"She?" Duncan asked, but then he saw the answer.

Hayes's former wife stood near the fading bonfire, looking at the Jewish tinker. It was not proper for a tribal wife to touch a male outsider, but she was directing her two sons to help the tinker, one offering him water as the other cut his bonds. The tinker ran to the river as soon as he was freed, standing at Ishmael's side as they forlornly stared over the moonlit water.

"The priest Tremblay was an agent for the French king," Duncan said.

"I know," Woolford replied. "Father LaBrosse explained."

"The missing French treasure was here."

"I know. Father LaBrosse explained," Woolford repeated.

The Mohawk rangers pulled away Mog's body and covered Brandt's with a blanket. Several of the Abenaki had hurried to release Father LaBrosse. Others had cut Munro and Conawago loose and were now prying the posts out of the ground, throwing them on the bonfire.

"One assassin is dead," Woolford said as they watched the priest run down to a man who was pulling a canoe onto the bank. "Maybe that should be enough. Come back with me to the Mohawk Valley. No one will find you."

"There's only one place left," Duncan said. "One place where all the answers await us."

"Not a chance!" Woolford protested. "Montreal is where Beck is, where the French spies are, where a regiment of infantry sleeps with your bounty broadside on their barracks door. Stop trying to throw your life away, Duncan. Give it time. In two or three months Beck will retreat back to London. I have friends in Montreal, some of them French. We can visit in the fall to pick up the scent of the spies. Go to the Iroquois villages and meet my new son. I will send for Sarah."

Duncan did not remember ever feeling so soul-weary. He knew Woolford was right. He barely had the strength to stay on his feet. He needed to be with Sarah. He needed to rest. There was a grave to dig in the morning, and he needed to make his decision with a clear head.

But suddenly Father LaBrosse ran up to them from the landing. "A messenger from Montreal!" he breathlessly reported. "Major Rogers is to be tried and hanged within the week!"

As the priest spoke, Ishmael cried out, and at first Duncan thought it was in response to the news, but then the young Nipmuc darted into the water, followed closely by Hayes and Will. Several of the Abenaki crowded in, then stepped back with exclamations of wonder, some of them crossing themselves. Ishmael and Hayes were supporting Molly as she staggered the last few steps out of the water. The big dog collapsed onto the sand, Sadie's long arms clenched around her neck.

19

MONTREAL LAY LIKE A THREATENING warship against the darkening sky, its river wall punctuated by cannon ports along the top and its lighted windows lined up like a row of portholes below. Duncan had been filled with foreboding the first time he surveyed the city eight years earlier. Then it had been filled with French soldiers who would have killed him and his companions had they been discovered infiltrating its walls. This time it was British soldiers who would seek his death.

Conawago touched his arm, and he followed his friend's gaze toward the file of canoes that hugged the south bank of the broad St. Lawrence. They had traveled with the Abenaki refugees from St. Francis for the past two days, and had waited on the island for darkness to fall before parting for their respective journeys. Theirs had been a surprisingly difficult farewell, for in their time together, the emigrating Abenaki and Duncan's party had grown unexpectedly close. According to Conawago, the natives who went west to avoid further contact with colonials were the "true tribes," and the old Nipmuc was impressed by their quiet determination to carve out a new, free life in an unknown land. They were undaunted by the terrible rigors of their long trek or by the threat of the hostile nations they would encounter before finding their new homeland. The forces of change they were fleeing would inevitably catch up with them, but their odyssey would keep one more generation safe from the influence of these forces. The women encouraged the children to sing harvest festival songs, and when they were not singing, the dozen Abenaki men chanted the old songs used to synchronize their long, powerful paddle strokes.

Hayes, still much diminished, his gaze often so distant it seemed he might not be aware of his surroundings, had stayed in the rearmost canoe with Noah and the injured Conawago, wordlessly doing his duty with the paddle. He did not react when, twice on the first day, Conawago had kindled a bundle of herbs and washed him with the healing smoke. At one point Duncan was so chilled by the abject way Hayes stared into the water that he pulled his own canoe close for fear the moribund tinker was going to leap in.

It was the wise Sadie who finally thawed Hayes's heart. At the camp the night before, Will and one of Rebecca's sons were playing fetch with Molly when Sadie grabbed the stick and ran with it to the solitary Hayes, pushing it under his leg as he sat staring over the water. Molly and the Abenaki boy raced to the tinker and, arriving at the same time, crashed into him. The boy was laughing so hard he seemed not to notice it was Hayes underneath him. Then suddenly he gasped with fear.

"*Pardon, monsieur!*" the boy cried in fright as he tried to untangle himself. "*Pardon, pardon!*"

He groaned as Hayes clamped a hand around his arm. The tinker's face was so dark that Duncan took several steps toward him; then his eyes cleared and he whispered "*Attendez*" to the boy. "*Attendez, attendez,*" he repeated more energetically as he rose and began sorting through the big pack he always carried. Hayes produced a little tin whistle, which he extended to Rebecca's Indian son. "*Pour vous,*" he said to the uncertain boy, then blew on it and pushed it into the boy's hand.

The boy's eyes lit with joy as he darted away to show the treasure to his older brother, who himself tentatively approached the tinker. Hayes reached not into his pack, but into his waistcoat, producing a small, multifaceted pewter object. On a flat stone he demonstrated, spinning it like a top until it fell on one of its flat sides. Duncan somehow knew it had belonged to Hayes's own dead son, and he smiled as the boy ran to show the trophy to his mother. He would probably be the only Abenaki boy in the world with his own dreidel.

Duncan had stopped breathing as he saw Rebecca's tall, silent husband approach Hayes with the two boys, as if to reject the gifts. Duncan had been terrified that Mog's brother would seek to harm the tinker, but the warrior stared uncertainly at Hayes, his own face now clouded with emotion. Then Hayes reached into his pack and produced a long clasp knife, probably one of the most expensive items among his trade goods, and extended it to the man.

"*Pour le voyage,*" the tinker declared. "*Vous devez la garder en sécurité,*" he added. *You must keep her safe.*

The warrior accepted the knife only after giving Hayes his own necklace of beads and bear claws. "*Elle aura une bonne vie,*" he solemnly vowed to Hayes. *She will have a good life.* Tetwanay had stood nearby, framed by her sons, tears streaming down her face again.

Now Hayes sat on a nearby boulder, silently watching the refugees leave their failing world for a new world, unknown, rife with danger but unconnected to anything European.

"The water gates all have marine sentries," Woolford declared after folding up his little brass telescope. "We should land to the east and go around to the northern gate, as if coming in from fur country." He turned to Father LaBrosse. "You're sure we will be welcomed?"

"The rectory was built for a time when new brethren for the missions arrived almost weekly," the priest explained. "Now, alas, your King George prohibits the entry of any Jesuits. Many of the rooms have been vacant for years. The vicar general will be happy to have them occupied by friends."

LaBrosse, having made certain they could find the side door of the rectory on Bonsecours Street, went directly across the river in a canoe with Noah and Conawago, whose wound was clearly causing him pain. An hour later Woolford, donning his officer's uniform and doing his best to give his Mohawk rangers a martial air, greeted the lethargic guards at the northern gate with a command that brought a surprised salute. No questions were asked as they marched through the tunnel in the high wall, with Duncan, Munro, Hayes, and Will flanked by the rangers as if being escorted on official business.

The heavy ironbound door, a vestige of days when Montreal was still threatened by Indian attacks, cracked open at Woolford's first knock. They stepped warily into a dimly lit corridor, and the hands of the Mohawks went to their weapons when it was closed and bolted behind them. The screen on the muted lantern held by their escort eased open, revealing a refined, scholarly looking man in a black cossack robe who towered a handsbreadth over Duncan's own six feet. He nodded his head, making a strangled, gurgling sound as he smiled, then gestured them down the hallway.

"Hurons!" Woolford's Mohawk corporal spat, as if it explained something.

Duncan gave up trying to puzzle out the statement as they entered a vaulted kitchen chamber where LaBrosse greeted them near a long table where a welcome meal awaited them. The silent friar who had met them proceeded to a sideboard, where he opened the tap on a cask and began filling crockery tankards with cider.

"Rogers is being held under guard in an old arsenal chamber built into the southern wall," LeBrosse explained as he sliced a fresh loaf of bread.

"Along the river?" Duncan asked.

"The major is regarded with high esteem by the French of this city, who knew him as a skillful but honorable opponent in the war. Sometimes people pass by and throw food up onto his window ledge. My brothers have been allowed to visit, to be sure he is receiving humane treatment." With those words Duncan had his explanation of how Rogers was getting messages out of his prison.

The silent friar distributed the cider as their party sat on the long benches at the table, encouraging the Mohawks to try it with a nod and a grunt.

LaBrosse picked up a slice of the bread for himself. "You've met Father Deschamps, then?" he asked between bites, nodding toward the tall friar.

"A man of few words," Munro observed.

"Oh, forgive me. I have known him so long and he is so expressive that I forget sometimes. He went among the Huron as a young missionary. They didn't like the words of God that came out of his mouth, so they cut off his tongue." LaBrosse paused to cut a slice of ham for himself. "They kept him as a slave for a dozen years before some voyageurs discovered him and traded some gunpowder for him. He is a most prodigious artist," LaBrosse added. "He illuminated a Bible in the Algonquin tongue, ironically enough, and now is painting murals on the ceiling of the chapel."

The Jesuit assumed his businesslike air again. "Rogers is to be tried in three days. They have already built the gallows on the parade grounds. The army believes in swift justice to traitors once sentence is passed."

"Surely there must be some effort to examine the charges against him," Woolford said. "Colonel Hazlitt of Ticonderoga is the presiding judge. Hazlitt is a reasonable man."

The Jesuit sighed. "Conspiracy with the French," he said in a pained tone. "Attempting to subvert the lands of King George. Such charges are severe. The army brings the charges, the army takes the evidence, the army selects the witnesses. The king is more inclined to set an example than to bother with tedious examinations. We tried to meet with the judge advocate charged with his prosecution but were refused. We tried to find him a barrister, but none will take his case for fear of offending the army. One of the charges is that he met secretly in the wilderness with French officers last August, a charge I am certain is not true."

"Certain?" Duncan asked as he studied the adornments on the walls of the room, including a partially burned cross and a crushed crucifix, remembrances of Jesuits who had been martyred in the wilderness.

"Can you really call a boat on Lake Huron the wilderness? And they weren't French officers."

Woolford lowered his fork. "They were French Jesuits," he suggested. "Discussing charitable work with tribes, no doubt," he added when LaBrosse did not disagree.

"Endeavors on behalf of the needy, yes," LaBrosse replied in a tight voice. "Neither Robert Rogers nor any of us would ever willingly meet with King Louis's government."

"We are not opponents, Father," Woolford said. "Can we agree we have two friends we do not want to hang?"

LaBrosse raised his tankard. "I'm an Old Testament man. Eye for an eye. I think too that those who falsely accuse should be compensated for their sin."

Duncan reached into his belt and pushed a slip of paper across to the Jesuit, the image of the Celtic cross from the powder horn at Ticonderoga.

"Exactly," LaBrosse said after glancing at the paper. "They must pay."

Duncan caught Conawago's eye, seeing that he shared Duncan's confusion. "You know this grave?" he asked.

LaBrosse gave a heavy sigh. "Everyone seems to." He pulled the paper closer and traced the nimbus, the circle, with a fingertip. "The stone itself was erected by a Scottish noble who came after the war to mark the grave of his son, an officer who died in the final battles. Perhaps he made the stone too distinctive. For a few years it was used for another noble purpose, you might say.

"And this week it was marked by the devil's disciples." The priest stood. "Follow me, if you would understand."

The Jesuit led them to a room up a short flight of stairs, probably once quarters for kitchen staff when the large rectory had been fully occupied. Two beds were in the chamber, each bearing a grievously wounded man, both asleep. LaBrosse pulled away the shutter on the muted lantern on the stand between the beds and gestured to the old native in the bed to his right.

"Moses has been the caretaker of the cemetery for years, even before the war. He and his wife have faithfully served the Society of Jesus for decades. He helped with the installation of that nimbus cross more than six years ago. Early this week he was disturbed in his sleep in the little cottage by the cemetery by two men digging into the grave. He challenged them, said they were defiling sacred ground, that he would call the watch if they didn't leave. But they accosted him, beat him with the handles of their spades. One was a soldier, but he carried a little hammer on a leather loop, and he hit Moses repeatedly with its knobbed end, demanding to know where exactly the chest was buried."

"Mallory!" Munro spat.

LaBrosse nodded. "They were not shy about using their names. The big one was a Sergeant Mallory, the other, his superior, is the man who questioned me years ago, the arrogant Mr. Beck."

Duncan leaned over the old Iroquois, who had awakened and was making a brave show of smiling despite his obvious pain. "Saguenay," the old man whispered. "Saguenay, Saguenay."

"That's what they kept saying to him as they beat him," the priest explained, then pulled back the blanket to expose the man's foot, which was elevated on a pillow. The bandage around the end was bloody. "Moses professed to know nothing, said there was nothing but a brave soldier and his casket in the grave. When Moses refused to say more, the one called Mallory put Moses's foot on a stone while Beck held a pistol to his head. Mallory used the spade like a cleaver, slicing off the end of the foot, including all the toes. The scream woke us, and they fled."

A terrible weight pressed down on Duncan as he realized he had led Beck to the graveyard by drawing the cross and the fortress on the wall of his cell. Once Beck knew to ask about the fortress and not the cross, he would have quickly learned the image was of Montreal. "What did they find in the grave?"

"A casket, which the blasphemers opened, only to find the mortal remains of the soldier inside. There had been nothing else there for years."

"Meaning there had been something else once," Woolford observed.

"Not for years," LaBrosse repeated, and shrugged, "Yes, apparently the chest had been there, but it was moved years ago. I do not know where it was taken. As I said, it is protected by layers of secrets." LaBrosse replaced the blanket and took Moses's hand, murmuring a prayer. "Blessed soul, even when we found him, all Moses said was 'tell my wife she is safe.'" He turned to the second man, a European with a large crucifix hanging from his neck. "And this is Father Andre, who replaced Moses and took the punishment the next night."

"They came back?"

"Three others, all Frenchmen. We hadn't even had time to fill in the grave, but when they saw the hole, they were furious. One was a rough character, a voyageur with a skinning knife. They toppled the cross itself and dug under it. And when they found nothing . . ." LaBrosse sighed again and gestured at Father Andre, whose haggard face showed that he had been struggling with great pain. Duncan pulled away the sheet. The man's arm, propped on a rolled blanket, had a loose bandage on it from elbow to wrist, which was seeping blood.

"The voyageur was called Regis," Andre explained, then groaned and stiffened.

"Regis," LaBrosse continued, "peeled away a wide strip of skin. Andre told them nothing. Indeed, he knew nothing. The night patrol heard his screams, and as they approached, the villains ran. But I know who the other two men were from their descriptions."

"The ones who beat you in St. Francis," Duncan said. "Henri Comtois and Philippe."

LaBrosse nodded.

Duncan examined the terrible wound, which was well cared for, and as they returned to the kitchen, he suggested to LaBrosse that the priests find laudanum for both men.

"These men must be stopped," LaBrosse said as they returned to the table.

Woolford raised the tankard he had left on the table. "We share your ambition," he confirmed, then leaned forward. "If you know the faces of King Louis's spies, they should not be difficult to locate."

"It's not King Louis's spies we need to see first," Duncan declared. "Tell me, Father, do you have a senior cleric here?"

"Of course, the Father Provincial presides from here. He is our vicar general for all of Quebec."

"Perfect. We must confer with him about a Jesuit apostate."

•

DUNCAN'S CALCULATIONS ABOUT THE JESUITS in Montreal had not been without some risk, but by midmorning the next day everything had fallen into place. LaBrosse had convened an urgent dawn meeting with several members of the province's mother church, and within an hour a small company of the devout, including converted Mohawks and several tradesmen, had been deployed into Montreal's streets.

Tremblay had not only been too arrogant to think about using a false name in Montreal, he had also enjoyed the prestige of having a bodyguard so much that he had kept his escort from St. Francis at his side like a servant. The word of an Abenaki with a faded stripe of war paint on his cheek had spread quickly through the Mohawk residents, and the two had been quickly located at an inn only five blocks away. Tremblay, confronted by two friars and four Mohawk rangers, had peevishly agreed to come to the rectory, leaving a note in French that one of the Mohawks stealthily retrieved.

Duncan and Conawago, their faces obscured by hooded cassocks supplied by the friars, were waiting in the dusty chamber into which Tremblay and his escort were ushered. Two large tables had been arranged in a T-shape. The man with short-cropped gray hair who sat at the center of the head table, flanked by LaBrosse and Deschamps, gestured Tremblay to the end of the other table and reminded Tremblay that he was the vicar general who received his credentials when the young priest arrived in Quebec the year before.

"Yes, yes. I haven't much time," Tremblay announced, listening with half an ear as he sniffed the contents of a pitcher on the table. He conspicuously straightened his fashionable new waistcoat before he sat. "We have engagements."

"We?" the vicar general inquired.

Tremblay gestured to the brooding Abenaki standing behind him.

"I see," the senior Jesuit said, and turned to LaBrosse, who reached into his robe and tossed an object on the table. It was a well-used knife in a moosehide sheath, adorned with a beadwork scene of a warrior carrying a pole of scalps.

"The owner of this died at St. Francis three days ago," LaBrosse said, looking up with an expectant expression at the Abenaki, whose eyes grew wide as he recognized Mog's scalping knife. He began backing away.

"No!" Tremblay barked at the warrior. "You do not have leave!"

The Abenaki did not acknowledge Tremblay. He spun about and fled. Corporal Longtree closed the door behind him.

Tremblay pushed his chair out, as if thinking of leaving himself, but then the chair would move no more as Longtree pressed his foot against it. The arrogance began fading from the young priest's face.

"We have much to talk about, Father Tremblay," the vicar general announced.

"No, no," Tremblay said, waving his hands in front of him. "There is a mistake. I am not a priest."

"Nonsense. You came to us with a letter from the superior general, dated just before the king revoked his authority. You confirmed what it said in the letter, that you were ordained in Paris. You brought us confirmations from other high-ranking members of the Curia. You are a priest, for if you are not, you have committed a grave sin before God. Heresy was once punished by burning, though that would seem awkward in Quebec since we have implored our native flock to abandon the practice." The vicar turned to speak briefly to the two figures beside him, who both nodded solemnly. "The garrote would be more appropriate. The tightened ligature around the neck was first used in ancient Rome, home of our blessed pope, did you know?"

What little color remained on Tremblay's countenance completely washed away.

"More experienced inquisitors than myself have used it to great effect, after all," the old priest explained in a conversational tone.

"Inquisitors?" Tremblay gasped.

"A harsh word, I agree," the vicar said in his very sincere voice. Duncan had taken a risk in relying on a senior priest he had never met, but after an hour's private audience with Conawago and Noah, the vicar had enthusiastically accepted his role and was playing his part perfectly.

Conawago had assured Duncan that they would be in good hands. "Jesuits may be committed to their last drop of blood to the conversion of the unblessed," the Nipmuc had said, "but there's nothing they love better than a good chess game."

The vicar was playing his part with Shakespearean aplomb. "We in Quebec are seasoned in the trials of this world," he declared, gesturing at one of the many plaques that hung on the rectory walls. "Alas, we have suffered so many martyrs, we cannot fit all their names on one memorial. We also understand about a crisis of the soul, Father. We would far prefer to focus on redemption for your sin rather than punishment, despite the severity of your act. We have a proven solution to problems like yours," he declared in a generous tone. "You will go under escort of our Mohawk brethren to one of the missions on the Mississippi. Kaskaskia comes to mind. The king in London has blocked new missionaries from coming from Europe, so it will be a blessing to have someone of your obvious capabilities join our brothers with the tribes."

Tremblay, who seemed to have trouble breathing, finally found his voice. "Impossible! You old fool, release me this instant!"

The vicar general ignored him. "You would need to remain for a period of reflection and penance, say two years, under the guard of converted natives—I hear the Illinois are almost as formidable as the Mohawks—and then you will be allowed to do as you please. There are voyageurs who call every few months." The old priest shrugged. "So you might make it back to Paris in three or four years." He aimed a beneficent smile at Tremblay. "Such an adventure, eh?"

"You cannot!" Tremblay loudly protested. "I am employed by the king of France!"

"No, you belong to the Society of Jesus. We have the papers to prove it."

"You fool! I will not put up with this farce!"

Two Mohawks pressed close to Tremblay. The vicar general sighed. "You need to appreciate your dilemma, Father."

"I am not a priest!"

"An intriguing proposition, sir. Your defense against being a priest is that you work for the French king. *Mais monsieur, nous sommes anglais.* The French king repudiated us. The French king gave this land to the British king." The vicar shrugged again. "So you are a priest who will make full confession and go west to atone for your sins. Or you are a spy to be delivered to a British hangman."

The defiance in Tremblay's eyes was quickly changing to fear.

"King Louis may have suppressed the Society of Jesus, but we are not without our supporters, both in Paris and in Rome. Imagine what an embarrassment it will be to Louis when it is revealed to the world that he engaged in lies about the suffering Jesuits to pursue his dreams of empire, that he actually created a false priest to inflict harm on his enemies. Lying about a man of the cloth is a sacrilege not even a king can live down. The pope will be outraged, I assure you. Louis is already in bad odor with the Vatican for seizing the assets of our order for his own enrichment. He will probably be forced to restore the Society in France. So please, Father, let us go to the governor and get you hanged so we can save our fellow Jesuits." The vicar general gestured to the plaque on the wall again. "We will add your name to our lists of martyrs."

Tremblay's hands started shaking. The vicar general called to one of the friars at the back of the room, "A drink for Father Tremblay. Claret, I should think."

More than claret was needed. Tremblay answered questions for an hour. Bread, cheese, and brandy were brought in, and as he ate, friars took turns writing down his every word. Deschamps finished a turn with a quill, doodled on a scrap of paper, and slid it toward Duncan. It was an expertly drawn image of a circus scene—a pig with Tremblay's round face walking on a tightrope.

Woolford, also in a hooded cassock, began asking questions; then Conawago and finally Duncan joined in. Tremblay lost all pretense and spoke freely of his conspiracy and his career with the Sun King's government. He had been taken out of the French military academy as a gifted student with perfect English, having lived in London as a boy. He had been given a commission as a lieutenant and reported to two army captains named Henri Comtois and Philippe Meunier, who worked out of a well-guarded chateau in Normandy, running special observers, as they called them, in and out of England. Tremblay had been trained at the chateau by a defrocked Jesuit, of which there were many in France, specifically to go to St. Francis and earn the trust of the Jesuits there.

"Why St. Francis?" Woolford asked.

"Because we had been told that St. Francis had never really been defeated, that it was still a French town with French sympathies, where the hatred of the Abenaki for the English could be harnessed."

"You mean used as killers," Duncan said.

"That wasn't . . . I wasn't sent for any of that. The mission for the ledger arose quite unexpectedly when news of its existence arrived from London, so my mission was adapted. But Comtois refuses all my questions about it, says I am not of high enough rank for such knowledge," Tremblay sulkily explained. "I was meant to collect information, look for signs."

"Signs?" Conawago asked.

"Of things that had been left behind in the confusion of war."

"You mean a few thousand gold pieces that had been misplaced," Duncan suggested.

"It was the king's money!" Tremblay hissed.

"More like spoils of war," Woolford suggested.

"It was meant to support another year of war in Canada," Tremblay said.

"It still could," Duncan observed.

Tremblay frowned, then shrugged. "I found no sign of it. But then we caught word that Major Rogers and the Jesuits of St. Francis had a different plan in mind. A different war, which would require much gold."

Duncan glanced at LaBrosse. "You mean a campaign for an independent nation of Saguenay." He watched the vicar general, who showed no surprise at his words. The credit extended to the French farmers had come from Montreal banks. Had it been based on deposits made by Jesuit clerics?

"Saguenay," LaBrosse corrected, "was the code for the mission, as Rogers called it. The name of the new state was to be Champlain."

"They've already started, right under your nose," Tremblay said with a gloating air.

"A few farms in Chevelure don't make a war," Duncan observed.

"*Imbeciles!* Every one of those farmers is a former officer in the Quebec militia! Ask LaBrosse. They signed articles pledging themselves to the state of Champlain!"

Conawago, Duncan, and Woolford all turned to LaBrosse, who gave one of the shrugs that seemed to be characteristic of many of the Jesuits. "We drank a lot of claret that night," LaBrosse explained. "The suggestion had come from Rogers. The first mission, he called it, 'a reconnaissance in force' was the term he used."

"A reconnaissance against the English enemy, you mean," Woolford said in an icy voice. He still held a commission in the British army.

"The tower at Chevelure," Duncan said. "It had been planned during the war but never built."

LaBrosse nodded. "As a gun emplacement. The positioning was perfect for sending shells over the walls of Crown Point. There are cannons hidden in a cave along the St. Lawrence." He saw the heat rising in Woolford's eyes. "Purely to discourage intervention," he hastily added. "We never intended violence. It's unclaimed land. We saw it more as a remote community of like-minded people, free of oppression."

"There were two conspiracies," Duncan reminded those at the table, and turned to Tremblay. "Something in your mission changed after you arrived in America," he suggested.

"I was summoned here to Montreal by my handler, our senior officer in North America, and told of the existence of a secret ledger that could change everything, that with it, France might take back all it had lost in America and more, all of New England even. My superiors were setting sail from Normandy, following it to America."

"And they seized it outside Boston," Duncan said, chilled once more by the memory of the bodies lying in a row on a beach. "Killing thirty-seven innocent men to obtain it. That was an act of war, a secret war. There is no forgiving those who did so."

"I knew nothing of that!" Tremblay gasped. He gripped his hands together to stop them from shaking. "Comtois spoke of it after he arrived here, laughed and boasted that there was no proof connecting them to the *Arcturus*."

"I don't believe you!" Duncan shot back. "You were in Boston, even New York perhaps, to help Comtois stalk Jonathan Pine. They had learned he was a messenger for the Sons of Liberty. You learned that Daniel Oliver would be on the same ship, and you took the news to Mog, who you knew would be the perfect agent for Comtois."

Tremblay shuddered and nervously twisted in his chair.

"And if *you* knew such things," Woolford interjected, "then there are spies among the Sons of Liberty."

"Just men who were willing to talk in exchange for a few coins or a jug," Tremblay said, and looked imploringly at Duncan. "I beg you, you must believe I did not know they would sink the ship."

"But you made it all possible. You sent word to Halifax so Comtois would know what ship to seek when he arrived there."

Tremblay said nothing.

"And you know where the ledger is now," Duncan stated.

Tremblay drained his fourth cup of brandy. "No! I told you, they won't trust me with all their secrets."

"But why did the ledger have to come north?" Conawago asked. "Comtois was bound to come north when he caught wind of the treasure, but he was planning to come north even before."

"I told you. The chain of command. Our senior officer is here. And customs inspections. The inspectors in the American colonies are most aggressive. In Canada, on the St. Lawrence, there are far fewer inspections. They thought it safer to ship the ledger concealed in cargo, then sail on the same ship."

Woolford, who often engaged in covert operations for the Department of Indian Affairs, leaned closer. "And your senior officer in Montreal. What is his name?"

"I am never given it. We just call him the field marshal. When I have to meet him, I go to a bookshop and remove a slip of paper left in a volume of Voltaire. It would say when and where we would meet, always at night, usually at the back of a tavern or along the river."

"Then surely you know his face."

"Comtois sometimes calls him the librarian. Meunier once laughed and called him the duke of dust, for he loves old books. Or sometimes even the cat keeper, for he often has cat hairs on his clothes."

"It must be the owner of that bookshop then."

"No. He is older than the owner there, perhaps the owner's father or uncle. A collector of books, I'd say, or a private dealer in old books. He has gray hair that he keeps long at the back and a hand often twisted with arthritis. He has a powder burn on one cheek from an old battle and usually wears spectacles."

"Find him for us."

Tremblay's face went bloodless, and he slowly shook his head. "I cannot! I would be killed if they suspected anything. There's a brute named Regis, a monster, a killer. He would torture me and leave my body in the river. Surely you understand they are ruthless men. No sacrifice is too great to achieve their goals."

Duncan held up the note Tremblay had left at his inn. "'Comtois,'" he read, "'I am delayed. The visitor arrives this evening. Victory is in hand!' you wrote. What visitor?"

Tremblay buried his head in his hands for several breaths. "Someone who had to be met at the Richelieu River, the river that connects with Champlain. Very secret. The man is traveling under some false name. They said it was the final piece, that the ledger was already working its magic. Comtois said the halls of Versailles will be ringing with the news of his victory, that he will be a colonel by the end of the year."

Duncan and Conawago exchanged a puzzled look. "The mission will be complete because of someone coming up from Lake Champlain?"

Tremblay nodded. "From the American colonies, coming to strike a deal, Comtois says. They said I should expect to go back with him with new orders, that glorious times lie ahead for us."

Woolford clenched a fist on the table and leaned forward. "Tell us this, Tremblay. What do they have you doing since you arrived in Montreal?"

"Watching. There is an Englishman named Beck, a spy for King George, and his deputy, Sergeant Mallory. I watch them."

"Where do they go?"

"To banks and finance houses mostly. I bribed one with whom he spent only a quarter hour. Beck told him he represents a syndicate of investors seeking to join those who are investing in new settlements in the Champlain Valley. When the banker said it was too risky, they moved on. And also to a graveyard where they dug up some soldier's grave."

Duncan rose and paced around the table. "You've told us so little that is of use to us, Tremblay. The army will be more persuasive when we turn you over to them."

"I can tell you where the bookshop is!" Tremblay cried. "And they use an old warehouse by the river, where that man Regis lives with a couple of guards."

"Regis, who applied his skinning knife to a priest's arm." The statement came like a curse from LaBrosse, who fixed Tremblay with a vehement stare.

Duncan put a calming hand on the shoulder of the Jesuit, who looked as if he were ready to do violence to the French agent. Duncan considered Tremblay's words for several long breaths, then retrieved one of the cassocks hanging on the wall. "I assure you, Father Tremblay," he said as he draped the robe over the Frenchman's shoulder, "you will soon realize what a blessing it is to have become a mere Jesuit outlaw."

DUNCAN LINGERED AT AN ALEHOUSE for nearly an hour with Tremblay before the Frenchman stiffened and put down his cup. "It's them—my masters!"

The two figures across the street indeed fitted the description of the French visitors to Worcester the night Chisholm had died. "Proceed with your business," Duncan reminded Tremblay. "Report about Beck, and add that he is asking about the missing gold. Find out the name of the stranger coming to meet with them. Do not alarm them, monsieur," he warned.

He watched, trying to control his emotions, as Tremblay crossed the rain-slicked street toward the inn where the French agents were staying. These were the men who had heartlessly taken the lives of the sailors on the *Arcturus*; these were the men who had used Mog to kill Daniel Oliver and Josiah Chisholm, who had intended to kidnap and probably kill young Will. A reckoning was long overdue, but Duncan knew there could be none until all the pieces of his puzzle fell into place.

Tremblay entered the inn with them, pausing in the open door to shake the rain off his cloak; then they disappeared inside. More than any city Duncan knew, Montreal was accustomed to the sight of tribesmen on its streets, so the appearance of Woolford and his Mohawk rangers out of the shadows caused no alarm to passersby. Duncan and Woolford conferred briefly, and the Mohawks were dispatched to watch the rear of the inn and assess whether the Frenchmen's upper-floor rooms might be easily accessible from the outside. Woolford slipped away with a nod, intending to make a brief passage across the front of the inn so he might better see the faces of the two spies as they lingered at the hearth, drying off.

But once at the window, Woolford froze, staring inside. Duncan, fearful that he would make the Frenchmen suspicious, darted across the wet cobblestones. He grabbed his friend's arm, but instead of moving, Woolford motioned toward the window. The three men were indeed at the hearth, but they had been joined by a fourth, their anxiously awaited visitor, who would complete their mission and take Tremblay back with him. The French spies were speaking with Robert Livingston, baron of the New York colony.

20

T HE JESUITS AND THE MOHAWKS were surprisingly adept at what Woolford had taken to calling urban rangering. Each in their way had been
evading, and watching, enemies for years, and now reports came in almost
hourly to Duncan and Woolford as they waited in the vaulted kitchen of the
old rectory. Between reports, they debated as to why Livingston would have
business with the French spies. At best, he was just another merchant being
asked about financial transfers supporting settlement in the Champlain Valley,
as the French tried to find the missing gold. At worse, he was an operative for
the French, though neither Duncan nor Woolford could imagine a goal that the
French would have in New York town or the Hudson Valley.

"But it isn't about the gold for Livingston. It's about the ledger," Duncan
said. "Livingston and Hancock were desperate to get it back, though I never
understood why. And Tremblay's bosses said the ledger was working its magic
already."

"The Frenchmen stole that ledger for their king," Woolford replied. "I
doubt Livingston has anything to offer that would outweigh the glory they
expect when they present it in Versailles."

"But why, Patrick," Duncan asked in frustration, "why do kings so desperately want some ledger concerning merchants of the British colonies? The
question has become like some black beast gnawing at my heart!"

They had learned that Beck and Mallory had called at two more finance
houses, Livingston had purchased some Brussels lace, and the French played
chess with each other, then had a rich meal and walked along the outer wall,

stopping for a time to sit on a bench opposite the cell of Robert Rogers. Corporal Longtree first reported that Colonel Hazlitt, commander of Fort Ticonderoga, had arrived and visited a violin maker behind the fish market then had a long talk with a furrier who was selling pelts of fisher cats. Later, two different Frenchmen wearing spectacles had called at Tremblay's bookshop.

DUNCAN AND CONAWAGO WATCHED FROM a leaded-glass window in the rectory's spacious second-floor library as a cloaked figure followed Father Deschamps up the steps into the rectory, leaving his kilted escort, one of Corporal Buchanan's squad, standing at the bottom of the steps. The visitor was engaged in lively conversation with the vicar general as the two men entered the long library chamber. Duncan and the old Nipmuc pulled up the hoods of their cassocks and took seats at a remote table as the vicar guided the visitor to a cabinet under the row of windows.

"You are most welcome, Colonel," the vicar graciously said as the commander of Ticonderoga removed his cloak, revealing his scarlet uniform.

"I am at a disadvantage, sir," Hazlitt admitted. "When your man—the poor fellow was mute, I believe—handed me this"—he produced a bright white skull with two long amber-colored teeth—"I was nonplussed. But then I saw the most amazing signature on it and had to learn more. I can tell it is authentic, from a letter I have in my possession."

"Most authentic, I assure you. Monsieur Bougainville was an avid natural philosopher even while serving here in the war," the vicar explained, "and he collected so avidly he had to leave many specimens in our custody, saying he would eventually send for them. But as we know, he has been most busy. You may keep the beaver skull. I am sure the good gentleman would not mind."

The colonel made an awkward gesture with the skull and seemed about to decline, then gave a gasp of delight as the vicar opened the top drawer of the cabinet, revealing a score of bird skins, all with the feathers intact, each with a small card in Bougainville's writing indicating the species. The vicar turned one over, that of a wood duck. "You can see he signed each one after preparing it. He was a skilled commander of soldiers, but I do believe this was his real passion. If you will allow me," the vicar said, opening the second drawer, of small skulls, then the third, of snakeskins and turtle shells.

"Heavens, sir, how you do tantalize me!" Hazlitt exclaimed. "But I don't understand why you honor me with this invitation."

"Someday," Conawago said over his shoulder, "I will take you to see a fisher on its hunt."

Hazlitt spun about. "Sir! How could you be . . . McCallum!" he exclaimed as Duncan approached, pushing down his hood. Hazlitt's hand went to his belt, but he had not brought his pistol.

"We ask only that you give us a few minutes, Colonel," Duncan said. "We have a tale you will want to hear. If you prefer to leave this instant, you are free to do so. If you wish to send troops to try to find us, that will be your choice, though we will not be here. We have alarming news."

"Most irregular!" Hazlitt groused, but the anger quickly faded from his eyes.

The vicar pointed to a decanter on a side table. "Colonel Bougainville always sipped on brandywine when studying his animals here." Without asking, the vicar poured four glasses, extending one to the colonel. "Our mute friar always accompanied him on his expeditions and still keeps his forest retreat for him. They would bring back specimens and sit here for hours, preparing the skins and making drawings."

Hazlitt's eyes drifted longingly toward the cabinet of specimens, then caught himself. "You are a fugitive from the king's justice, McCallum." He frowned at Conawago. "As are all those who helped you escape."

"I am a fugitive from a clandestine agent who manipulates charges and truths however they may suit him," Duncan replied. "We will not play his game. And we will not dishonor this house of God with falsehoods."

Hazlitt sighed. "I was content not to hang you, McCallum, but there are others who will exercise no discretion in that regard."

"There is an invisible war under way, sir," Conawago explained, "with invisible foes gathered here in Montreal."

The colonel grimaced. "We've had a taste of it, I fear. Corporal Buchanan was set upon by that brute Mallory. Mallory wanted to know where you were. Most likely the bottom of Lake Champlain, Buchanan said, and Mallory did not find the answer to his liking. Buchanan had to spend two days in the infirmary and was released just this morning." Hazlitt paused, silently studying Duncan. "But despite your obvious inclination for self-destruction, you apparently have some Celtic angel hovering over you." He turned at the sound of marching boots and watched as a patrol of soldiers passed the rectory, and for a moment Duncan feared he would open the sash and call out to them. Then he faced Duncan with a frown. "I make no promise other than that I will listen," he declared, and sat down.

THE RED-JACKETED GUARD AT THE door of the old arsenal was expecting two visitors, though clearly not one wearing the uniform of a captain of rangers. He rose to stiff attention, saluted Woolford, and nodded uncertainly to Duncan, who wore an austere suit of clothes borrowed from the rectory.

"Colonel says an hour, sir, no more," the guard said.

"How fares the prisoner?" Woolford asked.

"At first he would readily converse with us, speaking about his campaigns in the war and such. But now his tongue is stilled. He spends most days just staring out one of the windows."

The man inside the cell seemed disinterested in visitors. As they walked in, he did not turn from the small iron-barred window over the river. The chamber had been used for storing powder and shells during the war, and a hint of sulfur and saltpeter hung in the air. The furnishings consisted of a small cot with a straw pallet and blankets, three stools, and a table holding two candlesticks, several books, paper, and writing quills with a chipped pot of ink. The small hearth was empty, and the stone walls gave the room a dank chill.

"The winters at Michilimackinac are long, I hear," Woolford said to the prisoner's back.

Duncan had briefly met Robert Rogers and knew him to be fiercely strong, not only in body but also in mind, known for the intense determination that burned in his eyes. But the man who turned to face his visitors was haggard and dull-eyed. He seemed to have aged decades.

"The frigid air makes for good pelts," Rogers replied in a distant voice. He looked at the blank paper as he spoke, and Duncan realized that the man's usual visitors came to coerce written confessions.

"It's Patrick Woolford, sir," Woolford said. "I brought some Mohawk venison sticks." He dropped onto the table several pieces of the smoked venison that was a favorite of rangers when running the forests.

Rogers blinked; then gradually his face lit and his eyes found their focus. "Captain Woolford!" he exclaimed. "By Jehovah, Patrick, it *is* you!" The ranger sprang to Woolford's side and seemed about to embrace him but at the last moment halted and collected himself, straightening his soiled uniform and extending a hand. "I heard you took a civilian post with Sir William."

"Seconded, sir. I still maintain my captaincy and still run a dozen rangers for . . ." Woolford caught himself. "Special errands," he concluded with a grin.

Rogers still pumped his hand.

"I have brought an old acquaintance. You met Mr. McCallum years ago, I recollect."

Rogers cocked his head. "I confess to confusion. I do recall you, sir, but I had heard you were a fugitive on charges of treason and murder."

"Charges brought by the same men who have accused you, Major," Duncan said.

Rogers frowned, and his eyes clouded with suspicion. "If that were true, you could not be walking around this fortress as a free man. I am done being practiced on, sir."

"Colonel Hazlitt has granted me something of a truce."

Rogers lifted a piece of venison and took a bite, then retreated to the river window, where he turned his back on them. "First they brought in two grenadiers," he began, speaking toward the river, "who stood as some snot-nosed pup of an officer read statements that they had seen me on several occasions drinking with Colonel Bougainville after the capitulation of Montreal back in '60. I said bugger off, that he was a fine gentleman who only wanted to speak of the flora and fauna of the northern forest. They brought in some whore from a French tavern in Quebec City and read her statement that I had boasted to her of sheltering Jesuits when King Louis was suppressing them. They brought in some damned jealous Presbyterian missionary who said I had helped papist farmers of the Quebec colony move into new land along Champlain. They brought in a drunken voyageur who said I had him deliver secret messages to Frenchmen in St. Francis. Bugger them all. Bugger you if you come with more of the same filthy suggestions. An Englishman is entitled to confront the hard facts against him if he is meant to die, not just listen to the slander of drunks and whores. And now you. What do you offer, testimony that I was bedding the queen?"

"I can see how the formation of the state of Champlain would be a noble adventure, Major," Duncan said to his back. "But we'd rather choose to save your life."

Rogers went very still. He placed a hand on a bar in the window as if to steady himself, then turned, slowly stepped to the table, and sat. "On that particular subject," he stated with a thin, bitter smile, "I am open to suggestion."

Duncan spoke for nearly half an hour, explaining everything he knew about the conspiracy from Paris. He did not soften his words when he reviewed the separate Saguenay scheme Rogers had launched with disgruntled Jesuits and French colonists. The major silently listened, murmuring low curses when he heard of the loss of the *Arcturus* and the deaths of his former rangers.

"They arrived at the intersection of the schemes without knowing it," Rogers said with a sigh. "Oliver and Chisholm were gears that inadvertently clogged against that damned French machine. Oliver had declined my offer to come north, saying he had a new life at sea, though I suspect he had some hand in with Mr. Hancock's Sons of Liberty. Chisholm received my offer and said he would come north for Saguenay in a few months after taking care of some important personal business."

"Getting married," Duncan inserted. "To a woman who loved Shakespeare."

Rogers shook his head forlornly. "More's the pity." He clenched a fist. "Mog. That cunning bastard. He bragged of taking scores of scalps, of eating my friends' hearts. We tried to snare him more than once. He was as close to the proverbial bloodthirsty savage as ever you'd meet. I told my men to keep an eye for him at St. Francis and shoot to kill if they saw him."

Duncan had explained the struggle in St. Francis. "A ranger got him at last," Woolford reminded Rogers. "Somehow I think Brandt knew what would happen, as if their final encounter was predestined. Mog could have snuffed him out like a candle, but he wanted to play with Brandt. But Brandt played him too. The man didn't know that old rangers are the most dangerous ones," Woolford said pointedly.

Duncan glanced at Woolford, worried that he had just added fuel to the fire that they were trying to extinguish. Emotion did indeed swirl on Rogers's countenance. "The king knows nothing about this land," he said as he pushed the fire down. "The tribes are its greatest resource, and he treats them like inconvenient pests to be trod underfoot. The colonists are better educated and more diligent than men in England, and he treats them no better than a feudal lord treated his serfs. He prohibits them from manufacturing most things, so our riches cannot be put to use. He never earned the right to rule this land, it fell on him like some windfall from a horse race."

In the silence, they could hear commands echoing across the river as a ship bound for the Atlantic got under way.

"You would be mistaken if you thought we were here to argue those points," Duncan finally said. Both Woolford and Rogers cocked their heads at him in surprise. These were dangerous words Duncan was endorsing, yet he felt an unexpected catharsis, as if Rogers had released the sentiment that had been building in his heart. "There is no land like this land," he added, echoing the words he had heard from old tribesmen under a summer moon. "The king will fail if he keeps treating it like the Old World."

"Duncan!" Woolford warned in a whisper, glancing back at the door, as if worried that the guard might have heard.

But Duncan had finished. "We're not talking about the king's rights today, Major. We are talking about the king's power to hang you."

Rogers's face darkened again.

Duncan reached into a pocket and laid the pouch he had taken from Hahnowa's grave on the table. "I am completing Corporal Brandt's mission."

Rogers seemed to stop breathing. His eyes went round; then he extracted the contents of the pouch. He stacked the papers and withdrew the necklace of red and white beads with the quillwork image of a man and a woman holding hands.

Duncan waited with great anticipation for Rogers to consult the papers, to fully explain the mystery behind them, but he paid no attention to them at all. As the major pressed the quillwork image to his lips, realization struck Duncan. He had wanted only the necklace. Rogers was certain he was going to hang, and he wanted to wear the necklace, his link to his wife, in his death.

"Hahnowa would not want you to end this way," Duncan said after a long silence. "Let us take you back to her. Let us bring her Mohawk family and spirit talkers to her grave, to say the words that will bring her peace."

Something caught in Rogers's throat. He pressed his fist to his mouth with one hand and clutched the beads with the other. The storm on his face had broken. "It's too late, I fear," he said in a hoarse voice.

"No," Duncan said. "Tell us where King Louis's gold is."

Rogers's brow furrowed. "I don't know, McCallum, I swear it!"

Duncan stared at the man who had masterminded the disappearance of the gold so many years before. "Swear it on the eternal soul of your wife, Major."

Rogers's face clouded. He stared at the necklace and cupped both hands around it. "I so swear," he whispered. "Yes, LaBrosse showed it to me the night before the raid, and we agreed that it should be hidden from the French Army, and yes, I knew it was in a cave overlooking the St. Lawrence at first. But after the war I told him to move it away from St. Francis. He sent it to Montreal."

"You mean to the Jesuits in Montreal."

"LaBrosse is a very cautious man, and the Jesuits are cunning. We agreed that I would not be told and that, if possible, he should trust it to someone else, who would hide it without his own knowledge and shift it again later. Later I learned that it stayed for two years in the grave of a Scot who fell in the last battle."

"Marked by a Celtic cross," Duncan said.

"Yes, but I had said that each group who hid it must not know where the next group took it. When the time came, it would be made available to LaBrosse, but only in small amounts through merchants in Montreal, so as to not arouse suspicion."

"Made available by Jesuits."

"By men who had proved they could be trusted, men who respected vows as sacred trusts. Jesuits, yes, and perhaps members of their missions. LaBrosse once told me that he knew only that it was guarded by wolves. Once, in a letter, he mentioned that our great secret was held by one who would hold it forever in silence."

As Woolford questioned Rogers about bankers and merchants who might have been tapped to administer the funds used for the new settlers along Champlain, Duncan chewed on the ranger's words. They had no time to chase down every possible intermediary, as Beck was trying to do. They would be wrong, moreover, to think about the money the way the government would think about it. They had to think about it the way Jesuits and their particular allies would. A dim spark kindled in his mind and he grinned as it grew in brightness. He knew where the French gold was.

21

Hayes was playing the reluctant but polite companion as Duncan and Conawago escorted him down the shadowed streets. The tinker—for Duncan still thought of him as such—seemed to have melancholy permanently etched on his features, and Duncan worried that the man he had come to admire for his intelligence and compassion would now endure only as a hollow shell of his former self. The night before, Duncan had awakened to the smell of smoke and found Hayes in the kitchen, his beard gone. He had revived the fire in the large hearth and was feeding his letters to Rebecca, carried for years as a sign of his devotion, into the flames.

"Voyageurs!" Will Sterret exclaimed from behind them now, not for the first time, as they passed a group of compact, bearded men in leather tunics who wore their hair Indian fashion in braids woven with beads and fur. Duncan often felt a stir of excitement when he saw the spirited adventurers who traveled to far western reaches never seen by other Europeans, but he reminded himself that at least one voyageur was a brute who worked for the French spies and had tortured Father Andre.

As had become his habit, Hayes responded with a silent nod, then extended a hand into the pouch under his shoulder to stroke Sadie, who had become even more precious to him since the terrible blow he received in St. Francis and her own brush with death.

"This way," Conawago said, and they followed him down a cobbled alley to what looked like a sturdy but disused stable built of stone and timber. Conawago opened the heavy door as if familiar with the building, and they found themselves in an entryway that was filled with the scent of sawdust. A girl of perhaps thirteen years with a scarf wrapped around her head was on her knees, pounding wooden trunnels into fresh oak floorboards as a middle-aged tribesman stood by with an auger. The girl rose, swept dust from her long apron, and cheerfully greeted Conawago. She pushed a lock of brunette hair under her scarf and studied Solomon Hayes with an inquisitive expression, then curtsied and without introduction led them down the unfinished hallway to a newly hung set of double doors. She wiped her hands on her apron, touched a little box on the door frame, then cracked open one of the doors.

"Papa," she called. "Mr. Conawago is here with his friends."

From inside came what sounded like furniture scraping on a floor and tools being hastily put away. Hayes cast an impatient glance at his companions. He seemed to be barely tolerating this foray into Montreal's damp streets. Conawago put a hand on Hayes's shoulder as if to be sure he would not flee.

"A ship arrived with a crate from Portugal," the girl announced, as if it explained their delay. "Such places those sailors must see!"

"Rachel, it is well," came a tentative voice from inside, and the girl opened the door.

Half a dozen horse stalls had been reclaimed to create a large chamber, its freshly laid oak floor covered with a dozen wooden benches facing two simple tables. A black curtain hung from a rafter to separate two of the benches from the others.

Hayes, still uninterested, focused on Sadie.

"Welcome!" called a thin, energetic man standing in front of a tall cabinet along the back wall. He lifted a candelabra from a table beside the cabinet and brought it forward in one hand as he self-consciously adjusted the small cap on the crown of his head and straightened the fringed shawl draped around his waist.

"Honored, sir," the man said as Conawago introduced Duncan. "I am Jacob Cohen. As you see, we are still completing our little establishment and have received very few guests to date." Cohen turned to Hayes. "*Shalom*," he said in cheerful greeting, and extended a hand.

Hayes blinked, as if awakening from a deep sleep. His eyes fixed on the candelabra Cohen had set on one of the front tables. It was a menorah. A strangled gasp came from Hayes's throat. He seemed unable to reply.

"I am rabbi and chief carpenter," Cohen explained congenially. "We will be much better prepared on the Sabbath. But meanwhile, Mr. Hayes, welcome to Shearith Israel congregation."

Hayes fumbled for the cap he had stuffed into his belt. "I didn't . . ." he began as he awkwardly set the cap on his head. "I never thought. It's been . . ."

"A long journey," Cohen offered. "Your companion Conawago has been good enough to explain some of it. Such a propitious day for you to arrive! We have just received our Torah from Portugal, a week after finishing our ark for its home. There are only a score of us, but each has a New World tale of his or her own, each with its own lesson of how Jehovah guides us through tragedy. We are all about new beginnings here, Mr. Hayes." Cohen gestured proudly toward the ark and the menorah, then singled out the little lamp by the ark. "You can help us with the service to light our *tamid*, our eternal light. Our little synagogue is the first in Montreal, first in all of Canada."

Hayes advanced to the table and stood before the menorah. "The first north of Rhode Island," he offered in an awed voice. He had no words when he turned back to Duncan and Conawago, but his eyes had come alive, and the deep gratitude in them was all that needed to be spoken.

"Father!" the girl called from the back, where she stood with Will, and pointed to Hayes. Sadie, ever curious, was crawling up the tinker's shoulder.

Cohen laughed. "A capuchin!" he exclaimed, and offered a hand to the monkey. Sadie touched her forehead to it. "We welcome all denominations here!"

They could not pull Hayes away, and they left him with Cohen, examining the new Torah, speaking excitedly in Hebrew about his congregation in Rhode Island. Before they departed, Rabbi Cohen had been pleased to answer Duncan's questions about certain French residents of Montreal. He knew only one who was a private book dealer, and Cohen warned, "If you visit his home on Valcours Street, be aware that it contains many cats."

WOOLFORD AND DUNCAN WATCHED THE snug cabin that was built near a waterfall for nearly an hour after taking over from the Mohawk rangers who had followed Father Deschamps there and reported that the Jesuit had paused several times to light his pipe and collect wildflowers. The retreat Bougainville had built while serving in Montreal was a comfortable-looking structure in a clearing in the dense forest, surrounded by beds of flowers. Little platforms for bird nests had been fastened to several adjoining trees, and trout leapt in the pool at the base of the waterfall.

An old Indian woman, no doubt one of the Christian Mohawks, had met Deschamps when he arrived at the cabin, and after he had taken his pack of supplies inside, the two sat at a table under a hemlock to mount the skin of a pine marten on a stretching frame. Deschamps, continuing his work as Bougainville's assistant, had walked with the woman along the flower gardens, pulling the occasional weed, before heading back down the trail toward Montreal.

Duncan, after helping Woolford collect a pile of dried leaves and pine boughs upwind from the cabin, went in alone, greeting the woman as a solo traveler following the forest trail to Montreal. The old woman was a matronly Mohawk who wore a silver crucifix around her neck. She insisted that Duncan stay to join her in some good English tea, for which many Iroquois had developed a taste, and after she lit a fire in the hearth of the snug little cabin and swung the kettle over it, she gladly indulged his curiosity about the odd collections scattered over the mismatched tables and on the walls of the sitting room and the adjoining study, which she explained was the favorite room of the great natural philosopher who had entrusted her to maintain it during the monsieur's long absence. Duncan was shown rows of stuffed mice, voles, and shrews, the feathered skins of warblers and thrushes, butterflies, leaves and flowers pressed in the leaves of books, some of which, she explained apologetically, were disused hymnals. A long chest of drawers, so bulky Duncan wondered why they had taken the trouble to transport it miles into the forest, held a collection of skulls in its top drawer, then large feathers and samples of the clawed feet of birds of prey. The bottom drawer had its knobs removed, and on a bench pushed against it sat two expertly stuffed wolf cubs.

As the woman poured a second cup of tea, Duncan looked up in alarm and darted to the window. "Do you smell smoke?" he asked. Woolford had lit the mound of dried leaves a stone's throw from the cabin. Duncan ran outside with the Mohawk woman, into a cloud of thick smoke. The woman cried in alarm, then ran back inside. He followed her straight to the inner room, where she stood, stricken, next to the chest of drawers, staring at the pair of wolves.

"Do not trouble yourself yet," Duncan said to her. "It may be nothing. Do you have a bucket and perhaps a shovel?" In ten minutes he had the small fire reduced to smoldering leaves and was assuring the woman she had no need to worry.

"That pipe of his—" She sighed, shaking her head. "It will be the death of us," she added, as if she were Deschamps's scolding wife. But she wasn't his wife, he knew, for her husband lay in the rectory with part of his foot severed. Duncan finished his tea, thanked her profusely, and joined Woolford, who waited under a towering maple on the Montreal trail. The king's gold slept with wolves, and the one who held the secret would keep it forever in silence because he was a mute. Only one piece of his puzzle remained to be found.

A FINE MIST HAD SETTLED over the city by the time Duncan and Woolford reached its walls, conveying a scent of damp cedar over the cobblestone passages. Woolford nodded silently to the rangers who waited by the gate, and the Mohawks spread out as if on a forest mission, flanking and scouting ahead. The two men were so lost in conversation that Corporal Longtree had to whistle for them to stop when they reached the quiet inn where Duncan and Conawago, wary of bringing undue troubles to the Jesuits in the rectory, had just that morning taken a room. Agreeing to meet for a late supper, Duncan climbed the stairs to their second-floor room, then distractedly latched the door behind him as he entered.

"Not a movement, not a sound," hissed a voice near his ear as the cold steel of a pistol barrel was pressed against his neck.

Duncan twisted his head enough to see a face with a closely trimmed black beard. "I thought you would be on the way back to Normandy by now, monsieur."

"Comtois. My name is Henri Comtois. I think there is no longer any need for playacting."

"Good," Duncan replied in an even voice. "I will need the name for the stone we will mark over your grave. Or should I just bury you under that Celtic cross?"

The French agent gave an icy smile, then nodded toward the far side of the room. On the floor by his bed, Conawago lay unconscious, blood oozing from his head. Another man sat on the bed, pressing a narrow dagger against the Nipmuc's neck.

A blind fury ignited in Duncan. He took a step forward, then froze as the pistol cocked and pressed deeper into his flesh. "The old fool let us in," Comtois explained, "then tried to convince us to leave when we threatened him. He spoke good French, I admit, but he's no different from all the other annoying savages begging in the streets. Useless to the modern world."

Duncan, to his relief, could see the slow up-and-down movement of Conawago's chest.

"But apparently," Comtois continued, "you seem to value this creature as a servant or retainer or such. So if you do not resist, if we reach our destination and Philippe receives a message from me within thirty minutes, he will not drive that dagger into the old man's jugular."

"Philippe," Duncan said, "who came from Halifax with you."

"Philippe Meunier, *oui*, who came from Le Havre with me. Faithful servant of Louis Quatorze, as am I."

"Comtois and Meunier," Duncan said. "I want to get the names right. The murderers who sank the *Arcturus* for the sake of an old ledger book. Who manipulated an innocent boy for the secret and left him behind to die."

"Poor Will. But he survived."

"Even though you tried to kill him again."

Comtois shrugged. "There is no cost too high in the service of my king. And such a valuable ledger! Worlds can be transformed based on such pages!" He motioned Duncan to the door.

A full-bearded man with the broad shoulders of a voyageur waited outside, no doubt the man who had tortured Father Andre. He kept a hand clamped tightly around Duncan's arm as Comtois led the way down a series of alleys to an old brick building on a cul-de-sac under the eastern wall of the city. A guard holding a pistol opened the door for them, and inside, a boy waited by stacks of crates and bundles of pressed furs. Comtois bent to the boy's ear, dropped a coin in his palm, and the boy shot out the door.

"Your tame Indian will not die today," Comtois sneered, then led Duncan and his escort toward an inner door. The chamber he was led into had no windows, though Duncan thought he could hear lapping water, and he assumed they were near one of the long shipping piers that served the depots of the fur trade. The dank air was sour with the smell of unwashed men and their leavings.

Two wooden armchairs were chained to ringbolts in the wall. One held a bound, unconscious man whose head, covered with a sack, was slumped against his chest. As Comtois's voyageur tied Duncan to the empty chair, the French agent lifted away the sack and ladled water over the other prisoner, making clucking noises, as if to coax him awake. The second prisoner stirred, shaking his head violently and spitting a curse as he saw Comtois. It was Horatio Beck.

"At last, the convenience of having both my antagonists together at last!" Comtois said in a mocking tone.

Beck looked at Duncan with a dull, confused expression; then his eyes lit with recognition and he uttered a hoarse laugh. The effort caused blood to flow from a long, jagged cut down his temple. He had been pistol-whipped.

"The hounds are never ready when the clever fox turns on them," Comtois gloated.

Beck spat out blood. "Do not insult me with such an obvious ploy. McCallum is more fond of your pack than of mine."

Comtois replied by slapping Duncan so hard his lip split.

"*Bien sûr,*" Beck hissed. "Please do torment the bastard. I could care less if he dies here or at the end of an executioner's rope."

Comtois hit Duncan again.

"Ask him why he came to Montreal," Duncan gasped as Comtois raised his hand a third time. "His mission was to track you, to recover the ledger, but he questioned me at Ticonderoga, not about French spies but only about King Louis's gold. He is following the gold now. He wants it for himself. He may have been tracking spies when he left London, but now he is little better than a highwayman with a uniform."

The words silenced Comtois. He paced in front of his prisoners as the voyageur lit a fire in a small brazier and began heaping in coal. "As you say, McCallum," he said at last. "The gold belongs to my king."

"Does it? Odd that the treaty signed in Paris never mentioned it," Duncan rejoined. "Your government meant to smuggle it back to France, but it slipped away somehow. How embarrassing for you to misplace such a fortune."

"I was an officer in Quebec at the time," Comtois stated. "They were chaotic days. I would be a colonel now but for that embarrassment. But here we are. It is my destiny to recover it, you might say."

Beck struggled against his ropes. "McCallum conspired with Rogers!" he spat. "Rogers must have the gold, for his new land of Champlain!"

Comtois threw up his hands in mock exasperation. "Conspiracy this, conspiracy that. My world is very simple, Monsieur Beck. There are the friends of my king and the enemies of my king. You both work counter to the interests of my king. Therefore you are my enemies. Your lives are worth nothing to me, except to help me achieve my goals.

"I don't think McCallum was part of the Saguenay conspiracy," the French agent continued. "No one ever heard of him until you accused him of treason. My sources say he was a stranger to St. Francis until he appeared there with his most peculiar companions. He was your leverage, your stalking horse, though I still can't understand how you knew he was coming north in pursuit of us. He has proven most elusive."

"He had a spy with us," Duncan growled. "Masquerading as a deserter."

Comtois smiled and gestured toward the shadows along the wall. "Regis," he said. The voyageur stepped to what Duncan had taken to be a pile of rags and kicked it. The rags came to life as a man on the floor flailed out, earning another kick, then quieted as he recognized Duncan.

"McCallum!" the man spat.

"Sergeant Mallory," Duncan acknowledged with a chill, remembering that the last time they had been together, Mallory and his trained beast Wolf had been intending to blind and mutilate him. "And I had so hoped that you drowned that night on the lake. But you survived to maim an innocent Iroquois gravekeeper."

Mallory grinned. "Gawd, how he howled."

"And then an attempt on a corporal of the Black Watch."

"He should have died for helping you escape!" Mallory spat blood on the stone flags. "Another slab of Highland beef to be served up to the king. Too dense to know when he was bettered."

The voyageur Regis opened a tool chest, arranging several instruments along the edge of the brazier, then lifted a long set of pliers, and without warning slammed them into Mallory's jaw. "You talk too much, English!" he said, shoving Mallory, who was clutching his bloody mouth now, against the wall.

"I am sure your tales are most entertaining," Comtois said, "but sadly, I don't have time to listen to you ramble on to each other. Let's just acknowledge that we are at a confluence, a point where important knowledge has intersected. I will have all that knowledge, or I will have your lives. I am leaving this forsaken continent in less than two days. With the application of Regis's special talents, I will have my king's gold before I leave." The French agent examined the tools, then reached into the chest and handed the voyageur a wooden mallet.

Regis instantly spun about and slammed the mallet into Duncan's knee, then pounded it into Beck's shoulder. He stepped back and laughed as both men gasped. Beck muttered a curse, earning a second blow, harder than the first.

Comtois offered the voyageur a thin smile and continued. "Do we have your attention? The king is willing to pay a finder's fee, say five percent, to the man who takes me to the gold. And shall we say slow death to the one who does not. Slow death is rather a specialty of Regis's."

Duncan clenched his jaw against the pain that shot up his leg. "So we've established that you will pay for secrets," he said. "How far will you go?"

The French spy nodded to Regis, who began using a bellows to intensify the heat of the brazier. "I'm listening," Comtois said.

"The gold in exchange for the ledger," said Duncan.

"McCallum!" Beck shouted, and was silenced by another violent blow with the mallet.

"A steep price," Comtois replied, then smiled again as Regis lifted a pair of pincers that glowed red-hot at their end.

"A steeper price was paid by all those men in Boston. So which is worth more now? The ledger or a chest of gold louis?"

Comtois leaned against a table and extracted an enameled snuffbox, fastidiously inserting a pinch of powder into a nostril before replying. "A lost opportunity, Mr. McCallum. That particular package has embarked. It might have been an intriguing possibility. Perhaps we could have sold one page at a time." He produced a silk handkerchief that was scented with lavender and sneezed into it. "A pound of gold for each page of condemning evidence, eh?"

Beck twisted furiously against his bindings. "I can get you safe passage back to France, Comtois!" he shouted. "Do what you will to McCallum!"

Comtois pointed. The voyageur slammed the mallet into Beck's ear. As the officer's head sagged, Regis tied a gag around his mouth.

"You give me hope, McCallum. If you do indeed know where the gold is, we will have it out of you in an hour or two. It would be so much less messy if you could just—" Comtois paused.

A slow, rhythmic thumping was coming through the back wall. Duncan listened for a moment and grinned. It had the pace of an Iroquois war drum.

"*Qu'est-ce que c'est?*" Comtois asked his assistant. The voyageur opened the door, only to stumble backward as the unconscious body of the outside guard was hurled at him. Corporal Longtree leapt at Regis with a high-pitched war shriek. Two more rangers entered the fray before the voyageur was knocked unconscious.

"Comtois!" Duncan shouted as Woolford entered, the kilted and bandaged Corporal Buchanan behind him, his sword bayonet in his hand. In the confusion, Comtois had darted into the shadowed corner beyond his two prisoners. But when Duncan turned, there was nothing in the corner but an open trapdoor.

Duncan's heart sank, but then he quickly restrained Buchanan from untying Beck's gag. "The lieutenant has suffered grievous injury," he declared. "We need a ranger to escort him posthaste to the army infirmary."

Woolford grinned. "You mean you need him to be anywhere but with us—"

"Not so fast," an icy voice interrupted. Mallory had pulled himself up, leaning against the wall. "McCallum is mine."

Duncan ignored the sergeant for a moment too long, watching as Beck, still dazed, was led away. Mallory seized Duncan and pushed the red-hot pincers toward his face.

Longtree deftly knocked the pincers from Mallory's hand, then looked at Duncan, who gestured him away. "No, Sergeant. You are finished here." He considered the treacherous soldier a moment. "Is your man Wolf with you?"

"No," Mallory snarled. "Arrested by Hazlitt at Ticoderoga the night you escaped. By dawn he was gone too, leaving his long needle in a jailer's arm. He'll bolt into one of his caves in the wilds and disappear. Damn you, it'll take me months to find him now."

Duncan was weary of all the killing and somehow could not bring himself to do harm to a man whose life he had saved. "Then go, Sergeant." He extracted one of the gold coins from his pocket and extended it to Mallory. "Do what you will, just leave Montreal, and if you ever show your face in Edentown, we will not be so merciful."

Mallory's fierce gaze settled on the gold piece. "So you do have the treasure."

"Go," Duncan repeated.

The sergeant seemed to relax, and Longtree stepped out of the chamber to speak with Woolford. As soon as the Mohawk disappeared, Mallory leapt at Duncan. A dagger had appeared in his hand, and he pressed its blade against Duncan's throat. "The hangman will have his prize!" he spat. "We'll both go, you bastard, and you will give me the gold or I will see the color of your guts! Where do we find the—"

Mallory never finished the question. He groaned, then sagged, and the dagger fell from his hand as he collapsed to the floor. Buchanan had sunk his sword bayonet between his ribs.

"Beg pardon, sir, hope he spilled no blood on ye," the Highland soldier said in a gratified tone, then bent to extract his blade from Mallory's body. "Always did want to kill a sergeant."

Longtree reappeared, quickly assessing the situation, and directed his men to strip away Mallory's uniform and deposit him in the river with rocks tied to his limbs. As the body was dragged away, Duncan explained to Woolford what Comtois had said. "How many ships sail from Montreal to France?" he asked his friend.

"Very few, I should think," Woolford replied. "Two or three a month, perhaps."

"Then it should not be difficult. Comtois said the ledger had been put in transit, but he would not venture far from it. It will be on his ship, the vessel sailing for France the day after tomorrow. We need every man in his uniform." He turned to Buchanan. "Could you collect your squad of Highlanders to lend some authority?"

"Sir?"

"We will be doing a surprise revenue inspection of that ship. There's a crate of antiquarian books that needs to be confiscated."

22

THE CHAMBER ON THE TOP floor of the stone fortress had a scent of oiled leather and wig talcum. Half a dozen Highlanders led by Corporal Buchanan, betraying no sign of their sleepless night spent with Duncan and Woolford, stood in rigid attention at the back of the room as Major Robert Rogers, freshly shaven and in a clean uniform, was escorted before the stern triumvirate of judges. Horatio Beck, bruised but washed and well groomed in his lieutenant's uniform, sat at a table on the right, beside a nervous young officer who was apparently the prosecutor. Duncan, Woolford, and Conawago sat at the back. Sitting alone on the other side was Robert Livingston, whose beefy countenance had grown deeply worried, almost stricken, when he saw Duncan.

Presiding Judge Colonel Hazlitt called the chamber to order with a hammering of his pistol butt on the table and declared in a solemn voice that this was a hearing on the disposition of charges against Major Rogers. Beck leaned into the ear of the prosecutor, who stared straight ahead without reaction. Beck himself spoke up in an oily, chastising tone. "Surely you mean the commencement of the trial on capital charges of treason, sir."

Hazlitt fixed him with an angry gaze. "You have no authority in this room, Lieutenant. Nor do you have our permission to speak." He turned to Rogers. "Major, have you read the bill of particulars concerning the charges against you?"

The major replied in a steady, voluble voice. "I have, Your Honor, perhaps a score of times. And I have submitted my defense."

"Which I have shared with my fellow judges," Hazlitt confirmed.

Beck shot up out of his chair. "I have not seen any such statement!" he protested.

"You are warned, sir," Hazlitt barked. "Be seated!"

The colonel leafed through the papers before him. "The government's charges are based on a theory of conspiracy to defy the king's authority in North America by setting up a separate state in the lands east of Lake Champlain. But we now have reason to believe that this was a gross misinterpretation of evidence." Hazlitt fixed Rogers with a searching gaze. "You state that your actions were for the benefit of King George, aimed at discovering the location of a large sum of money that was secretly hidden by our enemies at the end of the last war. A fascinating tale, sir, if only we had proof of it."

"We have the best of proof, sir," Rogers answered. "The ultimate proof, if I may." Hazlitt nodded, and Rogers rose to drop two gold demi-louis coins on the judges' table. "We have recovered several thousand of these. As we speak, they are being handed over to soldiers under Captain Woolford's command, who will bring them to this very fortress before nightfall."

Beck gasped. "No! You can't possibly—" At a gesture from Colonel Hazlitt, a delighted Corporal Buchanan clamped an arm around Beck's neck and began dragging him out of the chamber. As his protests were choked away, he held up his hands in surrender, and Buchanan halted, holding Beck upright, still in his grip.

"And where exactly was this gold found, sir?" one of the other judges asked.

"In the forest cabin used by a Monsieur Bougainville, a senior French officer present at Montreal during the French capitulation, who remains a high-ranking officer in King Louis's army to this day. He secreted the gold there before leaving Montreal, unbeknownst to those who innocently maintained the cabin for him," Rogers added. They had agreed that they would keep the role of the Jesuits out of their tale. The old Mohawk woman had confessed to Corporal Longtree that she was happy to be rid of the gold, which had given her no end of worries over the years since Deschamps, no doubt with the vicar general's guidance, had brought it there.

Hazlitt ordered the sulking Beck brought to the judges' table. "The record further indicates, Mr. Beck, that you successfully uncovered two French spies in the course"—Hazlitt searched for words—"of all this. Spies named Comtois and Meunier, who killed thirty-seven sailors in Boston harbor. And then you cleverly arranged fictitious charges of treason against Mr. McCallum so he could bring added pressure on the pretense of clearing his name." He fixed Beck with a contemptuous gaze, daring him to protest, then lifted a page from the stack in front of him. "And a clandestine agent from France living here in Montreal has been identified. Very clever of you to leave him in place, unknowing of our discovery, so he can be observed by our most clever of watchers," he said with a glance at Woolford, who had agreed that his furtive team of Mohawks would keep the old book collector on Valcours Street under surveillance. The biggest threat raised by the French was, after all, in the western lands of the tribes. "Most excellent," the colonel declared in a hollow voice. "London shall hear of your efforts—no doubt the king himself."

Beck turned and glared at Duncan, then sighed and hung his head. He was beaten. "Yes, Your Honor."

"You will put your signature to our statement confirming so, and to a letter to the governor of Massachusetts that we have written for you."

"Yes, Your Honor," Beck repeated.

"And where are Comtois and Meunier now?" Hazlitt asked Rogers.

"They killed rangers, sir," Rogers stated flatly. "They are being watched by rangers and will be dealt with by rangers."

Beck's protest had a shrill, desperate tone. "No! You fools! You cannot! They must be interrogated! We can exchange them!" he shouted as he turned toward Duncan with a venomous glare. "We must find the—" His words ended in a strangled cry, echoed a moment later by Livingston. They had both spotted the small, soiled ledger that Duncan now held, resting on his knee.

Hazlitt ignored Beck. He exchanged a pointed glance with Duncan and turned back to Rogers. "You are saying, Major, that the threat to the Crown posed by these men has been eliminated?"

"They will no longer represent a threat to the Crown," Rogers quietly confirmed, looking down at the table. Hazlitt looked to Woolford, who offered a confirming nod.

"We thank you for your service, Major, and wish you swift passage back to your post in the Northwest. These charges are dismissed and this court adjourned," Hazlitt loudly declared, hammering the table again.

Rogers did not look up. The dream of the famed ranger had been broken, and in doing so, Duncan feared, a piece of Rogers himself had been broken. The colonel had inserted only one condition on the terms Duncan had proposed to him, that Rogers sign an unequivocal oath of loyalty to King George. Duncan had thought the old ranger was going to physically assault him when he brought the news to his cell, but then Rogers had looked out over the river for several long breaths. When he turned, he was fingering his wife's necklace. "We will go to her grave, as you said?" he asked. Duncan had solemnly affirmed his vow, and Rogers had signed. There would be no state free of kings, there would be no more money for French farmers, there would be no guns in the tower of Chevelure, there would be no free order of Jesuits, but Rogers would live, and no one would be punished for having embraced the dream of Saguenay.

DUNCAN DID NOT NEED TO press Robert Livingston for a private meeting. The New York merchant invited him to his inn for lunch after the hearing concluded and Rogers was released. Duncan declined, but set another meeting time, at Duncan's own choice of location for later in the afternoon, after he confirmed the sailing schedule for the ship bound for the Wine Islands and Le Havre.

Livingston was already nervous when he entered the old cemetery, and clearly he grew more uncomfortable as he passed the rows of tombstones to reach the bench Duncan sat on, not far from the restored Celtic cross.

"Was this really necessary, McCallum?" the merchant said as he sat, leaning on his walking stick. "We could have had a fine meal together."

"I find that the beds of the dead make for great clarity of thinking." In fact, Duncan had decided that for many Europeans, rows of tombstones were much like the rows of white wampum used by the Iroquois for solemn discussions, keeping conversations more truthful. "Even soul-searching," he added, suspecting that Livingston was not a man much given to the practice.

"So you have it, then," the New York aristocrat abruptly declared. "Comtois showed it to me, said he was sending it to France and that I should wait for instructions. He didn't take enough care in shipping it, apparently."

"He was arrogant in this as in all things. Hiding it in a crate of French books sent by a French book collector on a ship bound for France apparently seemed cunning to him."

"You've opened it, then?" Livingston asked in a thin voice.

"It is fascinating reading. So much effort to keep such remarkable secrets, undone by simple accounting clerks."

"These were family enterprises, you understand. John and I were too junior then to have made any meaningful mercantile decisions."

"Meaningful mercantile decisions." Duncan mouthed the words slowly. "You make it sound so ordinary. For how many years?" He answered his own question. "All the years of the war. I had friends who died in those years. I remember hearing again and again how the French would capitulate in North America because the Canadian crops kept failing, because their army couldn't get supplies of food and materiel from France. The war was going to be over in '57, then '58, then in '59. But soldiers and Iroquois kept dying, at Ticonderoga, at Duquesne, at Ligonier, at Niagara, all because the Hancocks and Livingstons and their merchant allies solved the French dilemma. What was the name of that harbor in Hispaniola? It has such a romantic ring to it."

"San Fernando de Monte Cristi," Livington murmured.

"Exactly," Duncan said, and repeated the name. "Judging by the ledger, Hancock and Livingston ships must have anchored there almost every week, for all the war years, moving goods in and out. Delivering supplies to French ships that sailed to Canada. So more British colonists and Highlanders and Iroquois could die."

"Duncan, it was just business. We had goods, and the French were ready buyers."

"No one else could have supplied them," Duncan said in an icy tone. "It wasn't business. It was treason masquerading in a mercantile cloak. You sent men from your own estates to the war, men who were killed by an enemy fed by the Livingstons and Hancocks."

"It wasn't John and me," Livingston insisted, though his voice was hollow. "It was our families."

"Right. I don't think you would hang. You would just be destroyed in every other sense if the ledger fell into the wrong hands."

"We didn't even know it existed until last year. One of the London bankers had kept it. When he died, his son found it and began making inquiries, all too openly, among London merchants and other financiers. We had to get it back."

"But the French found out. If King Louis had the ledger, he would own you. And he would think he owned the Sons of Liberty, or as good as owned them, for all the influence you have with the Sons. The Sons are furious with King George. With the right spark, they might be willing to oppose him more openly in the name of a new king. That's why Comtois and Meunier said the ledger could transform the continent. If they fomented a new war and had the Sons on their side, much of America could become French. On the other hand, if Horatio Beck had it, his superiors would think they could neutralize all opposition to the king in America."

Livingston wrung his hands in anguish.

"You met with them, had an entertaining evening here even though you knew they had sunk the *Arcturus*. And more good men have died since then. You were ready to sacrifice me and my friends, if it came to that."

The New York merchant shuddered, squeezing the handle of his walking stick as if for support. "I have nightmares every night. I wake up in cold sweats. I keep seeing those bodies on the beach. John suffers the same. How could we have known?"

Duncan did not reply. He looked out over the grave markers, many dating back to the prior century, and felt soul-weary again. Livingston and Hancock deserved their nightmares.

After a long silence, Livingston straightened and put his hands on his knees. "So the market has shifted," he said with a businesslike air. "What do you want, McCallum?"

"What do I want?"

"In exchange for the ledger. A junior partnership, perhaps. Five percent of my mercantile company. I think John would agree to the same terms."

A great sadness descended over Duncan. He was silent a long time. "What I want," he said at last, "is for you and Hancock to stop thinking of the Sons of Liberty as a personal enterprise. What I want is for others to have a voice in the affairs of the Sons." He thought for a moment and smiled. "And printing presses."

"Printing presses?"

"In New England and New York. Find educated men in half a dozen smaller towns willing to publish newspapers, and then provide them with presses."

Livingston winced. "An expensive proposition. I don't know if we could accept a full five percent for you then."

"Livingston, I do not want a percentage of anything. Just the presses. And some flowers," he added after a moment. "I want flowers planted for a woman in Worcester."

It was the merchant's turn to be silent. He too looked out over the lichened gravestones. The great aristocrat, baron of the Hudson Valley, seemed to shrink. "But you'll keep the ledger?"

"I'll keep the ledger."

Livingston gave a long sigh. "Done," he said.

THE MASTER OF THE THREE-MASTED ship headed into the Atlantic had reported to the harbormaster that it would weigh anchor an hour after dawn, which meant that at midnight the Jesuits and the rangers went to work at the waterfront warehouse used by the French agents. Munro had offered the suggestion when seeing that the French kept their own boats, including a wide bark canoe of the kind used by voyageurs, and before midnight the other two boats, both large river dories, were eased out of their berths and cast adrift.

The Mohawks had selected a ledge that overhung the river a quarter mile east of the city wall, nearly directly across from the anchorage of the big ship. As fingers of pink and gold began to stretch over the horizon, the calls of mates stirring the crew for their morning's work carried over the still waters of the St. Lawrence.

"You're sure about this?" Duncan asked Woolford, not for the first time.

"As Major Rogers told the judges, this is rangers' work. They killed good men in cold blood, sailors and men who wore ranger green. You heard Beck. If we turned them over to London, they would be used, not punished. The dead must have their due," he said, echoing words Duncan had used with him. Woolford studied his six Mohawks, each of whom was loading his rifle with extra powder and shot.

The canoe pushed off from the wharf a quarter hour later, with Comtois in the front while the paddles were worked by Meunier and the bearlike voyageur Regis who so enjoyed torturing captives. The river was wide and notoriously fast, and the canoe quickly reached the main current nearly a hundred yards offshore, steering for the ship.

Duncan and his companions had been there since before first light, and in the glow of a lantern Munro had unfolded a tattered list he had brought from Boston. "Jonathan Pine," he said, reading the first name on the list, then handing it to Conawago.

"Daniel Oliver," Conawago read, handing it around the gathered circle. The name of each victim of the *Arcturus* was read, and then two others.

"Josiah Chisholm," Duncan solemnly intoned.

Munro had recited the last name. "Corporal Ebenezer Brandt."

Now, as the canoe presented itself, Woolford turned to Longtree. "Corporal," the ranger officer said with a nod. Longtree acknowledged him with a grim smile and uttered a syllable in his tribal tongue.

At Duncan's side, Conawago spoke in the same tongue. "*Jiyathontek,*" he whispered, summoning the spirits to witness.

Three rifles spoke almost as one. They were aimed not at the men in the canoe, but at the birchbark at its waterline. The heavy pellets ripped into the thin covering, instantly creating three large holes. Comtois shot to his feet, shouting frantically. As the big man at the stern dug his paddle into the water, desperately trying to turn to shore, Corporal Longtree fired and the paddle in his hand shattered.

The remaining rifles spoke, and the canoe lost all headway, sinking fast. Duncan realized that Longtree was extending another rifle toward him, Duncan's own. Duncan aimed at a section of the canoe that had not yet been pierced. "Saguenay," he said, and fired.

It was over in seconds. The three men were standing in the canoe as it disappeared. They flailed in the violent current only moments before they too were gone.

Duncan turned to the two cloaked figures who stood silently at the back of the ledge. Colonel Hazlitt and the vicar general said nothing, just nodded at Duncan, then walked back down the trail.

The Mohawks too soon left, but Duncan, Woolford, Conawago, and Munro lingered, watching as the big ship weighed anchor and made sail for Europe.

Duncan reached into the pack he had left by a boulder and pulled out the soiled, water-stained ledger. It was thin, and tattered from long use. It was hard to believe it had caused such agony and changed so many lives. Kings had coveted it, merchant princes had been terrified of it, and Duncan could have grown wealthy with it. But he had come to understand it more as a symbol, of greed and empire-building, of the mindless exercise of power by men who had not earned the right to such power. The debt to the dead was not fully paid.

He looked into the face of each of his companions. They had talked the night before of keeping it secure, knowing it could be of value in the long struggle they sensed coming. But now each grinned and nodded. Munro touched his plaid. He had had the last word before dawn. "I don't entirely ken where this path of liberty is taking us," the battle-worn Scot had said, "but I do ken that we won't get there playing by London's rules."

Duncan stepped to the edge of the rock and with a mighty heave sent the ledger in a long arc that ended in the swift, bottomless river.

Epilogue

Early October 1768
Edentown

THE MOHAWK BROUGHT HIS STICK down violently on the wiry Scot, who rolled with the blow, muttering something quite rude in Gaelic and adeptly thrusting his own stick through the legs of the warrior to trip him. The warrior tumbled and slid, then paused as he rose, showing his assailant the brown smear that covered his arm and bared thigh. He had fallen onto a fresh cow patty. For a moment both men stared at each other; then both burst into laughter and sprinted down the field, where their teammates were fighting with racquets over a small buckskin ball.

"No, you don't," Sarah Ramsey said as Duncan took a step toward the lacrosse game. "You've played enough today. Who's going to mend the broken bones if the doctor gets one himself?" She slipped her hand into his and pulled him away.

The Mohawks and the Edentown settlers had been playing the game for hours and gave no sign of tiring. Hoots of joy and cheers rose from the on-lookers who sat on the fence of the big pasture. Some of the settlers, Duncan noticed, were cheering the Mohawks, who in good spirit had accepted the challenge when the settlers produced a team twice as big as their own.

Sarah looped her arm around his and led Duncan along the broad track that connected the community cattle barn, the horse stables, the smithy, and the cooperage, ending at the little schoolhouse where Duncan had once taught her to read and write after her years with the Iroquois. She greeted a tribal woman in Mohawk; then Duncan gave his regards in Gaelic to a red-haired boy and even boldly tried Welsh—"*Sut wyt ti?*"—when they passed the new cobbler just arrived from Cardiff. As they reached the horse stables, Sarah was knocked into Duncan's arms, laughing, by Molly as the big dog, Sadie on her back, raced out of the barn beside Will. They were followed by a gaggle of joyful children, the last of whom paused to shyly present Sarah with a brilliant feather that appeared to have been plucked from one of her hens.

Duncan could not recall when he last felt so content. The first harvest was in, the foals of the Belgian plow horses were all healthy and prancing around the back pasture, and judging from the sweet scent on the October breeze, the cider mill near the orchard had begun pressing apples. An inquisitive nickering caught his ear, and he turned toward a side pasture to see Goliath pacing along the split-rail fence, calling to him. He grabbed an apple from one of the baskets waiting for the mill and greeted the big thoroughbred with the treat. They had decided that the government owed him at least a good horse, and Ishmael was certain he could find a way to convert the military arrow brand into a spruce tree, which they would then affix to the other mounts.

As they approached the little schoolhouse, they heard a metallic hammering, then a curse that combined English and the Nipmuc tongue. The student population of Edentown had outgrown the compact structure, which was being converted to a new and unexpected use.

As they entered, Conawago looked up from a machine that occupied nearly a quarter of the chamber, and he raised a skinned knuckle. "She and I are still getting acquainted. A feisty lady." He grinned, tapping a leg that extended from under the machine, and Noah, ink staining his hands and face, crawled out, smiling sheepishly.

"Folks will be looking on the front page for a greeting from the proprietress," the Abenaki declared to Sarah as he wiped his hands on his apron.

The machine had arrived in large crates the week before, with a letter addressed to Conawago from John Hancock. He and Robert Livingston, the note explained, had made a charitable vow to equip some of the most literate men in the New England and New York colonies with the means to cultivate the seeds of literacy among their neighbors. Therefore, Hancock had written in his elegant hand, *please accept this gift, Conawago, so that your fellowmen may bask in the warmth of your erudition.*

The press was secondhand, but it was a sound German-made device with years of service left in it. Sarah, who had looked—to no avail—for an explanation from Duncan, had quickly offered the use of the empty schoolhouse, and Conawago immediately asked Noah to join him in the enterprise. Noah stepped to the typesetting table and lifted a page that was blank except for the masthead. The words *Beacon of the Wilderness* in large font were flanked by images of stags leaping between trees. The two old tribesmen were filled with a boyish energy that made Duncan's heart swell.

"It's perfect!" Sarah exclaimed.

Noah gestured to the large slate on the back wall, a vestige of the schoolhouse days. "Our first issue's content," the new editor declared, then motioned Sarah and Duncan to examine the list of articles and topics written in chalk. *Message from Sarah Ramsey*, read the first, then:

Alarming News from Boston
The State of Animal Husbandry in the Ramsey Grants
Status of Harvests
Reports of Family Events and Sojourners

Conawago muttered, then went to the last item, *Serialization of the* Aeneid *in Original Greek*, and crossed it out. "I've told you," he reminded his fledgling editor, "we have no fonts in Greek or Hebrew."

"Perhaps," Duncan suggested to Noah, "you could offer a different quote under the masthead each week."

The old Abenaki brightened. "We can start with Aristotle!"

"I was thinking of something more current," Duncan said, then lifted the chalk and wrote on the board.

When he was done, Noah stepped back and read his words aloud. "'If liberty is taken from men without their consent, they are enslaved,'" he recited with an approving nod.

"From Mr. James Otis of Boston," Duncan said.

"Perfect juxtaposition," Noah declared. "Speaking as an editor," he added self-consciously, handing Duncan a mock-up of the leading story. TROOPS

OCCUPY BOSTON, it said, and reported the news that had arrived with Munro the day before. The British Crown had finally lost its patience and dispatched the 14th and 29th Regiments from Halifax, who were now demanding quarters in Boston's private homes and public buildings.

Duncan felt Sarah's gaze, but did not return it. The warrant for his arrest had been withdrawn owing to John Adams's valuable assistance, but Duncan had promised her to stay away from Boston for now. Conawago lifted a type rack set with another headline. It took a moment for Duncan to read the reversed letters. PROPRIETRESS OF EDENTOWN BETROTHED, it announced. Sarah laid her head on Duncan's shoulder. John Adams had also been successful in overthrowing the order of extended servitude imposed by her father, and as soon as Adams obtained the signature of the magistrate, Duncan would be a free man, at least until the wedding could be arranged.

THE GREAT FEAST SARAH HAD organized under the autumn-tinged oaks and maples continued until dusk, punctuated by frequent toasts offered by lacrosse opponents. As sleepy children were being carried away, Ishmael tapped Duncan's shoulder. Duncan did not understand why he was being summoned, and as Ishmael led Duncan across the shadowed field, the Nipmuc youth, an expectant glint in his eyes, seemed disinclined to explain. Duncan saw flames as they approached the rim of the forest, and he realized that the tribesmen were using the old clearing once reserved for the Edge of the Woods ceremony, where Europeans had met periodically with Iroquois to confirm that they had come in peace and would speak only the truth at council fires.

Conawago and Noah sat at the far side of a rough circle of logs, their backs to the deep forest in the traditional position of tribal ambassadors. Woolford and his Mohawks were already seated in the circle. Ishmael fed the fire, then took a seat between Munro and a blond youth who looked vaguely familiar. Conawago indicated the stranger with the stem of the long ceremonial pipe he was lighting. "The wheel shop in Quinsigamond is closed for two weeks," he explained, and suddenly Duncan recognized the newcomer as Samuel, the nephew of Josiah Chisholm, the gentle soul who had yearned to become this boy's stepfather. Duncan clasped hands with Samuel and looked back at the old Nipmuc, who offered no further explanation. No one had invited Samuel to the festival, but Duncan had begun to realize that this council fire was not part of the festival.

Everyone seemed to be waiting for Conawago to open the council, but it was Noah who first cupped some of the fragrant smoke to his lips and spoke. "We have come to greet and thank the warriors," the former church elder intoned. "We have come to greet and thank the kindred. We have come to greet and thank the women." He was using the prayers that opened the ancient Edge of the Woods ceremony for joining strangers. But then he shifted to his own words. "We come to thank the gods in the heavens, the gods in the land, and the gods in our hearts. We come to thank them that we have become brothers who keep watch over each other in the night and stand at each other's side when foes approach."

Duncan studied the faces of those in the circle, who apparently knew more about their purpose there than he did. It was as if Noah were invoking some kind of secret brotherhood. The old Abenaki passed the pipe to Conawago, who puffed once and spoke. "We who keep the strength of the oak and the eye of the eagle," he said, and handed the pipe to Corporal Longtree.

"One stick alone breaks," the Mohawk solemnly stated after cupping the smoke to his mouth. "But the sticks bundled together never will."

Each man inhaled on the pipe in turn and spoke with the cleansing smoke wreathing his head. "The brothers of the bear," was all one Iroquois ranger said.

"There are bonds that can be thicker than blood," Ishmael offered.

"The wheel is strong because each spoke carries its weight," declared Samuel.

"The stag who outruns all enemies," intoned another Mohawk.

When it was Munro's turn, he nodded at Duncan as he inhaled on the Indian pipe. "Every man here has been living long enough with endings," the Scot declared in a contemplative tone. "It is time we looked to beginnings."

Woolford shared a quick smile with Duncan, who silently mouthed the words he knew his friend would speak. "'We few, we happy few, we band of brothers,'" the ranger captain said, no doubt hoping no one would point out that Shakespeare had put them in the mouth of an English king.

Duncan, still on uncertain ground, chose an old ballad from his childhood as the smoke blessed his tongue. "'God send each noble man at his end, such hawks, such hounds, and such friends,'" he recited, and handed the pipe back to Noah. As he did so, a small party emerged out of the shadows. Reverend Samson Occom, looking much thinner yet somehow stronger than the stiff pastor Duncan had met in Boston, was with Solomon Hayes, carrying between them the case of Bibles Occom had sent with Sarah when they parted ways in Massachusetts. Close behind them were Sarah, holding Will's hand, and several Mohawk women, who took seats beside the Indian rangers, apparently the wives of Woolford's warriors. At Will's side was Molly, who, with Ishmael's blessing, seemed to have adopted the boy.

"There are sons in Boston who are being forced to let the king's troops sleep under the same roofs as their own families," Munro suddenly stated, pulling out a tattered copy of the *Boston Gazette* and reading how warships had trained their guns on the city while columns of redcoats had unloaded from barges and marched through the streets to ominous drumbeats. The old Scot concluded with the newspaper's quote from a public dispatch sent from General Gage in New York, who, in ordering the occupation, described Bostonians as "mutinous desperadoes."

"We ask for compromise, and they instead order in troops, as if dealing with an enemy." To Duncan's surprise, the words had been spoken by Ishmael.

"I heard someone here say that the king did not deserve this land," Conawago pointed out.

"Words of anger," Duncan said. "I have no wish for another bounty on my head." Sarah, standing behind him, squeezed his shoulder as if to agree, but then she spoke.

"The king negotiates in a brutal way," she observed, "but still it is a negotiation."

Duncan glanced up in surprise at Sarah, who had so assiduously struggled to keep Edentown shielded from the conflicts of the outside world.

"The king has all the power," Noah said. "Even if the farmers and tradesmen and tribesmen were to call themselves the Sons of Liberty, what do they have to impress the king with? Plow horses and hay rakes? Spinning wheels and applejack? The Sons have no muscle, have no confidence, have no cohesion."

As if this were a cue, Hayes and Occom lifted the heavy crate between them and brought it closer to the fire. They both knelt and with borrowed tomahawks pried off the lid. Occom lifted out Bibles, which Hayes reverently stacked on one of the long benches. When the Bibles were removed, Occom began handing Hayes slats of wood. The crate had a false bottom.

"I spent two years of my life in England, a stranger in a strange land," Occom explained, "to bring back twelve thousand pounds for an institution that had apparently been only a figment of my imagination." There was a peculiar gleam in Occom's eye that Duncan had not seen before. "I prayed for hours after Reverend Wheelock told me he had other plans for my funds. That night, when I expressed my disappointment toward the altar, I heard something I had never before experienced. It was the sound of my God laughing. The conundrum was of my own making, he was saying, and the resolution was therefore in my own hands. He let me understand that I was only one of his many instruments, as was the money I had raised, so I acknowledged my debt to Reverend Wheelock and paid it. He will have his college in the New Hampshire grants, for I have surrendered to him nine out of every ten pounds I collected. The rest," Occom said with a nod to Sarah, "went west with Miss Ramsey. I most profusely apologize for the deception."

Duncan recalled the nervous way Occom had acted when the crate from Boston had been dropped to the ground in Agawam.

Sarah gaped at him in surprise. "I didn't . . ." she began. "I was waiting for the new minister to arrive to open the Bibles," she offered with a blush.

"It was Providence, fair lady," Occom assured her. "Many a night I have prayed that the crate had not been discarded or burned." He began extracting little sacks of coins from the bottom of the case, handing them to Hayes, who laid them in a line by the Bibles.

Duncan rose to heft one of the bags. There were more than two score of them, representing more than a thousand pounds, a fortune by any standard. "I don't understand," he said to Occom.

"My dream was snatched away by men who court favor with a government across the sea."

"But this is enough to build a new mission school."

Occom lifted one of the sacks. "This alone is enough for a new school in the western lands." There was an odd challenge in his eyes as he looked at Duncan. "I collected the money for God's work. There is another aspect of souls in the colonies that needs ministering, which I did not understand until I joined this company. The New World demands new types of ministers."

"There is no land like this land," Duncan said. The words had risen unbidden to his tongue.

"There are no hearts like those nurtured in this soil," Occom said. "Men need to find the voice of those hearts if they are to be heard in London."

Once more Duncan hefted the sack in his hand. "You cannot buy men's hearts."

"No. I am speaking of providing tools. The right tools empower a man in both body and spirit."

"Tools?" Duncan asked.

It was Munro who took up the answer. "Paper and ink for new printing presses," he said. "And muskets for militias who have only sticks to train with."

"Books," Noah put in.

"Shoes good enough for long marches," Corporal Longtree added.

"Cloaks for winter camps," Ishmael offered.

"You're suggesting that we secretly support the Sons of Liberty," Duncan declared.

"No, Duncan," Conawago said. "You speak as though the Sons were someone else. *We* have become the Sons of Liberty, for the frontier lands, for the remote farmlands. We will build a network of like-minded souls. Nipmuc, Scottish, Mohawk, Welsh, Oneida, Irish, Abenaki, English, whatever the blood."

Duncan glanced back uneasily at Sarah. "It would take a lot of hard travel to nurture such a network."

"We have that man."

Duncan squeezed Sarah's hand. "I am getting married."

Conawago smiled.

"A man and a boy," a determined voice rang out. It was Solomon Hayes. Will was standing at his side.

"And a monkey and a sea bear," Will added, raising grins all around as Sadie climbed from Hayes onto Will's shoulder.

Sarah stepped to the boy and put both hands on his arms. "We had hoped you would join us in our new school, Will."

"He wants to go to Rhode Island to meet my relatives," Hayes announced, "and I promised Rabbi Cohen we would bring some things from our synagogue there. But we hope to find a little corner here that we could call our new home, where we could stay in the winters, and where we could receive mail and inventory for my trading goods. The world will still know me as a tinker and trader."

"Of course," Sarah said, then cocked her head at him as if expecting something more.

"And if you but inform us of the primer you are using," Hayes ventured, "I promise that Will shall have his lessons six days a week, from me." Sadie, ever with perfect timing, leapt to the log and hoisted one of the little sacks of coins to her back.

"I suppose," Sarah said with a laugh, "that settles it."

Munro grew more solemn, and stood, followed by each of the others in the circle. "There be perilous times ahead," the Scot declared. "We'll need a leader to make plans, a spokesman who might go from time to time to confer with leaders of the Sons in Boston and New York, even Philadelphia."

Duncan realized they were all looking at him.

AUTHOR'S NOTE

I WAS IN PRIMARY SCHOOL when I first visited the Liberty Bell and pressed my hand upon it in wonder, feeling its cool bronze power. Through that touch, which would probably get me arrested today, I felt a link to the extraordinary years of the mid-eighteenth century, which pushed me toward more artifacts and venues of the American Revolution. It was only after many years of such visits and studying the chronicles of the era that I began to grasp that the Revolution is best understood not as a military event, but as a deeply complex social process. Battles didn't revolutionize America, it was scores of thousands of personal revolutions that transformed the colonists, who then transformed their colonies. Conventions and congresses amplified those transformed voices and focused them into a common political structure that bridged colonial borders, but it was these earlier, very personal struggles in the years before the Revolution that forged the new American identity. Individual colonists from vastly different backgrounds and cultures eventually translated their painful confrontations and frustrations with Old World mentalities into a common view built around taking ownership of their personal liberty.

In the final pages of this novel I provide a glimpse at the emerging role of the printing press, which became the most potent of all revolutionary weapons. Although the first presses had appeared three centuries earlier, only during the mid-eighteenth century did they become widely dispersed in America, resulting in a revolution in communication. Remote populations became, in eighteenth-century terms, instantly connected, launching a tsunami of change in education, literature, science, commerce, and politics. Old social and economic structures were rapidly crumbling by 1768, reflected, for example, in the dismantling of the vast baronial estates of the Hudson Valley.

The remarkable actors who walked on this stage provide rich material for the historical novelist, and I have drawn on many in creating *Savage Liberty*. Their diverse characters highlight how colonists discovered their American identity through strikingly different routes and experiences. Some learned to embrace liberty as a result of religion or education, others through experiences in commerce or politics, and some, I am convinced, by exposure to the original Americans who still inhabited the wilderness. While the figures of John Hancock and Samuel Adams stand tall in our history books, there are many lesser known, but no less authentic, players on this eighteenth-century stage who make their appearance at Duncan's side.

Samson Occom was very much the prominent, highly educated Mohegan pastor depicted here, and his tale of collecting a vast sum in England, only to have it diverted by his mentor, Eleazer Wheelock, for his own institution, is historically accurate, made all the more poignant by the fact that Occom lived in poverty all his life, never being paid as much as a pastor of European blood. The college Wheelock founded in 1769 with Occom's funds still thrives near the banks of the Connecticut River and is still known by the name of the benefactor who thought he was giving his funds to Occom's school for natives—Lord Dartmouth.

A few miles south of that renowned college, in Charlestown, New Hampshire, is the reconstructed Fort Number Four, to which Major Rogers returned after his raid on St. Francis. Sections of the 1759 Crown Point Road that linked Fort Four to Lake Champlain, on which Duncan and his company traveled, can still be seen in the forests of Vermont. The community of St. Francis itself had a rich history, not only as one of the most important Jesuit missions in New France but also as the base for many natives who had been dispossessed from their traditional lands. More than a few captives from the British colonies resided there, some intermarrying with the natives. Although the French suspected that Rogers was seeking to infiltrate Quebec in the autumn of 1759 with an expeditionary force, no one expected him to reach as far as this bastion near the St. Lawrence. When he arrived there on October 3, Rogers did indeed boldly enter the town on a clandestine scout before attacking it. Doubtlessly he would have seen Father Jean-Baptiste de LaBrosse, who was in the church that night, conducting a wedding. LaBrosse, deeply committed to the tribes of Quebec, was later renowned for his dictionary of the Abenaki language.

Members of LaBrosse's Society of Jesus, the Jesuits, had been actively working with northern tribes for more than 150 years by 1768, and their strong attachments to the tribes did not disappear when King Louis XV, jealous of Jesuit power and wealth in France, officially dissolved the order and seized its property in 1764. Canada had become a British dominion by then, but King George also prohibited the entry of new Jesuits into Canada. Jesuit allegiances to either king had thus been severely eroded. The most ardent of the "warrior priests," Father Roubaud, notorious for leading Abenaki raids against the English, actually switched loyalty and became a secret informer to his former archenemy, Sir William Johnson, superintendent of Indian affairs.

Henry Knox, only eighteen years old when Duncan met him in Boston, was fascinated by all things military; only seven years later he abandoned his bookshop to join George Washington in the Siege of Boston. Quickly rising to the rank of colonel with the help of his friend John Adams, Knox changed the early course of the war by his miraculous feat of retrieving cannons from Fort Ticonderoga in the dead of winter, after the capture of the fort by the frontier firebrand Ethan Allen and his followers in the Vert Monts. Although there is no evidence that Allen was conspiring in 1768 to form an independent nation called Champlain, the notion of carving out a separate country in those remote mountains is not a fiction. The Green Mountain Boys played a key role in establishing the short-lived independent republic of Vermont a few years later.

Robert Rogers, hero of the French and Indian War, was a brilliant leader of irregular troops but was ever rebellious toward the British military establishment and made many enemies among high-ranking officers. An enigmatic, restless man, he was feted as a hero for his wartime accomplishments, but his rapid descent into drink and gambling after the war led him to a New York debtors' prison in 1764. With the help of wartime companions, including the Highlanders of the Black Watch, he made a dramatic escape and fled to Connecticut, then eventually to London. In the hub of the British Empire he failed to obtain funding for his lifelong aspiration, an expedition across America to the Pacific that would have preceded that of Lewis and Clark by decades. He rehabilitated himself sufficiently, however, to get his command at Fort Michilimackinac in what was then the far Northwest. One of Rogers's fiercest foes, the senior military commander in North America, General Gage, had him arrested for treason for allegedly conspiring with French agents to help King Louis take back western lands. The wartime hero endured months of hardship in chains, ultimately being transferred to a cell in Montreal, where in late 1768 he was eventually acquitted and released under mysterious circumstances. Surprisingly—some say because of a feud with George Washington—he embraced King George's cause when revolution eventually erupted into combat. Although he was given command of the royal rangers, his career, and the remainder of his life, was overwhelmed by chronic drunkenness. Readers interested in further details of the extraordinary life of this frontier commando, with particular focus on the St. Francis raid, can find them in Stephen Brumwell's riveting *White Devil.*

Although it is not known for certain that the mysterious ledger that lies at the heart of this novel existed, the secrets it embodied are well documented. The merchant houses of Boston and New York, as well as those of Rhode Island and Pennsylvania, were actively engaged in secret, illegal trade with the French military during the French and Indian War. Their ships frequently called at the port of San Fernando de Monte Cristi in Hispanola, near French Haiti, delivering sorely needed supplies that kept the French war effort in America alive, extending it for several years. One observer reported seeing at least 150 American ships anchored in the port on a single day, many of them transloading cargo directly onto French ships. New York especially owed its wartime prosperity to trade with both sides of the conflict. Details of this clandestine traffic are described in Thomas Truxes's valuable book *Defying Empire* and Peter Andreas's broader chronicle, *Smuggler Nation.*

Many lesser planks in the scaffolding of this novel are also based on historical fact. Rhode Island did indeed host an active Jewish population, many of its members having been evicted by Massachusetts leaders who seemed to forget that their own colony had been founded by those fleeing religious intolerance. In the year 1768, the first synagogue in Canada, Congregation Shearith Israel, opened under Rabbi Jacob Cohen. Although the sinking of the *Arcturus* is of my own creation, John Hancock's ship the *Liberty* was seized in the spring of 1768 as described herein, and its captain did indeed mysteriously die after the ship was searched by overzealous customs agents. The *Liberty* was conscripted by the British navy and later played an important role in another chapter of this revolutionary era. The city of Worcester,

Massachusetts, was indeed built on the site of Quinsigamond, capital of the Nipmuc tribe, as Conawago vividly reminds an Irish sawyer. Louis Antoine de Bougainville was stationed at Montreal at the close of the French and Indian War, and his lifelong pursuit of the natural sciences led him to become the first Frenchman to circumnavigate the globe, taking with him Jeanne Baret, the first woman ever to do so. Bougainville would have heard with great interest the descriptions of the great water horse of Lake Champlain, which had circulated since Samuel de Champlain himself allegedly reported a sighting in 1609. The inhabitants of Chevelure, now known as Chimney Point, Vermont, no doubt must have kept an eye out for the mysterious beast. Although the creature was once held in reverent awe by the tribes around the lake, today the popular image has softened to that of "Champ," mascot of a minor-league baseball team.

A final historical element that I believe was a profound factor in many journeys to liberty is what I call "endings" in this book. There is powerful meaning behind Conawago's words that all those in Duncan's company are in their "ending times." The Highland Scots had suffered an eradication campaign that, in its intensity and violence, was unmatched until the twentieth century. The Jesuits had been disowned and were required to renounce their holy vows, although their order was finally restored decades later. The Jews had been enduring efforts to destroy them for centuries, and they often resorted to covert measures to keep their faith alive. The once-vital woodland tribes had become a pale shadow of their former glory, and many tribes, including the Nipmucs, were well aware that they were approaching extinction. Duncan and his companions, as well as thousands of other colonists, have to confront such forlorn realities, but they have begun to grasp that in every ending there is also a beginning.

—Eliot Pattison

ELIOT PATTISON is the author of *The Skull Mantra*, winner of an Edgar Award and finalist for the Gold Dagger; as well as *Water Touching Stone*, *Bone Mountain*, *Beautiful Ghosts*, *Prayer of the Dragon*, *Bone Rattler*, *The Lord of Death*, *Eye of the Raven*, *Original Death*, and, most recently, *Blood of the Oak*. Pattison resides in rural Pennsylvania with his wife, three children, two horses, and two dogs on a colonial-era farm. Find more at eliotpattison.com.